LENIN'S ROLLER COASTER

LENIN'S ROLLER COASTER

DAVID DOWNING

Published in the United States by

Soho Press, Inc.
853 Broadway
New York, NY 10003

Library of Congress Cataloging-in-Publication Data

Downing, David, 1946–
Lenin's roller coaster / David Downing.

ISBN 978-1-61695-604-2
eISBN 978-1-61695-605-9

1. Intelligence officers—Great Britain—Fiction. 2. Women
journalists—Great Britain—Fiction. 3. World War, 1914–1918—Fiction.
4. Espionage, British—Fiction. I. Title
PR6054.O868 L49 2017 823'.914—dc23 2016030515

Interior design by Janine Agro, Soho Press, Inc.

Printed in the United States of America

10 9 8 7 6 5 4 3 2 1

LENIN'S ROLLER COASTER

Author's Note

Almost a century has passed since the revolutionary upheaval in Russia that did so much to shape the politics of the twentieth century. As long as Soviet rule persisted and the Cold War dominated international affairs, some understanding of those upheavals was considered fairly essential, but since 1989 their causes and development have almost come to seem a historical irrelevance, and knowledge of even the most basic facts can no longer be taken for granted.

There were two Russian revolutions in 1917, one in March (February according to the old calendar, which was abandoned early in 1918) and one in November (or October). The first saw the czarist autocracy overthrown by a popular uprising and replaced by the so-called Provisional Government, an alliance of conservative, liberal, and socialist groups with few interests in common. This government shared power—or, perhaps more accurately, disputed its possession—with those "unofficial" elected councils or "soviets" that represented chiefly industrial workers, peasants, and soldiers.

This arrangement failed to deliver the three things most Russians wanted—a better quality of life, a speedy end to the war, and a functioning democracy—and in November the Provisional Government was forcibly overthrown by its soviet rivals in Petrograd and other

cities across Russia. At this point in time, Lenin's Bolshevik Party—
the Communist Party from 1918 onward—was the biggest party in
many of the city soviets. It formed a working alliance with the left
wing of the Socialist Revolutionary Party, which held a majority in
most rural soviets, and set about the task of revolutionizing Russia.

This book is set in the first year of that ongoing revolution, which
coincided with the final year of the First World War.

1
Excesses

As the horse clip-clopped its way up El Maghrabi Street toward Opera Square, Jack McColl let his gaze slip down the alleys on either side, wondering at the sheer volume of activity that each seemed to contain. Behind him the sun was almost down, the sky above the buildings a lurid orange. The heat, though, showed no sign of abating, and the shirt he'd only just put on was already stuck to his back. Every now and then, he swatted an arm at the posse of flies that seemed to have followed him all the way from his hotel.

The calash turned left across a corner of the square, its driver letting loose a string of curses at a tram that insisted on its right of way. As they passed up the western side of the Ezbekiya Gardens, McColl noticed palm fronds writhing above the perimeter wall, like ghostly spirits demanding release.

He'd been in Egypt for two days, long enough to notice a definite change of mood. First there had been the middle-class family on the train who'd all seemed so friendly until McColl spoke to the child in Arabic, and then the crowd of Egyptian Labour Corps volunteers at Cairo Station whose fervent singing only sounded patriotic if you didn't understand the words. McColl did, and he had spent enough time in India to recognize the signs—colonial rule might look secure on the surface, but the longer the war went on, the more dangers lurked below it.

Turning north away from the gardens, the calash clattered up a short street toward the Wagh el-Birka, which marked the southern border of the red-light district. The driver stopped to let traffic cross in front of them, and McColl had time to scan the street in both directions. It had been crowded with troops on his last visit, but maybe the night was still young.

It was Cumming's man in Cairo who had given him this errand. "All our Russian speakers were packed off to Russia," Randolph Considine had complained, "and anyone who talks to Linkevich in English or German always seems to get the wrong end of the stick. So do us a favor and find out what he knows about Prince Kamal's wife."

"Why's he still here?" McColl had wanted to know. "I thought the man was a revolutionary—why hasn't *he* gone back to Russia?"

Considine had laughed. "Well, he's been so useful to us that we put a few obstacles in his way. He kicked up a fuss at first, but since we doubled his usual fee, he seems to have settled down again."

Maxim Linkevich held court in an alley just west of the Shari' Clot Bey. Having arrived in Cairo from points unknown in late 1913—the rumor that he'd escaped from Siberian exile was probably his own invention—he'd soon made himself the city's one indispensable source for local intelligence. The British, always the last to know what their subjects were thinking or doing, were his main customers.

McColl had visited the café twice in 1916, and Linkevich was always at the same table, the one farthest from the door. The light seemed poorer than McColl remembered, the two kerosene lamps hanging in the smoky atmosphere like navigation lights in a fog. There were several other customers drinking either mint tea or Turkish coffee, but none gave him a second look.

"Jack McColl," the Russian said, rising with a smile and offering his hand. He looked much the same, his thick, dark hair brushed back and overlong, the quick black eyes behind the pebble glasses, a mouth that always seemed to be slightly open. Perhaps he had put on a few pounds—the lightweight tropical suit hugged him a little tighter. "I heard you were back in Egypt," he said in English.

"Of course you did," McColl replied in Russian, taking the proffered chair.

Linkevich offered him an expensive-looking Turkish cigarette and switched languages. "It's so nice to hear my own tongue. And from someone who doesn't butcher it. Some of your colleagues . . ." He shook his head sadly. "I wouldn't bet much on their chances if they've gone to subvert our revolution."

"As if," McColl said with a smile. These days he wasn't a regular smoker, but he'd always been fond of Turkish tobacco.

"So how I can help you?" the Russian asked, leaning back in his chair, cigarette arm aloft.

McColl got straight to the point. "The wife of Prince Kamal al-Din Husayn," he said carefully. "She's also the sister of the old khedive, as I recall—"

"The one you British got rid of," Linkevich helpfully interjected.

McColl looked hurt. "We relieved him of his duties," he conceded. "I'm sure he's enjoying a life of luxury on some Italian island or other."

"No doubt. Let me spare you a lengthy explanation. The old khedive's brother, whom you put in his place, is ill and probably dying, and it has finally come to your attention that Prince Kamal, who's next in line, will refuse to succeed him while you British are calling the shots. And you've probably heard that he and his wife are rather fond of the Germans."

McColl smiled. "And?"

"You want to know if the rumors are true and, if they are, whether the royal lovebirds are plotting with the enemy."

"Succinctly put."

"Thank you. So how much are you offering—the usual?"

"Plus ten percent," McColl said generously. No one had bothered to tell him what the usual was.

"Fine. But I also want a new passport. The nationality doesn't matter, as long it gets me home."

McColl considered. "We'll need something special for that."

"Have I ever let His Majesty down?" Linkevich inquired.

"Not yet."

The Russian tapped the ash from his cigarette into an already brimming saucer. "Well, I should begin by pointing your Mr. Considine in another direction altogether. These royal fools don't matter. Even if Kamal and his wife are plotting with the Germans, there's no chance they could ever be anything more than figureheads—they can only front for the Germans once the Germans are already in charge. They couldn't actually *put* them in charge. These people have no soldiers, no popular following—all they have is money, and I imagine they're only allowed to hang on to that providing they spend it on things that don't matter."

"So who should we be looking at?" McColl asked, guessing that Linkevich had other names to offer.

"We are agreed on the terms?"

"We're agreed."

Linkevich nodded. "The Germans have had someone in Cairo for more than a month." He smiled slyly. "So I've been waiting for your visit."

"What's his name?"

"Halberg. He's a Swede, an archaeologist before the war—I don't know if he still goes digging for that sort of treasure."

"Address?"

"I don't know. He was staying in the Rosetti quarter, but that was his third address in as many weeks. He may have left Cairo by this time. And Egypt."

"If he—"

Linkevich raised a hand. "He's not the one that matters. The ones who do are the Egyptians he talked to. They are the threat. The people who suffer real hardship from British rule, not the inbred peacocks who have their lives sent out from Harrods. And the Germans know this. The Egyptians never liked you British, but now they're beginning to hate you. There are just too many stories going around about the Labour Corps, and how all these volunteers are really anything but, and how badly they're treated the moment you get them out of Egypt. The Germans are looking for people who can channel all this anger—worker and peasant leaders, intellectuals, students. Looking and finding, I think."

"Think or know?"

"Well, I know about one man. He's a lawyer, quite young, I believe. His name is Safar, Abasi Safar. He has represented the families of several Labour Corps men who died in Palestine, supposedly in accidents but probably of ill treatment. Halberg made contact with him, and Safar has agreed to set up some sort of clandestine network. It was a good choice on their part. He's well known in his section of Cairo, very competent, very popular. And if you arrest him, you'll probably only make things worse."

"We can hardly just let him get on with it."

Linkevich shrugged. "It's not my place to say, but I thought you employed Theorides to take care of situations like this."

As was usually the case with Linkevich, McColl had to stop himself from asking, *How the hell do you know all this?* Theorides was another Cairo institution, this time of Greek origin. And while Linkevich employed an army of investigators to obtain his impressive results, Theorides relied on a gang of cutthroats. His results ended up entangled in reeds like Moses or stripped to the bone by desert winds.

Hearing McColl's report an hour or so later, Considine came to the same conclusion. McColl couldn't say he was happy about it, but treason was treason, particularly in time of war, and dying for one's country was hardly a rare occurrence. The manner of it, though, was something of a shock. Accompanying the local police to Safar's apartment in Bulaq on the following afternoon, McColl found himself staring at the aftermath of a supposed burglary, in the commission of which a man, a woman, and a child had all been stabbed to death. It would have been bad enough if McColl hadn't known them, but this was the middle-class family he'd sat and talked to on the train from Alex. The ones who'd looked worried when they realized he spoke their language. Now he knew why.

THE TRAIN HADN'T MOVED FOR over six hours, and there seemed no immediate prospect of its doing so. In the first-class carriage, the mood was more smug than angry. *This is what happens when you tinker with the social order,* the faces said, as if six-hour waits in the middle of nowhere had been unknown before the lower classes had the cheek to overthrow their betters.

The view through Caitlin Hanley's carriage window, like so much else in Russia, was open to interpretation. A peaceful-looking river ran parallel to the railway tracks; beyond it a couple of peasants had spent much of the day scything the lawn that sloped up to the elegant mansion. On several occasions two young boys in Lord Fauntleroy outfits had run out onto the terrace and been shooed back inside by their nannies. Out here in the country, the present still looked a lot like the past.

Or did it? Over the six hours, Caitlin had seen paintings and statuettes carried out to a waiting cart and sensed a real unease in the scurrying servants and grooms. Every now and then, one would cast a worried glance toward the peasants on the lawn, who spent more time staring at the house than swinging their scythes.

According to one of the ladies in Caitlin's carriage, the mansion belonged to Count Domontovich, whose prewar investments in Baku oil had tripled the family fortune. He was apparently away in Ryazan, contesting the local soviet's confiscation of his forests. "As if the peasants would know how to look after them," the woman had added dismissively.

The first-class carriage was replete with such opinions, and since leaving Tambov early that morning Caitlin had taken care to keep her own political views to herself. She'd been in Russia for several months but still felt far from sated—the endless debates, and the almost limitless possibilities they opened up, were like a drug she couldn't get enough of. And the more she understood the language, the more addictive the drug became.

She had started learning Russian the day that news of the czar's overthrow reached Brooklyn but knew that getting there might prove difficult. After leaving England under something of a cloud in 1916—the authorities suspected her of a more-than-journalistic involvement in the Dublin Easter Rising—she had lost both her job and her access to Europe. But America's entry into the war had changed everything—the New York papers were crying out for journalists with European experience, and the British government was bending over backward to please its new ally. The *Chronicle,* busy expanding its European desk, had not only taken her on but also put her in charge of following Russian affairs. As spring had arrived in Brooklyn, she'd boarded a ship to England.

She had hoped, without much expectation, to find her lover in London, but Jack McColl's flat was empty and felt like it had been for weeks. No letters had reached her since his departure from America early in the New Year, and none were waiting at their London poste restante. The arrangement they had come to after the Easter Rising was still in place: they would do their incompatible jobs—he as an agent of the British government, she as a journalist with radical views—until the war was over. They would meet up whenever they could, but only as lovers; they would not probe each other's professional secrets.

She had no idea where he was and had to admit that she didn't spend all her days wondering. The summer in Russia had been so absorbing, an emotional jamboree of people and happenings, of dreams and nightmares and everything in between.

It was getting dark outside. Feeling the need to stretch her legs, she walked to the end of the carriage and stepped down to the side of the track just as Dmitri Ezhov was passing. The young Socialist Revolutionary, whom she'd met only that morning, had taken a stroll down the line to see what was holding them up. A verst or so to the west, he'd found another train whose crew knew no more than their own. There were probably others in front of that one and others still bringing up their rear.

Farther down the train, passengers from the third-class carriages were collecting water from the river. Yellow lights glowed in several windows of the mansion opposite, and as she looked across, Caitlin heard—or perhaps imagined—what sounded like a gong. Was the Domontovich family being called to dinner? Having eaten nothing since breakfast, she felt hungry enough to swim the river and present herself, gracefully dripping, at the dining-room table.

She would probably find a welcome—Russians of all classes were inclined to be hospitable.

After wishing Ezhov good night, she climbed back aboard and curled herself up in her frayed first-class seat. Two groups of passengers were playing cards, several other people reading, but most seemed to be dozing. Caitlin felt her own eyes closing and offered up a silent prayer that the next thing she felt would be wheels moving beneath her.

She wasn't sure which woke her up—the voices full of anger and alarm or the orange light dancing in the varnished panels of the wall beside her. Through her window she could see that one whole wing of the mansion was on fire, and even as she watched, the other wing burst into flame. Anywhere else in the world, an accident would have been the natural assumption, but here in Russia, in this of all summers, that was the least likely explanation. Every week the papers carried news of one or more estates falling prey to arsonists, and several prominent families had either perished in their blazing homes or escaped the flames only to be skewered on their peasants' pitchforks.

Caitlin walked to the veranda at the end of the car and squeezed herself into the knot of watching passengers. The mood was black, one army officer muttering darkly about future revenge while his pretty young wife clung to his arm, two older men in business suits tut-tutting and shaking their heads at the madness of it all.

"Are we safe here?" the officer's wife asked, gazing out across the river.

"I'll shoot the first man who enters the water," her husband promised.

On the opposite bank, several motionless figures were silhouetted against the flames. A ring of watchers, a ring of arsonists. Several dogs were barking, and the shadowy shapes of horses were moving in the gloom. The unseasonal sound of sleigh bells mixed with the sharp crack of timbers.

No one was hurrying down to the river, not that doing so would have made much difference. The house was beyond saving, ablaze from end to end. In one of the upper windows, something moved—a curtain, Caitlin hoped, though the bloodcurdling cries that accompanied the apparition suggested something more gruesome. Windows exploded one after another, like a particularly virulent string of firecrackers. Someone screamed, though whether from pain or excitement was impossible to tell.

The young officer next to Caitlin was breathing heavily, like a dog straining at his leash. "Domontovich was a good landlord," another man insisted. "He even set up a school for his peasants' children."

Eager to get away from them, Caitlin shouldered her way into the next carriage and walked on down the train until she reached the third-class section. It was another world. A few of the older passengers were sleeping, but most were lined up by the windows, faces lit with exultation. That really was the only word for it. Tinged with guilt perhaps, though exultation nonetheless. They hadn't set the fire, but it was theirs.

She remembered the Bolshevik in Tambov who had seemed so unperturbed by the recent jailing of his leaders. In his opinion only fools thought the czar's departure would be the final word.

"What do you want?" a young soldier asked, tapping her on the shoulder. He didn't look particularly threatening, but Caitlin was suddenly aware of other eyes turned in her direction, examining her clothes, seeing what looked like the enemy.

"Nothing," she said automatically.

"She's a comrade from America," Ezhov said, appearing at her shoulder like a guardian angel.

"She doesn't look like one."

"Well, she is. She writes about our revolution for the American workers and soldiers. Writes about things like this," he added, encompassing the fire outside with a sweep of the hand.

"I do," Caitlin said gratefully. She did.

"They've had it coming for a long time," one woman said.

"I know," Caitlin said diplomatically. Perhaps the parents did, but the children?

Most of the faces seemed mollified.

"I'll go back to my seat," she told Ezhov.

He insisted on escorting her. "There are bound to be excesses," he said sadly as they reached her carriage. "After so many years of cruelty . . ."

"I understand," she said. "And thank you."

Once he was gone, she sat watching the flames rippling like gold dust on the surface of the river. Not long after, their steward announced that the train would soon be moving. The entertainment was over, she thought, and now they could be on their way. A few minutes later, without so much as a whistle, the train clanked into motion, and all that was left in the window was her own distraught reflection.

2

The Ever-Expanding Empire

It was a beautiful morning for a funeral, if such a thing were possible. The sun was bathing the distant hills in gold and drawing the deepest blue from the placid waters of the loch. It was chilly, but the lack of a breeze took off the edge; away to the north, the haze of smoke that always lay over the engine shed hung in the air like a miniature cloud.

Between fifty and sixty people were gathered around the waiting grave. As often seemed the case, the deceased had been more popular with his colleagues than with his family. Almost all those present were men that Euan McColl had worked with, either on the railway or in the union. Most had taken the early-morning train from Glasgow in their Sunday suits; the rest had walked up the cinder path from the depot in their work clothes. McColl had last seen some of the faces in their back room on Abrach Road more than twenty-five years before.

"It's a shame Jed couldn't be here," his mother murmured.

"Yes," he agreed, glancing at her. His brother hadn't liked their father any more than he had, but a week's leave to attend the old bastard's funeral would have been a damn sight more congenial than enduring seven more days of the endless Battle of Ypres, especially now that Mac was gone. Their friend had "drowned in the mud," according to Jed's last letter. As the war entered its fourth year, such brutal honesty was apparently much in favor, particularly among the younger soldiers.

As the thought crossed McColl's mind that his mother might go home from her husband's funeral to find news of her younger son's death waiting on the front doormat, he noticed a taxi draw up at the cemetery gates. Much to his surprise, he saw Caitlin step out. She was wearing a long plum-colored skirt beneath a high-collared black jacket, on her head a hat with a little veil, and she was carrying only a small black bag. She must have left her luggage at the station, he thought. As she walked across the grass toward them, tucking some stray tendrils of hair back beneath her hat, he felt his heart lift inside his rib cage.

She worked her way through the crowd of mourners, hugged his mother and then him. The vicar paused in his reading and gave them a mildly disapproving look before resuming. "Ashes to ashes . . ."

"How did you know?" McColl asked Caitlin in a whisper.

"I arrived back from Russia yesterday morning and found the telegram your mother sent you at the flat."

"Ah."

The coffin was about to be lowered. His mother had spared no expense, McColl thought, comparing this polished casket to the roughly nailed boxes stacked high on Scottish railway platforms awaiting shipment to France.

As this one went down on the ropes, McColl felt tears welling up in his eyes, and he almost angrily brushed them away. He wouldn't have cried for his father two years earlier, but the stroke that had almost killed him in 1915 had humanized the old man. Euan McColl hadn't suddenly become a loving father, but he had turned into someone to pity rather than hate. At moments there had even been glimpses of the man his mother must have fallen in love with, all those years ago.

The clunk of earth on wood mingled with a plaintive whistle from the direction of the station, as if one of the engines his father had driven in his youth were trying to say good-bye.

The railwaymen were lining up to pay their respects to the dead man's wife. She seemed coolness personified, greeting each man with a smile and a few words of reminiscence, almost like a politician. Over the last several years, Margaret McColl, like so many others, had had her life turned upside down, but in her case the changes had been generally positive. The cowering housewife had become a political activist, her name as widely known as her husband's had been at the height of his union career.

McColl's boss, Cumming—the head of the relatively new Secret Service—had mentioned seeing her name in *The Times* in connection with the rent strikes. He had given McColl an inquiring look, but a shrug in reply had sufficed to close the subject—Cumming was too old-school to openly pry into an agent's family affairs. Still, McColl had felt his boss's anxiety. Could an agent in thrall to two uppity women—Caitlin being the other—be relied on in the empire's hour of need? Then again, could Cumming afford to dispense with someone who spoke nine languages and had, over the last three years, served him with some distinction?

Heaven only knew, McColl thought. He had given Cumming reason enough to fire him in 1916, when his career and life had gotten so dangerously entangled with the anti-British activities of the young woman who now stood beside him.

"How are you doing?" Caitlin asked him quietly.

"Okay."

"He must have been liked," she offered, a hint of surprise in her tone. She'd only met Jack's father after the stroke, but she'd heard enough about his earlier shortcomings as a husband and father from the rest of the family.

"I suppose he was," McColl conceded, wondering if half this number would attend his own funeral. He very much doubted it.

THE THREE OF THEM TOOK the hired car back into town and, after collecting Caitlin's luggage, decided they might as well have lunch at the hotel.

"How are Jed and Mac?" Caitlin asked once they'd taken their seats in the nearly empty restaurant.

"Jed's okay, as far as we know. But Mac was killed a few weeks ago."

"Oh, I'm sorry." Caitlin was shocked. She hadn't known Mac well, but he'd been part of Jack's life for several years, first as his mechanic at the automobile firm and then as Jed's best friend in peace and war. And she'd liked him. "He was a nice boy," she added, conscious of how feeble it sounded. How many dead soldiers had received that epitaph in the last three years?

"He really was," Margaret McColl agreed. "And I think his death has hit Jed quite hard," she went on, looking at her other son for confirmation.

"I don't know," he said. "I suppose so. It's difficult to tell from his letters, particularly when half the words are blanked out by the censors."

After a few moments' silence, Caitlin asked Margaret how things were in Glasgow, and McColl was more than happy to let the two women spend most of the lunch swapping stories of the socialist and feminist struggle they both seemed to live for, here in Scotland and in newly czarless Russia. His mother had some welcome news for Caitlin—only the day before, the *Glasgow Herald* had reported that her home state of New York had finally granted women the right to vote.

Once they'd eaten, Margaret McColl announced that she'd go for a walk around the town. On her own. "Have a think about the man we just buried. Visit our old haunts. One last cry, maybe," she said, almost defiantly. "And if you two haven't seen each other for ten months, I expect you have a lot to catch up on," she added with what looked like a twinkle.

THEY HAD INDEED. AFTERWARD, AS they lay naked in each other's arms, Caitlin couldn't help thinking of all the men and women who'd been parted for a great deal longer. "We should be grateful we see each other as often as we do," she murmured.

McColl laughed. "Sorry, I just remembered something Jed put in one of his letters. One soldier in his unit was saying that every night he spent apart from his wife was a fuck the government owed him, so his mate turns and tells him that the government probably thinks they've fucked him enough already."

Caitlin shook her head. "That's too true to be funny."

"I suppose it is. Did you have any trouble getting back into Britain?"

"Less than I expected. They kept me for quite a long time, but the man asking the questions knew nothing about my history. As far as I could tell, the only thing that interested him was that I'd been in Russia."

"And Russia really was as wonderful as you told my mother?"

She heaved herself up onto one elbow. "You think I made it up?"

"No, of course not. But Russia's still in the war, and things can't be that easy over there."

"They're not," she conceded. "But there's a feeling of hope, of change, that I haven't experienced anywhere else. I know things are happening in Glasgow and other places, but this is a whole country we're talking about, and there don't seem to be any limits to what could happen." She lay back down. "I know I'm not supposed to ask, but have you been there since the revolution?"

"I was there in April. Weighing up the chances of Russia fighting on," he added in explanation.

"And what did you report?" she asked, pushing her luck.

"That the chances would be a lot better if we sent them some weapons to fight with."

"And have you?" she asked, knowing the answer.

"Yes, but nowhere near enough. You've only just come back— what do you think?"

"It's merely a matter of time. The soldiers are deserting in droves, and I don't think there's anything the government can do to stop them. And it's not only the lack of guns, not anymore. It's the lack of a reason. The soldiers have finally realized it's not their war."

"Even though their new government—the one most of them welcomed—says it is."

"I imagine a lot of them have realized that Kerensky's government isn't new enough. He and his cronies talk a good talk, but they haven't actually changed very much. The war's still going on, the elite still own the banks and the factories and most of the land. The czar's gone, but most of his supporters are still around, pulling what strings they can and waiting their chance to turn the clocks back. But I think they're dreaming. It's much more likely someone will speed it up."

"Another revolution? Led by whom?"

"The Bolsheviks, probably."

"But there are so few of them."

Caitlin shook her head. "Their numbers have probably multiplied by ten since you left in May."

McColl gave a low whistle.

"Kerensky won't last the year," she predicted.

AN HOUR OR SO LATER, they discovered how right she was. Standing at the hotel bar, waiting to order drinks for Caitlin and his mother, McColl overheard the barman tell two of the railwaymen who'd attended the funeral that there'd been a revolution in Russia.

"Aye," one of them replied with a deadpan face. "That news reached Glasgow about six months ago."

The barman gave him a look. "No, you idjit. Another one."

When McColl relayed the exchange, Caitlin insisted on seeking out an evening paper. She returned ten minutes later, holding it aloft. "I *was* right," she said triumphantly. "The Bolsheviks have seized power in Petrograd. Kerensky's gone into hiding."

"Is this good news?" Margaret McColl asked.

"It has to be," Caitlin told her. "But the report doesn't have any details. It doesn't say whether the other socialist groups are involved. Or what's happening in the other big cities."

"I suppose you'll be going back?" McColl's mother said, sounding almost envious.

"Yes, yes, I will. I must find a telephone," she told them both.

As McColl watched her rush from the room, he had a premonition of how this might pull them apart. If she'd just been going back as a journalist, there'd be nothing to fear, but she'd also be returning as a campaigner, as someone whose sense of herself was thoroughly entangled with her political beliefs. This, he realized, really might change everything.

She returned about half an hour later. "Why did I leave?" she asked herself and them as she sat back down. "I'm sorry. It's wonderful to see you both, even in such circumstances, but I knew that something like this was going to happen. I told my editor it would, but he wouldn't listen. He just kept saying that American readers are much more interested in what their own troops are doing in France, even though he knows that only a handful have actually arrived." She sighed heavily and took a sip of beer. "Anyway, I got the office in London to telegraph the States. I won't get a reply until tomorrow, but I know they'll want me back there. And there's a boat that leaves Aberdeen for Bergen on Sunday morning. How do I get to Aberdeen from here?"

Less than forty-eight hours, McColl thought. That was all they'd have. "There are plenty of ways," he told her. "And that's because none are easy. But I'll come with you."

"No, you should stay," Caitlin said, glancing pointedly at his mother.

"I'll be fine," Margaret McColl told them both.

THEY SET OFF FROM FORT William soon after nine, McColl trying not to let his disappointment at the shortness of their reunion spoil the day they had. Caitlin seemed to realize as much. "I wish we had more time together," she told him, "but there isn't another boat for at least a fortnight, and I can't take the risk of missing out on a story like this."

"I know," he said. And he did. But still . . .

That morning, as he waited for Caitlin to finish in the bathroom, a boy had arrived at their door with a telegram from London. Cumming wanted to see him, preferably yesterday. McColl had returned the slip to its envelope and offered it back to the boy. "I'll be leaving in a few minutes. If I give you a pound, do you think you could say I was already gone when you tried to deliver it?"

The boy had considered the proposition, but not for long. "Aye, I think I could manage that."

McColl had handed him the note and watched him skip back down the stairs.

Since then the day, too, had gone downhill. The two of them had started wading through newspapers while waiting at the station, Caitlin eagerly searching for fresh news from Russia, McColl scanning the latest war reports for any indication, no matter how slight, of a break in the murderous stalemate in France. There was none he could see and, with the new revolution in Russia, even less chance that one would turn up. He had hoped that America's entry into the war would finally tip the balance, but now it seemed that Caitlin's countrymen would merely take the place of the disappearing Russians. As their train steamed south across Rannoch Moor, McColl found himself wondering how long he and she could make their relationship work in a war that never ended.

IN THE SEAT BESIDE HIM, she was having similar thoughts. When she woke that morning, part of her didn't want to go. It was too soon. What could two people do in forty-eight hours? They could make love several times and swap news, but they couldn't find out how the other person really *was.* Jack seemed tired to her, not physically but mentally, emotionally, as if the war were wearing him down. Which was hardly surprising. The constant worrying over Jed must be exhausting, and now his father had died. She had no real idea of what the latter meant to him, and neither, she suspected, did he. He'd said he didn't want to talk about it now, but now was all they had.

THE TRAIN RATTLED ON, REACHING Crianlarich soon after eleven. They had an hour's wait there, another in Stirling. As their third train neared Perth, McColl realized that she'd fallen asleep, her head on his shoulder. Well, they hadn't slept much the previous night, and the stirring of desire evoked by the memory mingled with the scent of her hair and the warmth of her breath on his neck to conjure up a wonderful sense of completion. He could have died there and then, McColl thought, but of course he wouldn't.

The wait in Perth was closer to two hours. They ate a late lunch in the station buffet, which was crowded with soldiers and sailors. One of the former, apparently blinded, kept turning his bandaged eyes this way and that, as if seeking out someone to blame. His escort, whose facial features suggested a close relation, had only lost an arm.

Most of the other patrons were staring at McColl, and not with any affection. On each of his last two visits to Britain, someone had handed him a coward's white feather, and a third seemed in the cards. "Let's talk Russian," he told her in that language. Caitlin had surprised him the night before with the news that she'd become almost fluent during her four-month stay.

"All right," she replied in kind. "Any special reason?"

He explained that these days he was considered too young to be out of uniform. "And I can't actually announce that I work for the Secret Service."

"I was wondering why they were looking at you like that. I thought they were just jealous of your beautiful companion."

"I'm sure she makes things worse," he conceded. Looking around, he saw that the ruse had worked—thinking him a foreigner, the locals no longer seemed keen on a lynching.

"Does this happen often?" she asked.

"Not very," he told her. "And anyway, sticks and stones and all that . . ."

Storm clouds overtook them on the last leg of the journey, and it was still teeming when their train reached Aberdeen. During the taxi ride to the port, they could hardly hear each other speak for the raindrops drumming on the roof, and both got wetter than they bargained for in their dash to the shipping office. The clerk within confirmed the next morning's sailing and was happy to sell Caitlin a berth.

Twenty minutes later they were making love on a very bouncy bed in their fourth-floor hotel room. After sharing a bath in the outsize tub, they found themselves back in bed and reached for their clothes only when the chances of finding somewhere still open for dinner began to look less than certain.

By the time they got downstairs, the hotel dining room was closed, but the desk clerk knew of an Italian eatery only two streets away. There were no taxis outside, but the rain had almost stopped, so they walked. The restaurant in question was still surprisingly busy. And given the current level of war-induced privation, the food and wine on offer seemed more than acceptable.

"You couldn't do much better in Little Italy," Caitlin said. "I used to eat lunch there when I worked in Manhattan," she explained.

"There are a lot of Italian restaurants in Glasgow," McColl told her. "But I don't think my parents ever went to any. My father didn't trust foreign food, so my mother never got the chance to try it."

"How will she cope, do you think? Now that he's gone."

"Pretty well, if the last couple of years are anything to go by. As long as Jed survives," he added, as if the thought had just occurred to him.

"And you, too."

"Not in the same way. I can't explain it, but I think Jed dying would hit her harder. I don't think she loves me any less, but . . . I don't know. How are your family coping? Your brother Fergus is too old to be conscripted, isn't he?"

"Yes. And so is Finola's husband, Patrick. She's had another baby, by the way. A girl this time."

"And your Aunt Orla?"

Caitlin considered. "She seems to have aged a lot lately. She's healthy enough, but . . ."

"Colm's death must have been hard for her," McColl suggested with some trepidation. Caitlin's younger brother had been hanged in the Tower of London two years earlier, after taking part in an Irish republican plot to sabotage the transporting of British troops to France. McColl had caught and arrested him, albeit after offering to let him escape.

"Perhaps," Caitlin agreed. "She'll always feel she was partly responsible, favoring Finola and me—especially me—after our mother died, and neglecting him."

"She actually said that?"

Caitlin smiled wryly. "Repeatedly."

"Does she know my part in this?"

"Oh, yes. I eventually told her the whole story, and she was much more understanding of your behavior than I was. I think she made it easier for me to forgive you."

"And your father?"

"He doesn't know. And he would *never* forgive you."

"I'm glad you did."

"So am I."

Back at the hotel, a discarded evening paper was lying on the bar. There was a full account of the Bolshevik rising in Petrograd, which had apparently been virtually bloodless, and a much sketchier report from Moscow, where serious fighting was allegedly under way. A map of European Russia showed the wide sweep of towns now under Lenin's control.

"Have you met any of the Bolshevik leaders—other than your friend Kollontai?" McColl asked. Caitlin had known and corresponded with the Bolsheviks' most prominent woman for several years.

"Quite a few," she said. "I met Inessa Armand and Krupskaya—Lenin's wife—at the *Rabotnitsa* offices—that's the women's magazine. I interviewed Trotsky in June, after meeting him in the street. And I met Radek and Bukharin at friends' apartments."

He was impressed but hardly surprised. He knew how good a journalist she was. "What about Lenin?" he asked.

"No. I mean, I've seen him speak, but I haven't actually been introduced."

"And are they the fanatics our papers say they are?"

Caitlin smiled. "They're serious about real change. Does that make them fanatics?"

"That depends. Do they want it at any cost?"

She shook her head. "What does that mean? Would you call your General Haig a fanatic?"

"I might," McColl said lightly as they waited for the lift. "But most wouldn't."

"Well, he's hell-bent on defeating the Germans at any cost, and that wouldn't change the way we live."

"And the Bolsheviks will?"

"They want to. I don't know if they can, but . . ."

"Russia doesn't seem like the ideal setting for a new world."

She sighed. "Maybe not, but as we say in the States, it's the only show in town."

"I almost wish I were coming with you," he said as they got into the lift.

She smiled at that. "You know, I almost wish it, too. But you can't, and I must. And I think I'm ready for bed."

The lift door opened to reveal a uniformed constable standing outside their room.

"Mr. Jack McColl?" the man asked.

"That's me."

"I have a message for you. From London."

"Yes?" McColl responded, feeling more than a trifle irritated by how quickly they'd tracked him down.

The constable pulled a note from his pocket and reminded himself of the contents. "'Mr. Cumming requires your presence,'" he read.

"Thank you," McColl told him.

The young man consulted his watch. "You may just have time to catch the night train," he suggested helpfully.

"I don't think so," McColl told him. "I'll take one in the morning," he added, following Caitlin into the room and gently closing the door behind them.

HE WAS THE FIRST AWAKE and lay there watching as a patch of sunlight climbed the opposite wall. There were echoes of that last morning in New York, three and a half years before, when she'd accompanied him to the Hoboken ferry, the first leg of his journey to Mexico. And on that occasion he'd had no idea that they wouldn't share a bed again for almost two years.

He eased himself from this one and walked across to the window. The North Sea seemed bluer than usual, stretching beyond the docks under a cloudless sky. He hoped there were no U-boats waiting out there, hoped that the revolution she was going so far to report was as bloodless as the newspapers claimed. He hated the thought of her putting herself in any sort of danger but knew how useless it would be to say so. She was going, and that was that.

THE FOLLOWING MORNING WAS COLD, windy, and wet. McColl rode the bus south along Charing Cross Road, thinking how dour London was beginning to look after almost four years of war. The shop windows seemed sparse; the few umbrella-wielding pedestrians hurrying past them all looked anxious or grumpy. Trafalgar Square was virtually deserted, a scattering of empty bottles around the lion plinths left over from the drinking of the night before.

McColl got off the bus, put up his own umbrella, and started walking toward the river. The wind insisted on turning the brolly inside out, and he eventually gave up the struggle, arriving wet and somewhat bedraggled at the Service HQ in Whitehall Court. Cumming's office up under the eaves looked much the same, full of maps and models, the man himself ramrod straight behind his cluttered desk.

"Sorry to hear about your father," Cumming said gruffly. "The Russian army is disintegrating," he added without any further ado, almost conveying the impression that the two events might be connected. "More than half the units on the Eastern Front have stopped fighting, and the armies in Turkey have simply turned their backs and started for home. The Russians in northern Persia are holding their ground at the moment, but probably only because they're so far from the front. If either the Turks or the Germans head their way, we don't expect them to put up a fight."

"Have the Bolsheviks actually sued for peace?" McColl asked.

Cumming sighed. "Not yet. But the way they're talking it's only a matter of days. None of our experts think the Bolsheviks will survive much beyond Christmas, but the damage will be done by then. The main problem, of course, is that the Germans will be able to shift their armies in Russia to the Western Front. If they do that quickly enough, they'll have a significant advantage when spring comes."

"Won't the Americans make up the difference?"

"Not by then. And if the Germans win a major victory while the Yanks are still on the way . . . well, we're looking at another five years of war. And frankly, I'm not sure the country could stand it."

McColl was inclined to agree.

"But the Western Front's a matter for the General Staff," Cumming went on. "Our job is to shore up what's left of the Eastern Front and prevent the Germans and Turks from exploiting the Russian collapse." He paused. "I've lumped them together because they're allies, but they want different things. The Germans can make good their oil shortage if they occupy the Caucasus, and they can grab all the cotton they need for making munitions if they push on across the Caspian and take control of Turkestan, where this year's crop still hasn't been shipped. And that's not all. There are more than forty thousand German and Austrian prisoners of war in the area, who could also end up fighting our men in France.

"And then there are the Turks. They see Turkestan as a replacement for the empire they're losing in the Middle East, so they won't want the Germans to hang around, but they'll take what help they can get to push any opposition out of the way. And if they manage that between them, then the road to India will be wide open."

McColl shook his head. "Road?" he asked. "We're talking about a thousand miles of desert and mountains. Does anyone really think that the Germans could move a meaningful number of troops across that sort of distance and that sort of terrain? If they do, they've spent too much time looking at maps and not enough at the real world."

Cumming nodded. "You may be right, but some of our so-called experts are worried, and those are the ones the politicians seem to be listening to. I spoke to some government chap yesterday who insisted that Britain had to absorb Central Asia into the empire, as the last link in a crescent stretching from South Africa through East Africa, Mesopotamia, India, Singapore, and Australia. That if we don't take over the area, the Germans will."

"I'm sure he consulted his atlas," McColl said dryly.

Cumming smiled. "All right, but even if there's no real threat to India, we still have an interest in stopping the Germans and Turks from taking the Caucasus and getting across the Caspian. If we deny them the oil and cotton, we damage their whole war economy and compromise whatever offensives they mount in France."

"Okay," McColl said. "So what's in their way?"

"That's hard to say. The winter weather in eastern Turkey and the Caucasus Mountains is pretty severe, and they probably plan to use the next few months to get their supply chain in order, with a spring offensive in mind. The Caucasus has always been a hotbed of disputes. The Armenians, Russians, Georgians, the Azer-whatsits—the place has been divided on national and religious lines since kingdom come, and now it's divided on political lines as well. There are Bolsheviks and Mensheviks and God knows what else almost everywhere, fighting one another and what's left of the old order, and it's hard to keep track of who's in control of any particular place. But as far as we know, the Bolsheviks are in control of both the Baku oilfields and the cotton-producing areas of Turkestan. They run the soviet in Tashkent—you know what a soviet is?"

"An elected council."

"So they say. They run that one, but not the one in Ashkhabad, which the cotton shipments would have to pass through. The soviet there is theoretically subordinate to the one in Tashkent, but the two cities are five hundred miles apart and the Bolsheviks are only one of several influential groups in Ashkhabad. The other socialist parties resent being ruled from Tashkent, and the local Turks—Turcomen, I think they're called—resent Russian rule full stop. So anyone seeking to stir things up would have something to work with. How's your Russian?"

"Pretty good."

"Seems like a hell of a language to me. Strange alphabet, and it sounds like they all have bad colds."

McColl smiled. For someone who ran a global organization—and, as far as McColl could tell, ran it well—Cumming was remarkably insular. "It's not the easiest," he said diplomatically. "I had a lot of help. I studied it at Oxford, and I had a Russian friend who gave me lessons in return for improving his English. And I've been there three times. The job last year and twice before the war, when I was still selling automobiles."

"Can you pass as a native?"

McColl considered his answer. "Most of the time, in most places. My vocabulary's good, but the accent can wander a bit. The trick is claiming you're from a different region than the person you're talking to, because they put down any discrepancies to that."

"That shouldn't be too difficult in Turkestan," Cumming suggested. "If their empire's anything like ours, there'll be people from all over Russia."

"Probably. So that's where I'm going?" McColl asked, just to be certain.

"You and another agent, Audley Cheselden—have you run across him?"

"No," McColl said, hiding his surprise. He was used to working alone and generally preferred it that way.

"He's a good man. Young and a trifle rash on occasion, but sound enough. He's in South Africa at the moment, so you'll meet up in Egypt and go on to Persia together."

McColl nodded. The rain now hammering on the office windows made such places sound almost attractive. "I assume you have some specific tasks for us. Beyond just stirring things up."

Cumming grinned again. He seemed in a good mood. "First, we need up-to-date information. Who's in charge in Ashkhabad and how far does their writ run? Are there any people or groups among them who'll work with us against the Germans and the Turks? If not, are there any opposition groups who would if given the chance? Second, I want a report on how and where we could best put the Transcaspian Railway out of action. It's the only means of moving troops from the eastern shore of the Caspian to the border of Afghanistan—wreck it and we wreck any faint hope they might have of marching on India. Or of moving all that cotton in the opposite direction. We have to keep those stockpiles out of German hands, and it may well be that you'll need to destroy them. Is that specific enough for you?"

"It certainly is. One question, though. What if our best allies against the Germans turn out to be the Bolsheviks?"

"Then shake them by the hand. I doubt they'll last, but if they do, we can always deal with them later."

"Right," McColl said. He didn't need to wonder what Caitlin would say to that.

HIS MISSION DECIDED, McColl waited in London while others worked on the logistical details. Waited and waited. A second meeting with Cumming followed three weeks after the first, but all he learned was that his and his chief's superiors were still mulling over the many potential ramifications of the latest upheaval in Russia. No one, it seemed, could agree what to do about the Bolsheviks and their annoying aversion to war. Seduce them or step on them, that was the question, and if seduce turned out to be the answer, then annoying them first would be unwise.

The weeks turned into a month and that into almost two without a fresh summons dropping through the letter box of his Fitzrovia flat. He filled his time as best he could, reading the more serious newspapers from front page to back, paying particular attention to events in Russia, many of which he assumed Caitlin would now be witnessing. So far the Bolsheviks seemed to be doing all that she hoped, successfully keeping opponents at bay and introducing a raft of progressive legislation.

He kept a close watch on military developments elsewhere. The campaigns against the Turks in Mesopotamia and Palestine were clearly going well, but there didn't seem much change on the Western Front. The battles around Ypres and Passchendaele had ground to a halt without an obvious victor, and a new one had started around Cambrai in which armored vehicles had been used en masse for the first time. This had surprised the Germans, but no one expected the advantage gained to be anything other than brief. More depressingly still, the Italians were in danger of being routed by the Austrians, and Caitlin's Bolsheviks were suing for an Eastern Front armistice.

The one piece of really good news was that Jed had survived the latest Ypres battle and was resting with his unit some way behind the front. McColl heard this from his mother, who showed every sign of coping well with widowhood—her letters were full of Clydeside politics and Caitlin's good fortune in witnessing the future firsthand.

A letter from his brother arrived the week before Christmas. More words were blacked out than not, but Russia was mentioned several times, and always in splendid isolation. Reading between the lines, McColl was left in little doubt that the boys in the trenches were taking more than a casual interest in Caitlin's revolution.

3

A Fault Worth Cultivating

In Finland the snow had been several days old, but on the approaches to Petrograd there was little more than a dusting, a harbinger of winter rather than the real thing. The wide Neva Estuary might be the color of ice, but for now the water still rippled.

Caitlin had crossed into newly Bolshevik Russia at Tornio, after enduring a lengthy grilling from the Swedish border authorities. The Russians had been quicker and had contented themselves with a full body search, carried out with all due decency by a stocky young girl in overalls. Three days of Finnish lakes and forests had followed. Three days of endless pauses in dismal clearings, snow drifting down from darkened skies. Of black bread and coffee, the former so hard that it needed soaking, the latter so weak it barely deserved the name.

Some of her fellow passengers seemed unconcerned by the train's snaillike progress—Russians returning after years of voluntary exile were unlikely to begrudge a few extra days. Others bridled at the delays—they could hardly wait to reach Petrograd, if only to find out what was going on. Caitlin had heard nothing since Oslo—the Swedish press had been strangely silent on Russian affairs—and for all she knew, Lenin and his Bolsheviks had already been overthrown. Many of her current companions would rejoice if that proved to be the case; others would break down and weep. But most of those trapped in the slow-moving train had decided on returning before the second revolution, and they were suspending judgment. Almost everyone had heard of Lenin and his party, but few could say with any precision what the Bolsheviks actually stood for.

They were about to find out. The train was in the northern suburbs, and as it rattled through industrial Vyborg, Caitlin could see the chimneys flaunting red flags, the factory roofs emblazoned with slogans. She settled into her seat and smiled. She was back.

She wasn't expecting any help with her bags, but two young Red Guards insisted on carrying them out to the famous forecourt, where the prodigal Lenin had addressed his supporters that spring. This time it lay empty, and she waited several minutes for a droshky. As they crossed the river, the middle-aged driver happily answered her questions. Yes, the Bolsheviks were still in control. Yes, a few people had been killed—mostly young fools from the military academy. And yes, the Red Guards had given the reactionaries a bloody nose on the western outskirts.

As the driver seemed slightly surprised by this litany of successes, she asked if he thought the Bolsheviks would still be around at Christmas.

He thought about that for a while. "They do seem in a terrible hurry," he said eventually. "Maybe they know something that I don't."

Of the two hotels she'd patronized that summer, Caitlin preferred the Angleterre—the central location and the friendliness of its mostly youthful staff more than made up for the tawdry state of the rooms. Her old one was taken, but even this turned out a blessing—the new one had a wonderful view of the square and its cathedral. After dumping her suitcases on the sagging bed, she stood at the window watching the snowflakes drift by. Outside the cathedral a few soldiers in plain uniforms were talking in a group, their cigarettes glowing in turn. Beyond them two young girls were playing hopscotch, having drawn their boxes in the thin carpet of snow. She was here!

It was almost dark. Though she was dog-tired, her soul rebelled against simply going to bed. She had to go out.

On the pavement outside the hotel, she hesitated for a moment, wondering where to go. She knew the cafés and clubs where the foreign correspondents and their Russian friends gathered but decided she'd rather renew their acquaintance tomorrow. After three days with so little sleep, she was too tired for long conversations, and a strong voice inside her was pleading to be alone. With Russia and its revolution, if that didn't sound too silly. And even if it did.

She walked up toward the Admiralty, then right along the edge of the Alexandrov Gardens, where someone had already built a snowman. After taking a peek at the deserted plaza in front of the Winter Palace—a few Red Guards were standing sentry outside the darkened building—she went back to the top of Nevsky Prospect and started down the city's famous promenade. The streetlights were on, which seemed promising, but many shop windows were empty. Those that were not—one emporium specializing in jewel-encrusted dog collars, another in French cosmetics—bore eloquent witness to the class of residents now departed. Caitlin had encountered some of the women in Stockholm, bewailing their fate at Bolshevik hands while they bought new jewelry with the money their husbands had smuggled out.

The Club of the Noblesse, she noted with some satisfaction, was unlit and boarded shut. CLOSED BY HISTORY was daubed on the door, a length of red cloth looped across the brass doorknobs.

She crossed the Moika Canal and ambled on toward Kazan Cathedral. There were fewer promenading couples than she remembered, but that might be the change of season. There were more Red Guards, and she suddenly realized she hadn't yet seen a streetcar.

The dislocation that any political upheaval might leave in its wake? Or something more serious? This was going to be the hardest journalistic assignment of her career, if only because she felt so invested in what she was reporting. She would need to be constantly on guard against seeing only what she wanted to see.

Nearing the bridge over the Catherine Canal, she spotted an open café a short way down a side street. There was nothing but shchi, vegetable soup, to eat, and the tea proved as weak as the coffee on the train, but it was so quintessentially Russian—the smoky warmth and excited chatter, the bizarre mix of costumes all bathed in a kerosene glow. Perhaps there were fewer prostitutes, but there in the corner was the obligatory youth with burning eyes busy scribbling poetry. Every café had one.

The others at her table knew she was a foreigner—if the accent hadn't given her away, the clothes most certainly would have—but once she'd answered the usual questions—where was she from, and what was she doing in Russia?—no one insisted on knowing more. She sat sipping her tea, a smile on her face, quietly reveling in simply being there.

On the table in front of her, a small card advised against leaving a gratuity: "Just because a man must make his living by being a waiter, do not insult him by offering a tip."

Caitlin felt proud of herself for understanding the Russian, proud of the Russians for understanding the insult.

IT WAS LATE WHEN SHE woke the next morning, and she went down to the hotel restaurant with suitably low expectations. There was butter for the black bread, however, and two chunks of sugar for her tea.

The desk clerk wasn't sure there was a functioning foreign office at present but agreed that someone from the new government would want to check her journalistic credentials. He thought Smolny was her best bet—most of the new ministers had gotten such a hostile reception at their ministries that they'd retreated to the comfort of home, which for them was the former school for girls of the nobility where the Bolshevik had set up their party HQ.

Having been woken twice in the night by the sounds of distant gunfire, she asked if the streets were safe.

"Safe as they'll ever be," was the cheerful reply. According to him, there hadn't been any real fighting in Petrograd, "not even on the night they took over." And these days it was more likely to be

Red Guards firing on scavengers who'd found another abandoned wine cellar than anyone with a political ax to grind.

Partly reassured, Caitlin set off for the Smolny Institute, which she knew was a mile or more upriver. The sky had cleared again, which made for a pleasant walk, even if the pale lemon sun seemed reluctant to throw off any warmth. Staring across the Neva at the Peter and Paul Fortress, she wondered how many of the old regime were now enjoying its hospitality.

The walk proved longer than she expected, but after about an hour, a bend in the river brought the blue-and-silver domes of Smolny Convent into view. The institute was just behind it, a long, three-story building with a huge colonnaded entrance. The courtyard in front was teeming with people, mostly men and mostly armed, the sailors prominent in their singular caps and leather jerkins. Two armored cars, both still bearing the names of former czars, were parked to one side.

There were no sentries at the doors, so she went through into the entrance hall, which was twice as crowded as the courtyard and at least five times as noisy. The only people not talking were two soldiers fast asleep in their chairs, legs splayed and mouths hanging open.

She pressed on, picking one of the corridors that led away from the bedlam, then stopping at the first open doorway to inquire about foreign affairs. All but one man ignored her, and he just pointed her farther down the passage.

This happened several times, until she felt like Alice in Wonderland, lost in some vast and cavernous maze. Most people seemed so busy, and nearly everyone looked tired, including the famous Trotsky, who strode past her on one dark corridor, gesticulating wildly at an audience only he could see. The few idle hands belonged to the sleeping—curled up in office chairs and down among the stacks of pamphlets and books that lined so many of the dimly lit passages—often with rifles perched beside them.

She was beginning to despair of ever getting out, let alone finding Foreign Affairs, when someone she recognized came rushing around a corner and almost knocked her over. She had met this young man with the rounded glasses and short dark hair in the summer; his name was Volodarsky. A Jew from Ukraine, and an active revolutionary from an early age, he'd lived in the United States from 1913 until earlier this year. In that time he'd been active in the American socialist movement, and during their last conversation he and Caitlin had discovered several common acquaintances in Philly and New York City.

He did a double take when he saw her, then embraced her with a happy laugh. When she explained her reasons for being there, he volunteered himself as her guide. As they walked down corridors she was sure she'd seen before, he insisted on their meeting again, if both could find a minute to spare. "It's chaos," he said when he dropped her off at the office she needed. "But so exhilarating!"

After only a very few questions, the officials inside agreed to provide her with papers. Finding a typist and a typewriter took some time, but once this had been accomplished and her details put on file, an appointment was made with the press-liaison officer, who would tell her all she needed to know about sending dispatches home. She was welcome to use the mess hall while she waited.

She did so, sitting at a long wooden table on a long wooden bench, eating cabbage soup with a wooden spoon. Several Bolshevik leaders were having their lunch, including Bukharin and Kamenev, who seemed more interested in waving their spoons at each other than in sampling the excellent soup. There had to be several hundred people in the hall, and most of the others were eating at speed. There was a revolution to make, and only so much time in which to make it.

The one Bolshevik leader whom Caitlin could actually call a friend was conspicuous by her absence, and the thought of entering the maze for a second time was hardly welcoming. But this time she was luckier: another acquaintance from the summer—a young woman named Galina whom she'd met at the *Rabotnitsa* editorial offices—was entering the hall as Caitlin walked out. She learned from Galina that Alexandra Kollontai had been given the Ministry of Welfare to run and was the only woman in the Bolshevik cabinet.

Her ministry was on Kazanskaya Street, and that was where Caitlin would probably find her.

After seeing the press-liaison officer, she hailed a droshky and gave the address to its driver. He eschewed the route along the river, zigzagging his way eastward through a part of the city she barely knew. People were thin on the ground, but for a city that had just seen a revolution, Petrograd seemed virtually unscathed. There were no broken windows, no bullet-riddled doors, no bodies awaiting burial.

By a strange coincidence, Kazanskaya Street was where she had eaten on the previous evening. The ministry was housed in an old palace a quarter mile beyond the café, across from the canal. Two Red Guards kept vigil outside the massive doors.

One examined her papers with interest; both smiled when she explained that the new minister was an old friend. The young woman at reception was not so amenable—the minister was terribly busy, and there was no way of knowing when she'd be free.

"If you'd just tell her I'm here," Caitlin suggested. "I'm happy to wait." She took a seat in one of the two aging armchairs and looked around. The wall was covered in faded rectangular patches where paintings had been removed.

She sat back and thought about Kollontai. Caitlin had first met her Russian friend—who was actually half Ukrainian, half Finnish—in the summer of 1915. As the European correspondent of a neutral nation, Caitlin had been traveling to Germany to assess the situation there for her American readers. Her route had passed through Norway, and her British friend Sylvia Pankhurst had recommended that Caitlin stop off and visit the famous Russian feminist and socialist. The two women had hit it off immediately and spent the next three days in a whirlwind discussion of politics, love, and everything in between.

They'd corresponded ever since and had met on several occasions during Kollontai's American sojourn in the fall and winter of 1916. They had further renewed their friendship that summer, in the weeks between Caitlin's arrival in Russia and Kollontai's July arrest. At the time of their meeting in Norway, Kollontai had only recently resolved to join the Bolsheviks, and now here she was, less than three years later, a prominent member of Lenin's government.

A familiar voice was just about audible on the receptionist's telephone. "She'll see you now," the woman said, getting up. "Follow me."

They walked along a corridor and were about to ascend a wide flight of stairs when several children came barreling down. The receptionist's call for more decorum elicited a few shouted apologies but no appreciable deceleration.

Kollontai was waiting at the top of the stairs, a broad smile on her face. She looked none the worse for her summer in prison, and the blue-gray eyes were their usual riot of life. The two women enjoyed a long hug before Kollontai took one of Caitlin's hands and gently pulled her into the adjacent office.

"So this is a minister's office," Caitlin said, eyeing the tables stacked high with papers and files.

"And I am the minister," Kollontai confirmed with a shake of the head. "Who would have thought it?"

"I would," Caitlin told her. "Who were all those children?"

"Ah. They're from one of the city homes for older orphans. I have sacked all the people who ran it and proclaimed it a tiny republic. Now the children run the place themselves—they elect their own leaders, keep order, choose what food they want to eat . . ." She laughed. "When there's food to choose from, of course. But they come here to tell me how things are going—that was their executive committee."

Caitlin smiled. "It's good to see you. And to see things going so well."

"Don't count too many chickens. You should have been here a week ago. After Lenin gave me this job—much to my astonishment, I have to tell you—I was driven here in an automobile, full of myself and my mission, and I couldn't even get through the doors. There was this huge commissioner, dressed up like one of those hotel doormen, and he wouldn't let me pass. No matter what I said, he just kept repeating that visiting times were over for the day! I had to leave with my tail between my legs. I soon discovered that everyone inside was on strike, and when I did get through the doors next morning with the help of few Red Guards, I found smashed-up typewriters and torn-up documents and most of the staff gone, along with the keys to the safes and half the records."

Caitlin was shocked. "What did you do?"

"We tidied up, we tried to make sense of what was still there, and we waited for the staff to realize that they needed their jobs to live. And over the next few days, most of them came back. I called a meeting of everyone who works here, in the biggest hall we have. And I told them that everyone would be earning the same amount of six hundred rubles a year and that anyone—administrators, secretaries, cleaners—who had suggestions for improving our work would find a ready audience. Of course the few who'd been earning twenty-five thousand rubles a year were outraged, not least by the thought that the underlings they'd abused for years are no less important than they are." Kollontai leaned forward, her eyes alight. "And what a response! You wouldn't believe how many men and women have come to this office and pointed out better ways of doing things which hadn't occurred to *their* so-called betters."

Caught up in her friend's enthusiasm, Caitlin was already mentally writing her first dispatch from Russia. She asked who was most in need of help.

Kollontai sighed and seemed to age twenty years in the process. She counted off with her fingers: "Two and a half million maimed soldiers, another four million sick or wounded, 350,000 war orphans, 200,000 deaf, dumb, or blind. Heaven knows how many people in lunatic asylums. Elderly people who aren't being paid their pensions, others who never had a pension to begin with—there are bound to be some I've forgotten. This country was in dire straits in 1914, and three years of war have made everything so much worse."

"So where's the money going to come from?"

Kollontai delved into a drawer and brought out a pack of playing cards. "These," she told Caitlin.

"Those?"

"I forgot. You don't do this in America or England, but on the Continent it's quite common. Governments grant themselves a monopoly on production, and most use the profits to fund social programs."

"And there are that many people who want to buy them?"

"That's what I asked the veterans here, and they laughed at me. And it doesn't seem to matter how much you charge—I raised the price tenfold last week, and the orders are still pouring in. Next to a tax on vodka, it's the surest thing we have."

Caitlin couldn't help laughing. "I suppose that's wonderful, in a strange sort of way."

"Whatever works," Kollontai said. "We don't have time for anything else."

"So give me a rundown on what's happened in the last ten days."

Kollontai looked surprised. "Don't you know?"

"I was in Scotland when I heard about the revolution, and I've been traveling ever since. The Norwegian papers seemed confused by it all, and the Swedish ones had nothing to say."

"Wonderful," Kollontai said sarcastically. "The first government in history to really change anything, and no one's reporting it. Let me tell you what we've done in ten days. We've given the land to the peasants who till it. We've abolished private education—from this moment all Russians, no matter how wellborn, will attend the same schools. We've abolished the death penalty. We've published all the secret treaties that Russian governments signed with other nations, and we've demanded an immediate peace without annexations or penalties. How's that for a start?"

Caitlin could hardly believe it. "That's wonderful."

"And we're only getting started. There's a conference for women beginning on Monday—you have to be there."

"I will be." Caitlin hesitated. "As a journalist I have to ask this question—how secure is your government? Surely every other government in the world will try to bring you down. Do you really think you can survive?"

Kollontai took the question seriously. "It's a question we all ask ourselves. But if we are conquered, we will still have done great things. We are breaking the way, erasing old ideas. Blazing a trail that others can follow."

"Do you think your revolution can survive without others?"

"In the long run, no. But let's enjoy the moment we have."

"You seem like you are."

"Oh, I am. I know we talked about this for years—thousands of us imagined this moment—but I'm not sure I ever believed that the day would truly come." She laughed. "And wouldn't you know I would choose this moment to fall in love. What an idiot! You need leisure to fall in love, time together, time to breathe. Pavel and I—"

"Pavel?"

"Dybenko. The sailors' leader. Lenin has made him one of the three in charge of our defenses."

"How long have you . . . ?"

"Since May. And of course we're totally unsuited. Different class backgrounds, different ages—I'm fifteen years older than he is. But"—she threw out her hands—"I can't help loving him, and in that all-embracing stupid way." She laughed. "And how about you and Jack? Are you still together?"

"As far as I know. He knows I'm in Petrograd, although I haven't a clue where he is. But yes, we are still together, as much as the war allows us to be."

Kollontai sighed. "Such a time! And so much work! But how many people are given the chance to really change the world?"

THE WOMEN'S CONFERENCE WAS HELD at a small hall in Vyborg. Kollontai and the other organizers had laid on food and lodging for eighty delegates, but more than five hundred turned up, some having traveled that many miles. They had come as representatives of eighty thousand factory workers and union and political-party members. Inside the hall it was something of a squeeze.

The usual arguments soon flared up, the mostly Bolshevik leadership stressing the need for working through their governing party, the mostly middle-class feminists making the case for separate organizations. On the second day, Kollontai stressed the need for women to push their own issues—equal pay and paid maternity leave in particular—but not to expect an economically stretched

government to take immediate heed. What they could demand—
and expect to receive—was legal equality in family matters.

No one was completely satisfied, but neither did anyone leave in
a terrible huff. As an observer Caitlin was fascinated by the difference between this and all the other women's meetings she had ever
attended—this one had a government that was, at least in theory,
fully on its side.

THIS WAS THE SECOND STORY she filed; the first had been her general impressions of how the revolution was doing. As winter slowly
tightened its grip in the weeks that followed, there was no shortage
of things to write about; on the contrary, there seemed too many
stories clamoring for her attention. In the first half of December,
she attended at least a meeting a day, listening to workers debating
one another in vast factory yards, watching Austrian POWs pledge
themselves to the cause in the vast arena of the Cirque Moderne,
imbibing the arguments at the Tauride Palace or Smolny, as the
political stars of the revolution debated the course ahead.

There was new legislation to report. Having given the peasants
their land, the Bolsheviks stopped short of giving the workers their
factories, but the playing field between employers and employees
was leveled, with committees taken from both making all the important decisions. In some places this wasn't enough for the workers,
who simply took over their places of work and elected their own
committees to run the enterprise in question. These committees
then spent much of their time trying to lower inflated expectations.

There were new laws regulating the press. These were introduced
reluctantly, almost apologetically, the Bolshevik government pointing out that the wealthy few still owned the newspapers and were
using them to "poison the brains and consciences of the masses."
To leave the press "in enemy hands at such a time" was "out of the
question." But the restrictions were temporary and would be lifted
once the new order was fully established.

If Caitlin, as a journalist, found this a little worrying, her American editor and publisher seemed a great deal more concerned. She
was sure that Ed Carlucci felt that way for the best of liberal reasons,

but her publisher was another matter. She had met him more than once and knew how much he would loathe the new regime. He would want to print tales of Bolshevik crimes and panegyrics for the opposition martyrs.

There was little she could do to appease them. Whenever a vote was held, socialists of one stripe or another would win it, usually by a large majority. And disputes among the various socialist parties—important as some of these seemed—were not resolved by imprisonment or violence. The small parties of the wealthy, which had done so much to neuter the first revolutionary government, had lost all popular support and been reduced to inciting administrative sabotage, printing slanderous news stories, and generally whining about their present condition. To see them as victims required more sympathy than Caitlin possessed.

She did talk to them. The woman who thought her cook should be "beaten with a knout" for wanting a new pair of shoes; the family who burned their spare clothes out of spite rather than send them off to the front as their hated new government asked.

She talked to foreign diplomats, who all expressed their astonishment that the Bolsheviks were still in power. The Americans at the Red Cross Mission were less judgmental and almost made up for their embassy's undying antagonism. Foreign businessmen were unreservedly hostile, with one touching exception, an American millionaire so entranced by his experience of the revolution that he lost all interest in business. "If I were thirty years old and had no family," he told Caitlin, "nothing on earth would take me away from here."

She interviewed prominent members of the Bolsheviks and Left Socialist Revolutionaries, otherwise known as the LSRs. Most were highly educated men with years of opposition and exile behind them, who could hardly believe their luck at the opportunities now on offer. If any were taking advantage of their new positions to enrich or privilege themselves, Caitlin saw no sign of it—everyone ate the same food, earned the same paltry income, and dressed in the same shabby suits. Kollontai was the only Bolshevik who took any trouble over appearance.

Few of the leaders were women, but these all seemed extraordinary. The Bolsheviks had her friend Kollontai and the equally cultured French-born Inessa Armand, who held a high-ranking post in the Moscow Soviet and was close to Lenin and his wife. Konkordia Samoilova and Klavdia Nikolayeva ran the unofficial women's section. One was the daughter of a priest, the other from much humbler beginnings. Both had been Bolsheviks for more than a decade.

And then there was Maria Spiridonova of the Left Socialist Revolutionaries. All these women had stirring life stories, but Spiridonova's was the most dramatic. In 1906, aged twenty-one, she had shot and killed the czarist security chief then terrorizing the province of Tambov. Tortured and raped in detention, she had seen her subsequent sentence of death eventually commuted to life in a Siberian prison. The train that carried her eastward had been besieged by supportive crowds every time it stopped.

The first revolution had released her after eleven years of brutal incarceration, but the woman Caitlin met in the summer of 1917 seemed utterly unbowed by what fate and the czar had thrown her way. Though frail and tiny—Spiridonova was less than five feet tall—she radiated a rare combination of authority and compassion and was loved and respected in equal measure. She was the peasants' champion and, for many, the soul of the revolution. Her, and her party's, support for the Bolsheviks was what kept the revolution true, and Caitlin found herself dreading the prospects if Lenin and Spiridonova ever decided on taking divergent paths.

She also caught herself wondering what might happen if the two of them fell in love and Lenin gave up the admirable but rather stolid Nadezhda Krupskaya for Spiridonova's slow-burning passion. Not that it was likely—both were too busy changing the world to have any time for romance.

Caitlin's own social life was hardly exciting. She spent several evenings each week drinking, arguing, and swapping stories with one or more members of the English-speaking foreign press corps—the Americans Jack Reed, Louise Bryant, Albert Rhys Williams, and Bessie Beatty, the Brits Morgan Philips Price and Arthur Ransome—but the only Russians she actually thought of as friends were Kollontai and Volodarsky. She often met the latter for lunch, and she found him excellent company, sharp, well informed, and amazingly positive. If he wanted more than friendship—and occasional gazes of more-than-usual intensity sometimes suggested he did—he was clearly too shy to say so.

She saw her other friend as often as ministry work and Dybenko would allow, which wasn't very often. If Kollontai wasn't combating sabotage at the ministry, trying to conjure up loaves, fishes, and homes for Russia's hungry and dispossessed, or pushing through highly contested measures like the new marriage law, she was enjoying a few precious hours with her equally overworked lover. Caitlin met Dybenko at Kollontai's apartment—he was preparing to leave as she arrived—and was struck by how well matched they seemed, despite the obvious disparity in ages. The sailors' leader was certainly handsome, though not in a way that Caitlin found attractive—perfectly trimmed goatees, rolled mustaches, and rakishly perched Astrakhan hats were hardly the sort of keys to unlock an Irish-American heart. The two things that most impressed her were his obvious daring—something that Kollontai also had in spades—and how much in awe of her he was. Caitlin knew from others that he was thought to be less than faithful, but in her presence he seemed utterly spellbound.

Away from him Kollontai was a ball of energy belying her forty-four years, furiously intent on changing as much of the world as the hours allowed. There were still so many "great things" left to do.

December marched on, the days and food stores growing shorter. Lying awake in her icy bed at the Angleterre Hotel, Caitlin would listen to the occasional clip-clop of horses below or the rarer clang of a streetcar bell on Nevsky Prospect. There was no denying it—in most measurable respects, things were getting worse. And yet, for all that, there was still so much enthusiasm, so much hope.

The city, the country, were growing poorer, but life kept on getting richer.

ON DECEMBER 20 THE PETROGRAD press announced the setting up of the All-Russian Extraordinary Commission for Struggle against Sabotage and Counter-Revolution, otherwise known as the Vecheka, or Cheka for short. And all over the city that day, opponents of the Bolsheviks—from right-wing monarchists to Marxist Mensheviks—could be heard telling each other that this was it—the beginning of the long-promised terror. Caitlin, listening to three such conversations in three cafés patronized by the better-dressed few, couldn't help noticing how appealing they found the thought— they couldn't wait for blood to flow, if only to prove them right.

Which didn't prove they were wrong. So far the Bolsheviks had treated their opponents with breathtaking leniency, and given their leaders' fondness for quoting precedents from the French Revolution, she found it hard to believe that they'd make the same mistakes as Robespierre and company and erect a guillotine in front of the Winter Palace. But she understood what most of her compatriots would make of this new organization and decided that a preemptive investigation might be useful. She would interview one of its leaders.

The man in charge was unwilling to see her, but one of his deputies, the Latvian Yakov Peters, had employed some of the socialist American correspondents as part-time translators when he was a member of the Cheka's immediate predecessor, the Military-Revolutionary Committee. According to Albert Rhys Williams, Peters not only spoke perfect English but was usually willing to speak his mind. Caitlin phoned for an appointment and was given one the next day.

The Cheka offices were in the old police building at 2 Gorokhovaya Street, just around the corner from her hotel. Peters's room was on the third floor; the man himself, slimly built with a fighter's face and dark wavy hair, came out from behind his overloaded desk to shake her hand warmly. He didn't look old enough for his life story, but then few of the Bolshevik leaders did. Peters had spent four years as a revolutionary activist in Latvia and another nine in England, where he'd been arrested, tried, and acquitted in the famous Houndsditch murder case, which had ended in the equally notorious Siege of Sidney Street. When news of the first revolution had reached him in London, he'd immediately set out for Russia.

Rather to Caitlin's surprise, he knew as much about her.

"Am I right in thinking your brother was shot by the British?" was the first thing he asked.

"Yes," she said. "Almost three years ago now."

"Did you share his belief in the Irish Republican cause?"

She hesitated before deciding that openness might be reciprocated. "That's a difficult one to answer," she said. "My family is Irish, and I support Irish independence. But I'm not convinced that an alliance with Germany was the best way to get it."

Peters shook his head. "They accuse us of that. Just because the Germans let some of our leaders pass through their country in a sealed train, some people think that we're all German puppets."

"Well, they should know better by now."

"Ah, people believe what they want to believe." Peters smiled to himself. "When were you last in England?"

"Six weeks ago."

"And how are things there? My wife and daughter are still in London," he added in explanation.

"Life isn't easy, not after three years of war. But not as hard as it is in Germany. Or here."

Peters seemed pleased to hear that. "So how can I help you? You're writing a piece on the new commission?"

"In part. How would you define its role?"

"It's what it says it is—an organization to protect the revolution from enemies who engage in sabotage or secretly plot against us."

"What do you mean by sabotage?"

Peters sighed. "Everything from deliberately destroying official documents, which has happened at most of the ministries, to interfering with the transport of essential supplies. Things that prevent us from doing our job, which is to run the country in the interests of ordinary people."

"You know what some people are saying," Caitlin responded. "And not all of them bourgeois. That this is the thin end of the wedge, that the more opposition you face, the harsher you'll have to be, and that a reign of terror is only a matter of time."

Peters shook his head. "You can't have a reign of terror without a death penalty, and we've abolished ours."

"You could bring it back."

"We could, but I don't think we will—it would send out the wrong message. Admitted, there are some people whom we'll never win over, no matter what we say or do. But we need the vast majority to support us if we're going to achieve real change. Instilling fear is fine if all you need is obedience, but history shows that it won't get you anything more. We prefer giving wrongdoers a chance to see the error of their ways, to atone for their crimes and live a more useful life. Look, why don't you attend one of our tribunals and see how the system is actually working? I can arrange it, and if you stumble across a reign of terror, then please report it to me."

"I will," Caitlin said. "And I'd like something ordinary. We all know that Countess Panina got off lightly after walking off with the Welfare Ministry's funds, but she's a celebrity and one whom many people still admire. I'd like to see how you deal with the less sympathetic."

Peters reached for a ledger, licked a finger, and thumbed through several pages. "You're in luck," he said eventually. "There are several such cases coming up tomorrow morning. At the grand duke's Palace, starting at nine. You won't need a pass." He gave her a wicked grin. "You can even take part if you wish. Anyone present can speak, either for or against the accused."

"I doubt I'll do that, but thank you anyway."

"Thank the revolution."

NEXT MORNING, AFTER THE USUAL inadequate breakfast, Caitlin took the short walk through the snow to the Grand Duke Nikolay's palace. This lay on the other side of St. Isaac's Cathedral, not much more than a stone's throw from the frozen Neva. The grand duke himself had been dead for decades, and the palace, long a college for the daughters of the aristocracy, had been sequestered for government use.

The wood-paneled music auditorium, with its beautiful stained-glass ceiling and elegant red hangings, seemed a strange setting for a revolutionary tribunal, but a cynic might have noted the lack of a working electric light. The seven-man tribunal—one man in a suit, two in uniform, two in workers' overalls, and two in peasant blouses—was seated behind a large semicircular mahogany table, across which a sheet of gold-embossed red leather was draped. The accused were lined up on a long bench to one side, with the people—and presumably the lawyers—massed in rows of chairs facing the panel of judges.

Case followed case at a fairly rapid pace, the accused taking turns on a separate bench as those in the seats got up to support or denounce them. If any of the latter were lawyers, they spoke a lot straighter than those Caitlin remembered from court reporting in Brooklyn. And people seemed interested in more than the facts of who did what to whom—they wanted to understand motives and to judge how best the accused might find redemption.

At the end of each trial, the seven judges would move next door to reach their verdict and then return to deliver sentence. A man caught with a machine gun in his room, along with a pile of counterrevolutionary pamphlets—two years in prison. A man who had passed himself off as a commissar to collect "new taxes" from hotels—three years. A Red Guard who'd abandoned his post for a tryst with his girlfriend, a youth who had stolen a coat from an old man sleeping on a park bench—both sentenced to "the reprehension of society." And, in the youth's case, the return of the coat.

It all seemed quite astonishing at first, but by the end of the proceedings she was really glad she'd come.

That evening she found Jack Reed and Albert Rhys Williams in one of the cafés off Nevsky that they all patronized, and she recounted the experience.

"They're mad," was Reed's opinion. "It's not the small fry—I'm all for letting them off lightly and giving them another chance. It's the big guys—people like Kornilov, who led an *army* against them, for Christ's sake! And Krasnov. Both of them arrested, both of them released!"

"They're forgiving to a fault," Caitlin murmured.

"And in their case it probably is one," Reed said. "These people will come back to bite them, take my word for it. They'll go straight to the English and the French and beg them for help getting back into power. And once the big war's over—maybe even before—the English and the French will say yes. It's all very well being kind and understanding, but it's a recipe for civil war."

He might be right, Caitlin thought as she trudged home through the snow. But harshness also had its consequences, and on balance she liked those even less.

4

Disposing of the Dead

It was considerably warmer in Brindisi than it had been in London, but the rain seemed just as persistent, hardly abating from the morning McColl arrived until the evening he left, sixty hours later. His twenty-year-old steamship was one of five bound for Egypt under the protective eye of the Japanese destroyer *Hinoki*, which had strayed halfway around the world in the cause of Allied solidarity. The steamship's crew was French and North African, the passengers mostly Indian and English troops bound for Mesopotamia and the subcontinent, with a smattering of sappers bound for Aden, returning Indian Civil Service wallahs, and a few like McColl himself whose status and purpose were best left undefined. The only women on board were a group of nurses bound for East Africa, who were wisely keeping themselves to themselves.

There was a large contingent of horses and mules belowdecks, but their number went down with each passing day. The rough seas made them "troublesome," whatever that meant, and every morning several new cadavers were laboriously manhandled over the side. McColl had never been mad about horses, but he found their dumb sacrifice unexpectedly distressing, perhaps because it seemed so typical of the way the war was being run.

After five days of poor weather, the sun emerged from hiding, and everyone kept a close watch for the flocks of seagulls that were said to follow submarines. But none appeared, and only the appalling food spoiled the rest of the voyage. On the eleventh day out of Brindisi, McColl's ship parted company with the Suez-bound others and headed into port at Alexandria. The night train from there reached Cairo soon after dawn, and another week of waiting followed. When he finally received new marching orders, they came with the news that Audley Cheselden's ship had been delayed and that the man himself would now meet McColl in Aden.

The train to Suez took forever but finally shuddered to a hissing halt beside the *Malabar Khan,* a patchwork of peeling paint and rust that wasn't even upright at its mooring. The interior was worse. It was impossible to open a door without hearing the rustle of cockroaches scurrying for cover, and on more than one occasion a door came off its hinges. The vessel was also overcrowded with humans, not to mention the usual complement of troublesome horses, and Suez was barely out of sight when the first of these received a Red Sea burial. McColl asked several of the Indian army officers why they couldn't use French horses in France and Indian horses in India, but none came up with an answer.

The days that followed were cool enough for sitting out, and he ventured below only when hunger became acute enough to outweigh the taste of the food. Most mornings he read, swapping each finished book with one of his fellow travelers. In the afternoons he studied Farsi from a primer he'd picked up on Charing Cross Road, thinking it might prove useful in Persia and beyond. The hours went by, the distant yellow line of the African coast hardly changing at all, the sighting of other ships the only cause for excitement. When one hove into view, everyone rushed to the rail and waved at the pack of waving strangers a few hundred yards away.

It took the *Malabar Khan* seven days to reach Aden. This British outpost at Arabia's southwestern tip had been besieged since 1914, but the Turkish besiegers had long since given up hope of mounting a telling attack, and the British defenders were more than happy to leave the enemy where he was, out in the unfriendly desert. With Cheselden's ship still four hours away and his own busy taking on coal, McColl took a trip out to see the eleven-mile-long perimeter. He found a few sandbagged strongpoints connected by mile upon mile of thickly strung wire, plus a bunch of sun-bronzed soldiers almost mutinous with boredom. McColl found himself wondering what would happen to the barbed-wire industry if peace were ever declared.

By the time he got back to port, Cheselden's ship was inching in, and fifteen minutes later the man himself came bouncing down the gangway. The first impression was tall and gangly, but the cliché didn't do him justice—his movement seemed barely coordinated, as if each limb were out for a separate stroll. The face was pleasant enough, if spoiled by an overlarge nose. This latter was currently running, a condition that McColl put down to a cold but which turned out to be more or less permanent. Audley Cheselden's right hand was almost proof of perpetual motion—when it wasn't pushing back the hair that flopped across his forehead, it was usually wiping his streaming proboscis.

He had a lot of luggage for a man under twenty-five. Two suitcases and a trunk seemed more than a tad excessive for the mission Cumming had in mind, but it soon transpired that these were full of African artifacts bound for England. "My father's a collector," Cheselden explained as the native clerk in the shipping office filled out the requisite forms. "I only hope some wretched Austrian sub doesn't send them all to the bottom."

Not to mention the ship and its crew, McColl thought but didn't say.

However, the young man grew on him as their ship sailed east and north toward the gulf. Cheselden took the dreadful conditions in his stride, rarely complained about the bites soon stippling his body, and was once even heard defending the cooks. He was used to sleeping on decks, he said, having never found a cabin bunk long enough. He had a friendly word for everyone, whatever an individual's status or color.

He was of course keen on the job. Cumming had recruited him in 1914, after only a year trotting the globe for the world's most famous travel business. As Cheselden readily admitted, he had gotten that job on his father's recommendation—his studies at Oxford had proved something less than a total success. His qualifications for this one seemed similarly suspect. Though he claimed a certain fluency in French and German, he spoke no Russian at all, which McColl assumed ruled out any hope of their acting independently in Turkestan. Cheselden disagreed—"I'm good at improvising"—and he had studied the history of the region in question, which was more than McColl ever had. Tamburlaine, it turned out, was more than a character in some old play.

Cheselden assumed he'd been chosen for the mission on account of his expertise in handling explosives. McColl had trouble believing this but came to accept that it might be true. The young man's arms and legs might march to four different tunes, but his fingers were surprisingly nimble.

One night in the gulf, as they lay side by side on the slowly shifting deck, Cheselden told McColl he had a girlfriend back in London whom he hadn't seen for over two years. Her name was Sophia, but he called her Soph. "And she calls me Aud. Soph and Aud," he murmured to himself. "I hope she hasn't met some dashing swine in uniform." He turned to McColl. "Are you married?" he asked.

"Divorced," McColl answered curtly. "A long time ago," he added, thinking that Evelyn hadn't crossed his mind for months. He felt reluctant to mention Caitlin. Explaining her was difficult, and not doing so always felt like a betrayal.

EIGHTEEN DAYS AFTER LEAVING SUEZ, the *Malabar Khan* entered the Shatt al-Arab channel, lines of bright green palms edging the torpid brown waters. Arab dhows danced around the slow-moving steamship as it neared Basra, before finally weaving its way between a couple of vainly scuttled Turkish gunboats and drawing up alongside a long and crowded wooden wharf lined with towering cranes. The town itself was a mile inland, and the trip up a foul-smelling creek in the gondola-like *bellum* was definitely one to remember, albeit for all the wrong reasons.

Basra was the usual sea of sun-baked brick around a modern colonial core. The streets in the center were paved; the best hotel boasted electric lights and fans, which come summer would be something to die for. Over the next few days, as the two of them sorted out their ongoing travel arrangements, they came across the usual British landmarks—a racecourse, a church, and a cricket pitch. The locals had created a hybrid of soccer and rugby, which they played at all hours in flowing Arab robes.

A movie theater had been set up in one half-broken-down building. Attending it one evening, McColl and Cheselden found themselves surrounded by enthusiastic Arab males, who cheered and hissed the heroes and villains and fell strangely silent only when unveiled women appeared on the screen. The night before their departure upstream, there was a fireworks display in the adjacent square, which both of them watched from the hotel terrace. Rockets zoomed off into the night sky, creating new fields of eye-popping stars. Roman candles blazed and Catherine wheels fizzed, and as the display neared its end, several Arab men, festooned with squibs and presumably attired in fireproof suits, lit their own blue touch papers and somersaulted down the street, pursued by their sons and daughters.

As he and Cheselden were punted down the aptly nicknamed Shit Creek next morning, firmly holding their noses, McColl reminded himself that even an armpit like Basra had its happy children, and no doubt the sky above them occasionally coughed up a rainbow.

MESHED WAS STILL A THOUSAND miles away, the next leg of their journey a slow cruise up the Tigris on an old paddle steamer. The decks were packed with soldiers, the nights a litany of yells from woken men who'd just been stepped on. The days were long and boring, the river full of twists and turns, sometimes so severe that a boat upstream seemed to be gliding across the nearby desert. On clearer days the mountains of Persia were faintly visible on the eastern horizon.

A stop at Amarah offered some relief. McColl and Cheselden went ashore and followed the ship captain's directions to the local British officers' club, where drinks could be had in a roof garden overlooking the river. The three-month-old newspapers seemed like historical documents. Would the battle for Passchendaele be the breakthrough Haig had promised? Were the Bolsheviks yesterday's men?

Another three days brought the steamer to Kut, its final port of call. The soldiers were continuing north to the current front by train, McColl and Cheselden leaving from a different station for Baghdad. Kut was the town that General Townshend had surrendered to the Turks in April 1916, after his army had endured a harrowing five-month siege. It had been recaptured ten months later, and Cheselden insisted on paying Townshend's former HQ a visit, seating himself in the general's chair and arranging his jaw at a suitably heroic angle.

It was only a hundred miles from there to Baghdad, but the train took all night to reach the fabled city. McColl was not expecting much, having spoken to others who had, but Cheselden seemed almost insulted by the lack of flying carpets, their role usurped by Ford vans and Peerless lorries. The streets were certainly alive, the Arab cafés with their tiered seating, hubble-bubbles, and tiny cups of mocha, the eating houses full of boisterous Tommies. There were myriad signs in English, advertising everything from laundries to language lessons, but remarkably few in Turkish. The old rulers had been gone for less than a year, and they clearly weren't expected back.

After securing hotel rooms and eating their first decent meal since Basra—a chicken-and-vegetable stew with rice, richly savory with cinnamon—the two men walked over to the British Residency. No new instructions from Cumming awaited them, only confirmation that they should continue on into Persia. A short report on the political situation was appended but was almost as dated as the papers they'd read in Amarah. The local political secretary took them out onto the terrace for drinks and expressed his doubts as to their intentions.

McColl ignored them. "What we need," he continued, tearing his eyes from the pleasant vista of a river lined with beautiful villas, trees, and flowers, "is transport. A Peerless lorry would do, and petrol enough to reach Teheran."

"I'll find out if the army has one to spare."

McColl smiled. "If you tell them they do, then they do. And since we need to leave the day after tomorrow, perhaps you could have the lorry delivered to our hotel tomorrow afternoon. And a mechanic if possible, to talk me through the dos and don'ts." McColl had been working on automobiles since his return from South Africa, first as a hobby and then as a job, but he hadn't spent much time with lorries, and if the damn thing conked out in the middle of nowhere, he wanted to be able to get it started.

The following morning was spent gathering supplies, and by noon a serious pile of containers was waiting in the hotel's palm-shadowed forecourt for the expected arrival of the Peerless. It eventually turned up, driven by the mechanic McColl had asked for. As the two of them discussed the vagaries of the engine, Cheselden supervised some willing local youths in the loading of their bags and boxes. With several cans of petrol already on board, there was just enough room in the back for the two of them to sleep.

After another delicious stew—this one of ground lamb, potatoes, and eggplant—and an evening stroll through the still-busy Arab bazaar, they took to their beds, an early start in mind. By six they were out on the road, heading for the Persian frontier.

It took them all day to cover the hundred and twenty miles. The road was virtually empty of motorized traffic but not of civilians, and many of the latter seemed resistant to the notion of a British right of way. The surface also left something to be desired, making travel over fifteen miles per hour an unacceptable gamble. Even at that speed, Cheselden's head rebounded off the roof more times than seemed healthy, and McColl was relieved to reach the unmanned border, where abandoned Turkish and Persian watchtowers faced each other across a stretch of rock-strewn wasteland. They spent the night in the Persian one and were disturbed only by the single scream of an unknown animal somewhere close by.

The frontier followed the line of the foothills, and all the next day both road and lorry wound upward, glimpses of snow-draped peaks ahead, the Mesopotamian plain stretched out behind and below. It was around noon when McColl noticed that the road ahead was full of men and animals. He pulled the lorry off to one side.

The animals, he realized, were mules, and rolls of something were lashed to their backs. Rolls that looked like Egyptian mummies.

"It's a corpse caravan," Cheselden told him. "I read about them somewhere. These people are Shi'a Muslims, and their holy city is Karbala, which is near Baghdad. So they take their dead there for burial."

"There must be fifty bodies."

"They save them up. They bury them when they die, then dig them up and wrap them in sackcloth when it's time to go. The caravans make a lot of money for the people who run them, and people know that their relations are buried in the holiest ground. Everyone's happy."

Everyone but the mules, McColl thought. Some looked close to collapse as they trudged past the lorry.

THEIR OVERLAND JOURNEY TO MESHED took the better part of a month. Towns went by, each with its small colony of Europeans, eager for news of the outside world yet clearly glad to be keeping their distance. Kermanshah, Hamada, and on to Teheran, with its modern hotels and tramways and twice-weekly letters to Europe. Cheselden took the pile he'd written to Soph—each neatly numbered so she'd read them in the right order—down to the office on Khiaban-i-Lalezar and handed over a thick wad of Persian shahi. Then, just to be on the safe side, he continued on to the telegraph office, where he spent another small fortune on a cable telling her letters were on the way.

Their beds at the Hotel de Paris were a welcome change from the back of the Peerless, which of course seemed even less forgiving once they'd resumed their journey. But neither was a chronic complainer, and the amount of time they spent in close proximity provoked little in the way of irritation, let alone any real dislike. McColl knew that if he'd met Cheselden in ordinary circumstances, they'd have had precious little to say to each other, but the young man was a perfect traveling companion, almost unfailingly cheerful and equally happy in conversation or silence.

The Russian lessons didn't go well, to the point where McColl began to wonder about Cheselden's French and German. As the younger man freely admitted, he wasn't the sharpest pencil in the box. After announcing one night that his Soph was only five feet tall, he had gone on to conclude that their children were bound to be blessed with average height. His thoughts about what he might do after the war came down to a single sentence: "Oh, Father will think of something." His great idea for their mission in Turkestan was almost as simple: once they reached the Transcaspian Railway, McColl would go one way and he'd go the other, looking for bridges to blow up. Any problems he, as a non–Russian speaker, might encounter on his own—accessing the necessary explosives, feeding and housing himself—were airily dismissed as "details."

He increasingly reminded McColl of several young men he'd met at Oxford, whose breadth of knowledge had been matched only by their lack of practical intelligence.

THE FINAL STRETCH OF THEIR thousand-mile trek to Meshed was a tree-shaded road across a wide gray plain. The nearer they got to the gateway in the ancient city wall, the more McColl doubted that the Peerless would make it through, but despite the cries of alarm from watching locals, it did so with inches to spare. As they crept their way farther into the city, the astonished stares on the Persian faces told them how exotic a motorized vehicle was this far from their civilization.

In Teheran they'd been given directions to Meshed's British Residency, but more help was needed from the first passerby who could understand McColl's few phrases of Persian. The place, when they found it, was spectacular. After working their way through a maze of sand-colored walls and houses, they parked the lorry outside a huge gate bearing the British lion and unicorn and tugged on the hanging iron bell. A servant answered and ushered them in to a whole other world of lawns, rose gardens, orchards, and tennis courts. The main house—there seemed to be several within the walls—boasted a veranda entwined with climbing roses and hung with baskets of brightly colored blooms.

"This must be the Garden of Eden," Cheselden noted, wiping his nose.

"Here comes Adam," McColl murmured as a portly man in gardening clothes walked across to greet them.

"Reggie Cluett," he introduced himself. "Consul general," he added. "You must be the chappies from Whitehall. Come and meet the wife."

Lavinia Cluett was a thin, middle-aged woman with a pretty face and a slightly distracted air. She offered a limp hand to each of them before hurrying off to arrange their accommodation. As she vanished around one corner of the house, a man appeared, as if by magic, around the other.

"This is Colonel Aitchison," the consul informed them, with what seemed more than a hint of reluctance. "Our military attaché," he explained as Aitchison shook their hands.

"Miles," he introduced himself.

OVER THE NEXT COUPLE OF days, McColl realized that Cluett and Aitchison, while pleasant enough company, were not going to give him much help. Both were knowledgeable when it came to their Khorasan bailiwick, but the Transcaspian lands across the nearby border might just as well have been the moon. Cluett didn't consider it "his place" to spy on another great power, while Aitchison, whose job it most certainly was, seemed singularly inept. The latter had a neatly written list of spies and informers on the British payroll but virtually nothing to show for his money. He assured McColl that there were German, Austrian, and Turkish agents in Ashkhabad but had nothing to back this assertion up—no names, no addresses, no reports of any kind. For all McColl knew, these agents were creatures of Aitchison's imagination—they were there because they ought to be.

He and Cheselden sought out other sources of intelligence. Thinking the local Russians worth a shot, McColl duly presented himself at their consulate. The consul, a nervous-looking man of around fifty named Chudnovsky, freely confessed that he'd had no recent instructions from home. He had been appointed by the provisional government and was willing to concede that remaining loyal to this vanished entity was unlikely to help his career. But at least he was on foreign soil. The Bolsheviks could send a replacement, but they couldn't make him go home.

His wife, Galina, was hoping for better. She questioned McColl on the relative merits of France and Italy, noting in passing that Capri had been her destination of choice until the author Maxim Gorky—who had famously lived there for several years—had betrayed his class and joined the dreadful Reds.

"That *would* spoil one's enjoyment of a place," McColl agreed. He wondered how much money the Chudnovskys had managed to smuggle out and whether it would still be worth the paper it was printed on by the time they reached a new home.

Neither husband nor wife had anything useful to say about the government in Ashkhabad. It was almost a year since the pair had passed through the town, and those who left later had arrived in Meshed with nothing good to report. There was no real authority left, they claimed without exception, just a rabble intent on settling scores.

McColl walked slowly back to the British Residency, thinking that his and Cheselden's only option was to turn up in Ashkhabad and take whatever chances presented themselves. But as who? Official British emissaries seeking an alliance against the Turks? Or disguised as innocent travelers of one sort or another? Either way there seemed fair odds they'd be shot.

THE NEXT DAY BROUGHT BETTER news. A sizable party of Russians had arrived in Meshed that morning after fleeing across the border. According to one of Aitchison's informers, the newcomers were mostly from Tiflis in the Caucasus but had come by way of Ashkhabad. They were, moreover, eager for British help and should thus prove willing to answer questions.

McColl and Aitchison took the consulate brougham into the center of town, where the refugees were lodged in one of the smaller hotels. Seeing them crowded together in three large rooms, McColl could understand the Chudnovskys' reluctance to take them in. The seven couples with assorted children and grandparents might come from the requisite social class, but they had fewer items of luggage among them than the Chudnovskys had in their lobby. These families would not be choosing between rivieras.

The terms of a deal were quickly struck—information for hotel expenses and transport on to Teheran. McColl's first job was to pin down where each family came from, and, much to his delight, two were from Ashkhabad. The first, a handsome young Armenian named Tigran Sahakian, had lived there for four years. He was a doctor at the city hospital; his wife, the daughter of a local businessman, had lived there much longer. The family had given the first revolution a tentative welcome, and by summer things had seemed to be settling down. It was only in November, when news arrived of the Bolshevik coup in Petrograd, that their situation had markedly deteriorated. "By January we were cut off from the rest of Russia," Sahakian said. "And our so-called soviet was left to its own devices. It started redistributing wealth and property and arresting any of those who refused to accept their losses. My father-in-law was one of them. We spent six weeks trying to find out which prison he was in and then were told he'd been shot on the day of his arrest."

"Who's in charge?" McColl wanted to know. "The local Bolsheviks?"

"Not on their own. There are Bolsheviks and Mensheviks and Socialist Revolutionaries and other parties that someone thought up the day before and will forget again tomorrow. Most of them are railway workers. Railway workers!" he repeated, as if he couldn't quite believe it.

"What about the local Turks? The Turcomen, I think you call them."

Sahakian shrugged. "What about them? They spend all their time chasing each other across the desert. Or admiring their latest gold tooth in the mirror."

"They're not involved with the soviet?"

"God no. These socialists may be only railway workers, but at least they're white men."

"And the real Turks? Is anyone worried that they'll cross the Caspian and head for Ashkhabad?"

"I've never heard anyone say so. If they ever reached Baku, then maybe. But not until then."

"And what about Germans and Austrians? Are there any of them in Ashkhabad?"

Sahakian hadn't seen or heard of any, but one of the other men, a Russian named Poletaev, knew of some who had. Poletaev had owned a small clothes factory, and he had heard from friends in the local business community that a delegation of Germans had visited the city only a few weeks earlier. They had come to discuss the purchase of cotton stockpiles left stranded by three years of war. "No deal was done," Poletaev said, "because there is no way to get the cotton out. But if the Germans reach the Caspian, they can ship it across and train it home."

BACK AT THE GARDEN OF Eden, McColl talked matters through with Cheselden. His partner's Russian was unlikely to fool any half-competent authority, and spies, as McColl reminded his partner, were usually shot in wartime. Cheselden, however, had been working on his plan to head off alone once they were both across the border. He argued that while his Russian was dreadful, his German was much better, certainly good enough for him to pose as an escaped prisoner of war. If caught, he wouldn't be shot as a spy, just sent back to the nearest camp.

Which was a great idea, provided nobody asked him to describe the one he'd supposedly escaped.

McColl was inclined to think that the safest bet—for both him and Cheselden—was to leave the younger man behind.

Cheselden wouldn't hear of it. "What do you expect me to do?" he asked. "Just twiddle my thumbs while I wait for you to come back? I didn't travel halfway round the world to *wait*."

McColl raised his hands in surrender. "Okay. We'll go in together, waving the flag, offering the earth to any Russian who'll help us keep that cotton from the Germans. And the first hint we get that it's all going up in smoke, we either go into hiding or make a run for the border, whichever looks the better bet. Agreed?"

"Agreed," Cheselden said, wiping his nose on his sleeve and offering his hand.

5
Celestial Alphabet

Thanks to the Russian calendar, which was still running thirteen days behind its Western counterpart, the American correspondents in Petrograd had two Christmases to enjoy. The first, their own, was celebrated in some style. Invited to lunch at the Hotel Europe by the American Red Cross mission, they arrived to find a beautiful candlelit tree, a roaring fire, and a traditional table. Once turkey with potatoes and cabbage had been served, each guest was solemnly treated to the Russian chef's idea of a seasonal mince pie.

After digesting this feast, Caitlin and the other correspondents barely had time to get home and change for the evening entertainment—a full-scale party for the two-hundred-strong American colony in Petrograd. This was held at the old Turkish embassy, in a vast reception room lined with enormous mirrors. There was more turkey and real American layer cakes in place of the fake mince pies. Caitlin, like almost everyone else, spent time on the floor, dancing one-steps and waltzes with men she didn't know to the raucous music of a balalaika band. Several other guests expressed their admiration of her shimmering blue frock, which she'd borrowed from Kollontai's still-capacious wardrobe.

This singular day gave way to the worst week she'd had since arriving in Russia. Perhaps it was just a natural hangover, or maybe spending so much time in purely American company was bound to play on long-suppressed emotions. Whatever the reasons, four hours of daylight no longer seemed anywhere near enough, and the snow-draped city felt more like an icebox than a winter wonderland. The people were no less welcoming, her grasp of the language grew better by the day, but almost overnight, or so it seemed to her, Russia came to feel like a truly foreign country. She felt a long way from home, and achingly lonely. She missed Jack.

At this low ebb, she found that her political doubts began to multiply. If women were making bigger strides here than anywhere else, was that only because they had so much further to go? Was the Cheka as benign as Peters wanted her—and probably himself—to believe? With Finns, Ukrainians, and other nationalities all chafing at the old Russian yoke, could the country even hold together? And if it did, would the new democracy survive? The Constituent Assembly was due to meet in a couple of weeks, and most of the people she knew expected the Bolsheviks and LSRs to dissolve it. They had their reasons—ones she agreed with on her more forgiving days—but were they kidding themselves? Was she?

She didn't let these doubts seep into her writing—there would be critics enough back home—but as the year reached its end, she did sometimes feel they were seeping into her heart.

Salvation came in three installments: a magical walk, a message from Kollontai, and, most surprising of all, a speech by her own country's president. The walk was with her fellow correspondent Bessie Beatty, who had discovered the wooded islands just to the north of the city and taken to spending Sunday's daylight hours away from the ever-churning revolution. On the weekend after their Christmas, she invited Caitlin to accompany her, and the two of them spent several hours walking through the snow-clad pines and spruces, occasionally sharing a word but mostly enjoying the heaven-sent silence.

The message from Kollontai came two days later, informing her that the marriage law was about to be passed and urging her to attend. Caitlin was in the press seats next morning, watching her friend introduce her bill and seeing it duly voted into law. With gender equality as the guiding principle, marriage became a purely civil affair, requiring the couple concerned only to register their union. Securing a divorce was just as easy if children were not involved, and only slightly more difficult if they were.

That evening, at Kollontai's flat, Caitlin's friend was full of plans for turning one of the city's dreadful children's homes—often known, ironically, as "angel factories"—into a new model Palace of Motherhood, in which women could get the pre- and postnatal care they needed, regardless of how they came to be pregnant. And Kollontai also had other news. "Dybenko thinks we should set an example by making use of yesterday's new law," she said, "but most of my friends disagree. They tell me that after everything I've said about the slavery of marriage, people will think me a hypocrite."

"Then you should set an example of a slaveless marriage," Caitlin told her, to Kollontai's unconcealed delight.

The third thing that lifted Caitlin's heart was the speech that Woodrow Wilson gave to Congress on January 8, news of which reached Petrograd two days after the Russian Christmas. It wasn't his Fourteen Points for peace that inspired her—for all except European leaders these simply stated the obvious—but the depth of fellow feeling that the president shared with the Russian people and its current government. Clearly referring to the Bolsheviks' stand at the Brest-Litovsk peace negotiations, Wilson thought "their conception of what is right, of what is humane and honorable for them to accept, has been stated with a frankness, a largeness of view, a generosity of spirit, and a universal human sympathy which must challenge the admiration of every friend of mankind."

Of all the people Caitlin had expected to notice such qualities in the Russian Revolution, Woodrow Wilson was among the least likely, and she took his speech as a gift—one of those rare moments in which she felt truly proud of her country. And she wasn't alone in her surprise—even her fellow journalist Jack Reed seemed at a loss for words.

CAITLIN SPENT THE RUSSIAN NEW Year's Eve at an LSR party on Fontanka Embankment. The diminutive Spiridonova was much in evidence, her animated face more beautiful than ever. She introduced people to each other, enforced the evening's no-politics rule, and even blocked a stampede for the door when a kerosene lamp burst into flames and briefly threatened to burn the building down. There was roast pig and pasties to eat, candles in bottles for light, and a Christmas tree still tenaciously clinging to a few of its needles. There was dancing and comedy, and a moving hymn to fallen comrades, and, despite the rule, discussion of events in Ukraine and Finland, arguments over what if any terms the government should accept from the Germans. Everything, it seemed, was still up for grabs.

Back in her hotel room, and still warmly wrapped in her coat, Caitlin forced open an ice-encrusted window and stared out at the snow-covered dome of the cathedral opposite. It was almost 2:00 A.M., and Russia had finally welcomed in 1918, thirteen days after everyone else.

How much longer should she stay? Arriving in November, she'd naïvely assumed that a few weeks would be enough to take it all in, to identify the changes and the future they suggested. But as she'd just heard at the party, two months had passed and so much remained unresolved. This, the biggest story on earth, was still unfolding, with no clear end—no end of any kind—in sight.

Her place was here—she was certain of it. She couldn't understand why Louise Bryant and Bessie Beatty had already arranged their departures or why Jack Reed was staying only a week or so more. But she did know that convincing her editor and publisher that she should stay would not be easy. Since mid-December that editor and publisher had been alluding, with ever-decreasing subtlety, to those events across Europe that she wasn't reporting, indeed could not report, as long as she remained out on her frozen Russian limb. And when the war resumed after its unofficial winter break and the generals started feeding young Americans into their meat grinder, she suspected an ultimatum—Russia or your job.

THE NIGHT AFTER THE NEW Year's Eve party, someone took a shot at Lenin as he left an organized farewell for one of the first

Red Army units. Three bullets passed through the car he was in, slightly wounding a Swiss comrade who was sitting beside him. The man or woman responsible was not apprehended, but there was no sign of overreaction on the part of the Cheka—no roadblocks or combing of the city, no mass arrests. On the contrary, by the time Caitlin received news of the matter, her Bolshevik acquaintances were already laughing it off.

Which had to be good news, she thought. A less secure regime might well have lashed out.

On the following day, she met Kollontai at the building by the Moika Canal that was being transformed into the flagship Palace of Motherhood. The babies brought in from the streets, once known by the numbers inscribed on their knuckles, had all been moved into one wing, along with the countess in charge and the nurses who served beneath her, while an army of party volunteers scrubbed and painted the rest of the building. The plans that Kollontai proudly showed Caitlin included a model nursery, a library, a dairy, and extensive medical facilities. This was socialism in practice. This was the future.

The news from abroad was also heartening. Incidents of worker unrest had been proliferating across Germany in recent days, and on January 16 a near-general strike brought the Austro-Hungarian capital, Vienna, to a virtual standstill. In Petrograd, Caitlin heard Red Guards and party members eagerly discussing the latest reports, as if their own lives depended on these faraway events. As of course they did. She hadn't yet met a Bolshevik who thought the revolution could survive on its own, and a German revolution was everyone's great hope, offering both freedom from future attacks and the strongest of potential allies against the rest of the world.

Caitlin thought about the socialists she'd met there in the summer of 1915, the brave men and women who'd chosen prison or a life in hiding rather than support the war. Were they thinking their hour had come at last?

No one was counting chickens. On the day that the news from Vienna arrived, the Bolshevik government announced a state of siege in Petrograd: the Constituent Assembly elected in late

November was due to convene in two days' time, and trouble was expected.

It duly arrived. On the morning of the opening, groups of demonstrators refused to recognize the perimeter established by the Red Guards. Fights broke out, then shooting, leaving several dead in the snow. Caitlin heard the gunfire but only later learned that fifteen people had died.

Inside the Tauride Palace, she sat in the press gallery behind the podium watching the leaders of the various parties arrive. It felt like a reprise of the previous summer's high-level gatherings, with Kerensky the most notable absentee. Kollontai waved to her, then sat reading through a file of notes, apparently oblivious to the strange atmosphere. There were guns everywhere, Caitlin noticed—in the hands of the sailors and Red Guards who ringed the chamber, peeking from the pockets of many politicians.

This was just theater, she thought, and dangerous theater at that. Having overthrown the rightists and moderates in November, the Bolsheviks would never meekly relinquish their power, election results notwithstanding.

The proceedings finally began at 4:00 P.M., after an argument over who should kick things off. The Bolsheviks won by sheer force of voice, and their spokesman, Sverdlov, read out a list of their achievements in government. A member of the opposition was then elected chairman, and the next few hours were spent rejecting all the laws and decrees that the Bolsheviks had put forward. After Lenin and his party had finally walked out, Spiridonova asked that the assembly recognize the steps toward peace with Germany and Austria that the government had taken. When the majority refused, arguing instead for a comprehensive international agreement, the LSRs walked out as well, leaving the liberals and moderate socialists alone in the chamber, surrounded by government guards.

And that, Caitlin thought, was that. The people in front of her, who carried on debating as if it actually mattered, thought they had turned the clock back to October, when Russia was still at war, the peasants were landless, and the workers were still waiting for any real change. But the power had passed on. At four in the morning, the guards announced that the task they'd been given was to protect the whole assembly and not just a mere party caucus. They invited the remaining delegates to go home, politely at first and then with more insistence. The Constituent Assembly had apparently outlived its usefulness.

The following Friday the also-elected Third Congress of Soviets opened in the same chamber. Caitlin attended on the first day and thought the difference noteworthy. Yesterday's suits were gone, in their place a strikingly diverse group of workingmen and -women, come from every part of the country to discuss their mutual future.

Toward the end of the afternoon session, a hand tapped on her shoulder. It was Kollontai, silently urging her out of the gallery.

"You're invited to a wedding," her friend said once they were out in the corridor.

"Whose?" Caitlin asked, surprised.

"Mine. Mine and Pavel's."

"Congratulations! When are you—"

"In half an hour, in the office on Znamenskaya Street."

Caitlin started to say she would be there, but Kollontai was already gone.

The service was as short and sweet as the new law intended. There were about forty other guests, most of them women or sailors. Flanked by Dybenko and her grown-up son, Misha, Kollontai looked a picture of happiness.

A long line of droshkies was waiting in the darkened street, each with a sailor holding the reins and a lantern swinging beside him. Kollontai and Dybenko took the one at the front, and the guests all bundled into those lined up behind. Caitlin found herself sharing a two-seater with one of the sailor comrades, who introduced himself as Sergei Piatakov. He was a good-looking young man of about her age, with an air of confusion that probably stemmed from finding himself so close to a female who wasn't his mother or his sister.

The procession rattled across the Neva and up a broad avenue. Looking behind her, Caitlin could see the line of lanterns stretching back in the darkness, like a necklace of stars.

When they finally reached their destination, she could hardly believe her eyes. She'd ridden Petrograd's roller coaster—the "American Mountain," they called it here—back in early summer, but she knew that the park shut down in winter. It wasn't closed today. According to Piatakov, one of the sailors had heard Kollontai tell Dybenko how much she loved roller coasters, and a plan had been born. Over the last couple of days, this sailor and others had cleared the tracks of snow, deiced the machinery, and lit numerous braziers beneath the structure to keep it from refreezing. And here it stood, surrounded by snow-covered Ferris wheels and carousels, reflecting the light of the moon now rising above the city. The red cars had all been adorned with yellow hammers and sickles.

A laughing Kollontai climbed into the front seat of the first car and almost pulled Dybenko in beside her. For someone who'd defended a revolution, he looked a little nervous.

All the other guests piled in, save one woman whom no one could persuade. Caitlin claimed a seat in the third car, feeling both excited and nervous. Climbing in beside her, Piatakov offered her a reassuring smile.

The switch was thrown, and the cars began to climb, Petrograd slowly spreading out beneath them. A moonlit stretch of the Neva appeared above the snowy roofscape, then a glimpse of the gulf to the west and the silhouettes of ships at anchor, before the world fell away from under them and the tiny train plunged downward, the screeches of the riders fusing joy and fear.

ANOTHER WEEK WENT BY. ONE hand extended in front of her, Caitlin felt her way up the hotel's darkened stairwell. The electricity was out again, crippling the elevator, and candles were never left burning in untended areas. As a child she'd always rather liked the dark, but Petrograd had cured her of that. The long summer nights were entrancing, but winter's price was much too high.

She felt exhausted and dirty. There'd been no running water for a couple of days, and the jugfuls the hotel provided were often layered with ice. There was no doubt about it—conditions were still getting worse, with no sign they'd ever improve. Even cutlery was running short. At the table where she'd just eaten dinner—cabbage soup and black bread for a change—she and six other people had taken turns with three wooden spoons and a single knife.

And as for getting around . . . She'd spent the better part of the day struggling from place to place on foot, because most of the roads were blocked by snow and no streetcars were running on the few that were not. The authorities had no sooner cleared the rails and wires than the power stations had run out of coal.

The news from the outside world offered little in the way of compensation. The only good tidings of recent days had come from Britain, where women over thirty had finally been given the vote. But even this was soured, at least in Caitlin's mind, by the price that Emmeline and Christabel Pankhurst had paid for this piece of male largesse—their almost rabid support for the war. Elsewhere the outlook was thoroughly bleak. Serious fighting had broken out in Ukraine between the right-wing breakaway government and the local Bolsheviks, and the same seemed about to happen in Finland. A renewal of fighting on the Western Front was still a month or more away, but the Germans had already transferred enough divisions from the Eastern Front to shift the balance. There were now four American divisions in France, with many more to follow, but by the time the latter arrived, it might well be too late.

Russia's own military position remained precarious. Over breakfast that morning, Caitlin had eavesdropped on the conversation at a neighboring table between two long-term residents. The couple in question were minor aristocrats who had lacked the will or wherewithal to leave and were now pinning their hopes on the Germans. The woman would have preferred an English takeover, but as that seemed unlikely, she was willing to cope with the Kaiser. As long as the wretched Bolsheviks were gone and they got the chance to live the way they had.

It might still happen, Caitlin thought. Trotsky and his team had stalled the German negotiators at Brest-Litovsk for almost two months, but the latest reports suggested that the latter's patience had finally run out and that an ultimatum was in the offing. No one knew how the Bolshevik leadership would respond, including the leaders themselves, who seemed to be split three ways, roughly half urging defiance and revolutionary war, a quarter backing Trotsky's scheme to drag things out indefinitely, another quarter supporting Lenin's call for peace at any price. If the German negotiators called Trotsky's bluff and Lenin was outvoted by those of his colleagues who wanted a revolutionary war, then hostilities seemed set to resume, and German soldiers might well be marching down Nevsky Prospect before another week had passed.

Next morning Caitlin ran into Volodarsky at Smolny and solicited his opinion over tea in the noisy canteen.

He was worried, he told her, as much by the split in the party leadership as by the possibility of a new German offensive. "If you look at it from a pragmatic perspective, then it's easy to appreciate all three points of view," he told her. "Lenin's right—we do need a breathing space. The rebels are right—it would be a betrayal of the German working class to make a loser's peace. And since they're both right, then putting off the decision for as long as possible makes perfect sense. So Trotsky's right, too."

"And from an unpragmatic point of view?" Caitlin asked.

"Oh, we have to keep fighting no matter what. We always knew we couldn't stand alone, so saving our own revolution at the expense of others could never make sense."

"Then Lenin's wrong?"

Volodarsky smiled. "Not necessarily. It would all depend on how much we surrender and how long a breathing space we take."

Caitlin shook her head. "Maybe the Russian people have carried the torch as long as they're able."

"Maybe, but I'll tell you one thing." Volodarsky leaned forward, as if to amplify his words. "In these few months, I have had more joy than any other man should have in all his life."

THAT SAME AFTERNOON CAITLIN RECEIVED a cable from New York. The message was friendly enough in tone, but her editor had clearly reached the limit of his patience. The time had come to choose—stay in Russia or resign from her job.

It felt like an impossible choice. She wouldn't have gone quite as far as Volodarsky, but she had understood what he meant—she had never felt more useful, or more inspired by the people around her, than she had in this city. If she chose to stay, there would be other work that she could do, if not English translation, then something in Kollontai's welfare department or the women's organizations. Her Russian was probably good enough now, and it would only get better.

That evening she went to Kollontai's flat and was relieved to find Dybenko out at a meeting of fellow Ukrainians. After telling her friend about the editor's cable and her own inclination to resign, Caitlin was surprised by Kollontai's response.

"I don't want to lose you, of course," the Russian said. "But really, you must go home. The Germans are about to attack, and the British and French are already ganging up on us, and we need every foreign friend we have to trumpet our cause in their own country. And it's more than that. Remember what I said about us breaking a path for others to follow—well, they can only follow our path if they know about it, and it's people like you, my dear, who have to tell them. You have to tell the world what we've discovered here—that, for a short time at least, everything is possible. That selfishness and war and doing others down no more define human nature than selflessness and peace and helping each other out." Kollontai smiled. "And you know you can always come back."

Which of course was true. After she'd agonized for another couple of days, Caitlin's mind was made up by—of all things—a piece of unpublished fiction. She was talking to several young activists in a café when one insisted on outlining the plot of a new short story by the writer Yevgeny Zamyatin. The protagonists of the story were young revolutionaries who were trying to communicate with potential allies on either Mars or the moon—the narrator had heard the story thirdhand and couldn't remember which. Nor could he explain how people on earth had discovered the existence of this extraterrestrial population, but he insisted it was unimportant. "The point is that they were trying to communicate. And one of them has this bright idea of building a gigantic wooden "A" somewhere in the countryside and setting it on fire, the theory being that the people on the moon or wherever it was would see it and the two civilizations would gradually build up an alphabet between them with which they could converse. So they make the "A," they set it ablaze, and they wait for a reply. But none comes. They wait and wait, but no reply ever comes. And they can't understand it. They know that the "A" can be seen, so why is there no reply? The only reason they can think of is that the people on the moon just don't understand what the "A" means." The narrator sat back in his seat.

"And then?" one of the others asked.

"That's it—there is no more."

"Because that's where we are," another young man suggested. "We've sent out the message, and we're still waiting for a reply."

"I think Zamyatin is saying that we'll wait in vain," the original narrator said. "That no one else will understand the "A" we lit here in Petrograd."

"Because they haven't experienced what we have," a young woman said. "And their governments are telling them that peace and brotherhood are lies. We need to be better at sharing our experience and exposing *their* lies."

And not from this sort of distance, Caitlin thought.

The following afternoon she visited the Finland Station in search of a suitable train. One was leaving for the Swedish border in three days, which seemed ideal. She would still be able to attend the Palace of Motherhood opening on the thirteenth and have time to say her good-byes. At the central telegraph office on Pochtamtskaya Street, she cabled her editor, Ed Carlucci, with the news that she was on her way back to London. Her longer-term plan, which she didn't mention, was to do a catch-up job on any other major European stories, then sail for home. If Americans weren't understanding the "A," it wouldn't be for lack of a personal explanation.

Later that day she kept an appointment to see Spiridonova. Once the samovar had come to boil, they sat and sipped tea in the LSR leader's spartan room by the light of a single candle.

Caitlin was keen to understand why a big majority of the LSRs were now so opposed to signing a peace treaty with the Germans.

"Most of your support comes from the peasants," Caitlin said, "and they bore the overwhelming brunt of the war. Why would your party want it to continue?"

Spiridonova shook her head. "We don't want that war to continue. That was a war for the landlords and bosses and the nation they claimed we all belonged to. It wasn't our war, wasn't a war from which our people could derive any benefit. But a war for the revolution—my party believes that this would be a war for humanity, a war for us all."

"Some have told me that you're not completely convinced by this argument."

Spiridonova's smile was a sad one. "That's true. I do see both points of view, and sometimes I feel that a breathing space might be more important. But what really worries me is that this issue will split our government. My party will not accept the sort of peace that Lenin will. It will quit the government rather than sign such a treaty. And the Bolsheviks will be left to rule on their own."

This prospect was clearly cause for anxiety on Spiridonova's part, and as she walked her way back across town, Caitlin found herself sharing the feeling. Though largely sympathetic to Bolshevik views, she often doubted their commitment to democracy. The Bolsheviks were happy to accept the outcomes of their own internal votes but inclined—as in the case of the Constituent Assembly—to find reasons to ignore democratic procedures when dealing with opponents. If the LSRs were removed from the decision-making process, the revolution would lose its balance in more ways than one.

Back at her hotel, she found a message from Yakov Peters. Dzerzhinsky's deputy had learned that she was leaving and asked if she'd be willing to take out a letter for his wife in England. He assured her that the message was purely personal and would not lead to her being arrested should the "British Cheka" insist on reading it.

THE PENULTIMATE NIGHT IN PETROGRAD was undoubtedly her worst. In the early hours of the morning, Caitlin was walking up Nevsky Prospect, on her way home from a farewell party thrown by correspondent friends at the International Café, when she noticed an orange glow above the roofs to the west. She hastened her pace, with every step she took more afraid of what she might find, and as she turned the final corner, all those fears proved founded. The new Palace of Motherhood was burning, huge flames licking up into the sky. There were firemen in attendance, but she could see at a glance that the building was beyond saving—the middle section was a ruin of charred wood and shattered glass, its windows like the fire-filled eyes of a Halloween pumpkin.

Across the street a crowd had gathered, and one of the nannies from the old "angel factory" was loudly blaming the nurses whom Kollontai had brought in—"whores with their sailors, always dropping lighted cigarettes." Another woman was shouting that this was God's revenge on the Bolsheviks for removing all the icons.

"It was arson," one of the Red Guards told Caitlin. "Several fires were started in different places, all within a few minutes."

Why? Caitlin wanted to ask, but she already knew the answer. This was revenge all right, but not God's. Kollontai and her supporters had pushed too fast and hard for some people. Something that Kollontai, and Caitlin, considered self-evident—the belief that women who gave birth deserved the best the state could offer regardless of how they had come to conceive—was, to others, a condoning of immorality. To these ignorant bigots, Kollontai's dream was a nightmare, promoting indecency, corrupting children, and sanctioning blasphemy. And one or more of them had lit the deadly candles.

Kollontai would be devastated.

Caitlin found herself hoping that the Cheka would catch whoever was responsible and that the courts would sentence them to something worse than "the reprehension of society."

As she stood there watching the fire, Caitlin remembered the one she had seen from the train. Seven months had passed since then, seven months in which so much had happened. And if that first fire had told her that Russia's revolution was far from over, then this one carried the opposite message, that those who'd grown fat on the old status quo had not abandoned the fight.

6

Letters to Soph

Half a mile of rough track separated the disheveled-looking huts that housed the Persian and Russian border posts. After a sleepy official at the former had signed McColl's and Cheselden's passes, they said good-bye to their local guides and helpers, remounted their mules, and rode out across no-man's-land. As the Russian post slowly came into focus, McColl could see several soldiers sitting outside it, watching their approach. No one seemed particularly bothered, or at least not enough to reach for a horse or a gun.

As they dismounted outside the wooden hut, an officer in uniform emerged. McColl introduced himself and Cheselden and explained that they were on a diplomatic mission to Ashkhabad. The young man seemed to accept this at face value. He barely looked at their passes before waving them through with a smile. "You have three hours to reach the station," he added in warning. "The train only runs twice a day."

"Well, that wasn't too difficult," Cheselden remarked once they were out of earshot.

In front of them, a vast plain stretched to the horizon. Somewhere out there—allegedly twelve miles distant—were Kaakhka, its station, and the train to Ashkhabad. Behind them the mountains they'd crossed since leaving Meshed rose into the southern sky. The journey had taken four days but hadn't been hard. The worst nights of winter were over, the worst days of summer still some months away, and both walking and riding had proved easier than either man expected.

They had met several groups of refugees heading into Persia, and on each occasion McColl had swapped letters of introduction to the British consulate in Meshed for information on the state of affairs in Transcaspia. He had no idea how Cluett and company would react when these refugees knocked at the gates of Eden, but he was sure that Cumming would back him. The two men he had spoken to had provided the names of friends in Ashkhabad and Krasnovodsk who would be sympathetic to a British approach. One had been at the meeting that Poletaev had mentioned, between cotton wholesalers and potential German buyers.

So they had some cards to play. On more than one occasion during their thousand-mile trip from Basra, McColl had found himself speculating on what sort of idiots sent two men halfway around the world to infiltrate a country of which they knew next to nothing and still expected a happy ending. He hadn't shared this thought with his companion, since he knew that Cheselden would think he was joking. Because almost alone among those still fighting for King and Country, his partner, God help him, still believed that the authorities usually got things right.

The cluster of black dots lining the horizon had to be Kaakhka and its station. Closer at hand, another small farm clung to the side of the road, its small green garden like an island of misplaced hope in the dry brown immensity that surrounded it. The cottage was of sturdy construction, and the machines in the yard were definitely European. And all of it was Russia, McColl told himself. He remembered a line that Caitlin had quoted: "A country that refutes all preconceptions, a people that never fails to surprise."

"It's really quite civilized," Cheselden said, suitably disconcerted.

Kaakhka, when they reached it, was barely awake. They found a serai for the mules and paid for a fortnight's board—if McColl and Cheselden hadn't returned by then, the owner was welcome to keep or sell the beasts. The station was unpopulated, but there was shine enough on the rails to prove their recent use. McColl stared down the line in both directions, thinking that this was an arm of the old Silk Road, the track bed flattened by centuries of plodding camels. He felt a very long way from home.

Thirty minutes before the train was due, a man arrived on foot and promptly shut himself inside the station buffet. Minutes later smoke curled out of the chimney; a few minutes more and the door was flung open. A basket piled high with hunks of black bread sat on the counter; behind it a samovar and a cauldron of soup were heating on the stove.

As McColl and Cheselden were being served, the sound of a train became audible. They were still hurriedly eating, and burning their tongues in the process, when the engine wheezed into the station and what looked like all the passengers tumbled down from the carriages and swarmed into the buffet. McColl and Cheselden watched in awe as the motley scrum engulfed the counter, waving and shouting at the unperturbed proprietor. There were Russians and Turks and Persians and Indians, tribesmen and traders and farmers, wearing everything from sheepskin hats and boots to suits and dresses that wouldn't have seemed out of place on the prewar Champs-Élysées.

Out on the dusty platform, McColl bought tickets for himself and Cheselden. The guard-conductor insisted on seeing inside their suitcases but wasn't unfriendly. "The revolution has many enemies," he explained apologetically, as if he couldn't imagine the British playing such a role. Boarding the seven-coach train, McColl managed to find an empty window seat from which he could watch for any bridges seemingly ripe for destruction.

The eighty-mile trip took just over four hours, and all he saw were culverts of varying sizes for channeling runoff under the tracks. As they reached the outskirts of Ashkhabad, he and Cheselden scanned opposite sides of the line for any stockpiled cotton, but the only wagons on show were full of strange-looking logs.

"It's saxaul," Cheselden said, plucking another plum from his tree of esoteric knowledge. "A desert tree they use for fuel."

The station platform was lined with people waiting to board, but much the same number seemed to get off. The two of them took their time, Cheselden staying with their suitcases while McColl quizzed the Russian booking-office clerk about hotels. The two deemed suitable for Europeans were the London and the Germania, which didn't make for a difficult choice. By the time McColl rejoined his partner, the platform was almost clear, just a single man sitting on one of the benches. He wasn't staring at them, but McColl had few doubts that this was their official watcher. After hiring a phaeton and riding a hundred yards down the long road into town, he heard the sound of another horse behind them. There was no need to turn and look back.

The town was laid out on a flat grid, the few substantial buildings at its center surrounded by small streets and alleys lined with low-level mud-brick houses. The London Hotel had three floors, and the steel poles sticking out of its roof suggested a possible fourth in its future. The desk clerk was surprised to see two Englishmen but had no apparent anxieties about renting them a room. They took the first he offered, a mostly empty double with two large mattresses and windows providing a view of the Persian mountains. Once the young man had left them, McColl glanced down at the street below—their watcher's phaeton was still parked opposite, the man himself probably down at reception, reading their register entries.

Away to the west, the deep red sun was poised above the darkening line of mountains.

"I'm hungry," Cheselden announced.

"Then let's go and look for food."

Their watcher was talking to the desk clerk. As they walked down Annenkovskaya Street in search of a restaurant, he ambled along some fifty yards behind them. It was getting colder, and the light was rapidly fading, but most of the shops were still open for business and the streets by no means empty. Lights were shining in the posher Russian emporiums, kerosene lamps being lit in the narrower streets of the trading quarter. Above the buildings to their right, a minaret was silhouetted against the yellow-green sky.

There was no obvious police or military presence. Indeed, the only proof that the revolution had reached this far south was the red flags adorning the larger establishments; in all other respects, life in Ashkhabad seemed little different from life in Meshed or Teheran. When they did find somewhere to eat, the menu board was scrawled in Farsi, the sparse clientele a mixture of Russians and locals, whom Cheselden said were called Sarts. The place was clean, the food was good, and the other patrons showed a healthy lack of interest in who the two of them were, even when they tried conversing in German. That language was obviously not as rare in Ashkhabad as they would have liked.

Night had fallen by the time they finished, and the street outside was lit only by occasional lamps still hanging from storefronts. Their watcher tailed them back to the hotel, a moving shadow in the gloom, his footsteps barely smudging the silence. Though sorely tempted to turn and confront the man, McColl restrained himself. "You never force your opponent into making a hostile move" had been one of his father's favorite sayings, and what was good for Glasgow labor disputes was surely good for the mean streets of Ashkhabad. If the other side wanted a war, then let them declare it.

THE KNOCK ON THE DOOR came at seven in the morning, and McColl was encouraged by its civilized tone. It was a peremptory rap, no more. Not a frenzied hammering, let alone a splintering of wood.

The uniformed Russian whom McColl invited in was outwardly apologetic. About the early hour, about the need for them to dress and come with him at once. About the need for ablutions and breakfast to wait.

The two of them insisted on taking a piss but otherwise did as requested. A phaeton was waiting outside, its driver enjoying a particularly evil-smelling cigarette. Once the three of them had climbed in behind him, he jerked the horses into motion and the vehicle began rattling south along Annenkovskaya. There was no sign of their shadow from the previous day.

The town fell away behind, until only the station and its surrounding buildings were left between them and the distant mountains. These looked gorgeous in the early-morning sun, but McColl found himself wondering if, by the end of that day, he and

Cheselden would regret ever crossing them. The Russian beside him had refused to answer questions but had remained polite, and, in lieu of anything more positive, McColl was clinging to that. It didn't *feel* as if they were headed out into the desert for a summary execution.

A hundred yards short of the station, the phaeton abruptly pulled off the road and came to a halt outside a modern two-story building. According to the signs by the door, it housed the railway board and the telegraph office. After ushering the two of them up the stairs and into a room with a long wooden table and more than a dozen seats, their escort told them to wait and promptly disappeared.

McColl sat himself down in one of the chairs and gazed out the east-facing window at the receding ribbon of track.

"What do you think?" Cheselden asked him.

"An interview with the current powers-that-be would be my guess. Everyone tells us they're railwaymen, and here we are next door to the station."

A large clock on one wall loudly ticked the minutes away. Five became ten, ten became thirty, and soon a whole hour had gone by. They could hear people below, but it was almost ten o'clock when footfalls sounded on the staircase.

Five Russian men filed into the room, three in workmen's clothes and two in shabby military uniforms. The latter pair removed their guns from leather holsters and set them down on the table, then took seats on either side of the door. The other three sat themselves down at the head of the table, like a row of presiding judges.

"Your papers," the one in the middle asked, holding out a hand. He seemed the oldest of the three and had a darker complexion than his two companions. Like the man on his right, he was wearing a red enamel star in his lapel.

McColl passed them across and waited while the three men examined them.

"Which of you is McColl?" the middle one eventually asked, making the name sound like a glottal stop.

"I am. And whom am I addressing?"

All three looked surprised, by either the impudence or the fact that someone might not know. "This is Citizen Semashko," the middle one said, indicating the weasel-faced man on his right. "And this is Citizen Volkhov," he added, turning to the bulky, red-nosed man on his left. "And my name is Strakhov, Arkady Strakhov. We are the Emergency Defense Committee of the Ashkhabad Soviet," he concluded his introduction, with an admirable lack of self-importance. He turned to McColl's companion. "You are Cheselden?"

The latter looked to McColl for guidance.

"My partner does not speak Russian," McColl told them.

"But he does speak German?"

"Yes. And French."

Strakhov ran a hand through his thinning black hair. He looked Armenian to McColl, but the name was Russian. "So why have you come to Ashkhabad?" Strakhov asked. "To spy out the land for your army in Persia?"

McColl smiled and spoke slowly. "There are very few British troops in Persia, and there is absolutely no possibility of their crossing the border without the permission of the Russian government."

"You are expecting an invitation?" the one on the left—Semashko—asked sarcastically.

"We have been allies for almost four years in the war against the Germans and the Turks. Would it be so strange if we joined forces against an invasion of Turkestan?"

"A month ago no," Strakhov said, "but our government has made it clear that we are no longer at war."

McColl had heard in Teheran that the Bolshevik negotiator Trotsky had informed his German counterpart that Russia was adopting a "neither war nor peace" policy, which raised any number of questions. "I was not aware that a peace treaty has been signed," he told the three men, hoping that was still the case.

"Not yet, but it's only a matter of days," Strakhov answered, causing Volkhov's lips to pucker in what might be disapproval.

McColl wondered if the lack of a star in Volkhov's lapel meant the man was not a Bolshevik. A Left Socialist Revolutionary perhaps. Last he'd heard, they were all for fighting on. "What if it isn't?" he asked, looking at Volkhov. "What if the Germans and Turks take Baku and cross the Caspian and advance along your railway? Will you just let them walk over you?"

"That won't happen," Strakhov answered him, sounding almost too convinced.

"It may be unlikely," McColl conceded, "but if it does happen, would you let your revolution die rather than accept our help?"

"Why would the British ruling class help our revolution?" Volkhov asked, speaking for the first time.

"Because we share a common enemy. No more, no less. We don't have many troops in Persia, but those we have would double the number at your disposal," McColl continued, veering off into fiction. In truth he had little idea what forces either side possessed. "And we could provide more weapons for your troops," he added, "as we did for your first revolutionary government."

Volkhov's shrug was not entirely discouraging, but Semashko was having none of it. "And I suppose that once the battle was won, your troops would hurry back to Persia," he said scornfully.

"They would," McColl insisted. "We are only interested in stopping the Germans."

"And there's nothing else you would want from us?" Strakhov asked incredulously.

McColl admitted there was. "If we agreed to fight together, then my government would expect you not to sell your cotton stocks to the enemy."

Strakhov's smile was bitter. "The stocks left over from the last two harvests still belong to the mill owners. For the moment at least."

"But the soviet will have the final say," Semashko interjected.

"I don't understand," McColl said. "The cotton belongs to the wholesalers, but they need permission to sell it?"

"Something like that," Strakhov said with some irritation. "You make it sound stupid, but why should those with capital always have the final say?"

McColl didn't feel equipped for an ideological discussion. "Have the Germans approached you?"

"That is our business," Semashko said flatly.

"Is your government prepared to make an offer?" Volkhov asked, causing Semashko to roll his eyes.

"Yes," McColl said. "We have no way of transporting the cotton," he added, "but we will pay for the stocks to be destroyed."

"Pay with what?" Semashko asked.

"The weapons you say you need. Or notes of credit on a London bank. Whichever you prefer."

"I don't believe it," Semashko said flatly.

"If we ask for payment first, what do we have to lose?" Volkhov asked.

Strakhov considered. "The two of you will be taken downstairs while we talk this over," he eventually decided.

A samovar was bubbling in the office below. "So how much of that did you get?" McColl asked Cheselden in English, once they'd begged a glass of tea.

"Not a lot. Hardly a word, if I'm honest."

McColl went over the conversation.

"Do you think they'll bite?" Cheselden asked doubtfully.

"I've no idea. Volkhov—the big one on the right—He isn't happy about Russia quitting the war, but I don't know why. It might be ideological—some of the other socialist groupings are against any sort of peace with what they see as reactionary governments—or he might have personal reasons for hating the Germans or the Turks. A dead brother, something like that. The other two—I don't know. Strakhov seems far from stupid, and I can't see him wanting to close any doors until he's absolutely sure. As for Semashko—he'd just as soon see us shot."

"Well, let's hope the others don't listen to him."

"You could say that."

It took the troika upstairs only fifteen minutes to reach their decision. Which was, in effect, to put one off. The matter would be referred to the regional soviet in Tashkent, which, as Strakhov now informed them in a studiedly neutral tone, was the ultimate authority for all of Turkestan. It might take several days for that body's reply to reach Ashkhabad, and in the meantime the two Englishmen were forbidden to leave the city.

No lift was offered back to the town, so they strolled across to the station in search of a phaeton. Finding none, they started walking.

It was Cheselden who eventually broke the silence. "That was a strange experience," he said. "Meeting those men back there. I mean, I didn't understand much of the conversation, but you get a feeling for people. Those men seemed decent enough—well, two of them did—but . . ." He laughed. "It was like being taken to task by servants. Nothing wrong with that, I suppose, but it felt strange. To them as well, I thought. I mean, they're railwaymen—they can't find it easy suddenly being in charge."

"My father was a railwayman," McColl said.

Cheselden stopped in his tracks. "Oh, no offense, old chap."

"None taken. When I was growing up, there were plenty of men like that who came to our parlor for one reason or another. Some of them were thick as planks, some were every bit as clever as anyone I met at Oxford. They probably knew less, but only because their lives had given them less opportunity to read or travel. And men like that are not used to being in charge, as you put it. But that doesn't mean that none of them could handle it."

"I'm sure you're right," Cheselden said, eager to minimize any slight.

McColl didn't answer. What had struck him was the depth of hatred that Semashko had plainly felt for them both. And not because they were foreigners. This went deeper than that.

When they finally reached the hotel, their watcher was back in position on the far side of the street, apparently sharing a smoke and a chat with his driver.

"So what now?" Cheselden asked once they were up in their room. "Do we just wait?"

"No," McColl told him. "I thought Semashko looked a lot happier than Volkhov about referring the matter to Tashkent, which probably means that hard-liners like him are in control there. In which case we won't get the answer we want. So we need some other irons in the fire."

"The names we were given."

"Yes."

"We'll have to lose our shadow."

McColl nodded. "Once will be easy—it doesn't seem to have occurred to his bosses that the two of us might choose to head off in different directions."

"True. We're assuming he works for our railwaymen friends, but what if he actually works for the Germans? We know they're here somewhere."

"Maybe. But that would mean they were meeting every train just in case an Englishman stepped off. It seems more likely that the local police would have someone there, looking out for anyone suspicious."

Cheselden shrugged. "I don't suppose it matters. They're all enemies."

McColl extracted a crumpled sheet of paper from the lining of his suitcase, smoothed it out on the solitary nightstand, and carried it into the sunlight. "It looks as though our cotton wholesaler's office is only a couple of streets away." He turned to his partner. "I suggest that you take another trip to the station. While you're there, you can make a copy of the timetable and maybe check the yard for any cotton. If our friend below goes with you and I take the back way out, then our railwaymen friends should be none the wiser."

"How do you know there's a back way out?"

"I was awake in the middle of the night, so I had a good look around. There's another staircase at the back and a way out through the kitchen."

Cheselden was surprised. "I didn't think the hotel had a restaurant."

"It's knee-deep in dust, just like the kitchen. Which makes it all the easier."

"Okay, I'm on my way."

Standing at the window, McColl witnessed the watcher's reactions when Cheselden came out alone. The man stared at the door for several seconds, willing McColl to follow, then glanced up at the window, hoping to see him still in the room.

McColl obliged, but not too obviously, standing still with his back to the window for the better part of a minute. When he finally looked out, Cheselden and the watcher were almost out of sight.

He met no one on the back stairs. The disused kitchen's outside door led into a dusty alley and this to a small street of mostly shuttered shops. Several men suggested that he stop and peruse their wares, but he passed them by with a smile, his eyes in search of street signs. As far he could tell, there were none, and by the time he found a Russian speaker who knew where Azadi Street was, he had walked two blocks past it. The office, when he eventually found it, was on the ground floor of a small brick building.

Opening the door, he found a young Russian woman typing at her desk.

"I'm looking for Alexei Lutovinov."

She gave him a worried smile. "You are . . . ?"

"A friend of a friend," he said reassuringly.

At that moment a door opened and a middle-aged man walked in.

"This is my father," she said.

McColl offered his hand, explained how he'd come by Lutovinov's name and the purpose of his visit.

The Russian gestured for his daughter to leave the room. "The British government will pay me to destroy my cotton," he said once the door had closed behind her, in a tone that suggested he couldn't quite believe his ears.

"As far as we're concerned, anything's better than having it fall into German hands."

"I am only one owner."

"We will offer the same deal to all the owners. I am hoping that you could tell me who they are and how to contact them."

Lutovinov gestured McColl to a chair and sat down himself. "I understand what you want," the Russian said, "but you must appreciate that this is not a simple matter. The current government would have to approve such action."

"So I was told this morning." McColl explained Strakhov's description of the current situation.

Lutovinov made a wry face. "That is where we are. The government has not taken ownership of the cotton lands or industries, but it has passed new laws giving the growers and workers greater influence in how these are run. How *much* influence remains unclear and in practice varies from place to place. This state of affairs might last, but I doubt it. Only last month the Tashkent soviet seized several mills, only to hand them back a fortnight later, presumably at Petrograd's behest, but my colleagues and I think it's only a matter of time before we find ourselves ousted completely. So if a deal could be done at all, it has to be done very quickly. How will payment be made?"

"Accounts will be opened for you and your colleagues in a London bank," McColl explained, knowing that this would prove acceptable. Lutovinov and friends would be well aware that they had no future in a Bolshevik Russia.

"I will talk to people. The other owners, at least the ones I can reach. And there are people in the new government—the soviet—whom I can sound out. But don't worry—I will be careful."

"Have the Germans already approached you?" McColl asked.

"Of course. They've had agents here in Ashkhabad for several months and have built up quite a network of informers. And they're not only offering money. They have promised to reinstate the old regime here in Turkestan."

"That must be tempting," McColl suggested.

"It would be if we believed it possible."

"Have they also approached the soviet?"

"Of course." Lutovinov grinned. "And promised support for their regime."

"What was the reply?"

"The soviet is divided. Those three you met this morning—Strakhov and Semashko are Bolsheviks, but of very different types. I knew Arkady Strakhov at school—he has more sense than most, and he seems sincere enough. I'm sure he believes he's changing the world for the better."

"And Semashko," McColl prompted.

Lutovinov grunted. "He'll say the same, but what really excites that man is tearing the old world down."

"He did seem resentful," McColl agreed. And perhaps with good reason, he thought—the old Russia had been a punishing place. "What about Volkhov?"

"Sergei Volkhov is the local leader of the Socialist Revolutionaries. And like his leaders in Petrograd, he's in favor of continuing the war. He's our best chance of doing this deal."

"Strakhov told me the three of them had agreed to ask Tashkent for instructions."

"Hmm. I doubt Volkhov was in favor of that." Lutovinov paused. "And other things may happen first," he added mysteriously. "We may see a change in who controls the soviet before too many weeks have passed."

Having offered this hint, Lutovinov refused to elucidate. "You should talk to Volkhov," was all he would add.

McColl elicited the relevant address, then took his leave.

HE WENT FOR A WALK around the town, aware that this was likely to be his last chance to do so without a shadow. The streets were pleasant enough but essentially uninteresting, and the only building he came across of any aesthetic value was a Baha'i temple. McColl had vaguely heard of the Baha'i but had no idea what they believed in or why they should have built a temple in a city as remote as this one. The man at the gate spoke just enough Russian to refuse him entry, so McColl wandered around the perimeter, peering through gaps in the balustraded walls at the surprisingly lush vegetation and the mosquelike dome and minarets.

Half an hour later, he let himself in through the hotel back door and ascended unobserved to their room. On the other side of the street, a new watcher was busy biting his nails, and McColl had to stand in the window for several minutes before his presence was registered with a twitch of the head. He thought it unlikely that his absence had been noticed and was sure of it once he'd checked the hair in the clasp of his suitcase.

His partner soon returned. Cheselden had made a note of the passenger-train times—there were two a day in each direction, west toward Krasnovodsk at 1:00 P.M. and 10:00 P.M., east toward

Tashkent at 3:00 P.M. and 2:00 A.M. He hadn't come across any mountains of cotton.

After hearing McColl's account of his meeting with Lutovinov, he had only one question: "Was the daughter pretty?"

"Yes," McColl told him absentmindedly. He was wondering whether to follow Lutovinov's suggestion and pay Volkhov a visit.

"I'm not really interested in other girls," Cheselden was saying, having laid all he could of himself on his mattress. "I really miss my Soph," he added, flexing the feet that hung over the end.

LATE THAT AFTERNOON THE TWO of them used a stroll around town to pinpoint Sergei Volkhov's home, a one-story bungalow on the southern edge of a built-up area that reminded McColl of the India cantonments. They ate once more at the same Persian restaurant—chicken and rice heavily flavored with saffron—then returned to the hotel and waited for darkness. Once that had fallen, McColl slipped down the back stairs, out through the disused kitchen, and zigzagged his way across the town, using only the smallest streets and alleys.

As he walked, he rehearsed his pitch to Volkhov, a promise of British support for the Ashkhabad Socialist Revolutionaries, against the Germans and the Turks on the one hand and the Bolsheviks on the other. Such a promise would, he hoped, encourage Volkhov and his party to take control of the local soviet. And, once they were in power, permit the destruction of the cotton stockpiles.

His hopes were misplaced. Volkhov was certainly surprised to see him, but there was anger there, too, and more than a touch of fear. Rather than invite McColl into the house, he gestured him toward the seats on the dimly lit veranda. When McColl tried small talk, asking after the various plants in pots and barrel bottoms, the Russian merely grunted, "My wife would know."

It was easier to find common ground when it came to the war. Volkhov was vehemently opposed to a "shameful peace"—"How can we tell those millions of mothers that their sons died in vain?"—but had nothing new to offer in the matter of the cotton—"Tashkent will decide." When McColl casually suggested that the soviet in

Ashkhabad might choose to go its own way, Volkhov stared at him in silence for almost a minute before saying McColl should talk to the wholesalers. "Discreetly," he added, as if to himself.

Behind the soviet's back, was the implication. "Discretion is difficult when our every movement is followed," McColl said.

Volkhov again looked surprised. "Not by us," he insisted.

"Are you sure?"

"I am in charge of the local police. We have no men watching you."

Cheselden had been right, McColl thought as he made his way back to the hotel. The Germans had been keeping them under observation, using local helpers.

He reentered the building as he had left it and wearily climbed the stairs. Their door was slightly ajar, and the smell of blood hit him as he pushed it open. Cheselden was facedown on the floor, his head surrounded by a large and glistening pool. Dropping to his knees, McColl could see that the throat had been cut.

A sudden noise spun him around, but it was only the door's rusty hinge.

He moved across to close it, keeping his head low to avoid being seen. As he did so, one of the two candles gutted out. Crawling over to the window, he inched an eye around the frame to scan the street below. One watcher was still there, the other probably reporting in.

Checking his bag for the Webley service revolver, he found only the oilcloth in which he'd wrapped it.

He went back to Cheselden, lifting him up and away from the puddle of blood. After closing the young man's eyes, he sat and stared at the body, trying to take it in. In death the gangling young man looked no more than an overgrown boy.

On the other side of the room, the pages of an unfinished letter to Soph were scattered across the mattress.

"Good-bye, Aud," he murmured.

What to do? It seemed certain that Cheselden's killers would come back for him once they knew he was there. And now they had his gun. He had to get away from the hotel.

There was nothing he could do for the boy. Except take the letters he had written to Soph.

He gathered those up and placed them in his own bag, then rummaged through Cheselden's valise for anything that might prove useful. There was nothing.

One last look around the room—still nothing. He grabbed his bag and half crouched his way across the room, rising to his full height when he knew that he couldn't be seen from outside. Pressing his ear to the door, he heard only his own thumping heart.

The corridor was lit by just a sliver of moonlight, the stairs so dark that he twice almost lost his footing, but memory guided him down to the kitchen and through to the hotel's back door. As he stepped outside, it occurred to him that the other German might be covering this exit, but no blade or bullet leaped out of the shadows.

He hadn't yet decided where to go, but he started walking anyway, intent on putting some distance between himself and the men who had killed his partner. German-paid assassins. Who else could it be?

He didn't pause for breath until he'd crossed three streets. The town was almost wholly asleep, with only an occasional window revealing a candlelit glow. The streetlights were out, a thin veneer of moonlight glinting on the edges of the box-shaped buildings and turning the scene into a life-size cubist painting. Struck by the beauty of it all, McColl reminded himself that the moon would still be around tomorrow, whereas he might not be.

Where should he go? He wasn't far from Lutovinov's house—would the cotton wholesaler help him, if only with advice? He didn't believe that the man would shop him, so there seemed no risk in asking.

He located the house without too much difficulty and was surprised to find a light burning behind the downstairs curtains.

His rap on the door was answered in a heartbeat, the same amount of time it took for the young girl's face to switch from hope to accusation. "What do you want?" she almost shouted at him. Her eyes looked red from crying.

"To see your father—"

"My father has been arrested! Only hours after talking to you!"

The door slammed shut in his face. He stood there for a moment, stunned by the suddenness of the exchange. He thought about knocking again and decided there wouldn't be much point.

So now what? The only way out of Ashkhabad was by one of the four daily trains—what time did they run? He seemed to remember that one of the Tashkent trains left at three in the morning, about three hours from now. If no alarm had been raised and no one stopped him boarding the train, then the horses were waiting at Kaakhka, and by noon tomorrow he could be back in Persia.

Their mission would have ended in abject failure, but he would be alive.

He owed Cheselden more than that. He probably owed his country more than that.

He needed to go west. To Krasnovodsk, where he knew there were stockpiles of cotton ready for shipment across the Caspian. Where he knew of two possible helpers.

But how?

Volkhov, he thought. A slender hope, but the only one remaining. McColl didn't doubt the man's hatred of the Germans, and only a railwayman could smuggle him out of Ashkhabad.

He started walking again, hugging the sides of the empty streets now that the moon was brighter. A wind had risen in the last half hour, chilling his skin and coating the back of his throat with dust.

He rehearsed what he wanted to say.

This time the house was in darkness. He banged on the door and waited, banged again and heard movement inside. A few moments later, Volkhov appeared, his ample form wrapped in a blanket.

McColl was getting used to frosty welcomes. "I need your help," he said without preamble.

Volkhov laughed. "You have nerve, I . . ."

"My partner is dead. When I got back to the hotel, I found that someone had cut his throat. The Germans—it had to be. Who else had a motive?"

Volkhov actually looked shocked. He stepped out onto the veranda and shut the door behind him.

"I assume they also want to cut mine," McColl went on. "I could run back to Persia, but that would mean they had won. I don't want that, and I don't think you do either."

"No," Volkhov conceded, "but I don't see what I can do. You can't stay here."

"You can get me on a train to Krasnovodsk. There are stockpiles of cotton there already, and all the rest will be shipped there sooner or later. I can destroy at least some of it, especially if I get some help. You must know people there who still believe in fighting the Germans."

Volkhov shivered and pulled the blanket tighter around his shoulders. "You ask a lot," he said at last.

"I know."

The Russian nodded. "Wait here."

He returned fully dressed a few minutes later. "We are going to visit a friend," he announced, leading the way out onto the empty street. "Your Russian is good enough," he said after they'd walked in silence for a while. "From this point on, you must cease to be an Englishman. Some kind of Russian, but we will talk with my friend about that."

"He's a railwayman?"

"Of course. And a comrade. He will get you to Krasnovodsk."

It took them about fifteen minutes to reach the friend's gate. "Wait here," Volkhov said, and walked on up the path. McColl could only just hear his rap on the door, but it opened a few seconds later. Volkhov disappeared inside.

McColl watched and waited and told himself that Volkhov would not betray him. That this wasn't Semashko's house and he wasn't about to be offered up as a sacrifice in some local power struggle.

If he were, there was nothing he could do.

He wasn't. The door opened, and the man who walked up the path with Volkhov was a young, fair-haired Russian with a flat nose and a wide smile. "Leonid Kuskov," he introduced himself.

"And you are Georgiy Kuskov," Volkhov added. "Leonid's uncle."

"Who is interested in fighting Germans and Turks," Kuskov said, looking him in the eye. "And only Germans and Turks?" The question mark was infinitesimal but impossible to ignore.

McColl took the point. "Your revolution is your business," he said flatly.

Kuskov seemed happy with the answer. "I will get you to Krasnovodsk. Do you know Moscow at all?"

"I've been there."

"Well, you are my uncle now, and that is where our family comes from. From south of the river, in Serpukhovskaya district. Later I will give you some details to remember. You are here because you have been visiting your brother Gennady—my father—here in Ashkhabad, and you are now returning to Moscow. Understood?"

"Yes."

"Good," Volkhov said. "I must go. You asked about possible allies in Krasnovodsk. The leader of my party there is Grigori Tsvetkov, and he has long argued against making peace with the Germans. I cannot say for certain that he still believes this, but I would be surprised if he did not. And he has never been one to keep his opinions to himself, so you need not fear approaching him."

And you need not fear my betraying him, McColl thought. Which was fair enough.

"I wish you good luck," Volkhov said in farewell.

"Thank you," McColl said.

Kuskov led the way into the house, offered him an armchair for the rest of the night, and disappeared into the bedroom, where murmuring Russian voices soon gave way to creaking bedsprings. McColl struggled to get comfortable in his armchair and wondered whether Caitlin was still in Russia.

He was awakened by the sound of an infant howling and soon greeted by a young woman with long dark hair and striking green eyes, holding the quieted child in her arms. "I am Vara," she told him. "And this is Demyan Leonidovich."

She told McColl that he should stay in the house, that her husband would return before nightfall. After serving up tea and bread, she got on with the family laundry and left him to his own devices.

With nothing for McColl to do but wonder what was happening elsewhere, the hours limped slowly by. Surely someone would have found Cheselden's body by this time and the hunt would be on for the other Englishman. McColl realized he had no idea what had happened to the Russian police over the last few months. Were the same men still in uniform, or had the soviets recruited their own law enforcers? If they had, he only hoped the Keystone Cops were their main inspiration.

There was more black bread for lunch, along with a strange but not unpleasant-tasting soup. Vara's Russian sounded worse than his own, but she smiled a lot and didn't seem the slightest bit unnerved by his presence.

It was just after four when Kuskov returned. "There's a train tonight," he told McColl. "Mostly empty wagons, so we'll have no trouble finding you a spot. If anyone challenges you, then refer them to the guard. His name is Rozhnin, and he thinks you're my uncle, so he'll vouch for you."

"Wonderful. When does the train leave?"

"Not before nine. It will pick up more wagons in Kyzyl-Arvat, but you should be in Krasnovodsk about this time tomorrow. Here," he added, reaching into his bag, "I've bought you bread and two bottles of Narzan water. Make the water last, because tomorrow might be hot."

He wouldn't accept any payment. "When the war is over and our revolution has put down its roots, then come and visit us," Kuskov said. "Bring Vara something pretty from London."

THE TRAIN LEFT THE ASHKHABAD goods yard around one, after what seemed an interminable wait. McColl was riding in one of many American-style boxcars, somewhere near the center of the train. It had sliding doors and a straw-covered floor, and it smelled vaguely of horses. Army transport was his best guess.

Once the train had been in motion for a couple of minutes, he eased one of the sliding doors open and sat himself against the jamb to scan the line for bridges. But as the night grew colder, his resolve began to weaken. Telling himself he would hear a bridge beneath the train, he slid the door shut and sat there in the darkness, thinking about Audley Cheselden. Just one of millions who'd been killed in the war, but what a difference it made when you knew the man in question, when you'd listened to his hopes and dreams, when you'd known him in life before seeing him dead. If McColl got back to England, he would take the letters to Soph and hopefully find her in thrall to some dashing swine in uniform and not have to break her heart.

The train reached Kyzyl-Arvat as the day was dawning. This, Kuskov had told him, was where the Transcaspian Railway had its main workshops, and here they were, plunked down on the empty steppe like factories on the moon. The train shunted this way and that with many a jolt and jerk, but no one slid back the door of his boxcar, and an hour or so after arriving, the train was headed west once more. Soon it was warm enough to sit by an open doorway, and as McColl watched the desert roll past, he wondered how Strakhov and company were doing. Were they still questioning Lutovinov, eliciting the names of the business contacts that the Russian had promised to pass on? Had Lutovinov implicated Volkhov and raised the suspicions of the latter's Bolshevik partners? All that really mattered to McColl was whether they knew he had left Ashkhabad. The lack of a search at Kyzyl-Arvat suggested they probably didn't.

The train rumbled on, pumping sparks and smoke out across the desert. Every hour or so, it would pass through another small settlement, another genuine contender in a middle-of-nowhere contest. McColl tried to put himself in the minds of the ragged children who noisily ran alongside it—did they know of different worlds farther down the line, or were they just chasing an iron dragon?

It was late afternoon when a wide bay came into view, and what looked like the open sea beyond. The train hugged the shoreline for a few miles before pulling up in a fan of sidings, most of which were occupied. With the door just cracked ajar, McColl could see cranes in the distance and a line of roofs beneath a rocky backdrop. Krasnovodsk.

He was wondering whether to wait there for darkness when he heard the sound of voices. It was too late to push the door shut, so he just stood behind it, holding his breath.

Boots crunched in cinders, then stopped right outside. "Georgiy Kuskov," a voice said hopefully.

McColl slid back the door. Two men looked up at him, one in uniform, the other not. Neither appeared armed.

"There he is," the former said to the latter, as if the matter had been in doubt. Without further word he turned and walked back up the train.

The guard, McColl realized. He lowered himself gingerly to the ground and reached back for his suitcase.

"My name is Karelin," the other man said. "Anatoly Davidovich. I have been asked to take care of you here in Krasnovodsk."

He was a studious-looking young man with longish fair hair, glasses, and a neat mustache. About twenty-five, McColl guessed. "You are a Socialist Revolutionary?"

"Of course."

"My friend in Ashkhabad told me I should talk to your leader, Grigori Tsvetkov."

Karelin nodded. "I know. I am one of his deputies. But he has had to visit Kyzyl-Arvat. He may be back tomorrow—we shall see. In the meantime I will look after you. Tonight you will stay in my house."

"That's very kind of you," McColl said automatically. He was disappointed not to be dealing with the top man, but Karelin seemed intelligent enough. "Do you work on the railway?" he asked.

"No, but my father and brother do. I am a teacher at the town school."

It took them about fifteen minutes to reach Karelin's home, a small, one-story house not far from the sea. Krasnovodsk was possibly the worst-lit town McColl had ever seen and seemed little bigger than a village.

"The population is around eight thousand," Karelin told McColl, as if divining his thoughts.

The Russian lived alone, but apparently not for much longer. A plump young blonde was standing by the stove and stirring their supper—Alisa and he would be married in spring. She was friendly enough, but McColl detected a few uncertain looks, as if she didn't quite trust him with her husband-to-be. After serving their supper, she went home to cook for her parents.

Karelin clearly wanted to talk, and the exhausted McColl did his best to oblige. They discussed the war, its causes, conduct, and consequences. Karelin believed that any peace deal with Germany would be a betrayal of the German working class and found it hard to believe that the Bolsheviks would sign one. "I used to think the story about their being German agents was ridiculous, but sometimes now I wonder."

They talked about the revolution and where it might take Russia and the world. According to Karelin it was only a matter of time until other nations followed their example—"Why would the worker and the peasant continue working for the industrialist and the landlord when they saw they didn't have to?"

Eventually McColl brought the young Russian back to the business of cotton. He told Karelin that he supported the revolution and that he had taken this job for the British government only because he truly believed that defeating the Germans in Transcaspia was in both their interests. And most of that was true. McColl didn't see how a German or Turkish invasion of Central Asia would serve any local interest, and unlike his boss and most of his colleagues, he was still keeping an open mind as far as the Bolsheviks were concerned. Caitlin's enthusiasm had rubbed off, at least to the extent that he was willing to give them a chance.

He told Karelin about Nikolai Ostrovsky, the cotton exporter here in Krasnovodsk, who one of his refugee contacts had thought would be willing to help.

The expression on Karelin's face was not encouraging. "Who told you about Ostrovsky?" he asked.

McColl named the source, who by this time would be in Teheran. Recalling the man in question, he had to concede that his loathing of the Bolsheviks had more than matched his loathing of the Germans.

According to Karelin, Ostrovsky was less evenhanded. "The rumor here in Krasnovodsk is that he's already made his deal with the Germans," the Russian told McColl. "Rumors are only rumors, true, but this one I believe. I will check it out tomorrow just in case, but you shouldn't approach this man until we know for certain. Agreed?"

McColl nodded. "I'm happy to wait. Just so long as you agree that we need to do something about the cotton."

After consenting to that, the young Russian, with annoying but commendable precision, went on to list the difficulties they would face. How could they stop the transfer of cotton? By destroying the railway? Impossible. By destroying the ships? They would sail for Krasnovodsk only when the Germans seized a port on the Caspian's western shore. By destroying the cotton? Well, that was stored in many locations, and burning the biggest heaps, here on the Krasnovodsk wharves, would hardly make much difference. And even they could not be destroyed without burning down the port and threatening the town with starvation. "But do not despair," he concluded, seeing the look on McColl's face. "Tomorrow I will talk to Tsvetkov, and we will find a way."

"At some point I'd like to talk to him myself," McColl said, hoping this wouldn't offend Karelin. "I want to make it clear that my government is not expecting something for nothing. If it looks as though the Germans or the Turks are planning to cross the Caspian, then the Krasnovodsk soviet can ask for our help in resisting them, and we will do all we can."

"And what if the Bolsheviks disagree?" Karelin wanted to know. "Would you fight with us against them?"

"If you side with us and they side with our enemies, then yes." And this, McColl thought, was the rub. Supporting one Russian revolutionary faction against another, even if only to further an anti-German agenda, was meddling in Russian politics. And he would have to live with that, or he might as well go home.

Caitlin would see things differently.

His eyes were beginning to close, and Karelin was a kind enough host to notice. "I imagine the train was too cold for sleeping," he said. "Come, I'll show you your bed."

MCCOLL AWOKE TO FIND HIS host gone, the familiar meal of bread and Narzan water waiting on the table. A note alongside informed him that Karelin would return around six.

After visiting the outhouse, McColl noticed a mirror hanging on the wall and took some time to examine himself. He'd lost weight over the last few weeks, and his cheekbones seemed sharper than he remembered, even under two days of stubble. "Jack of Gaunt," he murmured to himself. "A desperate character."

Strakhov and company had only seen him in a relatively clean-shaven state, so he decided to leave the beard alone, at least for the moment.

With a sky free of clouds and the edge already off the morning chill, it seemed criminal to spend the day indoors. Karelin hadn't said he should, and a real Georgiy Kuskov would surely have gone for a stroll. Somewhere in the town, there might be something other than bread to eat.

He first explored the docks, walking out onto the long wooden jetty beneath the towering stacks of cotton bales. They wouldn't be hard to set ablaze—a few splashes of kerosene and a single match would suffice—but Karelin had been right: the jetty would go up, too, and the cranes would drop into the water, leaving no means of unloading the food the town would need to survive.

Should he do it anyway? McColl thought he knew what the generals back home would have said, but until he was sure that there was no alternative—and probably even then—he didn't think he could. There had to be another way.

A hanging haze of smoke led him on to the railway station and yards. There was more cotton in the latter, two long lines of cars packed with the stuff.

Perhaps he could torch these trains. A drop in the ocean certainly, but the gesture would be noticed and might encourage the locals to do more. He would suggest it to Karelin.

The town looked as boring in daylight as it had darkness. There was no hotel that McColl could see and only a scattering of shops, none of which had much to sell. The bazaar was open but had already run out of food. It was going to be a long day.

Rather than go home, he walked on beyond the last few houses and found himself on a beautiful beach. There was no one else about, so he stripped off his clothes and waded out through the gentle surf. The water was cold, but no colder than Loch Linnhe on a bright spring morning. And for the first time in weeks, he felt thoroughly clean.

KARELIN CAME HOME LATER THAN predicted, and the look on his face was grim. "Bad news," were the first words out of his mouth. "The Ashkhabad soviet has put a team of police on tonight's train. An executive committee member named Semashko is in charge . . ."

"I've met him."

"I thought you might have. Once his men have searched every house in Krasnovodsk and weeded out everyone who doesn't actually live here, he'll be the one to identify you."

"Fuck," McColl said in English.

Karelin recognized the tone. "It is not as bad as it sounds. The train is due at eight in the morning, but friends will ensure that it doesn't arrive before ten. Too late to catch the morning boat to Baku, which you must be on."

"And the cotton?"

"You must leave that to us. This is a small town, and if you're still here when they arrive, they will certainly find you. And one way or another, that will be the end of your war."

The Russian was right, and McColl knew it. There was no escape across the desert, and a train would simply take him back to Ashkhabad. A ship was his only hope.

NEXT MORNING KARELIN WALKED HIM down to the quay. According to the Russian, the two men by the gangplank were Bolsheviks and probably there to check those departing. "But don't worry, I've known them since school. Let's go and introduce ourselves."

Praying that the Russian knew what he was doing, McColl followed him across the quay. "My friend's uncle," Karelin said in reply to their questioning looks. "Georgiy Kuskov," McColl introduced himself, shaking both their hands.

"What are you doing here?" Karelin asked them.

"Looking for an Englishman," one of the men said, his eyes scanning the dock.

"Well, good luck."

McColl could hardly believe his own, but managed a comradely smile. As the two guards carried on scanning the quay for the wanted spy, Karelin saw him onto the ship, which hardly seemed big enough for a sea crossing, and helped him buy the necessary tickets for his passage and meals. "And for once there will be something to eat," the Russian told him; "I just saw the cook come aboard with a big bag of cabbages. But don't leave it too long," he added, "or they'll all be gone."

"Thank you," McColl told him. "For everything." Listening to Caitlin's tales of Russian generosity, he had half suspected she'd simply been lucky. Apparently not.

"I will tell you something to make your journey easier," Karelin said quietly after checking that no was in eavesdropping range. "Something you must not repeat to anyone. Do I have your word?"

"Of course," McColl said, hoping he'd be able to keep it.

"The Bolsheviks in Ashkhabad will not be in power much longer. It is probably a matter of weeks, a few months at most. And once we control the soviet, there will be no deals with the Germans. We will burn the cotton rather than sell it to them."

"That is good to hear."

After they embraced, McColl watched Karelin bound down the gangplank, share a few words with the bored-looking Bolsheviks, and stride off down the jetty. He was an impressive young man, McColl thought. As Kuskov had been. Russia's future might be brighter than people thought.

It was almost half past nine, but there was no sign of anyone lifting the gangplank. As he waited, McColl kept his eyes on the far side of the bay, where the line from Ashkhabad skirted the shoreline. And there, to his distress, a plume of smoke appeared above the rocky outcrop, heralding the coming of a train.

It was distant enough to look toylike, but seemed to be barreling on as if eager to make up lost time. Ten more minutes and it would reach Krasnovodsk.

When was the damned ship leaving?

Looking down from the rail, he could see that the gangplank

was at last being hoisted aboard. The two Bolsheviks were walking away.

The gangplank was soon stowed, but there was still no sign of movement, and the smoke from the locomotive was now rising above the warehouses that lined the tracks on their way into town.

The ship just sat there by the jetty.

"Please," McColl murmured, and some god or other decided to listen. No ship's horn had ever sounded so sweet, no revving engines quite so melodious. The ship edged out from the quay and slowly turned its bow toward the mouth of the bay.

He had gotten away, and Semashko could gnash his teeth in vain. In the joy of the moment, McColl almost forgot the fullness of his failure.

Almost.

7

A Different Drum

Twenty days after leaving the Finland Station, Caitlin saw the upper floors of Manhattan's skyscrapers poking out through the fog that lay across New York Bay. Her journey had been quicker than expected, and quicker by far than that of poor Jack Reed, who had left Petrograd a fortnight before her, only to be marooned in Norway by their government's refusal to allow him home. "It's flattering to be considered so dangerous," he had told Caitlin over dinner on the eve of her sailing, "but I think I'd kill someone for a night out on Broadway."

She knew what he meant. After so long away, the sight brought tears to her eyes. The world might call, but this was home.

The Brooklyn quays seemed full of ships, most of them no doubt Europe-bound, carrying men or munitions. Hers moved on past a blurry Statue of Liberty and up the Hudson before edging into a berth just beyond the Hoboken Ferry terminal. Having telegraphed ahead with the ship's anticipated time of arrival, Caitlin was hoping there'd be someone to meet her.

There was, but not the someone she wanted. After looking at her passport, the young immigration officer checked a list on his desk, told her to wait, and asked, with minimal courtesy, if she'd accompany him into his office. Ordered to sit, she watched as he methodically emptied her suitcases onto a large, flat table.

He was about her own age, Caitlin thought. Short black hair, wiry build, probably of Italian parentage. His New York accent inclined her to like him; the look in his eyes and the twist of his mouth did not.

Her clothes and toiletries were put to one side, her notes and newspaper clippings to another. After unrolling a revolutionary poster in which Woodrow Wilson, dressed as Uncle Sam, was looking down on Europe with dollar signs for eyes, the man gave Caitlin a nasty look.

"Wait here," he said, leaving the office and closing the door behind him.

A uniformed woman came in and ordered Caitlin to strip off her clothes.

"Completely?"

"That's what "strip" means."

"It's freezing in here."

The woman nodded her agreement. There was anger in her eyes, too.

Refusal, Caitlin knew, would merely prolong matters. Swallowing her indignation, she took off all of her clothing. The woman went through each item twice before handing the whole lot back. As Caitlin re-dressed herself, she caught a flicker of movement behind the door.

The man returned and took the seat across from hers. "I have some questions," he began.

Which was something of an understatement—he had hundreds. Questions about Russia: What she had done there, whom she had met, who had paid her expenses? Questions about the Bolsheviks: How well did she know Madam Kollontai—this with a leer—and what had they asked her to do in America? There were questions concerning the war and how she felt about her own country's involvement. Did she consider herself a patriot, or did she agree with traitors like Eugene Debs and Bill Haywood, who claimed that the war was a trick on the American people?

None of it was subtle. Quite the contrary, in fact—it was all so glaringly obvious that she even wondered for a while if she might be missing something. But she knew she wasn't. The man reminded her of the stupider Bolsheviks she'd met in Petrograd, young men who'd swallowed a creed whole and felt compelled to resent those who hadn't.

There seemed no point in lying, and giving him honest answers felt almost as good as slapping his face would have done. She was a socialist and a feminist, she told him, with socialist and feminist opinions. And the last she'd heard, freedom of thought and speech were guaranteed by the Constitution. So long as that was the case, she would continue to promote those causes. The Russian Revolution was an inspiration, not a paymaster.

The questions moved back in time. What had she been doing in Paterson in 1913? In China in 1914? Who had paid for that trip and why? What about her family's links to the Irish republican movement, and what about her younger brother, whom the British had executed as a German agent?

After spending several hours with this idiot of a man, Caitlin found herself wondering how the authorities managed to keep themselves in power. The answer, of course, was simple—they made use of the power they had. All her notes, journals, and souvenirs would, he told her, be taken away for "examination," to determine whether or not they "contained anything contrary to the interests of the American government." The fact that he was unable to offer any date for their return clearly gave him a great deal of pleasure.

A probably foolish sense of disbelief helped her keep a lid on the upset and anger, but it was still a close-run thing. His final flourish was to hand her a copy of the 1917 Espionage Act. "If you haven't been home for a year, you need to read this," he said. "Your country is at war now."

Four hours after reaching Immigration, Caitlin was finally allowed through to the arrival hall. This vast space was empty, save for two people sitting on a bench, almost fifty yards away.

"Caitlin!" her Aunt Orla cried as she clambered to her feet, her Irish-American brogue bouncing off the high brick walls.

- ← ←

ON THE SUBWAY TO BROOKLYN, there were several occasions when Caitlin caught her aunt and brother-in-law giving her worried looks. Back in her old room in the East Fourth Street brownstone, which felt a bit like a museum exhibit after such a long time away, she examined herself in the mirror. It had to be admitted that the last four months had taken a toll: her face was thinner, cheeks paler, hair less lustrous. When she changed out of her traveling clothes and into ones she'd left behind, the looseness of the latter was almost startling.

Her older brother, Fergus, was now living in Washington, but her sister, Finola, and brother-in-law, Patrick, were waiting at the house with their two children—the four year-old son Caitlin knew and the baby daughter she'd never met, who'd been christened Bridget after her late grandmother and who was altogether delightful. Finola and Patrick seemed utterly self-absorbed and almost absurdly happy, with each other, their children, their new house just two blocks away. Caitlin envied them and didn't.

Her father was his usual gruff self. He made a few welcoming noises—more, Caitlin thought, for Orla's sake than her own—but expressed no interest in where she'd been and no joy in her return. Over lunch he offered a few opinions on the state of the world, catching her eye in the process, as if defying her to argue. He gave no sign of mellowing as he aged; if anything, he seemed to grow a little sourer with each year that passed.

He soon went off to his "study," leaving the others to greet and take care of the stream of relations and neighbors who dropped by to welcome Caitlin home. Most suggested she needed "feeding up" and took for granted how relieved she must be to be back. Several asked about Russia, but few listened hard to her answers. Imagining herself in their place, it did seem far away. As far as the moon, she thought, remembering Zamyatin's story.

But with Russia now such a huge part of her life, she couldn't just keep quiet about it. And she knew that her aunt was curious, particularly when it came to feminist issues. When Kollontai had visited the house in Brooklyn two years earlier, she and Orla had gotten on well, so Caitlin's tale of her friend's ministerial travails, recounted on a wintry walk around Prospect Park, was listened to with interest. But when she tried to explain the split in the Bolsheviks over peace with Germany, she saw her aunt's eyes glaze over. "I'm sorry," Caitlin said. "I've been so wrapped up in it all."

"I can't deny it sounds exciting," Orla said. "I've been following the news there as best I can, but most of the stories are just sensational, about the dead not being buried and all the churches being burned down. What has happened to the priests?"

"They're having to earn a living like everyone else. No, really," she said, noticing her aunt's expression, "the priests in Russia weren't like the priests here. They were part of the establishment. One day, about two months ago, I was on a tram in Petrograd, and the priest refused to buy a ticket, because he and the other "men of God" always used to travel free. When the driver said no, the passengers all backed him up and threatened to take the priest before a revolutionary tribunal. These days all men are equal, they told him, including "men of God.""

Orla shook her head in wonderment. "It will be strange for you, being back here," she said, looking out across the tranquil park.

Caitlin gave her aunt's arm an affectionate squeeze.

"And how's Jack?" Orla asked.

"I've no idea. We're fine," she added. "We just don't see each other very often—November was the last time."

"At his father's funeral."

"Yes. Four months ago," Caitlin murmured, as if she'd only just realized how long it was.

Orla was silent for a few moments. "I can't help wondering if you two will ever be able to settle down together," she said eventually. "You'll find it difficult, dealing with each other all the hours God sends."

Caitlin often wondered the same. She wrote to him that evening, sure for the first time in months that a letter would reach his London flat. Whether he'd be there to read it was another matter.

✦ ✦ ✦

MONDAY MORNING, ON THE SUBWAY into Manhattan, Caitlin familiarized herself with the Espionage Act. It had come up in several discussions with the other American correspondents in Petrograd, so she already knew the gist, which Jack Reed had defined as "Don't mess with the US war effort!" Reed had also been fond of quoting the act's provisions, most notably the one that targeted any opponent of the war who might "willfully cause or attempt to cause insubordination, disloyalty, mutiny, or refusal of duty in the military or naval forces of the United States, or shall willfully obstruct the recruiting or enlistment service of the United States." Reading through the act on the wildly lurching train, she decided that everything would come down to how loosely or not the law was interpreted. Or, to put it another way, how far up the government's backside the judiciary was meaning to climb.

Turning to her newspaper, she discovered that a new and harsher version of the act was already under discussion. "And you almost had me liking you," she muttered to herself, thinking of Woodrow Wilson.

Buried on an inside page there was confirmation of what she'd heard on the wireless the previous evening, that the Bolsheviks had finally signed a peace treaty with Germany. What she wanted to know was what damage signing it would do to the coalition with the LSRs, but nothing was said about that. The Germans, meanwhile, were advancing on Petrograd, and the government had shifted the capital to Moscow.

Emerging onto the sidewalk across from her newspaper's office, she took a few seconds to drink in the sights, sounds, and smells of Manhattan. Reassured that nothing much had changed in twenty months, she jinked her way across the busy street and pushed through the revolving doors. The elevator man was one she hadn't met before, but several of the secretaries upstairs jumped out of their chairs to welcome her home. They all looked slightly strange to Caitlin, and for a moment she couldn't work out why. But then she realized—the fashions had all changed. Tired of looking dowdy, she had actually made an effort that morning, but what had been smart in 1915 now seemed as passé as Kerensky.

Her editor, Ed Carlucci, was surprised to see her at all. And on his way out. "It's lovely, of course," were his first words, "but I expected our European correspondent to be in Europe."

Caitlin explained. "When I arrived in Christiania, there was a boat for home on the very next day and none to England for weeks. So, rather than maroon myself in Norway for the rest of the war, I thought I'd come home for a few days' vacation. Now that our army's off to France, there can't be any shortage of ships heading east."

"It seems a long way around," Carlucci said, massaging his gray mustache with his right forefinger. "But you do look like you could use a rest."

"So everyone tells me." She reached inside her bag and passed across the article on "Peace, the Bolsheviks, and America" that she'd written on the boat.

Carlucci gave the first page a brief and, Caitlin thought, almost apprehensive look. "I expect it'll go in tomorrow or Wednesday," he said, glancing at his watch. "I have a meeting, so we'll have to wrap this up." He managed a smile. "And since you have come back, you might as well take some time off. The rest of this week, at least. Why don't you come in on Monday, and we'll talk about the next few months? With the Germans moving all those armies west, this summer's going to be a doozy."

Caitlin had never heard the word before, but she had no trouble guessing what it meant.

BACK IN BROOKLYN, SHE NOTICED how much emptier the house felt. With Colm dead, Fergus and Finola buying homes of their own, and herself almost always away, on weekdays her father and aunt had the place pretty much to themselves. Her father clearly found this unsettling; like a coin in an otherwise empty tin, he rattled rather noisily. It was mostly self-directed, but early that evening it was Caitlin who bore the brunt.

"So have you finished your gallivanting in foreign parts?" he asked out of the blue as they passed on the stairs.

"Probably not," she said.

"Well, it's time you found yourself a husband. Either that or earned a proper living, one that doesn't require you to take so many handouts from your aunt."

Caitlin was shocked by the virulence. "I haven't asked Aunt Orla for a cent since the day I left college," she replied coldly. Which was strictly true, she told herself; the subsequent checks had all been unsolicited.

Her father shook his head, as if he knew her denial for the half-truth it was, and carried on down the stairs.

He was on his way out of the house, which was where he spent most evenings, leaving Orla and Caitlin to sit and talk or listen to the wireless. In the daytime Caitlin would read in her room or go out, lugging a clutch of newspapers to a bench in Prospect Park or walking the empty beach at Coney Island. She devoted one day to trawling through a year's worth of papers at the local library, trying to get a proper handle on what had happened to her country. The war was the simple answer, but how had it made itself felt?

There had been a marked lack of enthusiasm for joining up in the early weeks and months. Reading between the lines, Caitlin thought it obvious that the government had adopted a dual approach, on the one hand introducing a draft to compel participation, on the other setting up a vast propaganda machine to discourage dissent and encourage compliance. The Committee on Public Information was the principal official organization established to sell the war to the American people, but there were other semiofficial ones, like the American Protective League. Both had enlisted tens of thousands of volunteers, whose sole aim seemed to be the demonization of anyone less gung ho than they were.

This was not surprising—after three years of reading about the slaughter in the trenches, even the most patriotic American was unlikely to be blindly in favor of this particular war. Far easier, then, to accuse those who opposed it of being unpatriotic. German-Americans had been the most obvious target, but those Irish- and Finnish-Americans who balked at sharing sides with England and Russia were also considered fair game. Many individuals had been attacked, some killed. Homes and businesses had been burned to the ground, sauerkraut rebranded as "liberty cabbage."

While a few hardy souls had gone underground, most of these "enemy Americans" had learned to fly the flag and keep their thoughts to themselves. The socialists had been less discreet. Most had opposed the war from the word go, and America's entry had not made it any more acceptable. But that entry had created a political problem, because if they persisted in opposing the war, American socialists faced the charge of being unpatriotic and, once Congress had passed the Espionage Act, rendered themselves liable to prosecutions, fines, and long periods of imprisonment. Such prospects had created the usual divisions between those who took the longer view and those who insisted on a principled stand, but most of the leaders, like Eugene Debs and "Big Bill" Haywood, had opted for the latter and were now in jail awaiting trial.

Oh, my country, Caitlin thought as she stepped back out onto a sunlit Brevoort Street. If no one else had noticed Zamyatin's burning "A," her government certainly had.

That evening was just as depressing. After ringing around to a few old friends, she arranged a gathering in one of their old Greenwich Village haunts. About a dozen people turned up, and for the first half hour it felt like one of those nights she'd spent before the war, when she was working on a city desk and knew a good proportion of New York's rebels. But it soon became apparent that these were different people—older, more cynical, more cautious. The magazine writers and editors talked about their problems finding backers, about how conservative their readers had become and how careful they had to be when deciding what to print. An artist once known for his political daring told Caitlin that politics was boring before launching into an aggressive defense of his latest work. Talking to another friend, she discovered that after a Protective League volunteer had informed on this particular artist, he'd been blackballed by several galleries and had seen pickets outside his front door.

The only bright spot of the evening was an invitation from her old journalism professor Ed Morrison to give a talk on the Russian

Revolution at the college where he now worked. Even this arrived with a sting in the tail. He warned her that the students would likely be hostile.

WHEN FRIDAY CAME AND THERE was still no sign of the piece she'd given Carlucci, Caitlin rang the office. The editor was out, and his secretary had no explanation to offer. Caitlin could ask him on Monday.

She did.

He almost squirmed in his seat. "Our lawyers had a problem with it."

"Yes?" she said coolly. She'd half expected something like this and was determined not to lose her temper.

"Nothing definitive," Carlucci said, scratching his head. "But these days . . . well, we want to pick our battles, and Russia is not a good choice. There's a new act coming from Congress, and the more responsible we look, the less draconian it'll be."

"Why Russia?" she asked, knowing the answer but wanting him to spell it out.

He grunted. "Because the public's had enough of it. You know how short the attention span is these days. People are more interested in what our boys are doing in France. And people feel different about Russia now that it's out of the war. They see Russia the same way they see our socialists—unsupportive at best, traitors at worst."

"Shouldn't we be putting them right?"

"Right? Is it really that simple? Look, I'll be straight with you, Caitlin. You're a good reporter, one of our best. But I think you've become too invested in Russia and its revolution. I think you need to stand back a little, be a little more objective. And in the meantime I want you in Europe again, concentrating on the war. That's what Americans want to read about in 1918."

Caitlin took a deep breath. "I *have* been covering the war," she said quietly. "This war is about more than men killing each other. It's about a new world. Isn't that what Wilson has been talking about? A world in which people get to determine their own governments and their own lives?"

Carlucci looked uncomfortable but quickly recovered. "Of course it is. But for most American families—the ones who have boys out there or fear they soon will have—the men-killing-men part is pretty damn important. And they don't want to read that their boy is dying in a war of rival imperialisms, or whatever it is Lenin calls it. Dying for nothing, in other words."

"That *is* what they're doing."

He took a deep breath. "You may think that, and I'm not sure you're wrong, but it's not what this paper will say."

Caitlin wanted to argue but knew it was futile. "I understand," she said. "How soon do you need an answer?"

"I'll give you another week." He showed her both palms. "But after that . . ."

"Fair enough," she said. "I'll let you know."

On her way out, she visited the paper's legal department and asked one of the lawyers if he'd see what he could do about retrieving her notes from the government.

He wasn't optimistic.

THE JOURNALISM SCHOOL'S LECTURE THEATER was a small-ish tiered affair, the seats rising nickelodeon fashion toward a tall ceiling. There were only a couple of high windows, on which the evening rain was audibly beating.

As Ed Morrison introduced her, the harsh lighting gave the rows of faces turned toward Catlin an almost spectral cast. Most of them did look hostile, she thought. And would have done in any light.

She rose to stand behind the lectern, half expecting a chorus of boos. After she and Morrison discovered that the microphone was out of order, they looked at each other and laughed, as if to say, *This can't be happening.*

Paranoia, she told herself. This was a room of journalism students, of young men and women who knew the importance of reason, who could be swayed by cogent argument.

There were, she realized, very few women. And several of the men were wearing Protective League badges.

She began by describing the often comic difficulties of her last journey to Russia and was rewarded by a few smiles. Her first impressions of Petrograd in the aftermath of the Bolshevik Revolution were received in silence, as were her descriptions of the various measures the new government had introduced. Many of the new laws had simply given Russians rights that Americans took for granted, she pointed out, and when it came to those measures that were even more progressive . . . well, perhaps Americans could learn something from the Bolshevik example.

"Socialist garbage!" someone at the back shouted.

A medley of insults followed, causing Morrison to stand and raise his hands. "You'll get your chance to respond during questions!" he shouted back. "Now, show some courtesy to our guest."

Caitlin plowed on. The US should recognize the Bolshevik government, because it reflected the will of the Russian people. Brest-Litovsk was not a betrayal—after three years of appalling suffering, the Russian armies and people were simply unable to fight any longer. Their own President Wilson had acknowledged as much in his speech the previous January, and even now, at the end of their military strength, the Bolshevik example was doing more to undermine the Kaiser than was any Allied army. Americans should support the Bolsheviks because they, unlike Britain and France, preferred a fair and lasting peace to a world of feuding empires.

The silence by this time was truly stony, and Caitlin decided enough was enough. "That's all I have to say," she said. "I'm happy to answer questions."

The applause was decidedly thin.

A dozen hands went up, and Morrison picked out a suited youth who wasn't wearing a badge.

"According to our newspapers, the Germans paid Lenin and Trotsky to take Russia out of the war," the young man said. "Doesn't that make nonsense of everything you've just said?"

The shouts of support coalesced into a wall of noise.

"It would if it were true," Caitlin said once the clamor had subsided. "But it isn't."

"You've been to Germany and Russia!" another youth shouted. "Maybe they're both paying you!"

Again the noise took a while to recede. "I'm paid by the *New York Chronicle*," Caitlin said coldly. "And no one else."

Morrison's next choice was one of the few women in the audience. Her question about women's voting rights in Russia was jeered by most of the men, Caitlin's answer drowned out by hooting. It was getting ridiculous, and not a little scary, but she didn't want to give her hecklers the satisfaction of driving her out.

She sat back down beside Morrison, waiting for the tumult to fade. "I'm sorry!" he shouted in her ear. "I expected better of them."

She could see that her old professor was close to tears. On the benches in front of her, some of the eyes were shining with hatred.

As the noise died down, someone shouted the essential question—"Do you support American participation in the war?"

Caitlin stood up slowly, weighing her answer. "I believe that a just peace, without annexations or reparations, will serve the world—and America—better than continued slaughter."

"But isn't that just what a German would say?" the same voice shot back. "Now that we're in the war and your Kaiser's on the ropes, isn't that just what he wants?"

Her dry rejoinder, that the Germans had rejected such a peace, was drowned out by the baying students.

"That's enough!" Morrison was yelling at her side.

"Enough treason!" someone screamed back at him. It sounded like a twelve-year-old to Caitlin, but she was probably biased.

Morrison hustled her out the side door and insisted on seeing her into a taxi, apologizing all the way.

"Don't," she said. "I think I've learned more about my country in the last hour than I have in a week of wading through the newspapers."

"It's not pretty, is it?"

"No, it's not."

She gave him a farewell smile as the taxi started up, then told the driver to stop at the first subway station. If only the Kaiser *had* been paying her, she could have sat back in comfort all the way to Brooklyn.

Sitting on the subway train, she realized how shaken she was. And how angry.

And, more than either, how disappointed. In her fellow Americans for their parochialism. In herself for forgetting that and other realities. Had she really believed that the American establishment would suddenly grow a conscience and abandon its power and privilege? The Bolsheviks would never have been so naïve.

She'd returned to America high on the hope she'd found in Russia, wanting to share it, wanting to spread it, wanting to grab people's shoulders and point their eyes at the sky and at Zamyatin's bloody great "A." But the ways she might get her message across seemed to be fast disappearing. Her newspaper would let her write on anything but Russia; the socialist magazines were either walking on eggshells or being closed down. A speaking tour had seemed a feasible option, but that evening's experience had not been encouraging. Which left only writing a book, and for that she needed her notes.

How else could the bastards obstruct her?

AT SEVEN THE NEXT MORNING, there was a thunderous knock on the door. While Caitlin's father was still reading the assorted papers with which he'd been presented, half a dozen young men in plain clothes started rampaging through the house in search of documents "prejudicial to the interests of the United States."

They found nothing fitting that description but took away a few books just in case—some novels of Caitlin's and two Fenian tracts of her father's. The man in charge—fortyish and fat, with a New Jersey accent, glasses, and thinning black hair—insisted on talking to Caitlin alone before he left. "Be grateful we're not taking you with us," he said. "And know that from this moment on, you won't say or write anything to anyone, in public or in private, that we won't know about."

He turned away, and Caitlin just stood there watching as he crossed the street and squeezed himself into the passenger seat of a gleaming black Ford. When the car turned off East Fourth Street and vanished from sight, it felt like a foreign body had been expelled and Brooklyn could get back to being itself.

Inside, her father was seething. His sense of himself as a rebel obliged him to blame the invaders, but Caitlin knew he was just as angry with her for giving them the excuse. As she and Orla tidied up the gratuitous mess the searchers had left behind, Caitlin realized she could no longer stay there. Her aunt was too old for more days like this.

Only a few hours had passed when a telephone call offered Caitlin another, more positive, reason to leave. Jack Reed, whom *The Masses* magazine had assigned to cover the upcoming trial of International Workers of the World (IWW) activists in Chicago, was still trapped in Norway. The Wobbly trial would probably last several months, the editor told her, and Reed should be back for most of it, but he wondered if she would step into the breach and cover the opening week. "It starts on April Fool's Day," he concluded dryly.

She told him she'd think it over and let him know the next day. Carlucci would want her back in Europe before that, so it was one or the other. It was time to decide.

Listening to the wireless that evening, she and Orla heard that the Germans had launched a massive new offensive in France. And, it appeared, broken through.

This was their last throw, Caitlin thought. If they were going to win, they had to win now, before they faced a million Americans. "Ed Carlucci will be on the telephone first thing tomorrow," she told her aunt, "insisting I take the next boat."

Orla put down her sewing and looked at her niece.

"So do I go?" Caitlin asked.

"Only you can answer that."

Caitlin sighed and ran a hand through her hair. "I know. The *Chronicle* has been good to me—Frank has been good to me—and giving up a job that others would pull out their back teeth for—it's not something I could ever do lightly. It might be the end of my career as a journalist, and I'd hate that. I feel I'm letting you down, for one thing. You've been—"

"You're not," Orla said firmly, almost crossly. "Whatever you decide, you could never do that."

"It's wonderful of you to say so. The thing is, the war in France, I know it's important—of course it is—but in my heart of hearts I know that what's happening in Russia is more important. And not just to Russians, to all of us. And I know that there are dozens of reporters who could do just as a good a job as I could in France, but—and I hope I'm not kidding myself—I don't think there's anyone better qualified to tell the rest of the world what's happening in Russia."

Orla smiled. "Then there's your answer."

"I suppose it is."

"Do you need money?"

Caitlin held up her hands. "I can't take any more from you," she said, her father's voice in the back of her head.

"Whyever not? I have more than I'll ever need, and what better use could I have for it?"

Caitlin was almost in tears. "I'm sure I can get some commissions, and there's nothing to spend on when you're there, but I could do with some help with the passage and train tickets."

"That's settled, then. Tell me how much you need, and err on the generous side—I don't want you not coming home because you can't afford the fare." She smiled. "I must be soft in the head, paying for you to go away again. It feels like it was only yesterday you came home."

"It does, doesn't it?" Caitlin went to sit with her aunt on the sofa and laid her head on Orla's shoulder. "I don't deserve you."

"Ah, not many people get what they deserve."

"And I do have to go."

"I know. If you stayed, either you'd kill your father or he'd kill you."

Caitlin laughed.

"I want you to know how proud I am of you, my girl. How proud I've always been. I won't pretend I understand the politics, or would agree with them if I did, but I know a brave heart when I see one."

And that, Caitlin thought, was far and away the nicest thing that anyone had ever said to her.

NEXT MORNING SHE TOOK THE Brooklyn Rapid Transit train to Park Row and walked the short distance to the newspaper office. Thinking it prudent to ask the paper's lawyers about any efforts they'd made to retrieve her notes before she handed in her resignation, Caitlin stopped off on the second floor to see the young man she'd spoken to earlier. He sighed, gave her a helpless look, and explained that he hadn't yet found the right person to ask—each authority he contacted passed him on to another. "They're giving me the runaround, and no mistake. Another week or so and I'll be back where I started."

Unsurprised but still unhappy, she went up a floor to see Carlucci and handed in her resignation. He was neither shocked nor angry, which was something of a relief—although certain she was doing the right thing, Caitlin also felt she was letting him down. When she told Carlucci as much, he just waved the notion away. "If I was twenty years younger, I'd probably do the same."

Back home in Brooklyn, she called the *Masses* editor and told him she'd go to Chicago.

The trial began in ten days, and once she'd established—through several long-distance calls—that there was no chance of interviewing any of the prisoners ahead of the proceedings, she booked a seat for the following Saturday on the 20th Century Limited. More calls provided information on transpacific sailings; the first of those she could easily catch left San Francisco on April 11, arriving in Tokyo two weeks later. There was no scheduled onward service from there to Vladivostok, but something was bound to turn up.

Having planned her immediate future, she hoped to enjoy her last week in Brooklyn. There were no more visits from the authorities, which rather surprised her. Perhaps they were biding their time; perhaps they'd decided that a journalist lacking a public platform—something she now was—warranted less intimidation. Or maybe they knew she was heading back to Russia and were simply thinking good riddance.

Her father was almost nice to her on those rare occasions their paths happened to cross—Caitlin guessed that Orla had given him a talking-to. Finola and Patrick were utterly mystified by her decision to leave again so soon, her sister unconsciously twisting the knife when she said how much their aunt had looked forward to Caitlin's return.

Orla insisted on seeing her off at Grand Central on a suitably overcast Friday morning, and both were in floods of tears long before the whistle blew. Her train was out in open country when Caitlin finally dried her eyes and sought the distraction of the newspapers she'd bought for the journey.

But after reading the first front page—the German offensive seemed to be petering out, albeit after reducing the Brits and French to a state of near panic—and searching in vain for any concrete news from Russia, she put the paper down again and stared blankly out the window, her mind a jumble of warring thoughts and feelings. It was on this train in 1914 that she'd realized she was falling in love with Jack McColl. Four years go, almost to the day. She'd shied away from the prospect, saying something glib about enjoying each other until they went their separate ways and not crying when they did.

Was she being selfish now? Did Orla need her more than the world did? Did Jack? Kollontai would say—had said—that women who acted independently would always be called selfish. By men, by other women, by themselves. Especially by themselves. That self-doubt was one of the prices they paid.

Long separations were another. They might make reunions sweeter, but they were still so hard to bear. Yet what choice was there? If traditional love affairs obliged women to accept limits to their independence, then independent women had to deny themselves traditional love affairs.

HER CHICAGO HOTEL WAS BETTER than she'd expected, and probably somewhat inappropriate for a left-wing journalist reporting a political trial. But seeking out something less salubrious would hardly help the defendants, and there'd be plenty of sackcloth and ashes in Russia, not to mention black bread and unsweetened tea. The three weeks of Brooklyn home cooking had been wonderful, but she was still ten pounds below her usual weight.

Other than one short walk on the wintry lakeshore, she spent Sunday in her hotel room, reading up on the background to the trial. It was being held in a huge federal courtroom only a few blocks away, and on Monday morning she was one of the first to arrive, half expecting problems with her press accreditation. There were none. As she waited in her excellent seat for the proceedings to begin, she could only conclude that the government needed socialist journalists like herself to spread the word among her comrades that their traitorous jig was up.

The vast courtroom slowly filled. The hundred and one defendants filed in and took their places on the rows of benches provided for them. Most had already spent several months in Cook County Jail, but resigned expressions were few and far between. This was their chance to tell the world, and most looked eager to do so.

They were charged with various conspiracies, all of which boiled down to jamming their sticks in the spokes of the government wheel. The kind reading was that IWW practices deemed acceptable in peacetime had begun to interfere with the nation's war effort and therefore needed to be curtailed. The unkind reading—Caitlin's— was that the war and the new legislation had given the bosses the chance they craved to smash the union once and for all.

It was the IWW—not these hundred and one individuals— that was really on trial. The lead prosecutor said as much in his three-hour opening speech before extensively quoting from IWW literature and the speeches of its leaders. It was no surprise to him that the union had waged "unremitting warfare" on employers—hadn't their leader Big Bill Haywood stated categorically that employers and employees had no interests in common? Several defendants nodded their agreement with this and with the prosecutor's next accusatory quote, that the war was a "capitalist trick."

Looking at the rows of union men—lumberjacks, longshoremen, miners and field hands—Caitlin was struck by the similarities to their comrades in Russia, the workers and peasants who populated the Red Guards and soviets. The same scorn appeared on their faces when the prosecutor said something they knew was utter nonsense. And they knew because they'd lived it, not read about it in books.

Over the next few days, that scorn was often visible. Witness after witness was called to support the prosecution case, and it didn't take long for Caitlin to realize two things. One was the palpable thinness of that case and the almost insulting inadequacy of the evidence produced—incidents outside the time frame of the charges were introduced as if they weren't, statements were assumed to prove things when they clearly did not. The second point Caitlin grasped was that none of that mattered. The guilt of these men had already been taken for granted, and there was no chance that they would be sentenced to the "reprehension of society." They were going to prison for a very long time.

She hadn't felt so depressed since the last days of her brother's incarceration. And not just about the suffering these men would endure. It felt like an end to something. Of the Wobblies, most probably, but not just them. Of hope, perhaps, that her country might rise to the challenge, might override the legacies of slavery, Indian slaughters, and tenement squalor and actually place itself at the forefront of human progress. As an American she'd been proud of the Wobblies. Hell, only three months earlier she'd been proud of Woodrow Wilson. And now here his government was, grinding the best into dust.

AFTER A WEEKEND WRITING THE piece for *Masses*, she found herself boarding another train. As it chugged past the teeming stockyards and out onto the Iowa plains, she had the sudden feeling that she was heading out into a void, the past cut loose and abandoned. If she got into Russia and managed to get her stories back out, then a number of magazines had agreed to buy them, but after several years of working for a paper, she had to admit she missed the security. And true independence, as her father had rather cruelly pointed out, also required that you earn your own living. If, after the war, she and Jack got together on a day-to-day basis, then she wanted to earn as much as he did. Which might be silly, but he hadn't thought so. Which was one of the things she loved about him.

That evening the prairie played host to a brilliant storm. She could barely hear the thunder above the sounds of the train, but streaks of lightning snaked out of the sky like heavenly spears, as if badly aimed at the lonely farms they fleetingly brought into view. When the storm had passed, Caitlin took to her bed and lay there in the dark, remembering the compliment her aunt had paid her. She hoped Orla was right about her having a brave heart, because chances were good she'd be needing one.

8
Chaplino Junction

McColl gave the door a vigorous knock, as he had the day before. The lack of response was the same, but his nose detected something different. A smell he recognized and wished he didn't.

The door seemed unlikely to resist a frontal attack. Ramming his shoulder against it, he could feel the lock giving way. Another thrust and he was in, the jamb torn from the wall.

For a moment he thought he was back in Ashkhabad. The positioning—facedown and spread-eagled—was almost identical, the pool of blood surrounding the head much the same size. But this corpse had been here for longer. This blood was dry, the flies eating rather than drinking.

Steeling himself, McColl rolled the body over for a look at the face. The eyes were caught in shock, the mouth half open. The blood from the exit wound below the chin had created the illusion of a long red beard.

More to the point, the still-visible tattoo of a sea serpent on the dead man's neck confirmed it was Lyubov Nakoryakov, McColl's proposed point of contact here in Sevastopol. London had sent him the name and description more than a month earlier, while he was still in Baku.

He got to his feet and walked across to the single window. There was no sign of fresh activity in the street below, no indication that the house was being watched. Nakoryakov's killer either had not considered waiting for his contacts, or had simply run out of patience.

He looked around the room, which gave new meaning to the word "bare." There was nothing under the mildewed mattress, nothing in the drawer of the bedside stand. There was a suit hanging up in the cupboard, but nothing in its pockets. The rest of the dead man's wardrobe was stuffed into the canvas bag by the door, presumably bound for a laundry. There was nothing in those pockets either.

There were no books or papers, no tickets or receipts. There was nothing under the threadbare rug, no loose floorboards to pry up. If the pattern of squashed mosquitoes on the walls was an elaborate cipher, then McColl didn't have the key. This, as the Americans would say, was a bust.

He took one last look at the corpse. It was Audley Cheselden all over again, and yet it wasn't. Seeing the body of someone you knew was worlds away from seeing the body of someone you didn't. This one brought back the sudden, piercing grief he'd felt in Ashkhabad, but not on its own account.

He had no intention of reporting his discovery, but he didn't suppose Nakoryakov would be unduly inconvenienced. And no doubt someone else would find him before too long—the smell would see to that. After propping up the door as best he could, McColl walked back down the stairs, opened the front door, and warily stepped outside. There were no curtains twitching—no curtains at all, come to that—and no one lurking in the narrow street. Fifty yards to his right, an electric tram glided by on its way up Bolshaya Morskaya.

He walked that way, crossing the tree-lined boulevard and continuing on past the Cathedral of Peter and Paul until he reached the road that skirted Southern Bay. The naval barracks on the far side of the inlet seemed a hive of activity, but that was to be expected. With the Germans only a few days away and the Russian authorities still apparently split on where to send their Black Sea Fleet, a certain level of hysteria seemed appropriate. McColl himself had been feeling more than a trifle anxious when he woke up that morning, and the discovery of Nakoryakov's body had done nothing to relax him.

Who had killed Nakoryakov? The German intelligence services seemed the best bet—the local Bolsheviks were no shrinking violets when it came to political murders, but private throat slittings were hardly their style. It might have been personal, but somehow McColl doubted it. He would have to assume it was the Germans and take care not to let his guard slip.

It was spitting rain by the time he reached the Streltsky Café, the only place in the city where a cup of coffee could still be obtained. The precipitation had emptied some of the outside tables, allowing McColl to gamble, successfully, on the swift return of the sun. He recognized several of the other customers from previous days, almost all of them middle-class Russians from places farther north. They'd been seeking a southern route into exile, but the imminent arrival of the Germans had thrown them into confusion. Might their erstwhile enemies help them back to power, or should they get themselves onto a ship and give up their country for lost?

It was hard to feel sorry for them, or at least for the adults. It was hard to feel sorry for anyone in Sevastopol, a beautiful city with a dreadful recent past. Here, and in several other Crimean ports, naval officers in the hundreds had been executed by the sailors they had once commanded; according to the local British consul Pyotr Torovsky, they'd been tangled up in chains and tossed into the sea. He held all Bolsheviks responsible, but others said the leaders in Moscow had been equally appalled and had jailed those directly involved in the murders. McColl had no way of knowing how widespread such atrocities were in Lenin's new Russia, and he hoped that these would prove an exception. He hated the idea that Cumming knew the Bolsheviks better than Caitlin did.

TWO MONTHS HAD PASSED SINCE his escape from Transcaspia. He had sent for fresh instructions soon after reaching Baku, but they hadn't arrived until early April, leaving him plenty of time to sample that city's delights. These had included bucketloads of intrigue and a full-scale pogrom, in which local Armenians had murdered thousands of their Muslim neighbors. McColl had always considered "streets running with blood" a figure of speech, but now he knew better.

His next stop was Ukraine. Since the signing of the Brest-Litovsk Treaty, the Germans had been steadily advancing across this new and supposedly independent country, occupying the grainlands that could feed their own hungry cities and securing the railway links to the Caspian that would carry the oil and cotton their war machine needed. Several train-watching and sabotage units had already been set up in major cities, and McColl, with his experience of similar work in Belgium, was expected to lead one.

The journey had been long and occasionally dangerous. The Georgian capital, Tiflis, had been swarming with German agents, the port city of Batumi awash with their Turkish equivalent. After several fraught encounters with men who examined papers, the ten-day ride on a fishing boat, heading north up the Black Sea coast, had seemed like a holiday.

A second boat had carried him from Kerch to Sevastopol. The telegraph had been operational when he arrived, but only for a couple of hours, and he hadn't received any fresh instructions. What should he do? According to that morning's paper, the Germans were less than sixty miles away and would be in Sevastopol by Wednesday. The only ships he could take were bound for Odessa or Romania, the first already in German hands, the second a country currently lacking an exit. And since staying in the city was out of the question, his only real option was to head northward, somehow evade the Germans, and try to make contact with those colleagues already in Russia. He supposed he could whistle "Rule, Britannia!" Or wave a Union Jack.

NEXT MORNING HE WOKE WITH a hangover—Sevastopol was running out of many things, but alcohol wasn't one of them. He had done most of his drinking in the relative safety of his hotel room, staring at the bay and its silhouetted warships until night had swallowed them up. Before passing out on the surprisingly comfortable bed, he had written another letter to Caitlin, which he now tore up.

He should destroy Cheselden's as well, but he couldn't bring himself to do it. God willing, he would see Caitlin again, but his dead partner's letters were the only thing left for Soph.

At least the sun was shining—the spring weather in this part of the world was uncommonly pleasant. After washing in the communal bathroom at the end of the corridor, he went downstairs to the restaurant, which was virtually empty. The only other patrons— a middle-class family and a group of angry-looking sailors—were sitting at opposite ends of the long room; McColl, not wishing to suggest an allegiance, took a table halfway between them. The usual plate of bread and jam appeared, and for the second morning running, a jagged lump of sugar accompanied the tea. More surprising still, the waiter soon returned with a single chunk of what had to be meat. It tasted like nothing McColl had tasted before, but he ate it anyway, remembering the long-gone days when his mother had called him a fussy eater.

Once outside, he stood on the Count's Quay steps for several minutes, enjoying the warmth of the morning sun and the deep blue stillness of the bay. The obvious upsurge of activity on two of the anchored warships was probably a sign of imminent departure; if so, and if they were heading east to Novorossiysk, the Allied command would be pleased. McColl didn't see how the Germans could make much use of the Russian ships, but why give them the opportunity?

It was past ten. Reluctantly tearing himself away, he walked back across the square and onto Yekaterinskaya. The mood here was febrile—even the gulls wheeling above the street seemed unusually raucous. Sevastopol was in the last throes of something, but no one knew quite what.

The British consulate was on a side street behind the Church of St. Nicholas, two rooms on the first floor of a yellow limestone mansion. Acting consul Torovsky was an English-speaking Russian who dreamed of owning a cottage close to Shakespeare's birthplace. He greeted McColl with the usual downturned mouth—no, there was nothing new to report.

Nor did he think there would be. The telegraph line to the west ran through Ukraine and was now effectively blocked by the Germans. The Bolsheviks were still allowing ordinary traffic on the roundabout route via Moscow but had forbidden the sending of coded messages since "our troops" landed at Murmansk early in April. If Cumming had new instructions for McColl, he had no way of passing them on.

"But I do have something to tell you," Torovsky told him, reaching for his cigarette box. "The consuls from Kiev and Kherson both arrived last night, and I'm sure they will have all the latest information." After examining the inside of the box, he gently closed it again. "They are staying at the Grand Hotel. But I wouldn't call on them just yet—I expect they'll still be sleeping. It was three o'clock this morning when they woke me up to announce their arrival."

"Where do they mean to go from here?" McColl asked.

Torovsky shrugged. "They didn't say."

McColl took his leave and resisted the temptation to double back and catch the consul lighting up one of his precious cigarettes. He bought a local paper and took it to the Streltsky Café, where the clientele looked much the same and the coffee still flowed from its precious unknown source. The war news was suspiciously good—the second German offensive of the spring had slowed to a halt after more impressive gains. How much more did they have? McColl wondered. And what was keeping the Americans?

He had another task that morning, one that required him to take the short ferry ride across Southern Bay. He hadn't needed a gun in Baku, and being caught with one on his journey across the Caucasus might have proved fatal, but now, with Nakoryakov's death and the prospect of venturing behind German lines in Ukraine, he was eager to replace the one he'd lost in Ashkhabad. And according to his favorite waiter at the Kist Hotel, there was a healthy market for firearms in Sailor Town.

The bar the waiter had suggested was a fifteen-minute walk from the Pavlovsky Point landing stage, on a corner of the crossroads just beyond the naval hospital. It was closed when McColl arrived, which might have been a blessing—and a knock called forth a boy of not much more than ten, who gave him another address in exchange for a ruble. He walked on through the gridlike streets, seeing only women and children—the sailors were doubtless on their ships, still arguing over where to take them.

It was a young woman who answered the door and an older one who showed him four guns, each complete with ammunition. Officers' pistols, he guessed, taken from those about to be drowned.

"Who do you want to shoot?" the old woman asked as he examined them.

"No one," he said shortly. "I'm traveling to Moscow, and the country's not safe."

"Nowhere is," she said, with evident satisfaction.

He chose the Mauser C96, partly because he'd handled one before but mostly because he knew that its widespread use in Russia would make ammunition easy to find. And it was a good gun. Winston Churchill had carried one in the Sudan, and rumor had it that T. E. Lawrence was currently tucking one into his belt.

It was the most expensive of the four, but still a bargain. Walking back to the landing stage, McColl felt comforted by its physical presence in the small of his back.

He spent the long wait for the ferry watching the myriad boats scooting this way and that across the waters. Hills rose on all sides, basking in the sunshine under a pure blue sky, reminding McColl of one of those rare days when the weather gods smiled on his Scottish homeland.

By the time he reached Count's Quay, it seemed reasonable to assume that the fugitive consuls would be up and about. He took the short walk to the Grand, where the diplomatic duo had taken the Governor's Suite, presumably at the British taxpayers' expense. The two fortyish men were indeed awake, if not yet dressed for the outside world. Breakfast and lunch had apparently been eschewed in favor of early pre-dinner drinks, taken in resplendent silk dressing gowns on a balcony overlooking the confluence of Sevastopol's two bays.

McColl suspected the effusive welcome had little to do with himself, and thought about coming back later. But with nothing to suggest that later would be better, he took the proffered drink and tried to get what information he could from the two diplomats. It was hard work. Both were intent on reaching Romania—"There are worse places to sit out the war," as the man from Kherson put it. "Try Kherson," he added with a giggle that swiftly turned into a snort.

Kiev had apparently been better, particularly before the revolution went and spoiled it all for the consul and his Russian friends. But the latter's fate paled into insignificance when compared with the love of the consul's life. "A dark blue twelve-cylinder Pathfinder two-seater," the man enunciated carefully, actually drooling as he did so. It was locked away at his dacha, and he hoped to God it would still be there when the Bolshevik scum had all been taken out and shot. If McColl were ever near Bucha, the consul begged him to check that the car was all right.

When asked about British-organized sabotage units in their area, both disclaimed any knowledge of such activities.

"Skulking around in alleys," as the man from Kherson put it. "Complete waste of time."

"Worse than that," his colleague boomed. "We should be letting the Germans get on with clearing up the mess."

If he'd needed advice on having a suit pressed in Kherson or a billiard cue mended in Kiev, then these would have been the men to ask. McColl took his leave without regret. It wasn't often he met Englishmen who made the prospect of losing the war seem almost attractive.

HE WAS NO NEARER A firm decision on what to do when he woke up the following morning. According to his restaurant waiter, three full trains and two empty boats had arrived during the night, leaving a sizable surplus of would-be émigrés with no chance of an onward ticket. As McColl moodily dunked the harder-than-usual bread into his tea—there was no fresh fruit that morning—he wondered whether he should simply cut his losses and pull whatever strings he could to get a berth. A German POW camp held no attractions, particularly one in Russia.

After the usual visit to Torovsky had proved the usual waste of time, he decamped at the usual café and sat with his coffee, watching that morning's array of desperate Russian faces. And then—lo and behold—there was an English face, and one he recognized to boot. Miles Pryce-Manley saw McColl at the same moment, his stern, patrician features dissolving into an unlikely grin. Grabbing an unattended chair, he plunked himself down beside McColl. "I've been looking for you," he said in Russian.

"You've found me," McColl responded in the same language. He hadn't seen Pryce-Manley since the previous spring, when they'd both been stationed in Petrograd. As a fellow agent, he'd seemed intelligent and careful, not inclined, as some of their colleagues were, to see all Russians as either dim but well-meaning aristocrats or wild-eyed nihilists armed with bombs. "And where have you popped up from?" he asked.

"Thataway," Pryce-Manley said, jerking a thumb toward the north.

"Just arrived?"

"In the middle of the night. I dozed on the station platform until it got light, and then went in search of a boat . . ." He paused to order a coffee from the hovering waiter. "I haven't had a decent cup in weeks."

"Did you get a berth?" McColl asked.

"I did. The ship leaves tonight, allegedly for Constanta."

"You said you were looking for me."

"Yes. I found your hotel—it was the first one I tried—but you'd just left." He stopped to admire the cup of coffee that the waiter had just placed in front of him, then took a first sip. "Oh, excellent. Yes, I have things to tell you, but this is a trifle public," he added in a low voice. "Have you got a few hours to spare?"

"Yes."

"Well, I always wanted to see the place where the Light Brigade came to grief, and the clerk at your hotel told me there's a place down here where you can hire a carriage with rubber wheels."

"I know it. Yes, but—"

"It's only an hour's ride."

"Oh, all right," McColl agreed. Taking time off from one war to visit another seemed a bit much, but he had nothing better to do.

The carriage company's owner was pleased to see them—so pleased that he offered to charge them ten times the appropriate fare. Once that misunderstanding had been sorted out, driver and carriage were summoned from the stables, and soon they were heading down past the station and up into the hills that lay to the south of the town.

"Look over there," Pryce-Manley said loudly in English. "There's a naked woman in that field."

The driver's motionless head suggested he wasn't a linguist.

"So what do you have to tell me?" McColl asked Manley-Pryce.

"I got orders for you just before I left. They couldn't get them to Sevastopol, and Cumming's man in Moscow hoped you'd still be here when I arrived. The old man wants you in Kiev."

"As your replacement?"

"More or less . . ."

"What made you leave?"

Pryce-Manley grinned. "The Rada police got a photograph from somewhere—not a very kind one, but sadly recognizable—and they passed it on to the Germans. And strange as it may seem, secret work gets a trifle difficult when your face is pinned onto hundreds of lampposts. I was more of a danger to my own people than I was to the enemy."

"Well, let's hope they don't have my picture," McColl said. Romania suddenly seemed a more enticing destination.

"No reason they should have," Pryce-Manley said cheerfully. Their carriage was passing the gates of a large cemetery, and he asked the driver whose it was.

"*Frantsuzskiy*," the man said, drawing out each syllable before aiming a gob of spit in the cemetery's general direction. He clearly wasn't fond of the French. "*Vostochnaya Voyna*," he added in explanation. The Eastern War. Which was presumably what the Russians called the Crimean War.

"So tell me about Kiev," McColl said once they'd left the graveyard behind.

Pryce-Manley did so. He'd run a network of train watchers in the city, gathering information about the movement of German troops and providing the Allied military leaderships with a clearer idea of how many were being shifted westward. But the flow of trains had slowed in recent weeks. In Pryce-Manley's opinion the Germans had moved all the troops they could, if they weren't to leave their grain and oil shipments unprotected. "So sabotage is the name of the game now. Stop the traffic. There are three groups in Kiev that we're involved with—not running them but helping with things like documentation, money, coordination. And with the actual operations—you have experience with explosives, right?"

"I do." McColl had a mental picture of the Belgian railway bridge collapsing into the Meuse.

"Good. Your main problem will be getting there in one piece. The Germans have taken a real grip on the railways, and there are no roads to speak of. Someone told me there were only twelve automobiles in Odessa—can you believe that?"

"'There's about that number in Sevastopol. The commissars drive round in them."

Pryce-Manley grunted. "How's your memory for names and addresses?"

"Not bad, but I'll write them down when we stop and burn the paper before I leave Sevastopol."

"All right."

"Now tell me about the situation in Ukraine."

Pryce-Manley grimaced. "A mess. How much do you know already?"

"Assume nothing."

"Well, you know that Ukraine declared itself independent soon after the Bolshevik takeover? The new government, the Rada, is a mishmash of nationalists and moderates and socialists, rather like the old Kerensky government. The Bolsheviks in Petrograd said they accepted Ukrainian independence, but a lot of Ukrainian Bolsheviks weren't at all happy with the Rada, so they're at war with each other. The Rada people welcomed the Germans as allies, only to find that the Germans had other ideas—so now they're just set on holding on until the Germans leave. The Ukrainian Bolsheviks never stopped fighting the Germans, even when Lenin told them to, though some people say he egged them on in private. So they're all at each other's throats. And I haven't even got to the Russian nationalists, the Socialist Revolutionaries, and the anarchists. There are thousands of anarchists in Ukraine—God knows why. A Russian I met thought it was the flat horizons that drove them to it."

McColl laughed. "What about the bigger picture? What's happened since the treaty was signed?"

"Apart from the Germans sending half their troops to France? Well, the Bolsheviks dropped us like a hot potato. No cooperation at all."

"You don't think that had anything to do with us landing troops in Murmansk?" McColl asked innocently.

"Oh, you heard about that, then?"

"That was front-page news, even in Batumi."

"Ah. And yes, I guess it did. Not that they've done anything since they arrived. Worst of both worlds, really—we've pissed the Bolsheviks off without achieving a damn thing. And more than that—they stopped us using code and forced us back on couriers, who keep getting arrested."

"Which hardly encourages Lenin and company to trust us," McColl noted wryly.

"Oh, that ship has sailed. We're going to have to fight the Germans without any help from the Bolsheviks. The best we can hope for is them staying neutral."

"And once the Germans are beaten?" McColl asked. "Do we just get out of Russia?"

Pryce-Manley looked surprised by the question. "I don't know," he said. "Up to London, I suppose." He thought a bit more. "If it were up to *me*, I would. It's not our country, and I'd have trouble choosing a side. I've met decent chaps on all of them. And some right bastards, too." He hesitated. "But I don't get the feeling that's the way things are going. Some of our people in Moscow . . . You've met them, you know what their politics are. Their idea of a revolution was killing Rasputin so that the czar and his wife would come to their senses."

McColl smiled, but only briefly. "There's something you need to let London know," he told Pryce-Manley before recounting his gruesome discovery two days earlier.

"And you've no idea who killed him?" Pryce-Manley asked.

"None whatsoever."

"Speaking of killing, I think we're here."

The driver had brought the carriage to a halt where the road ran along the crest of a ridge. "There," he said in Russian, sweeping an arm to embrace the land to their left. "*Idiot soldaty*," he added, which didn't need translating.

It certainly looked like the ideal spot for a suicidal charge—a flat, narrow valley, plugged at one end by a hill and flanked by two long ridges. McColl had no trouble picturing the host of thundering horsemen, drawn sabers glinting above an unrolling carpet of dust. Or the cannons lining the higher ground, gouging holes in their ranks.

"I used to charge my lead soldiers between two lines of books," Pryce-Manley said, gazing out.

"'Theirs not to reason why, Theirs but to do and die,'" McColl quoted softly.

"'Honour the charge they made! Honour the Light Brigade, Noble six hundred,'" Pryce-Manley responded.

"*Idioty*," the Russian driver muttered under his breath.

A WEEK LATER. THE SUN had just cleared the horizon, bathing the steppe in a golden glow. Most of the station's transient population were still asleep, the platform thick with bodies wrapped in shawls or newspapers, a couple of men smoking their first cigarette of the day. There was no sign of activity in the small German billet that lay beside the single copse of trees, the soldiers still in their motor lorries, the officer in his tent.

This was Chaplino Junction, and McColl didn't think it owed the name to Charlie Chaplin. Behind him two lines diverged, the one heading east toward the Donbas, the other south toward Crimea. Up ahead, beyond the nondescript station, the tracks forked west and north, the former to Kiev, the latter to Kharkov and Moscow. It was a place for changing trains, if there were any to change to.

Without them it was merely a village lacking any obvious means of support.

There were signs of traffic past—a line of rotting wooden wagons in one of the overgrown sidings, in another the rusting remains of a locomotive whose boiler had exploded. The train McColl had arrived on was now stabled in the shunting loop, lacking the engine it needed to proceed.

Beyond the station the steppe stretched away in all directions, its flat immensity disturbed to the north by a line of hills so low they barely deserved the name and to the east by the distant silhouette of the nearest settlement. Perpendicular columns of smoke were already rising from a few of the village chimneys, one no doubt the bakery's; in a couple of hours, the daily cartload of loaves would struggle down the earthen track toward the station.

The air was rapidly warming, the makeshift camp beginning to stir. People were sitting up and stretching on the platform, tumbling out of the abandoned coaches and joining the queue at the station well. Several babies were crying, and the overall buzz of conversation was steadily rising. The fields around were slowly filling with people in need of their morning crap.

And there was no sign of a train.

THE DAY AFTER THE VISIT to Balaklava, McColl had taken a local train to Simferopol and hidden away in a crummy hotel. As he'd hoped and expected, the bulk of the German occupation force had moved straight on to Sevastopol, dropping off units as they went to guard the lines of supply. Those soldiers assigned to Simferopol station were mostly older men, content just to go through the motions, and once the trains were running again, passenger checks were cursory. After four boring days in the city, McColl had presented his papers for their inspection and been airily waved through. As his train had chugged northward, he'd thanked his lucky stars that his fears had proved unfounded.

But they hadn't. At some point in the night, the train had been diverted and on arrival at Chaplino Junction had endured the ultimate slight—its engine had been stolen by a passing German transport.

It was time to see if there was any fresh news. The station's only employee couldn't conjure trains out of thin air, but that didn't stop the several hundred stranded passengers from behaving as if he could. His office was usually under siege, his parentage often in question; as far as McColl could see, only the presence of German troops had saved the hapless soul from being lynched. They needed him to man the telegraph.

At this hour of the morning, there were only a few angry people leaning over his shoulder as he sought the latest news from up the line. There was none to appease them. Several German troop and freight trains were expected on the east-west line, and Russian trains would have to wait their turn.

Was there any alternative? That morning, in the scrum around the bread cart, McColl overheard a couple talking. Like him, they were heading for Kiev and in lieu of a train were considering walking to Ekaterinoslav on the Dnieper, where one could still catch a boat upriver. Seventy miles, the man thought. More like a hundred was his wife's best guess.

A hell of a trek either way. Doable, but McColl didn't think he'd leave just yet. He remembered waiting for omnibuses in London—after a while impatience would start you walking, and the damn thing would always turn up the moment you'd gone too far to get back.

Early that afternoon two of the promised German trains steamed through, neither even stopping for water. A third clattered through the points near his bed on the loading bank soon after dark, and he was still wide awake an hour or so later when lightning flashed on the eastern horizon. A brief rumble of thunder followed, but neither was repeated, and as far McColl could see, there wasn't a cloud in the sky.

ANOTHER TRAIN ARRIVED SOON AFTER first light. Once it had stopped a hundred meters short of the station, soldiers poured out of the four boxcars and hurried off in different directions, like people escaping a building on fire. When it became obvious that a perimeter was being drawn around the station area, the sense of disappointment that had accompanied the train's arrival swiftly turned to alarm.

There were about eighty of them, McColl guessed. While half formed the cordon, the rest marched down the track toward the station, where they split into small units, some herding those on the crowded platform, others beginning to empty the buildings and vehicles. As he obeyed a German soldier's order to get down off the loading bank, McColl noticed that two groups were being formed—one of men and older boys, the other of women and children.

The latter group was herded toward the overgrown sidings on the other side of the water tower, where the derelict engine and wagons stood. The men, McColl included, were harried and hustled into a single line, until all were standing between the two rails with their backs to the platform. About a hundred of them.

"This happened to my brother," someone was whispering. "When they need laborers, they just take people away."

"If we're lucky," the man on McColl's left muttered under his breath. He was probably in his thirties, with dark hair and beard. On the previous day, McColl had noticed him penciling notes in the margins of a dog-eared copy of Turgenev's *Fathers and Sons.*

Would his papers pass muster? McColl wondered. But only for a moment—the Germans were showing no sign of running a check. Which might be good news but probably wasn't.

A German major was walking down the line, mostly looking straight ahead but occasionally glancing to his left at the red and barely risen sun. McColl and the Russians might have been invisible for all the interest he showed in them.

At the end of the line, the major halted for a moment, staring out across the steppe. And then he turned abruptly, causing the sunlight to glint on his shiny boots, and started retracing his path.

A finger was pointed at the first man, who was swiftly shoved forward across the rail by the major's subordinates. The finger carried on wagging and was raised again a few seconds later.

"Every tenth man," McColl's neighbor muttered. "Fuck."

McColl's stomach contracted like a balloon expelling air. In Belgian villages the Germans had sometimes taken one of every ten men hostage and then shot them in reprisal for resistance attacks.

He suddenly remembered the singular thunder and lightning of the night before. Had someone blown up a bridge or a train? Were they the reprisal?

The officer was about halfway down the line. Behind him four men stood forward of the others.

Looking to his right, McColl counted out ten men. If the young man with the shock of blond hair was chosen, then he would be, too. And there'd be absolutely nothing he could do about it. The nearest cover—the station house—was more than twenty yards away, and in the unlikely event he reached that, there was still the circle of soldiers beyond and a world as flat as a pancake.

Was this it? Had his luck finally run out? Would Caitlin ever know what had happened to him?

A fifth man was pushed forward. A sixth.

The finger went up and down, counting off lives.

Counting off the blond young man's.

Dread seemed to drop like a curtain, and he had the strange sensation that his feet were clinging to the earth.

The finger reprieved another two men, then suddenly stopped in midair. A young woman had broken away from those guarding the women and children and was running toward the line of men. Two soldiers rushed to intercept her and each managed to grab an arm, sweeping her feet off the ground. She began to scream, just the one word—"Pyotr!"—over and over.

The blond young man managed only a single step in her direction before soldiers hauled him back.

As she was dragged away, still screaming her husband's name, the German resumed his counting.

And a sliver of hope pierced McColl's heart. Was he imagining it, or had the distracted major taken an extra step? Had he missed a man? As the German drew nearer, McColl could hear him softly counting: "*sieben*"—the next but one man along, "*acht*"—his neighbor, "*neun*"—himself, "*zehn*"—and the finger raised at the old man on his left.

The wave of relief was so intense that McColl felt his bowels on the verge of loosening. The old man, who obviously hadn't been counting, shuffled forward with grim resignation.

McColl's other neighbor had. The bearded man's look—half smile, half disbelief—suggested McColl was the luckiest man in the world.

The major reached the end of the line. Turning, he nodded to the sergeant beside him, who shouted an order down the track. The pairs of soldiers guarding the men who'd been selected now hustled them off toward the dock. Most went quietly, but a couple had to be forced. Soon they were all in line, their backs to the low brick wall. Several looked in shock, one was openly weeping.

Looking at the old man who'd been chosen in his place, McColl was seized with a sudden urge to put things right.

He couldn't do it.

A German soldier stepped forward, carrying a weapon that McColl had never seen before. At first sight it seemed like a cross between a shotgun and a rifle, but the small, drum-shaped magazine suggested a handheld machine gun, and that was what it was. At a nod from the sergeant, the trooper tightened and held the trigger, hosing the line from end to end with a deafening hail of bullets. The bodies jerked this way and that like puppets on strings, then collapsed in a heap when the firing stopped.

The ensuing silence was eerily complete. And then the wails of grief rose up from the corralled women and children, punctuating the steady plod of the sergeant's boots on ballast as he checked each man for signs of life.

I should be dead, McColl thought. He was still thinking it when a German soldier appeared in front of him, holding out a spade.

Twenty of them were chosen, two for each grave. McColl found himself with his bearded neighbor, digging a hole on the edge of the fallow field that lay behind the loading bank.

"You saw him fuck up his count," the Russian said after a while.

"Yes," McColl admitted. For a moment he expected a lecture on doing the right thing, but the Russian just laughed.

"History must have work for you," he said. "I am Semyon Nikolayevich Kerzhentsev," he added, holding out a hand.

"Georgiy Romanovich Kuskov," McColl said, shaking it.

They worked on. The Ukrainian soil was dry without being hard, and the Germans were impatient enough to accept a mere meter in depth. When all the graves were dug, the bodies were laid alongside, the relatives allowed to say their good-byes.

No one came to see the old man, most of whose face had been ripped away. McColl stood over the Russian for a few seconds, thinking he should say something but having no idea what that might be.

"It was just luck," Kerzhentsev said beside him. "Good for you, bad for him. I wouldn't lose any sleep over it."

"I don't expect I will," McColl said. There were enough things he felt responsible for without adding fate to the list.

The order was given to infill the graves, the relatives pulled away. After the first few shovels of earth had been thrown in, the Germans left them to it. They were heading back toward their train, leaving only the original group to guard the junction.

"Where are you headed?" Kerzhentsev asked him.

"Kiev."

"Me, too." Kerzhentsev was staring at the motor lorries parked in front of the trees. "I don't suppose you could drive one of those?"

IT WAS A TEMPTING IDEA, one they came back to several times that day, albeit with less and less confidence. After the executions and burials, local hostility was further stoked by the posting of a notice threatening additional reprisals, and the small German garrison wisely showed no inclination to relax its vigilance. The soldiers stuck close to one another and to their transport and gave McColl no chance of a closer look at the lorries. Not that he really needed one—he was pretty sure he could get one started, with or without a key, but what would be the point? There was bound to be noise, and an outcry would follow. If by some miracle they managed to outrun the rifles and the second lorry, how far would they get before a

German airplane tracked them down? There was nowhere to hide on the steppe.

It was a nonstarter, and both of them knew it. Either they could wait for a train and risk falling victim to another reprisal or they could start walking.

They weren't prisoners, but it still felt prudent to leave unobserved. Soon after dark they picked up their bags and slipped away across the field behind the station house. According to the locals they had asked, Ekaterinoslav and the Dnieper River were almost directly east of Chaplino Junction, but the railway that connected them took a big loop to the north, almost doubling the distance and increasing the probability of unwanted encounters with Germans. So they'd decided on the direct route, navigating their way across the open steppe by a sky that they hoped would remain open.

Their progress was slowed only by the uneven ground. There were few obstacles of any kind, natural or man-made, the occasional stream to ford, the even rarer fence or hedge to climb. They circled the small settlements that appeared in their path, only once attracting the attention of dogs, whose incessant barking seemed to follow them for what felt like hours. Above them the sky behaved, rarely clouding the Pole Star from view, and then for just a matter of minutes.

By 3:00 A.M. Kerzhentsev reckoned they had walked around fifty versts. "Let's sleep now," he suggested, "and do most of our walking by daylight. We'll need to find food and water."

McColl was only too happy to get off his feet and was asleep within moments of hitting the ground. The return of daylight brought him briefly back to consciousness, but the next thing he knew, it was ten in the morning and Kerzhentsev was waking him out of a nightmare in which he couldn't find his brother, Jed, who was loudly screaming for help.

During the day's walk, he learned some of the Russian's personal history. Kerzhentsev was an engineer by trade. He had a wife and two daughters, aged seven and four, the second of whom he'd not yet seen. Called up in 1914, he'd managed to survive three years on the Eastern Front and in the process had become a Bolshevik. He had grown up in a small town west of Minsk, and it was there that the German occupation authorities had hanged his fifteen-year-old brother for allegedly stealing a hunk of bread and left the corpse in situ to serve as an example. His father and mother had been clubbed to death by drunken German soldiers when they tried to cut it down.

No wonder the man hated Germans.

But why had he become a Bolshevik? Hadn't they signed a peace treaty with the Germans?

"Only because there was no army left to fight them. It was just tactics, yes? We all want our revolution to survive, and we will do what is necessary. Some will sign pieces of paper, some will continue to fight. And those who sign the paper will be as pleased as the fighters when we kick the beasts out of our country."

They saw no Germans that day, and the villagers they met said the enemy rarely strayed far from the safety of their trains. All were women or much older men—those younger men not killed in the war were away fighting for some group or other. One old man told them that both his sons were fighting with an anarchist group led by a local woman. "Marusya," he said. "Remember that name."

Kerzhentsev had already heard of her. "They say she commands several hundred men," he told McColl. "And has magnificent breasts."

She probably had a horse as well. At each village they asked how much farther it was to the Dnieper, and the answer was always depressing. Walking what felt like ten miles usually seemed to advance them five and on one occasion left them even more distant. When they sank to the ground on the banks of a small river soon after ten that evening, the Dnieper still seemed as far away as ever.

Kerzhentsev was sitting with his back against one of the trees. "So who are you really?" he asked out of the blue.

McColl just stared at the Russian, hoping he'd misheard.

"And what are you doing so far from home?" Kerzhentsev continued.

The Russian knew. Somehow he knew. Had someone finally

heard the foreigner in his accent? "Fighting Germans," McColl said simply.

"You are English, yes?"

"Yes." McColl considered reaching for the Mauser in his bag, but there was nothing threatening in the Russian's voice. He sounded more amused than anything. "How did you know?"

"This morning you talked in your sleep. Shouted, in fact. I did enough in school to recognize your language when I hear it."

"What was I shouting?"

"Ah, I didn't learn enough to understand it. One thing you kept yelling—'Jed, Jed, Jed!' What does that mean?"

"It's my brother's name. He's in France. Also fighting Germans."

"Ah, the stuff of nightmares. Well, any enemy of the Germans is a friend of mine." The Russian smiled. "Until they are defeated, of course. Then we will have another conversation."

"I have no interest in fighting Russians," McColl said. "Now or in the future."

Kerzhentsev was silent for a moment. "I would love to believe you," he said. "But I presume you work for your government—why else would you come all this way to fight Germans, when you could just take a short trip to France?"

"I do work for my government."

"The same one that has landed troops in Murmansk."

"To fight the Germans and Finns, as far as I know." Kerzhentsev still looked unconvinced, so McColl played his hole card. "My wife is a Bolshevik," he said, wondering what Caitlin would say if she heard they were married.

"Your wife is a Bolshevik," Kerzhentsev repeated, as if he could hardly believe it. "You are married to a Russian?"

"An American. She is a journalist. Have you heard of Alexandra Kollontai?"

"Yes."

"Well, she is a friend of my wife's. They met in Norway a few years ago, then in America, and again here in Russia."

"But you are not a Bolshevik."

"I'm not anything. I was never very interested in politics."

Kerzhentsev grinned at that. "Then you're in the wrong country, my friend. Or will be once the Germans are gone." He stroked his beard. "So what does your government want you to do in Kiev?"

McColl told him about the train watching and the sabotage campaign. "We mean to make it difficult for the Germans to send any more troops west, and we want to stop them shipping your oil and grain to Germany. We're working with Russians—it's an Allied campaign. Like you said last night, there's enough of you who still want to fight, whatever treaty Lenin signs."

Kerzhentsev sighed. "Then maybe it's fate we met up at that godforsaken junction. For all I know, your friends may be working with mine by now. I've been away from Kiev for a couple of months." He laughed. "Well, I guess it's time to sleep. Who would have thought I'd be walking across Ukraine with an Englishman whose wife knows the great Kollontai? I don't suppose you have a picture of her?"

"My wife? Yes." McColl passed across the watch he carried, with the picture of Caitlin inside it. It was cut from a larger photograph of her and her New York friends, which she'd given him a year earlier.

Kerzhentsev struck a match against the sole of his boot and studied the face. "She's beautiful," he said.

"Yes," McColl agreed, fleetingly bereft.

"My wife is, too. But the only picture I have is the one in my head." The Russian passed back the watch and laid himself flat on the ground. "It's enough."

THEIR EARLY START NEXT MORNING proved fortunate. Another half hour's sleep and chances were good they'd have walked straight into the German billet that lay a mile to the east. Or at least they assumed it was Germans inside the tumbledown hut that stood twenty yards from the river. Who else would have three horses tethered outside and two men with Slavic faces roped to the nearest trees?

McColl and Kerzhentsev hunkered down in the tall grass and took a long look. One prisoner was clearly asleep in his bonds, and the other had given no indication that he'd noticed their approach. Both men wore lengths of black cloth around their necks.

"Anarchists," Kerzhentsev whispered.

"Our enemy's enemies," McColl reminded him.

Kerzhentsev sighed. "I know. But there's no point freeing them without killing their guards. And we have no idea how many men there are inside that hut."

"There are only three horses," McColl pointed out.

"True, but I have only one knife."

"I have a pistol."

Kerzhentsev gave him a look. "Why didn't you say so? Let's go."

Their second dose of luck was as telling as the first. Halfway to their feet as the hut door swung open, they were back on their haunches by the time the men emerged. There were two of them, both with German-style close-cropped hair, wearing long johns, vests, and boots and carrying rifles. They glanced casually this way and that, in the manner of men who weren't expecting surprises.

Their appearance had awakened the other Russian, who wanted untying so he could have a crap. The Germans ignored him. After checking their horses—one soldier giving his an affectionate nuzzle—the two of them sauntered down to the river and started stripping off. A few seconds later, four pale buttocks were bouncing into the river, both men whooping with distress at the coldness of the water.

"I'll take care of them," Kerzhentsev whispered. "You make sure there's no one else inside."

It seemed a fair division of risk. Keeping low, McColl began working his way through the grass toward the back of the hut. He had just reached it when one of the bathing Germans suddenly burst into song.

McColl circled the hut, ears pricked for the sound of movement inside. He heard none, which made it all the more surprising when a third German stepped out through the door, almost into his path. With no time to think, McColl lashed out with the Mauser, catching his opponent on the side of the head and dropping him to the ground. The man groaned and tried to push himself up. McColl hit him again, and this time he stayed down.

There was no reaction from inside, but McColl eased an eye around the jamb to check that the hut was empty. It was.

The Germans in the river were now chorusing together. They sounded happy.

He was picking up the fallen man's rifle when he heard the first shot. Kerzhentsev, he thought. And hoped.

The singing had stopped.

As he hurried toward the river, two more shots rang out.

He found the Russian staring at the two naked bodies floating facedown in the water. "Were they alone?" Kerzhentsev asked.

"One more. He's out."

The Russian strode off toward the hut. McColl followed, knowing what to expect. He arrived in time to see Kerzhentsev lift the man's head by the hair, and drag the knife across his throat.

The reek of blood brought back the day in Ashkhabad.

Kerzhentsev was already sawing through the ropes that bound the two anarchists. They were both in their twenties, McColl reckoned, one much stockier than the other. The thinner man went off to have his crap, leaving his friend to explain their recent predicament. A month or so earlier, Marusya's anarchist army had been forced to retreat in the face of the German advance, and they'd been one of several pairs left behind to monitor the enemy's movements. Two days ago they'd awakened to find their house surrounded, its location betrayed by a local villager who wanted her hostage husband to live. These three Germans had been given the job of escorting them all the way back to Ekaterinoslav, because a public hanging there would have a more salutary effect than a private one out on the steppe.

"How far is it to Ekaterinoslav?" Kerzhentsev asked.

The anarchist shrugged. "Twenty miles. Maybe less. But it's full of Germans. If you have to go there, better arrive after dark."

His partner returned, a great deal wetter. "I pulled out the bodies," he said. "We should bury them. If the Germans find them, they'll take reprisals."

"Or even if they don't," Kerzhentsev said. "But I suppose it's worth making them wonder."

The lack of a spade seemed like a problem, but the riverbanks were soft enough to scoop away. Once the three naked corpses had been wedged in a line beneath the lip, some tufts of grass were used to hide them from above. Someone wading down the center of the stream would get a shock, but the bodies couldn't be seen by anyone walking the riverside path or looking down from a plane.

Back at the hut, they removed all traces of its temporary German occupation. The empty food tins were buried among the roots of a tree; the comb, uniforms, and army service haversacks were all claimed by the anarchists as compensation for their ill treatment.

"Where are you headed now?" Kerzhentsev asked them.

"South," the stocky one said. "We still have a job to do." He hesitated a moment. "You could join us."

Kerzhentsev shook his head. "We have our own job to do. In Kiev."

"Fair enough. Will you give us one of the horses?"

"Take all three. Riding into Ekaterinoslav on stolen German horses doesn't seem like a great idea."

"No." The thinner anarchist laughed. "Well, have a nice walk. And thanks for saving the hangman a job."

Watching the two men ride away, trailing the third horse behind them, McColl asked Kerzhentsev if the anarchists had known he was a Bolshevik.

The Russian shrugged. "They knew I wasn't an aristocrat or a German lover. Anything else they could live with."

"What do you think of anarchists?"

"They're romantics. You know that thing people say about their wives—can't live with her, can't live without her. I used to feel the same way about anarchists, but I'm beginning to think I could live without them. If I had to." He smiled. "It's too early in the morning for politics."

The hours went by. The two of them sat outside, Kerzhentsev reading his Lermontov, McColl writing mental letters to Caitlin, Jed, and his mother. "Just hidden three naked Germans . . ."

In midafternoon the Russian suggested they set off. "Arriving in the middle of the night would be worse than arriving in daylight."

The river grew more serpentine as it headed east, and the farmhouses became more frequent. The only airplane they saw was flying north, away from their anarchist friends, which had to be good news.

The Dnieper appeared with disconcerting suddenness. After rounding a tree-lined bend of their small river, they found themselves gazing out across at least a mile of water. For a fleeting moment, McColl felt like one of those famous explorers he'd hero-worshipped as a child.

The chimneys in the distance had to be Ekaterinoslav. They walked toward it, keeping as close to the river as the terrain allowed, until the first of the outlying buildings was only a quarter mile away. After the light had faded, they walked on into the town, which seemed eerily empty of both locals and Germans until they reached the center, where some sort of ceremony was underway.

"The German are crowning a puppet," was Kerzhentsev's guess, one that the bored faces of the Russian bystanders did nothing to refute. There were a lot of German troops on display, but no obvious tension in the air.

The local landing stage was a half mile to the west, and almost as crowded as Chaplino Junction. The good news was the paddle steamer anchored in the middle of the river, scheduled to leave for Kiev at eight the following morning.

9
Museum of the Future

Caitlin's third Pacific crossing was very different from the first two. The westward journey in 1913 had felt like a rite of passage, her first taste of life outside the white man's rich cocoon. Four months later she'd been in love, though still reluctant to admit it to herself. She and Jack had left her stateroom only to stretch their legs and eat.

This time the hours passed slowly, day after day of cold gray seas and skies. Her fellow passengers seemed a strange and mostly dreary mixture—returning Chinese students and Japanese businessmen, polite young Americans who worked for some unnamed arm of the government, the usual handful of well-meaning Christians intent on saving Asians from themselves. She spoke when spoken to and tried to be pleasant, but she had nothing in common with any of them. Four years of war and revolution had apparently left them wholly unscathed, and she found that inexcusable.

Was she being unfair? Probably. She felt alone and profoundly depressed. Her country's latest slide into vicious bigotry was nothing new—as the descendants of slaves and the original natives knew only too well—but there had always been something noble ranged against it, some overriding sense that individual people really mattered. Until now. Something was dying in that Chicago courtroom, and she didn't know how it could be saved.

Maybe it was only her. If she was alone, she had no one but herself to blame for that. If she always put those she loved second, what did that say about her own ideals? She remembered Ed Carlucci's words, that she'd invested too much in Russia and its revolution. When the torch burned out, what would she be left with? Might-have-beens? Some days she knew that politics was all about embracing life; on others she feared that it was one more way to avoid living in the here and now. On really bad days, she found herself wondering if her sister, Finola—whose world stretched barely a few city blocks—understood life a lot better than she did.

Maybe she just had too much time to think. Arriving at Yokohama cheered her up, and two nights in a Tokyo hotel provided the opportunity to explore somewhere new, which was always one of her favorite pastimes. The local English-language papers brought her up-to-date with the news, none of which seemed good. The British and Japanese had both landed troops in Russian ports, and neither seemed likely to leave it at that. The German armies in France were still advancing, which she knew would upset Jack. For one thing his brother, Jed, was in the firing line, and for another he cared who won the war.

Where events in Moscow were concerned, the papers had little to say. Caitlin knew that Kollontai and Spiridonova's LSRs had left the government, both, as far she knew, over the issue of peace with the Germans. She hoped and prayed that this was the case and that nothing more crucial had come between the women she most admired and the revolution they had helped to bring about.

Spring had come to Japan, filling the streams with melting snow and coating the valleys in blossoms. It rained throughout her three-day wait in Niigata, but on the morning of her ship's departure the sun at last emerged, and it was shining again when Vladivostok loomed into view late on the following day. As the ship drew closer to the hill-surrounded port, a line of warships at anchor appeared on the starboard side: the British *Suffolk*, the USS *Brooklyn*, two Japanese cruisers, and an ancient Chinese destroyer. Here was the enemy, she thought; up ahead, in the town festooned with crimson flags, was where she would find her friends.

✦ ✦ ✦

OVER THE NEXT WEEK, VLADIVOSTOK fed both her hopes and her fears. After depositing her luggage in a seafront hotel, Caitlin put herself through the two obvious hoops, reporting in at her country's consulate and at the city soviet. The man at the former asked what her plans were and promptly disclaimed all responsibility should she foolishly choose to carry them out. Her first contact at the latter, a chirpy young woman named Zoya with short, spiky hair, not only recognized her name but insisted on offering her somewhere to stay. "There's lots to write about here," Zoya said more than once. Which was just as well, because the trains to the west had stopped running. A Cossack bandit named Semenoff was blocking the route through China, a broken bridge had severed the line up the Amur Valley.

The accommodation was in a large stone house that Zoya shared with other activists. These were eager to hear about Caitlin's experiences in Petrograd over the winter, the women particularly keen to know about Kollontai. In return they were happy to explain the current state of affairs in Vladivostok, which all agreed was fast turning into a crisis.

Most of what these young Bolsheviks told her made sense and proved easy to verify over the next few days. The city was dividing into two camps, one better armed than the other. Five hundred Japanese and fifty British marines were stationed within the city limits, along with a small but growing number of soldiers from the Czech Legion. This force, some sixty thousand strong, had originally been formed from Czech prisoners who wished to join the Allied struggle against their Austro-Hungarian overlords. The army had been fighting on the Eastern Front, but with Russia's withdrawal from the war, arrangements had been made for sending it east to Vladivostok and then by sea to France. Those Czechs already in the city were waiting for ships to take them away, but so far none had appeared, and no one knew when they would.

There were more marines on the warships anchored in the bay and probably more warships just below the horizon. There was organized opposition both inside and outside the local soviet. Over the last few months, the Trans-Siberian had deposited trainloads of the revolution's opponents on this eastern edge of Russia, and many were still there, clinging to the hope that Allied intervention would obviate the need for emigration. Meanwhile ships like Caitlin's were arriving with adventurers and businessmen keen to tap Siberia's legendary riches while the region lacked a government that would stop them.

The anti-Bolshevik forces were waiting for the chance to move west. The money was already moving in that direction, funding Cossacks like Semenoff and anyone else who was willing to take on the Reds, as the Bolsheviks and their allies were now universally known. One nation's agents were much in evidence—wherever Caitlin went that week, she saw Frenchmen and Russians in conspiratorial huddles and more than once saw bundles of notes changing hands. When she asked a local Bolshevik to explain this Gallic interest, he just laughed. "The French were the czar's biggest creditor," he told her, "and they want their money back."

The American government was the only one still holding out against a full-scale intervention, but when Caitlin was invited to dine on the USS *Brooklyn*, she found her hosts and fellow guests united in hoping for a change of heart. Now that Prince Lvov—the March Revolution's first prime minister—had formed a new government-in-exile in Peking, the Allies had someone they could get behind, and no one else at the table could understand their president's reluctance.

All of which boded ill for those who wished the revolution well. If the Bolshevik experiment ended in failure, Caitlin thought the failure should be their own. If Lenin and the party went down to defeat, it should be at the hands of the Russian people, not a cabal of foreign interests in league with past oppressors.

When all was said and done, there was still so much to hope for. Zoya was eager to show Caitlin the scale of the transformation they had already wrought, taking her to factories and shipyards, introducing her to those who now ran them in their former owners' stead. There were many problems, but no one tried to gloss these over, and the levels of enthusiasm were almost scary.

Most of those she met on these visits were workers born and bred, unlike Zoya and her friends, who were mostly from bourgeois homes. It was these better-educated young men and women—most of them younger than Caitlin—who supplied the political organization, who called the meetings, wrote the agendas, got out the leaflets, who kept the city ticking even as they changed it. Most touching of all, at least to Caitlin, was the way they held themselves to account, constantly checking their own motivations and striving to be the best advertisement their revolution had. When they weren't at work or singing revolutionary songs in some café, they were arguing with one another, about everything from Brest-Litovsk to Kollontai's writings on love and sex.

One such after-work discussion in the city hall's chamber had only just finished when Aidan Brady walked in through the door. Caitlin didn't recognize him at first—the way the big man moved was strangely familiar, but she needed to mentally add a mustache before she realized who it was. He didn't see her right away, and she took some time to bring her emotions and thoughts into some sort of order.

They had met in the spring of 1914, in another hall on the other side of the world. A demonstration had been called in Paterson, New Jersey, a year after the broken silk workers' strike, and he'd given a short speech on recent events in Detroit. Seán Tiernan, her brother Colm's friend from Dublin, had brought Brady over before the speech, but she didn't know whether or not they'd already known each other before then. Their subsequent partnership was certainly no surprise—Tiernan was on the socialist wing of Irish republicanism, Brady a longtime Wobbly; both were lifelong renegades, and neither shrank from violence, as they would demonstrate several months later in England, mounting the failed operation that saw Caitlin's brother arrested and eventually shot in the Tower of London. Tiernan had died in the course of the operation, but Brady had escaped his pursuers and somehow returned to the States.

He was striding toward her. "My God, it's a small world," he said, taking the chair next to hers. "Are you on your way out or in?"

"In, if I can get a train. How about you?"

"In. Most definitely in." He turned toward her. "I'm sorry about Colm," he said softly.

"Thanks," she said, believing him sincere. Brady had his faults, but being devious was not one of them. And the fact that he seemed genuinely pleased to see her meant that he didn't know what had happened in Dublin two years before. Her rescue of Jack McColl, the British agent who'd thwarted his earlier plot, was not something he would have forgiven.

"The goddamn English," he said. "I won't be sorry to be fighting them again."

His face was harder without the mustache, but also younger.

"I can guess what you're doing here," he went on. "I've read some of your pieces over the last year. Good stuff."

"Thanks. It's actually been a privilege just being here."

"I can imagine. And being on the winning side for once in our lives can't be bad, eh?"

She knew what he meant. "What have you been doing since—"

"The fiasco in England? I went back to Ireland for a while—have you heard the latest news?"

She hadn't.

"The English have finally introduced conscription, and everyone—the Volunteers, Sinn Fein, the old Citizen Army people—they've all agreed to fight it. And the people are supporting them."

"That's great," she said, trying to sound enthused. These days Ireland seemed more a source of sadness than hope. "So where else have you been?" she asked.

"After Ireland I worked a passage to Mexico. I was with Pancho Villa for a few months, but the revolution down there had run out of steam and Villa's no better than a bandit. So I snuck back home across the border and reached Montana just in time for the IWW's bust-up with Anaconda."

"I know about that," Caitlin said. The big mining corporation had waged a vicious war against its own workers.

Brady sighed. "Yeah, well, after the company goons lynched Frank Little, I laid low for a while, and when Bill Haywood and the other leaders decided that a Chicago courthouse was the best podium they were ever going to get, I washed my hands of the IWW. Why put yourself in a jail cell when there's a real revolution to fight for? It took almost six months to work my way across the goddamn ocean, but here I am. And from what I can see, probably just in time. Next couple of years, the Bolsheviks are gonna need every gun they can get."

Caitlin agreed with that but didn't share Brady's obvious pleasure at the prospect. The Bolsheviks she knew had taken such pride in their almost bloodless revolution, and not without reason. As one had once told her, "You don't get real change at the point of a gun. Obedience, perhaps, but nothing more."

They talked about practicalities. Brady had arrived only that morning and still didn't know where the station was. "I'll walk down there in the morning," he told her. "Tell me where you're staying, and I'll let you know if I hear of a train."

IT WAS THREE EVENINGS LATER when he called at her lodgings. She and the others were singing revolutionary songs and didn't hear his knock on the door, so he simply walked in and joined them.

"There's a train at six in the morning," he told her when the opportunity arose. "I've booked places as far as Chita, which is where our control runs out. We can wing it from there."

She noticed the "our"—after only four days in Russia, it was already his revolution. Which was fair enough. "All right," she said. "I'll be there." After everything that had happened in the States and in England, she felt more than a little wary of Brady, but they both wanted to reach Moscow, and traveling with a man who didn't take no for a answer might be a good way to get there.

The others seemed to like him, and he ended up sleeping on the floor.

Lying on the rather more comfortable couch, she wondered why he wanted her company. She hadn't felt he'd liked her that much in 1914—his opinion of journalists, though never spelled out, had clearly been low. Did he feel guilty for surviving what her brother had not? She doubted that.

There was always the usual reason a man went out of his way to help a woman.

Brady was good-looking enough, better without the mustache. Their political beliefs weren't that far apart—a damn sight closer than hers and Jack's—and she didn't doubt his bravery. Colm had never lost faith in him; Zoya and her friends had seemed almost starstruck. But there was something about him. Something cold.

On the day of the demo in Paterson, McColl had seen him knife a cop to death in an alley. The cop had also been intent on violence, but still . . .

And then there was the night watchman at the English quarry, who'd stood between Brady and Colm's group of renegades and the explosives they needed. One of them had killed him, and if she had to put her money on who . . .

A committed revolutionary would claim that the end justified the means and that killings like these were regrettable necessities. Caitlin accepted that they might indeed be necessary; what she doubted was that Brady found them regrettable.

Men like him might save her revolution, she thought. But what would be the price?

THE FOLLOWING MORNING THE TWO of them boarded their train. The distance to Moscow, as the sign at the station told them, was 5,768 miles. In 1914 the journey had taken ten days, in 1918 it sometimes took that many weeks.

The latter seemed more likely as the train worked its way northward along the Ussuri Valley, stopping frequently for no apparent reason and generally spending more time at rest than in motion. Once Brady found out that the locomotive's boiler was leaking, their fitful progress became easier to understand, but the need for repairs at the next major stop was bound to cause a further delay. The springtime scenery offered some compensation—often the landscape was a carpet of flowers—but did nothing to lessen the general discomfort. The train was crowded, the toilets disgusting, and sleeping in a seat had never been one of Caitlin's favorite pastimes. The food was basic but plentiful,

alcohol in ample supply, both on the train and out on the platforms. If the number of peasants selling hooch was any guide, the
region could match Kentucky for stills.

It took three days to cover the five hundred miles to Khabarovsk
and another thirty-six hours to patch up the boiler. As the train
rumbled across the new Amur Bridge, Brady did some calcula-
tions—at their current speed they should reach Moscow sometime
in early June.

Few of their fellow passengers seemed overconcerned. They
were another mixed crew—locals making short trips, businessmen
bound for central Siberia, party men and women with meetings to
attend in distant Moscow. There were several young men and women
who seemed more like pilgrims than anything else—inspired by the
revolution, these youths were simply heading toward its heart, with
what intention they scarcely knew.

Brady talked to everyone. Like Caitlin, he had started learning
Russian the moment the czar was overthrown, and once he was
surrounded by native speakers, his fluency grew with remarkable
speed. He would come back to their seats full of some story he'd just
been told and insist that she include it in one of her pieces, behaving, in Caitlin's jaundiced eyes, like some kid who'd just enjoyed
another visit to the revolution's candy store.

There was something about him she couldn't trust, something
she couldn't quite explain, but she had to admit he was never boring or, indeed, ever bored. It wasn't a comforting thought, but she
could see why her brother had found him easy to follow.

The next thousand miles, winding through forested hills with
occasional views of the Amur plain to the south, were traversed in
only four days. According to the drivers, their engine was practi-
cally reborn, and it wasn't mechanical failure that brought the train
to a halt in Nerchinsk. The junction with the route across northern China was only a hundred miles ahead, and no one knew who
held it. Their Red Guard protectors would venture no farther—this
was the end of the line they controlled. Travel any farther and they
risked ending up one of Semenoff's captives, who rumor claimed
were sometimes burned alive in locomotive boilers.

Having recognized the name of the town and been assured that the train would not proceed that day, Caitlin decided she would visit the prison camp where Maria Spiridonova had been incarcerated for almost a third of her life. The office of the local soviet was impressed by the arrival of a foreign woman journalist and offered to supply a cart and driver-guide for the journey, but they pointed out, almost apologetically, that visiting even one of the seven *katorga* prisons would take a week—all the camps were close to the Mongolian border and at least a hundred miles away. Perhaps madam would prefer to visit the Museum of the Katorga, which was under construction here in Nerchinsk.

"Under consideration" might have been a better description, but it was moving nevertheless. Two rooms of the old local governor's house had been requisitioned for the task. The first had several exhibits—a wad of picture postcards from friends and relatives, paper flowers made by women prisoners, a zither with broken strings, a pile of thick gray trousers, tunics, and caps. The second held nothing but chains. They overflowed from baskets and trunks, hung from hooks on the walls, lay coiled like rusty snakes in every available space. Picking up an iron hobble and giving it a gentle shake, Caitlin was unexpectedly reminded of a day trip from Wesleyan College and the marching road gang they'd passed in the jalopy, much to their teacher's dismay. The classic sound of oppression, the one that Spiridonova and so many others had heard on their long walk into exile.

"'Man is born free, and everywhere he is in chains,'" Brady muttered behind her. "Well, no one's in these anymore."

"They should melt them down," Caitlin said, letting the links drop noisily onto the floor.

"Don't be too hasty—we may need them for the bourgeoisie," Brady joked.

Back at the station, there seemed little likelihood of an early departure, but returning to the train after a better-than-usual meal in town, they found it ready to leave. Word had reached the authorities that Semenoff's forces were farther away from the junction than they were and that a quick departure should see them through before the dreaded Cossack arrived.

It took five hours, and dusk was falling when the tracks from China came into view, empty as far as the eye could see. The junction station was almost deserted, but there was coal enough for the locomotive and no news of any recent trouble between there and the next big town, some fifty miles ahead. This was Chita, which had changed hands several times over the last few weeks.

THEY ARRIVED NEXT MORNING TO find Red Guards in charge of the station, but according to Brady the town was full of other armed groups, all trading hostile stares. Many people boarded the train during the day, and from the looks they gave the nervous Red Guards, Caitlin deduced that few of the newcomers were Bolshevik supporters. As night fell, a palpable rise of tension offered further proof that this was the case.

Leaving would have helped, but the crew seemed in no hurry, despite unconfirmed news that Semenoff's men had seized the junction behind them. The situation up ahead was equally unclear— certainty, Caitlin realized, was something they would have to learn to do without. As day turned to night and the train continued to sit there, she drowsily wondered if she'd ever reach Moscow.

When she woke, it was almost light. Brady was snoring beside her, and the train was running through a wooded valley, alongside a fast-flowing river. A walk through the crowded carriages showed most of the passengers still asleep, a condition that suited them if the next twelve hours were any guide. The usual debates were soon underway in every car, but the customary tolerance of other views was conspicuous by its absence. Some arguments turned violent, and though no actual shots were fired, for most of the day it felt like only a matter of time.

But somehow no one was killed, and the next day the differences that had threatened a minor civil war turned into the train's salvation. The many tunnels punctuating the route along Lake Baikal's southern shore were held by different groups, some by Bolsheviks, others by Socialist Revolutionaries or Kadets, some by enterprising local bandits, and all but the last had supporters on the train who could argue their right to pass. The bandits, of course, needed buying off, but a hat was passed and filled. The passengers might have nothing else in common, but all them wanted to reach Irkutsk.

When they did so on the morning of May 13, they were told that the train would go no farther, at least for a couple of days. After almost a fortnight of sleeping in a seat, Caitlin felt that the prospect of a hotel bed offered ample consolation for this new delay, and while Brady took out his frustration on some hapless railway official, she inquired as to where she might find a good one. The Central was recommended but was probably full. If so, the Metropole was just as comfortable.

Brady shared her droshky to the hotel, then disappeared in search of something less expensive. She stood outside the entrance for several moments, gazing up and down the bustling street. Irkutsk felt like a real city, the first since Vladivostok.

After taking a room and enjoying her first hot bath in almost a fortnight, she went back downstairs and asked about getting her clothes washed. Informed of a Chinese laundry just around the corner, she dropped off everything she wasn't wearing and went for a walk around town. There was still food in the shops, and the restaurant menus seemed almost extravagant.

A late lunch required a siesta, which turned into a fifteen-hour sleep. A second bath, somewhat colder than the first, certainly woke her up, and she was drinking tea in the marble-floored hotel restaurant when Brady came by with news he'd just picked up at the station—at least one train would be leaving for Moscow the next day. Two hours later he was back with less welcome tidings. There had been a major incident in the Ural city of Chelyabinsk, a violent fracas of some kind involving Bolshevik Red Guards and soldiers of the Czech Legion, which seemed to put their travel plans in doubt.

As the day wore on, the news grew worse. The Czechs in Chelyabinsk had taken control of that city, and their units in other towns were also up in arms. All travel west was suspended until order was restored.

Over the next few days, all sorts of rumors abounded. According to one, Trotsky had ordered the disarming of the Czechs after receiving orders to that effect from the Germans. Another claimed that the Czechs had decided against evacuation, choosing instead to fight with the "Whites"—as the conservative opponents of the Bolsheviks were now known. The Bolsheviks' enemies thought the former story more convincing; their supporters favored the latter.

"How many Czech soldiers are there?" Caitlin asked Brady one evening.

"Between fifty and a hundred thousand. It's the biggest army east of the Volga, but it's strung out over thousands of miles."

"And why in God's name would they want to stay and fight for the Whites?" she wanted to know.

Brady shrugged. "Any number of reasons. I don't expect that their officers like the Bolsheviks any more than the czar's officers did. And you can bet they're being paid, one way or another. I expect that the English and French have promised them independence once the war is over."

"They'll get that anyway."

Brady shrugged. "But they're stuck, and maybe that was the Allied plan all along. If there aren't any ships to take them home, what else can they do but stay and fight?"

"I wonder if they'll let a couple of neutrals through. I've got my press credentials, and if you say yours are lost, I can vouch for you."

"Hm. Maybe. But we still need a train."

Another week passed before that wish was granted, a week in which the city grew increasingly tense. The Bolsheviks paraded their troops at every opportunity, but the anxious looks on the soldiers' faces subverted the intended message. The meetings of the city soviet were one long shouting match, and the hotel lobbies were full of intriguers, many speaking Russian with thick French accents. One in particular haunted the Metropole and insisted on saying hello to Caitlin whenever they met, his leer wrapped up in good manners.

When their train finally left, he was on it, along with several of his countrymen. "He's a spy," Brady said simply when Caitlin pointed him out. "Next place we reach where the party's in full control, I'll hand him over."

He never got the chance. Three mornings out from Irkutsk, beyond Krasnoyarsk but a long way short of Omsk, their train drew into a wayside station. It was a cold, clear morning, and Caitlin was looking out the window when another train slid into view. It was standing in a parallel siding about twenty yards away, and the side of each car bore illustrations of one kind or another—paintings of long-ago battles, ornately crafted lists of names, childlike pictures of cottages with flower-filled gardens. Like a line of Gypsy caravans, she thought until she noticed the open doorways and the snouts of machine guns pointing her way.

A CZECH COLONEL COMMANDED THE train and its soldiers, at least in theory. The passengers selected for interrogation in the command carriage saw a thin, gray-haired man in legion uniform sitting at his desk while two other men—a plump young Russian with a monocle and the Frenchman from the train—stood sentry at either shoulder.

Caitlin was one of the first.

"You're an American," the colonel declared after looking at her papers, his tone suggesting that was all he needed to know.

"What are you doing here?" the Russian asked accusingly.

His tone and the looks on all of their faces—the Czech uncomfortable, the others hostile—told her she had to be careful. "I'm a reporter, and I'm on my way to Moscow."

"Who do you work for?"

"The *New York Chronicle*," she said, feeling sure that news of her resignation hadn't yet reached Siberia.

"And where do your sympathies lie?" the Frenchman asked her in Russian.

"What do you mean?" she asked, working on her answer.

"Do your sympathies lie with the Whites or the Reds?"

"With Russia and its people. And with people like yours who want to go home," she added, addressing the colonel.

He gave her a thin smile.

"You talked to the Bolsheviks on the train," the Frenchman insisted.

"I talk to everybody. As a journalist should."

The Frenchman's look was contemptuous, leaving Caitlin with a sudden, terrible feeling that her life was hanging by a thread. The hiss of the engine outside, the birdsong in the trees—was this where she would die?

The Czech seemed her only hope. "I would be interested in interviewing you," she said. "On how your soldiers have been treated and what hopes they have for the future. With a history like ours, Americans are always interested in others who are fighting for independence."

"Perhaps on some other day," the colonel said, rising to his feet and offering his hand. "You may go now."

She went, descending the veranda steps on decidedly shaky legs. Had he saved her, or had she only imagined the threat? She would never know.

Brady was next. She walked back to their carriage, not worried about him. The man could talk his way out of anything.

Sure enough, he was back within minutes.

"What do you think?" she asked him.

"I think we'll be losing some comrades."

He was right. In midafternoon she was just dozing off when the salvo was fired.

"Rifles, not a machine gun," Brady said.

There was nothing visible from the window.

Another volley, and this time a hint of smoke above the roof of the parallel train.

And another.

She was reaching for the door when Brady placed a restraining hand on hers. "Don't," he said. "They won't want any witnesses."

She knew he was right. If it felt like cowardice, then so be it. Dead journalists didn't file stories.

Their train jerked into motion. As it slowly gathered speed, she and Brady walked through the carriages checking for absentees. The party officials and Caitlin's young "pilgrims"—all were gone.

10
The Price of Cabbage

The three-hundred-mile journey upriver took four days. The paddle steamer *Kutuzov* stopped at all the scheduled calling points and quite a few places besides; according to its captain, the aging engines needed frequent respites just to override the current.

McColl enjoyed it. The food was better than expected, and there was room to sleep on deck. The weather was beautiful, days clear and sunny, the nights just cool enough. If the views weren't that interesting, neither were they hard on the eye: yellow-green grasslands and rickety jetties, occasional white churches with polished domes of blue and gold.

His fellow passengers were the usual hotchpotch. Rumor had it there were a couple of princes locked away in one of the cabins, and there was certainly no shortage of paupers lining the decks. According to Kerzhentsev, most of the crew were Bolsheviks, but they, unlike their brothers in Sevastopol, bore no great grudge against their officers and captain. McColl's Russian companion spent much of the trip proselytizing among the other passengers, with, as he cheerfully admitted, precious little success.

When they reached Kiev early on the morning of May 13, Kerzhentsev suggested a place—a café in the Old Town—where both could leave messages under false names, should either need help in their anti-German ventures. McColl readily agreed. He had no idea what reputation the Russian might have among Cumming's people in the city, but he'd seen for himself how effective the man could be. And truth be told, McColl rather liked him.

There were German soldiers hovering close by the gangplank, but no general inspection of papers, which suited McColl. The ones he'd been given in Ashkhabad were almost in shreds, and if Georgiy Kuskov was still on his way home to Moscow, he'd chosen a round-about route.

The center of town was a couple of miles to the south, so he and Kerzhentsev clambered aboard one of the droshkies that were waiting outside the dock gates and sat back in the sunshine as the horse trotted briskly down the riverside road. McColl had never been to Kiev, and his first impressions were favorable—the city was built amid a clutch of wooded hills rising up from the river's west bank. The distant slopes seemed thick with churches, and away to the south what looked like a statue was crowned by a huge white cross, ablaze in the morning sunlight.

At Tsarskaya Square they paid off the driver. So far they'd seen very few Germans, but here in the center several groups of officers were taking their morning stroll. There were also Ukrainian troops, the lower ranks standing sentry outside some of the bigger buildings, the officers parading in their many-colored comic-opera uniforms, complete with gaudy epaulets and ludicrous cockades.

"Independence!" Kerzhentsev muttered scornfully. "They have a hetman now, the first since 16-something. A man named Skoropadsky. A German puppet, but a willing one." He broke into a laugh. "What times, eh? Well, I guess this is good-bye. For now at least. I wish you luck in your endeavors."

"And you in yours," McColl said, shaking the Russian's hand and watching him walk away.

One thing he had noticed on the latter stages of their ride was the number of cafés and restaurants that seemed to be open. Unlike the cities he'd been to thus far, Kiev didn't look as if someone had emptied it out, and he felt like indulging himself.

He found a suitable café almost instantly, and lo and behold, there was coffee and cake. Terrible coffee admittedly, and the cream on the cake was more than a little sour, but after four years of war and revolution the layers of flaky pastry might have been the fragmentary remains of some long-lost civilization.

And there were newspapers, too, in both Ukrainian and Russian. McColl took one of the latter, rifling through the pages for news of the Western Front. He couldn't find any, which was probably a good sign. If the Germans had entered Paris, that would surely merit a line or two.

The lead story was the forming of a new Russian government in Peking, which seemed rather a long way off to actually influence matters. According to Manley-Pryce, the Japanese were itching to invade Siberia, so maybe they would take this government with them and drop it off at the Urals. Or maybe it was all just wishful thinking, like the stories heralding the imminent collapse of Lenin's regime in Moscow.

Looking around, McColl took note of his fellow patrons, all dressed much better than he was and no doubt smelling a good deal sweeter. The empty tables around him were probably a comment on the number of days since he'd last had a bath. Sevastopol, he remembered. Two weeks ago.

It was too late to throw himself in the Dnieper. The address that Manley-Pryce had given him was a few streets away on the edge of the Old Town, and he found it easily enough. The pastel blue building, which butted up against a steep ridge, had five stories, the second of which contained the offices of the Zheltaya Luna film company—one of only two such companies in Kiev, according to Manley-Pryce. The local owners thought their chief accountant was a Muscovite named Andrei Golubev. To the better-informed McColl, he was an Englishman named Patrick Davidson.

The secretary on guard was blonde, young, and attractive. "I'm here to see Golubev," McColl told her. "About an automobile he wants to borrow," he added, following his instructions.

Davidson was around thirty and already losing his dark brown hair. His eyes were also brown and his body, when he rose from behind the desk, rather too plump for a fourth year of war. The smile was brief and harassed.

"How freely can we talk?" McColl asked quietly in Russian.

"Freely enough at this volume," Davidson whispered back in the same language. "I was afraid you'd never arrive—the railways have almost ground to a halt."

McColl offered a brief summary of his journey and mentioned Kerzhentsev's willingness to consider joint action against the Germans.

Davidson scowled. "Perhaps," he said. "Generally speaking, we give the Bolsheviks a wide berth. Of course we don't want to burn any bridges, but . . . you understand. Anyway, I'm glad you got here in one piece. I've arranged a temporary billet with a Russian family who live not far away, the Drobolyubovs. They're old friends of mine. The father's dead, so the son's the head of the family. And there's the mother and two sisters. All three children are in their twenties. All pro-Allies. I'll take you over there now and introduce you. And then you must stay indoors until your new papers are ready. It shouldn't be long, and after the trip you've had, you'll probably enjoy the rest. The girls are excellent company."

As they walked on into the Old Town, Davidson gave McColl some personal background—he'd grown up in Russia as the son of an expatriate businessman—and a brief résumé of the situation in Kiev. "There are refugees pouring in from the north—the cafés and theaters are full of them. They all have their stories of Bolshevik cruelties, and they see the Germans as their protectors. The people working with us tend to be locals. Most see themselves as Russian patriots, and they wouldn't dream of turning their guns on the Bolsheviks until after they've beaten the Germans."

Their destination was a faded yellow house on a small street behind St. Sophia Cathedral. A diminutive servant girl answered the door and ushered them through to a lovely room at the back, where the family was sitting in a circle of chairs. The acacia visible through the French windows filled much of the tiny garden.

Golubev made the introductions. The mother, Evdokia Drobolyubova, was a handsome woman in her fifties, graying hair coiled in a bun at the nape of her neck. The son, Yakov, was a dark-haired, bespectacled, and mustachioed young man in his late twenties, with the air of someone who took himself very seriously. The daughters, Tanya and Alisa, were dark and pretty, with small teeth and big eyes. McColl shook hands and returned smiles. They all appeared delighted to see him, which, given the circumstances, seemed a trifle odd.

McCOLL STAYED WITH THE DROBOLYUBOVS for four days and couldn't fault the family's hospitality. He was given a pleasant room overlooking the garden, with a comfortable bed and several shelves of books. The quality of the meals depended on what the servant girl, Irina—"She's almost part of the family"—could scavenge on any given day, but there was always something worth eating.

The state of the house—the fine but threadbare carpets, the eclectic sets of expensive china—suggested a shortage of funds that no one seemed inclined to admit, let alone attempt to reverse. Both father and son had been soldiers. The former was killed at Tannenberg in 1914; the latter had resigned his commission the previous year when the socialist Rada declared Ukraine independent and now spent much of each day wondering whether he should join General Denikin's army in the northern Caucasus. Neither mother nor daughters had ever earned a kopek and, though now obliged to do occasional household chores, insisted on dubbing such efforts "volunteer work."

All the family members spent most of their days where McColl had first encountered them, in the still-splendid living room. The women read novels and sewed, Yakov perused the newspaper and various histories. They all enjoyed listening to music on their precious gramophone, which they played ever so quietly for fear of attracting a thief. They conversed a great deal on a surprisingly wide range of subjects and were clearly determined to make the most of their visitor. Yakov was keen to know McColl's opinions on the war and how it was going, on Russia's future and the other Allies' role in helping to shape it. He was disappointed that McColl knew less about General Denikin than he did and was convinced that once the Germans were beaten, the Allies would sort his country out. The British troops in Murmansk, the Japanese in Vladivostok—these were just the beginning. "They'll help us set up a proper democracy, one based on Russian values."

Tania and Alisa were more interested in England and what life there was actually like. Neither ever talked about leaving their home and their country, but it was perhaps in the back of their minds—it certainly was in the back of their mother's. "We raised them to live in a certain world," she told McColl in the garden one day, "but that world is gone, and despite what Yakov says, it's never coming back. A year from now, I fear that people like us will feel more at home in a foreign country than we do in our own."

But on they read, on they sewed, reminding McColl of characters in a Jane Austen novel. He knew what Kerzhentsev would make of the Drobolyubovs—what Caitlin would, come to that—and the two of them wouldn't be wrong. And yet. None of the four were unthinking or unkind, all had their hearts in more or less the right place. McColl felt sorry for them, probably more than he should.

They shared the outside world on only one occasion, when the older daughter, Tanya, asked him to accompany her on a shopping expedition. They were close to the café where he'd enjoyed his coffee and cake when local police began clearing the street, and a few minutes later a mounted German regiment came trotting through, all polished blades and helmets, stern eyes straight ahead. Tanya's eyes were shining, but not, McColl thought, for the Germans. This was how her father and brother had gone to war; this was the past in all its glory.

DAVIDSON ARRIVED AFTER DARK ON the fourth day and took his time getting around to the business at hand. He was clearly besotted with young Alisa and apparently oblivious to her lack of interest in him. McColl found himself wondering whether she might be the price of a future escape to the west.

After tea had been served in the mismatched cups, Davidson brought forth the fruits of his labors. McColl had two sets of new papers, each with a new name and history. One was for Arkady

Vostyovich Belov, a Russian born in Kiev who had just returned to the city after several years in Petrograd and was staying with his Uncle Anton, a dispatcher at the goods yard. He was a teacher whose teachings the Bolsheviks had found objectionable. The other set was for Khristian Vissotsky, a photographer from Moscow, who was hoping to start a new studio here in Kiev.

"Why two?" McColl asked.

"The first is easier to prove, because you really will be staying with the uncle. But if you're caught by the Germans, we'd prefer you use the latter and keep Belov out of it. Understood?"

"Yes," McColl said, saving his doubts for later.

There were also new clothes—two whole sets—to add to the outfit that Yakov had lent him. And new digs. "Not so convivial, I'm afraid," Davidson told him after they'd said their thanks and good-byes. As the droshky carried them southward, Davidson took frequent looks over his shoulder, just to make sure there was no one behind them.

After skirting the botanical gardens, they turned east, eventually diving under a railway bridge and entering a neighborhood of neat workers' cottages. "This is Solomenka," Davidson explained. "It was built in the 1890s for the railway workers. My father had a hand in the design."

It was pleasant enough, McColl supposed, as they drew up outside one of a hundred identical dwellings. Belov's, he noted, had the advantage of backing onto the railway line, and if McColl wasn't mistaken, those clanking noises in the distance were the sounds of freight being shunted. A train watcher's paradise.

Anton Belov was a change from the Drobolyubovs. The greeting was friendly enough but didn't extend to the eyes. A monkey in a suit, McColl's father would have called him, a white-collar man who worked in a blue-collar world. He didn't drive trains but told those who did where and when. He gave off that quiet sense of confidence that the Drobolyubovs appeared to have lost.

The new room was barely long enough for its bed—Cheselden's feet would have stuck out the door. But the goods yard and depot were visible through the window—a line of German wagons, newly converted to the Russian gauge, were standing in one of the sidings. It was Belgium all over again, and for one heady moment McColl thought he scented the perfume his Resistance contact Mathilde had often used. He wondered if she was still alive.

Davidson was leaving, anxious not to have the droshky outside for longer than was necessary. "Anton Vostyovich will fill you in on the details," he said in English. "I'll be seeing you every few days when you bring the reports. Anton will tell you where and when."

"A drink?" Belov asked once Davidson was gone.

"Thank you," McColl said.

The Russian poured him a generous measure and passed it across. "To the czar," he said, raising his glass.

"The czar," McColl echoed. In Belgium it had been King Albert, and the drink homemade anis. Here it was homemade vodka tearing a strip off his throat.

THE NEXT FEW DAYS WERE spent familiarizing himself with his new role. There were about a dozen men involved in the Kiev train-watching network, all of whom worked for the railway in some capacity or other. Around half were train watchers of the classic sort, simply noting the composition and cargoes of trains that ran past their points of vantage; the rest had jobs in the goods depot and signaling section that provided them with access to current and projected German movements. None of them knew one another, and McColl had weekly meetings with each individual at different workers' cafés in the area around the station. He then collated the reports and passed them on to Davidson for onward transmission to Moscow and eventually London.

It was a smooth-running operation, and by the end of the week McColl felt as if he'd been doing the job for much longer. There appeared to be little in the way of danger—the Germans seemed thin on the ground, and those in evidence were mostly involved in guarding critical infrastructure. They wanted their trains to run and didn't seem to care who knew what they were carrying.

The job rarely took up more than half of any given day, which gave McColl plenty of time to pursue Davidson's more general request, of assessing the political mood among the city's lower classes. This also involved sitting in cafés and bars, often for hours on end to little apparent effect. As many of the overheard conversations were in Ukrainian, his lack of that language was a handicap, but enough were conducted in Russian, or a mixture of the two, to convince him there was no such thing as a uniform mood. On the question of Ukrainian independence, those he listened to seemed equally divided between those who'd always been in favor, those who were now disillusioned, and those, like the local Russians, who'd always been against. On ideological matters there was an even wider spread. The Bolsheviks, Mensheviks, liberals, and monarchists all had followings, but all were also split: the Bolsheviks over Brest-Litovsk, the monarchists over who they wanted for their monarch, and so on and so on.

In the more well-to-do parts of the city, anti-Bolshevism reigned. McColl had two rendezvous with Davidson in the first ten days and on each occasion took the opportunity to explore the central area, eating at restaurants packed with refugees from Moscow and Petrograd. Their conversations revealed the men as bankers, landlords, and sundry businessmen, the women as their proud, indignant, and overdressed chattels. Outside on the streets, the pavements were full of expatriate prostitutes, less proud, less indignant, but just as overdressed, with dark red lipstick and drug-filled eyes. On Nikolayevsky Street, McColl was intrigued enough by the clientele to spend a couple of hours in the Dust and Ashes nightclub, where a succession of male poets in extravagant makeup declaimed the evils of Bolshevism.

After that the cafés around Kiev Station seemed almost like home, but as the days went by, the job and its risks seemed harder to justify. The number of troop transports had shrunk to almost none, and there were no westward movements of oil or cotton, or at least not through Kiev. There was some grain traffic—spring wheat, McColl assumed—but not on a scale that would feed many German villages, let alone towns or cities. He had no way of knowing what was moving on other routes or what might soon be moving on this one, but he couldn't help thinking that there must be better uses for his talents and time.

ONE WAS SUGGESTED AT HIS next meeting with Davidson. It was another beautiful early-summer morning, and they were sitting in the pavilion of the Merchant's Garden, looking out across the quarter-mile-wide Dnieper.

"The gasworks in Dvortsovaya," Davidson said, in the manner of someone announcing a prize. "It supplies the whole southern half of the city, including most of the German barracks and command centers. There are two big holders—blow them up and half of Ukraine will see the flash. Our people in Moscow are keen." He gave McColl an expectant look.

"Are they indeed?" McColl said dryly. "I don't suppose they know how well these works are guarded."

"No, but I do," Davidson said almost smugly. "There's a military post by the front gates and a regular patrol of the perimeter, but there are no guards inside the walls at night."

"And the walls?"

"Ten feet high, with barbed wire on top. Not easy, but far from impossible."

"Not if you're only interested in getting in."

"There'll be time to get out again. In Poltava a few weeks ago, one of our teams destroyed a holder by starting a fire alongside and then firing a few rounds into it from about a hundred yards away. It blew up all right, but every man's nose bled for days. So now we're using time bombs. Much more efficient. They'll be coming in from Kharkov, and all you and your Bolshevik friends have to do is collect them from the station."

"My Bolshevik friends?"

"Kerzhentsev and his comrades. You talked about taking joint action against the Germans, right?"

"Yes."

"Well, this seems an ideal opportunity."

McColl was suspicious. "Why this sudden desire to work with the Bolsheviks?"

Davidson shrugged. "There's no one else available," he said. "I've got saboteurs in every German-held town but this one. Didn't you see the morning paper, the gas holder blown up in Kursk? Or last week's in Cherkassy? You and your Bolshevik friends are all I've got in Kiev."

"They may be busy."

"They may, but there's no harm in asking."

"I suppose not. And if we succeed, what then? The Germans will go berserk."

"Ah, that's the other thing I have to tell you. Once this business is taken care of, Cumming wants you in Moscow—"

"What in God's name for?" There weren't any Germans in Moscow.

"Not a clue. Ours not to reason why, eh? But we'll get you there on the double. I'm sure Belov can smuggle you onto some sort of train."

"And Kerzhentsev's men?"

"I doubt they'll want to leave. And it's up to them how they ensure their own survival. We're at war with the same enemy—it's not as if they're doing us a favor."

AFTER REACHING THE TOP OF the steps, McColl needed the time to get his breath back. The view from the Vladimir Monument was an elevated version of the one from the Merchant's Garden, but this time the sky was clouded over, the receding steppe wreathed in haze. A well-dressed couple were standing arm in arm at the edge of the drop, and McColl had the sudden feeling that they were about to jump. A moment's hesitation and he was hurrying toward them, wondering what to say.

There was no need. He was still several yards away when the twosome suddenly turned around, their faces wreathed in smiles, leaving McColl to stifle a laugh at his own relief. Kiev might be a city where despair was becoming commonplace, but here were two members of the Russian bourgeoisie whose world hadn't turned black with the Bolsheviks.

"Speaking of the devil," he murmured to himself as Kerzhentsev strode toward him. He looked a lot better turned out than when they last met, but then so did McColl. They warmly embraced, McColl aware of the gun in the Russian's side pocket, Kerzhentsev of the belted Mauser in the small of the Scotsman's back. Men who were more than they seemed, McColl thought. And maybe less.

"It is good to see you," the Russian said as he took in the panoramic view. "How does the train counting go?"

McColl smiled. "Well enough. But I have a proposition for you," he added, glancing around to ensure there were no listeners. "How would you like to blow up the Dvortsovaya gasworks?"

"Very much. We have been thinking about it for couple of weeks, ever since the one at Kursk was destroyed, but we haven't yet found a way of doing it without sacrificing at least one of our men."

"It was our people at Kursk. They used time bombs, which made all the difference. When the bombs eventually went off, everyone was miles away. And we can get the same devices for the works here."

"So why do you need us?" the Russian asked.

"We're overextended, and you and I did talk about joint action."

Kerzhentsev gave him a searching look and seemed satisfied with what he saw. "We did. And anything that hurts the Germans . . . But first I must convince my comrades. They're not all as broad-minded as I am."

McColl laughed. "Neither are mine. Shall we meet again here, same hour, in two days' time?"

Kerzhentsev nodded. "I'll be here."

"So how are your wife and children?"

The Russian sighed. "They left for Moscow this morning. It's safer there, but I miss them already." He smiled at McColl. "But this business—it will be my consolation. I will persuade my friends."

As he watched Kerzhentsev walk off, McColl realized he was hoping that the comrades said no. Why? The gasworks appeared to be a target worth hitting, the attendant risks hardly excessive. Was it because the operation seemed such a win-win for the British—if he and the Bolsheviks succeeded, it was one in the eye for the Germans, and if the Bolsheviks were subsequently caught, then who in London would shed a tear? McColl liked Kerzhentsev more than

Davidson and half suspected he would find the Russian's colleagues more to his taste than the Englishman's.

As he made his way back down the steps, he wondered where it would end. The day he favored Bolshevism more than the system he worked for was the day he should hand in his notice.

TWO DAYS LATER KERZHENTSEV REPORTED his comrades' agreement to the sabotage mission. McColl told Davidson, who passed on the news to Kharkov, where the time bombs were being put together. Delivery was promised in ten days or less.

June had arrived, and the weather was suddenly hotter, as if the gods had belatedly noticed the date. McColl continued to collect reports from his train watchers, but the only significant event was the transit of a large cotton shipment—the Germans had finally started moving the stuff across the Caspian. He also had another meeting with Kerzhentsev, who was fretting at the wait. The Russian had enlisted three comrades, two of whom were not much more than boys. "Orphans," he added. "Their parents were killed by the Germans."

McColl tried, without much success, to keep up with news of the wider war. A third big German offensive had begun toward the end of May, but finding out how successful it had been—or still was— proved beyond him. The Marne was mentioned in one report, which he hoped was a mistake. That was the river that had marked the German high tide in 1914, and if they'd reached it again, then Paris would be in their sights.

He supposed he would find out in Moscow, if he ever got there.

The big Russian news was the revolt of the Czech Legion. The process of moving the Czech force east to Vladivostok had started in early spring, but over the last few weeks things had gone badly wrong and a substantial chunk of the legion had taken up arms against the Russian authorities. The Kiev newspapers—anti-Bolshevik to a man—were ecstatic.

ON THE EVENING OF JUNE 7, Belov reported that the train carrying the time bombs was leaving Kharkov at seven that evening and was expected to arrive in Kiev twenty-four hours later for overnight remarshaling. The bombs were hidden among the disassembled parts of a Russian engineering works, which the Germans had decided could be more profitably sited in their own country.

The necessary details arrived the following afternoon. On Davidson's orders Belov met McColl and Kerzhentsev on a prearranged street corner a few hundred yards from the goods depot. "Line 8, Car 17, the crate numbered B24," Belov said succinctly, as McColl leaned in to light his cigarette.

"Thank you," McColl said, but his dispatcher host was already on his way. "Get that?" he asked Kerzhentsev.

"I did," the Bolshevik said, staring at Belov's back with ill-concealed disdain. "Is that why he couldn't just carry the damn things out in his lunch box?" he demanded. "Because he hates Bolsheviks?"

"Probably. But he's given us the train, and he's spent the last week checking the timing of the German patrols. We couldn't have collected the bombs without him."

"We haven't yet."

THE NIGHT WAS CLEAR BUT mercifully lacking a moon. Soon after ten, Kerzhentsev cut a neat flap in the wire fence the Germans had erected around the goods depot. There were only four points of entry, two for trains, two for carts and motor lorries. All four were gated and guarded. Searchlights illuminated the long stretches of unguarded wire that separated the depot as a whole from the through lines and surrounding streets. Thanks to the shadows cast by two towering birches, the spot they had chosen for ingress was darker than most, but McColl felt far from invisible. As they hastened across the stretch of open ground that lay between them and the nearest line of wagons, he half expected a shout of alarm, swiftly followed by gunfire.

Once under a wagon, they took a few moments to check that they hadn't been seen. All McColl could hear was the clanking of buffers elsewhere in the yard and an engine in steam much farther away—no running feet, no guttural voices. They were safely in. Now to find the bombs and then get safely out.

Track 8 was the eighth of fourteen sidings, counting up from the main line. The two of them began working toward it, carefully checking each walkway between trains for signs of movement, then ducking under the nearest pair of couplings and checking the next. The train, which McColl had watched arrive soon after seven, was easily recognizable, some thirty unmarked boxcars topped and tailed by wagon-mounted machine guns. There had been at least thirty soldiers on board, but according to Belov the usual procedure was to allow them all off once the train was inside the fenced-off area.

He seemed to be right. The train on Track 8 stretched a long way to their left and almost as far to their right. The locomotive was gone, presumably for coaling.

"I can't see any markings on the wagons," Kerzhentsev said in a whisper.

McColl tried the other end, and there it was—a large number 5. He beckoned the Russian over and pointed it out.

They started walking down the train, keeping as close as possible to the left-hand rail and wheels. The sound of something passing stopped them in their tracks, but as far as McColl could make out, it was only an engine running light, probably bound for the far end of the yard.

Car 17 was distinguished only by its neatly scrawled number, under which someone had scrawled "*siebzehn*," as if Russian numerals were rendered differently from German ones. The door was well oiled, sliding back with hardly a sound. As agreed beforehand, Kerzhentsev interlinked his fingers to receive McColl's foot and helped hoist him up through the opening. Once inside, McColl slid the door shut before striking a match and finding a place to wedge the candles he'd brought along.

There were upwards of a hundred boxes in the car, stacked by size rather than number. After whispering a warning to Kerzhentsev that the search might take a while, he began working his way through the piles, starting with those of the smaller crates. Ten minutes later he had—as his father would have said—more wax burns than a drunken Catholic. He was beginning to doubt he'd ever find the damn box when a stenciled "B24" popped into view. It took another minute to lever off the lid, but there, neatly nestled among several boxes of mysterious steel castings, was a small canvas bag containing three pipe-shaped time bombs.

Dousing the candles, he slid the door open and passed the treasure down to the waiting Russian. Once he was on the ground again, they headed back the way they had come. The urge to hurry was intense, but they managed to overcome it, treating each gap between trains like the firing range it might turn out to be. It was only when they reached the last line of wagons that everything fell apart.

"Halt!" a German voice shouted, nervously shrill.

It wasn't directed at them. Crouching down, they could see both hunters and prey. Two German soldiers, their rifles raised, advancing on two small boys. The older one, who was carrying a bag, looked around ten, his companion about two years younger. Both looked panic-stricken, and with good reason—as McColl knew from Belgium, the Germans were not shy when it came to murdering children.

"We can take them," Kerzhentsev said in a whisper. And without giving the surprised McColl a chance to argue, he squirmed out from under the wagon, gun clasped behind his back, and cheerfully asked, "What have we here?"

It clearly hadn't occurred to the Russian that the Germans would not understand him. One of the soldiers must have noticed the hidden hand, because he barked out a warning and opened fire just as Kerzhentsev pulled his own trigger. The other German went down, but so did the Russian, still clutching the bag full of bombs.

The surviving soldier turned his rifle toward McColl, who was still only halfway out from under the wagon. As a bullet pinged off the metal side above him, he pulled himself back behind the curve of a wheel, took careful aim at the soldier's torso, and tightened his finger on the Mauser's trigger.

The soldier uttered a squeal of dismay as he sank to his knees, then a heartfelt grunt as he folded forward, head kissing the cinders like a Muslim at prayer.

There was a moment—perhaps even several—of stillness and silence. Three prone bodies, two boys gaping. And a partridge in a pear tree, McColl heard himself think.

And then there were shouts in the distance, and a bell began tolling as if the end of the world were nigh. The two boys seemed to wake from their trance, turning tail and haring off into the distance before McColl could say a word. Their bag lay abandoned, having spilled what looked like a trio of cabbages.

McColl strode across to where Kerzhentsev was lying and found to his surprise that the Russian was still alive. But he was breathing his last, and he seemed to know it. There was no fear in the eyes, though. "Buggered that up, didn't I?" he whispered. "Get the kids away," he said, forcing each word out like it might be his last.

"They're gone—" McColl started to say, but the Russian's eyes had stopped moving.

There was no sign of the boys.

Grabbing the bag containing the bombs, he headed for the fence. There were sounds of movement away to his right, but buildings blocked the view. His prospective captors were still out of sight.

Reaching the wire, he walked toward the stand of trees, searching for the hole they'd cut. It wasn't there. Retracing his steps, he finally found the well-disguised flap and forced himself through. Picking up the bag again, he resisted the thought of just leaving it there—if the boys were caught and tied to sabotage, their chances would be minimal. This was his risk to bear.

There was a yard-wide gap between the German fence and the walls of the properties beyond. He made his way along it, conscious of the lights now weaving patterns above the goods yard to his right and the incessant ringing of the sonorous bell.

No one had seen him, he told himself. No one but the boys. If they were caught and questioned . . .

There was no future for him in Kiev, but that didn't matter—Cumming already wanted him in Moscow. It was just that getting from the one to the other was likely to prove more difficult than either of them had envisaged.

After hesitating for a moment, he turned left along a narrow passage between houses. This opened onto an empty street, which sloped down toward a bigger road. The one, he hoped, that passed under the lines near the southern end of the yard.

It was almost midnight, and there was no one about. At the bottom of the street, he paused in a shop doorway, then squeezed himself deeper into the shadows as a German motor lorry rumbled past. The driver seemed in no hurry, and the lorry's presence was probably coincidental.

He assumed that the Germans would scour the depot and hoped they'd finish doing that before widening their search. He hoped the boys had gotten out the way they'd gotten in and weren't huddling in some dark corner, praying the Germans would pass them by.

The street ahead was clear. He walked on, keeping to the shadows as much as he could, trying to avoid an impression of haste. Passing the road that sloped up to the depot, he saw the gate office blazing with light. A few yards more and a rifle cracked in the distance. Just the once. So . . . maybe a soldier shooting at shadows.

The bridge that passed under the yard was at least fifty yards long—a tunnel in all but name. Its dark mouth felt like a death trap, but the only alternative was walking across the open tracks. McColl hurried into the gloom, boots slapping on the stony ground. The place smelled of mold, even in June.

Somewhere in the middle, a memory of almost drowning appeared out of nowhere, and emerging at the other end he felt the taste of Loch Linnhe water on his tongue. How old had he been? Seven?

He turned right into the Solomenka railway colony. The bell, he realized, had stopped tolling. It must have done so while he was inside the tunnel. As he passed down the first row of houses, he could imagine the faces at windows on the opposite side, all wondering what was happening in the depot across the tracks.

Belov, of course, was able to guess. His host of the last three weeks looked appalled to see him, and maybe a little surprised.

"You can't stay here," the Russian said.

"I won't," McColl reassured him. "But I need my things," he added, pushing his way in and heading for his room.

The thing he wanted most was the map of the local area that he'd finally acquired the previous day, after three long weeks of searching. "Always know the way out" was a maxim that had saved his life on more than one occasion.

There wasn't much to pack—the map and a spare set of clothes, the letters to Soph and his two sets of papers.

Belov was waiting by the front door. "Are you leaving Kiev? Golubev will want to know."

It took McColl several seconds to remember that Golubev was Davidson. "Yes, of course. I'll head west," he lied. "They won't expect that." He had left the other bag by the door. "I don't suppose you want the bombs?" he asked Belov.

"Hell no!" the Russian exclaimed, taking an involuntary step back. "Why in God's name did you bring them here?"

There was no answer to that. "Thanks for the hospitality," McColl said, picking up the other bag and slinging it over his shoulder. After quick looks up and down the empty street, he pulled the door shut behind him and headed north in the direction of the station. He could almost feel Belov's eyes on his back.

Once out of sight, he took a left turn. Five minutes later the houses were all behind him, and he was walking down a tree-lined track between fields. Here, at last, the reality of Kerzhentsev's death came home, and he found himself wiping away tears. Perhaps it was the shock—and the fact that it could just as easily have been himself. But he knew it was also more than that. He'd known the Russian for only a few weeks, but in that time they'd shared things that mattered, things he hadn't shared with many others. They'd been comrades in the best sense of the word.

McColl remembered Kerzhentsev saying that the picture of his wife that he carried in his head was all he needed. And the love in his eyes when he said it.

Stopping in the middle of the empty lane, McColl stared up at the heavens and said good-bye, then resumed his onward march. According to his map, which he'd studied at length the previous night, there was a ferry some twenty-five miles to the south.

✦ ✦ ✦

WHEN HE REACHED THE DNIEPER an hour before dawn, an almost-full moon was hanging low above the steppe beyond, casting reflections the color of clotted cream across the slow-flowing river. It was beautiful beyond words, but all McColl could think of was Kerzhentsev's wife and children. He didn't even know their names.

As the world grew lighter, he studied the landing stage below. There was no one waiting for the ferry, but he saw a simple rowboat tethered to a similar stage on the eastern bank. The river was about six hundred yards wide, the current difficult to judge. A hard row, but better than swimming.

When a man appeared on the other side, McColl went down to the empty stage and rang the bell that hung from the wooden post. The man waved back but showed no inclination to cross. He was, it seemed, waiting for someone to share the oars.

McColl sat down and waited, trying to keep his impatience in check. He wasn't expecting to see any troops, but the local commander might have ordered a plane or two aloft. The shooting of two German soldiers wasn't something he could afford to take lightly.

If McColl were caught up in a sweep and the boys had not been captured, the Khristian Vissotsky papers might be enough to keep him free. He had ditched the Arkady Belov papers in a foul-smelling pool not far from the river and after some thought had dropped the bombs in after them. Anyone taking a swim in such water was bound to have a death wish.

After about an hour, two would-be passengers arrived on the opposite bank and the ferry started off. The crossing took about twenty minutes, the ferryman steering the boat in a wide half circle to compensate for the current. By the time it arrived, the passenger who'd shared the rowing duties looked utterly exhausted.

The ferryman wanted to wait for another passenger and refused to proceed until McColl agreed to pay double. The trip was conducted in silence, which was fine by McColl, who needed all his energy for pulling on the oars. A sleepless night and a twenty-five-mile hike had not been the ideal preparation.

It seemed wise to get some distance from the river, so he walked for almost an hour before laying himself down in a small copse of trees. He was almost out when he heard the plane and blessed his luck in getting off the open road. The sleep that followed was fitful, but when he finally opened his eyes, the sun's position suggested that six or seven hours had passed. He stayed where he was, eating half the bread he'd kept in reserve. A stream running along one edge of the copse provided some brackish water.

There were about two hours of daylight remaining when he decided to risk going on. The station he wanted to reach—the third to the east of Kiev on the route to Moscow—was around forty miles to the north, and by the time darkness fell, he should have managed ten. Another thirty overnight, and he'd be there by dawn, waiting for a train. Always assuming some were running. If none were, he had no idea what he'd do. Walk all the way to Moscow? He didn't know how far it was, but five hundred miles seemed optimistic.

The sun was well below the western horizon when he came to the crossroads and saw the signpost. Many had mysteriously disappeared when the Germans invaded, but this one had somehow survived. There were four villages named, and one of them was Bucha.

Where had he heard that name?

The consul from Kiev. The dark blue Pathfinder.

McColl laughed. Surely it couldn't still be there.

And if it was, there wouldn't be anything like enough petrol.

And even if, by some wonderful chance, there was fuel enough to reach Moscow, surely the last thing a fleeing British agent should do was drive across the German-occupied Ukraine in a huge, shiny automobile.

If there were an easier way of drawing attention to himself, he couldn't think what it might be.

It was a daft idea, but he couldn't resist it.

According to the sign, Bucha was three versts—two miles—away. An hour or so later, having asked directions and bought some bread from a woman in the nearby village, McColl was gazing at the consul's dacha, a cottage of around four rooms with verandas on three sides. It looked abandoned but was still in one piece, the windows shuttered, front door locked and chained.

The garage was around the back, a recent addition built in brick. This had also been padlocked, but someone had levered it open.

And presumably stolen the consul's beloved car.

McColl pushed his way into the darkness and immediately walked into something metal. A lighted match confirmed it was the Pathfinder, which looked as splendid as its owner had claimed.

Noticing a pair of candles, he applied a match to each. And there, stacked against the far wall, were at least a dozen cans of Russian petrol.

The only complication was the boy in the Pathfinder's passenger seat, now rubbing his eyes in the sudden glare.

11
Czars of All Sizes

After the mass shooting of the Bolsheviks at the wayside halt, the nightmarish quality of Caitlin's journey across Siberia grew no less intense. Over the next twenty-four hours, her train arrived at two stations liberally littered with corpses, in one case those of Bolsheviks, in the other of their local White opponents. On each occasion a mass grave was dug by volunteers, the bodies all tipped in and thinly covered with earth.

Over the next hundred miles, she and her fellow passengers came across four armored trains—two Bolshevik, one White, and one Czech. Each delayed them for several hours, as far as Caitlin could see for no other reason than that they could. Only the Whites bothered to check the passengers' papers, and then in perfunctory fashion. All were keen to hear about the other armored trains: where they'd been seen, how many men they carried, what sort of guns they had. Caitlin was spared the last question. As a woman she was not expected to know one gun from another.

Omsk, when they finally reached it, was still held by the Bolsheviks. The line divided here. The fork heading northwestward toward Yekaterinburg was in Bolshevik hands but closed for the moment, allegedly on account of a broken bridge. The other fork, which ran westward to Czech-held Chelyabinsk, was wholly under Czech control and supposedly still open for civilian traffic.

After their last experience with the Czechs, Caitlin and Brady were willing to take that route, but the Bolshevik-led railwaymen in Omsk, wary of losing a precious train, decided to suspend all further westbound traffic until the next meeting of the local soviet. This was in four days' time.

Though frustrated by the delay, Caitlin lost no time in seeking out a decent bed and bath. Her Baedeker recommended the Rossiya Hotel, which was just as well, because most of the others seemed closed. From her window Omsk had the air of a ghost town, an impression confirmed when she went for a walk. The general post office was open for business, but only if the business was local—the world beyond was out of reach, whether by letter, phone, or telegraph. Letters for America—here a sad shake of the head—would be better posted from Moscow. Or perhaps from Vladivostok, depending which way madam was headed.

Madam was beginning to wonder. In Nikolskaya Square she found two elegant churches and a military school, all bedecked in slogans, all having suffered serious damage. She walked the length of Lyubinski Prospect, passing the closed Museum of the Imperial Russian Geographical Society and a boarded-up municipal theater. Some of the original fortress was still standing, but not the part where Dostoyevsky had spent his four years of imprisonment and written *Buried Alive: Or, Ten Years of Penal Servitude in Siberia*. Retracing her steps, she sought out the US consular agent, whose address was listed in her Baedeker. He was gone—several months ago, according to a neighbor—and Caitlin found it difficult to blame him. For those who weren't locked up, Omsk didn't seem like a hard place to leave.

The hotel was just about acceptable. There was hot water on only two occasions during her four-day stay, but the food was better than anything she'd eaten in Petrograd over the previous winter, and the bed, though lumpy, was a good deal more comfortable than any train seat. The Cheka officer who called to examine her papers was courteous to a fault and much impressed by her personal acquaintance with Yakov Peters. If he also seemed nervous and tense, then so did the town. Some of the people she spoke to were eager to welcome the Czechs, hoping, perhaps naïvely, that these foreign soldiers would protect them from their own warring countrymen.

The day of the scheduled meeting arrived. It was held around the turntable at the locomotive depot, the soviet delegates filling the adjoining tracks and cinder paths, a host of interested onlookers lining the footplates of the stabled engines. "Industrial theater" was the phrase that came to Caitlin's mind. A workers' Delphi.

The evening was hot and humid, and no one seemed in a very good temper, but all were determined to have their say. Caitlin had been to several such meetings in Petrograd, but this one felt different—in what way she wasn't quite sure. Almost all those present were Russian, so why would the Siberian setting make any difference? It was, she decided, more to do with the passage of time. The Bolshevik revolution was now over six months old, and the papers she'd read in Omsk were full of the threats now facing Lenin's government. The revolt of the Czech Legion had emboldened all its enemies, from anarchists and dissenting socialists to those who dreamed of restoring the czar. Add a few Allied troops to the mix, not to mention pots of Allied money, and further reverses seemed more than likely.

Bolshevism was on the defensive, was fighting for its life, and she could hear it in these voices. The joyous optimism had vanished, at least for the moment. Now there was defiance, and not a little fear.

Compared to this, the business of running which trains on which lines was something of a footnote. The decision was made to resume services on the Chelyabinsk section, partly to create some space in the overfull yards but mostly in the hope of securing a working alliance with the Czechs who held the western part of the line. The Bolsheviks were still in charge of Omsk, but without new friends or reinforcements their chances of remaining so were much in the balance, and they knew it.

The vote was almost unanimous—the first train would leave at seven the next morning.

～ ～ ～

IT LEFT AT TEN. THE endless forest seemed to be behind them; now it was steppe and occasional trees stretching into the distance. There were fields of wheat and rye close to the widely spaced settlements, but the overriding impression remained one of emptiness, of a land so vast it could never be filled.

They met their first Czech train in early afternoon and were soon given leave to proceed. A second encounter took longer, but the result was the same, and by the time darkness fell, Caitlin was thinking the Urals might soon be in reach. She woke around dawn to the ominous sensation of the train running backward.

This was Kurgan, and they were being shunted into a siding. It was midmorning before an explanation was forthcoming—all civilian traffic between there and Chelyabinsk was suspended, and their train would be held for an indefinite period. Brady went off to investigate and returned an hour later with even worse news. The Czechs had decided to use the train, suitably armored, on the diverging line to Yekaterinburg, most of which remained in Bolshevik hands. Its passengers were effectively stranded in Kurgan.

Brady went off again without saying where he was going. Uncertain what to do, Caitlin decamped to the station's restaurant and sipped her way through two glasses of tea while she waited for his return. Heaven, she decided, would be a place where trains ran on schedule.

It was early afternoon when he finally came back. "I've found some comrades," he told her. "And they're heading north tonight. The front line between the Czechs and the Bolsheviks is about ten versts up the line to Yekaterinburg, and they say we can walk around it. Are you game?"

BRADY'S NEW FRIENDS WERE THREE in number—two men in their thirties and a woman who seemed slightly younger. All had vaguely Asiatic coloring and features; all were wearing Russian trousers and peasant tunics. The men also wore caps, the woman only a bright red head scarf wound around her braided black hair. They looked nervous, and with reason.

According to Brady they had returned from an out-of-town trip in time to see some comrades led away by local Whites. Hoping to find other comrades at the office of the town soviet, they had hurried in that direction, only to realize, as they rounded the last corner, that the enemy was already ensconced. They had ducked back into the shadows, kept the building under observation, and let themselves into the ransacked rooms when the Whites had finally left. Guessing that the place was unlikely to be searched again, they had opted to stay until nightfall, when darkness would cover an escape from the town. And then Brady had arrived and taken it upon himself to explore the seemingly empty building. The woman, whose name was Olga, had managed to persuade her comrades that shooting the lone intruder would only draw attention to their presence. Instead she had gone out to talk to him and discovered they were on the same side. A little more conversation and Brady had convinced the Bolsheviks to take him and Caitlin along that night.

How did he do it? she wondered that evening as the five of them filed through the office's back door. The man had such a forceful air about him that he was almost irresistible. She could see how Colm had been swept away, not that that excused the sweeper.

With the gas lamps unlit and the moon still low, the streets were truly dark. There were bursts of gunfire in the distance, but not from the direction in which they were heading, and soon they were leaving the town's last houses behind. After traipsing through several fields of crops and passing a single unlit cottage, they finally reached the relative safety of the woods. The rising path seemed barely marked to Caitlin, but Olga strode on without hesitation, and after a while they could see the railway line down to their left.

They had walked only a couple of versts, Caitlin thought—ten would take some doing. When one of the comrades had offered to carry her suitcase, she'd fought off the feminist urge to refuse, thinking she might slow everyone down. One of her better decisions.

The path wound on, passing through stretches of forest and clearing. The humid air stuck Caitlin's blouse to her back; the cloying smells of the grasses and trees tickled her nose and made her want to sneeze. Small clouds of insects would rear up in her face and cause her to duck, but she never saw any of the unknown animals who rustled away through the undergrowth as human feet drew near.

It was almost two in the morning when Olga called a sudden halt and pointed out two faint orange lights in the distance. Ten more minutes of walking brought a better view—the lights were fires, lit by the Czechs on either side of the line below. A short train was also visible, a locomotive and a single carriage, motionless on the track. Heavy guns of some sort were positioned on either side, and what looked like trenches had been dug from the line to the edge of the trees.

A hundred yards or so to the north, the single track passed over a small river, and some way beyond the low bridge there was another small cluster of lights. The Bolsheviks, Caitlin assumed. That two small forces should be facing each other across a probably nameless river in the middle of nowhere seemed more than a little absurd, but she supposed that every battle counted.

After stressing the need for quiet, Olga led them on, moving away from the tracks and eventually reaching the bank of the river a few hundred yards downstream from the bridge. They waded across, making less noise than Caitlin had feared and attracting no attention from the soldiers up on the line.

As they approached the Bolshevik positions across a grassy meadow, the sense of relief was intense. And premature. They were no more than fifty yards away when an animal—most likely a rabbit or hare—leaped out from under one of the Russians' feet, causing him to yelp in shock and someone else to pull a trigger.

As Caitlin threw herself to the ground, she heard a grunt of surprise.

"Stop! We're comrades!" Olga was screaming. "Comrades!" she kept yelling, until the firing abruptly stopped.

Caitlin lay there trembling while one of the Bolshevik soldiers demanded names and proof of loyalty.

"Stand up," Olga was saying, her voice much weaker. "They want us to stand up."

Caitlin was unhurt, but it took everything she had to get back onto her feet. Brady was still in one piece, as was one of the Russian men, but Olga's blouse was black with blood, and the other man was lost in the grass. Dead, as they soon discovered, a bullet through either cheek and the back of his head blown off.

OLGA WAS CARRIED OFF THE train at Shadrinsk, where the doctor hoped there might be enough blood to save her. Her comrade stayed with her, but Caitlin and Brady traveled on in the Red Guard train as guests of its commander, a middle-aged Ukrainian named Mantsev who claimed he had danced with Kollontai before she discovered politics.

Caitlin's own escape had left her shaken, but the commander's vodka had a calming effect, and the man's most interesting story— told when he was well in his cups—took her mind off everything else. According to Mantsev, the czar and his family had recently been brought to Yekaterinburg and were now imprisoned in a big mansion on Tolmacheva Street. The house had belonged to an old Ukrainian school friend of his, but the local Cheka had ordered him out.

This was all top secret, he added sternly, a finger placed across his lips to reinforce the message.

A bit late for that, was Caitlin's opinion. The thought of interviewing the fallen czar was an intoxicating one, and after the journey they'd had, another short stop would barely register.

Brady was keen to press on, and when he suggested that they meet again in Moscow, she didn't demur. She couldn't say she felt any warmer toward him, but there were so many points of connection—the Wobblies, Colm, their recent journey—that she found it hard to imagine not keeping in touch.

Once they'd said their good-byes, she took a droshky into town. The American Hotel still bore that name, but probably not for much longer—once Wilson joined the other Allies in their military intervention, a rechristening seemed likely. A room was available, and there were no raised eyebrows when she asked after Tolmacheva Street. If the czar and his family were there, the receptionist was not aware of it.

Up in her room, she opened the window to let in some air, and then she lay on the bed, trying to work out how best to make her pitch. Nothing persuasive occurred to her, and pictures of Olga kept popping into her mind. Standing in the tall grass with blood coursing from her side. Pale as death when they lifted her out of the train at Shadrinsk. Caitlin didn't even know the woman's second name.

AT NINE THE NEXT MORNING, she presented herself at the Regional Soviet of the Urals. After showing her press accreditation, she was ushered into another room and made to wait no more than a few minutes before a young official arrived. He brusquely refused her request for an interview and denied the facts on which it was based. The czar and his family were not in Yekaterinburg, and spreading such a dangerous falsehood could land her in serious trouble.

She could see the lie in his eyes but knew there was no point in calling him out. She thanked him and left, feeling more determined than ever—as her aunt had often told her growing up, she didn't take well to being told no.

At the very least, she would find the house. The northern end of Tolmacheva Street, as the hotel's map of the town informed her, was less than a verst away. After walking to that point and staring down the suspiciously empty street, she decided that she would be less conspicuous in a carriage. When a droshky finally appeared, she asked the driver to carry her down to the church that was visible at the end of the road.

The mansion was easy to spot: the sentries at the gate, the new wooden fence, and the whitewashed upstairs windows all suggested a place of confinement. The house was two stories high and at least a hundred feet long, with arched dormer windows at either end of the roof. It was also built into a slope, which offered the prospect of better views from behind.

At the church she paid off the driver, waited until he was out of sight, and started walking back toward the mansion. She was resigned to not gaining entry—though climbing the fence wouldn't be difficult, the chances of getting in and out without being seen were vanishingly small, and the consequent punishment might be severe. But as far as she knew, there wasn't a law against looking through windows.

As she walked on, she found herself wondering why the czar and his family were here in Yekaterinburg. The fact that it was far from any border—and thus from any would-be foreign rescuers—had no doubt played a part in the original decision, but the march of events had moved on. Now that the Bolsheviks had lost their grip on large chunks of Siberia, a domestic rescue, by the Whites or their Czech allies, seemed a much more likely possibility.

What would the Bolsheviks in Yekaterinburg do if the enemy closed in? They couldn't let the czar become a rallying point for their opponents. They would have to move him again—or kill him. And killing him would be effective only if they also killed his heirs. Every last one of them.

Caitlin felt no sympathy for Nicholas and his wife, who had ruled Russia with a criminal lack of human feeling. But whatever political logic dictated, she couldn't condone the killing of children.

She was drawing close to the mansion. There were others on the street now, just ordinary people going about their business—a couple of men, a woman with a small daughter. And rain was beginning to fall, just a few spots so far, but the dark clouds threatened more. There was only one sentry at the gate, and he was looking inward, talking to someone inside the courtyard.

As she walked along the front fence, she saw no gaps to peer through. Reaching its end, she stopped to look back; seeing no one, she started up the grassy slope between the mansion and its neighbor. The fence remained impervious, so she kept walking up, toward the trees that stood atop the hill. When she turned to take a second look, most of the mansion's rear façade was visible, but on this side, too, the upper windows had been rendered opaque, and there were no signs of any residents.

The hand on her shoulder was far from gentle.

"What are you doing here?" one of the Red Guards asked as the other yanked her purse from her hand.

"Just looking," she said, like a guilty child.

They each grabbed an arm and hustled her back down the slope to the street. For a naïve second, she thought they intended to let her go, but another quick march past a couple of dumbstruck locals brought them all to the gates. Once inside the courtyard, she was stood against a wall and ordered not to move. Was she about to be shot? Her mind refused to believe it, but her heart seemed less convinced, beating at twice its normal rate.

As the Red Guards returned with a single companion—surely not enough for a firing squad—two stable doors swung open to reveal a garaged car. It was the first she'd seen since Omsk, and it was flying a Cheka flag.

She was bundled into the back, the new man up front by the driver, holding her purse in his lap. When she asked him where they were going, he simply ignored her.

Not that she had any doubts. The Cheka headquarters were in the old czarist police station, a few hundred yards to the north of her hotel, which they passed on the journey. She hadn't seen much friendliness in the eyes that followed their car, and there wasn't much here, the duty officer holding her papers up to the light as if expecting forgeries.

A long wait ensued, during which several Chekists walked past without so much as a glance. Either they'd all been neutered or the month on the Trans-Siberian had finally destroyed her looks. When allowed to use the bathroom, she peered at her face in the badly cracked mirror and had to admit there was much to deplore. But there was no sign of any lasting damage. She hadn't lost her beauty, merely mislaid it.

The thought didn't cheer her up for long. When she was finally taken in for interrogation, the man across the desk seemed like every White's stereotype of a Chekist—all sneers, threats, and ready assumptions of guilt. To make things worse, his quick speech and strange accent were hard to understand.

The questions came thick and fast. What had she been doing there? How had she known that the czar and his family were held there? Who was she working for?

She tried to explain. A Red Guard had told her about the czar being in a house on Tolmacheva Street, a Red Guard on the train from Kurgan—she had never learned his name. And she had guessed from the fence which house it was. As a journalist she had simply been curious. Her American readers might not like the czar, she added disarmingly, but they would be interested to know what had happened to him. And she herself—she had to admit it—had been intrigued by the possibility of actually seeing one of the family at a window.

He smiled at that. She was lying, of course. Only a White spy would have thought up such a story. A spy in league with those who wished to rescue the autocrat and his brood. A spy taking notes on the house and its defenses.

Here he picked up her reporter's notebook and waved it in her face.

"No," she said. "Absolutely not."

He just looked at her.

"I have important friends in the party," she said, playing what looked like her only card. "I am a friend of Alexandra Kollontai. And of Volodarsky. I know Yakov Peters."

Peters's name rang a bell.

"They will all vouch for me," she said confidently. "Yakov Peters will." She knew that Kollontai and Volodarsky would and saw no reason that Peters wouldn't. She had carried his letters.

"We shall see," he said. "In the meantime you will be held downstairs."

"Why not let me return to my hotel?" she asked. "I promise not to leave."

He laughed at that, and two minutes later one of his men was showing her into a cell. It had one small window high in the wall, an upturned bucket in the corner, a couple of unlit candles lying on a badly stained mattress.

Once the door had slammed shut behind her, she lowered herself to the floor and fought the urge to cry. She knew she'd behaved like a fool and could only hope that the men upstairs would realize the same.

12

The Boy in the Front Seat

His name was Fyodor Vladimirovich Rozmirov, but he told McColl to call him Fedya. Once the boy realized that the intruder not only wanted his bed but also planned on driving it away, he insisted on being taken along. When McColl refused, Fedya threatened to wake the nearby village and have him arrested for theft.

McColl considered pulling out his gun, but only for a second. Fedya would assume he was bluffing, and Fedya would be right. And it occurred to McColl that the boy might provide useful camouflage—what sort of foreign agent would travel with a child?

"What's *your* name?" Fedya asked with some truculence.

"Khristian Sergeyevich Vissotsky," McColl told him. "And if I take you with me, you must pretend to be my son."

Fedya thought about that for a second, then nodded his agreement. "Fyodor Khristianovich Vissotsky," he said, trying it on for size. "Do I have a mother?"

"She died five years ago."

Fedya looked like he might burst into tears. He was painfully thin, with tousled light brown hair, large eyes, and a face that seemed too old for his body. His clothes and shoes were falling apart. "My mother died at Easter," he said solemnly. "Before we go, I must visit her grave."

"I'm sorry," McColl said. "You must do that. But first we need to know if this automobile will run." He looked around for the starting handle and found it hanging on a peg. After checking the oil and petrol, he gave the handle a hopeful turn, and much to his surprise the engine roared into life.

Fedya looked astonished—and not a little frightened.

"How old are you?" McColl asked, turning the engine off again.

"Eleven?" It was as much a question as an answer.

"And are you from this village?"

"No. We came from our farm, a long way away. That way," he added, gesturing toward the west. "The nearest town was Jitomir."

McColl had no idea where that was.

"My mother and father were Russians, not Ukrainians," Fedya insisted, in a tone that suggested he thought that highly significant. "We escaped from the Germans. But my mother was sick, and she died on the road, not far from this village."

"What about your father?"

Fedya shrugged. "He went off to the war, and my mother said he died. My sister died, too. There was only my mother and me."

"And the village took you in?"

The boy gave McColl a telling look. "They didn't drive me out."

"So where do you want to go? I'm only going to Kozelets and the railway station there."

"Will there be trains to Moscow?"

"I hope so. But why would you want to go there?"

"My uncle is in Moscow. Look." He produced a piece of paper from his pocket, on which someone had scribbled an address. "My mother had it," he said. "One of the men in the village told me it's where he lives."

McColl had never heard of Grocholski Street. "It's in Moscow?"

Fedya shrugged. "It must be."

McColl handed back the piece of paper. Moments like this he felt torn between weeping and shooting someone.

"Let's say good-bye to your mother," he suggested.

It was almost fully dark, the stars providing only a glimmer of light, but Fedya led the way across the fields at a brisk pace. The graveyard was a few hundred yards distant, a small fenced area with fifty or so plots on the edge of the village. The same ground was probably reused every few generations—why waste land on the dead when the living needed food? The grave of Fedya's mother was off to one side, a mound that seemed too short for a grown-up, a simple cross of birch twigs at its head.

Fedya sank to his knees, put his hands together, and began a one-sided conversation. He was going to Moscow, he told her, and there he would find her brother. He would come back and see her as soon as he could.

There were tears on his cheeks when he got to his feet, and McColl could feel a few on his own. "We'll drive in the dark," he told Fedya as the two of them made their way back to the dacha. "The Germans don't fly at night."

Relighting the candles, he searched the garage shelves for things that might prove useful. A hammer and wrench were discovered, along with a British army water flask that reminded McColl of his time in South Africa. Best of all, a large tarpaulin was already folded up in the trunk—the consul hadn't wanted his precious car to get wet.

It was time to go. After sending the boy to fill their flask at the dacha's well, McColl put his shoulder to the back of the car and rolled it out of the garage. Waiting for Fedya's return, he thought about taking more petrol. They wouldn't need more to reach Kozelets, but what if there weren't any trains? If the car was their only way onward, it would be stupid to run out of fuel.

He added three cans to the boot, using the tarp to buffer them. With that much petrol, they might reach Moscow, if no one got in their way. Which of course someone would.

Returning with a full flask, the boy took his place in the passenger seat.

"Don't you have any . . . possessions?" McColl asked.

Fedya just looked bewildered.

McColl turned the starting handle again, with the same impressive result. He could see why the consul had liked his car.

The track that had brought him to the dacha was in good

condition—presumably at the owner's insistence—and the starry sky was bright enough for navigation, provided he kept below ten miles an hour. Once they were a decent distance away from the village, he turned on the lights, and Fedya let out a gasp of delight. McColl was more pleased with the engine's satisfied purr.

"Could I do what you're doing?" the boy asked.

"Drive the car? Not until you're bigger—your feet wouldn't reach the pedals."

Fedya was crestfallen for a moment but soon recovered. "Are you from Moscow?" he asked.

"Yes. And so are you, remember?"

"I remember. So why are we here?"

It was a good question. "Visiting relatives," McColl decided. He needed to get the boy some better clothes, he realized, if they were traveling to Moscow together. Clothes like his own, which looked as though they might stay on.

"Are your mother and father alive?" Fedya asked.

"No."

"What work do you do?"

"I'm a photographer," McColl remembered.

"What's that?"

"I draw pictures with a special machine."

"Oh. Where is it?"

"In Moscow."

"So what are you doing here? Really, I mean."

"Fighting the Germans," seemed a safe enough answer. "But they almost caught me in Kiev, so I had to escape in a hurry."

Fedya took a while to absorb this information. "Are there Germans in Moscow?" he asked eventually.

"No. Now, why don't you get some sleep," McColl advised.

"I'm not tired."

"Well, just stop talking, then. I need to concentrate."

Fedya did as he was told but showed no sign of dropping off. He had probably never been in a moving car before, and the circumstances were such that even McColl found the drive absorbing. Motoring down dark Ukrainian tracks at ten miles an hour, the headlights illuminating an ever-changing world of insects and scurrying mammals, was an almost hypnotic experience, not one he'd expected to have, particularly with an eleven-year-old child in tow.

He made frequent stops to consult his map and took to dousing the headlights whenever they passed through a village of any size, lest it harbor a German outpost. What the locals awakened by the Pathfinder's engine made of it all was an interesting question—no doubt some knew of motorized vehicles, but few would have actually seen or heard one. McColl could imagine the pillow conversations after the noise had faded—what in God's name was that?

Progress was slow, and by the time the first hint of light appeared on the eastern horizon, he reckoned they had traveled only about twenty crow-flying miles. Dog-tired and aware that driving in daylight would be asking for trouble, he pulled the car off the track beside one of many copses and carefully inched it in among the trees, where, draped in the tarpaulin, it would be hard to spot from the air.

THERE WERE NO SCARES DURING the day. If a plane flew over, it was high and quiet enough not to wake them. If anyone passed on the road, whoever it might be was either wearing blinkers or thought it wiser to leave people in strange machines alone. When McColl awoke that afternoon, the Mauser was still where he'd cached it and there wasn't a peasant in sight.

They left an hour or so later, stopping in the first village to beg water and buy some bread. The automobile's appearance caused a few mouths to gape, but the villagers were friendly enough and willing to take McColl's kopecks. Getting the local children off the running boards took a while, but eventually the two of them were able to leave, heading north through the twilight as a huge red sun sank into the western horizon.

Fedya had been saving up questions. "Why are the Germans here in Ukraine?" he asked McColl. "What do they want?"

"Grain for their people back in Germany, who are hungry because of the war. And oil to run their armies and factories. They don't have enough of their own."

"Because of the war?"

"Yes."

"But didn't they start the war? If they hadn't started it, they wouldn't need more food and oil, would they?"

McColl couldn't help smiling. "No, they wouldn't."

"So why did they start it?"

McColl considered. "You know there are some men who can never get enough. Of food or possessions or land or whatever. Well, if one of those men ends up in charge of a country, then it becomes the country that can't get enough. And when it tries to take what it wants from other countries, then you end up with a war."

Fedya thought about that. "When I asked my uncle why Germany attacked Russia, he said it was because someone was killed somewhere else—I don't remember where he said it happened, but the man who was killed wasn't a German or a Russian."

"It was an Austrian that was killed. By a Serbian. In a place called Sarajevo."

"So why . . . ?"

"Because Austria was friends with Germany and Serbia was friends with Russia."

Fedya was silent.

"Do you understand?"

"Yes. I understand. But I've never met a Serbian. And I don't think my father did either. It seems stupid."

McColl sighed. "You're not alone in thinking that."

IT TOOK THAT NIGHT AND another to reach the outskirts of Kobizhcha, the small town on the Moscow line where he hoped to catch a train. Once he was sure he was in the right place, McColl turned the Pathfinder around and found somewhere safe to leave it while he did a reconnoiter. Persuading Fedya to stay with the car was the hardest part—the child needed more than a little convincing that his protector was coming back, and it was only when McColl pointed out that he was leaving all his things behind that the boy decided to acquiesce.

It was a three-mile walk to the town and half a mile more to the station. Kobizhcha seemed unusually busy for five in the morning, with lights burning in many windows and several people out on the street. Those that noticed McColl seemed unsurprised, as if used to the presence of strangers, and the railway station, observed from a discreet distance, confirmed as much. It had all the appearance of a semipermanent camp, and the German vehicles parked to one side offered a stark reminder of Chaplino Junction. Eyeing the platform and its carpet of still-sleeping bodies, McColl wondered which would arrive first—a Moscow-bound train or some monocled caesar hungry for hostages.

In less than an hour, he was back with Fedya and the Pathfinder. "Too many Germans," he told the boy. "And no sign of a train. We'll find somewhere to sleep, then go on tonight in the car."

"IS IT A REAL BORDER?" Fedya asked. Two more days had passed, and according to the villager whom McColl had just questioned, it was only fifty versts away. "I thought Ukraine was part of Russia," the boy went on when McColl failed to answer.

"Not anymore. Or not for the moment at least. Everything's up in the air until the war ends. If the Germans lose, they'll have to leave Ukraine, and then I don't know what will happen. Some people here like being part of Russia, some like being independent. I don't suppose most people care one way or the other, but the ones who do will probably fight each other."

"Another war?"

"I wouldn't bet against it."

"What do you know about the Socialist Revolutionaries?" Fedya asked, apparently changing the subject.

"They're a political party. They and the Bolsheviks were the two main parties in the new Russian government until a couple of months ago. Then there was a big falling-out, and the Socialist Revolutionaries left. Why do you ask?"

"My uncle is one. Why did they fall out?"

"The Bolsheviks wanted peace with the Germans at any price, but the Socialist Revolutionaries didn't."

"Why did the Bolsheviks want peace?" Fedya asked, sounding almost indignant.

"Because millions of soldiers had died and the ones who were left didn't want to fight anymore."

Fedya thought about that and agreed it sounded sensible. "So why did the Socialist Revolutionaries want to carry on?"

"Well, that's more complicated. I think they believed that ending the war would strengthen the German czar and that doing so would weaken the revolutionaries in Germany. And that if there were no German revolution, then the Russian Revolution would have a hard job surviving on its own."

"So who was right?"

McColl shook his head. "I don't know. Maybe they both were."

"I expect my uncle will know."

"Probably."

"So what do the Bolsheviks want? Are they good people?"

"Some of them must be. They say their revolution is for ordinary people, and so far that looks true. They've given the peasants the land they work, and they've given workers more say in how their factories are run."

"So who doesn't like them?"

"Well, the people who used to own the land and run the factories for a start. And . . . well, it's complicated."

"It doesn't sound it."

"It is. For example, sometimes the workers don't know as much about running their factory as the people who ran it before."

"They can learn."

McColl laughed. "You may be right. I hope so."

And he did, he thought later, driving through the night with Fedya asleep at his side. It would be wonderful if something truly good came out of the war, if the terrible slaughter proved an unintended midwife for something better to be born, a world in which men—and women—had more control over their work and their lives, in which they weren't forced or fooled into fighting for people with whom they had nothing in common and into fighting against those who lived similar lives and shared much the same concerns, albeit in a different language.

Why did that seem so unlikely? Why did he find it so hard to believe? Two questions, he realized. They always got put together, but were they really one and the same? Should the world change? Could it change? Those who thought it should often assumed it could, as if right would always find a way. But what if it didn't? The struggle might last a hundred years and then only end in defeat.

He and Caitlin had often talked about this, and he found himself wondering how, and in what directions, her experience over the last few months had influenced her thoughts. Was she still in Russia, and, if so, might she be in Moscow? He knew of course that he shouldn't seek her out. What was the phrase?—a conflict of interests. He didn't know what Cumming wanted of him in the new Russian capital, but it was hard to believe that the Germans would still be his principal foe. And any association with a foreign enemy of the Bolshevik regime would render Caitlin's situation as a journalist impossible, if not downright dangerous.

HE DROVE ON THROUGH ANOTHER night, tacking this way and that down the lanes and tracks, keeping the mostly visible polestar at roughly ten o'clock. There wasn't enough light to drive without the headlights, and driving with them on was like boring through an endless tunnel. After eight hours of that, dawn came as a revelation. The plain opened up around them, dotted with trees and occasional settlements. Some of the latter seemed dead, as if war or something worse had drained them of life, leaving the cottages vacant and forlorn amid a sea of dried-out crops. Others seemed the opposite, as if the war had passed them by and things went on as they always had, smoke curling up from the chimneys, fields of golden wheat shifting in the breeze.

The roads were mostly empty—a few carts, the odd peasant on foot, an occasional group of refugees. Each time they inched their way past one of the latter, McColl expected pleas for assistance, but none were ever forthcoming. For all the relevance the Pathfinder had to their lives, it might have been one of H. G. Wells's Martian spaceships.

The only motorized transport they saw belonged to the Germans, and they were lucky the Germans didn't see them. They had started off early, hoping to reach the Moscow highway before night-fall. McColl was driving down a tree-lined lane that reminded him of France when he spotted what looked like a moving dust cloud above the low rise to their right. There was no hiding place available—all he could do was bring their car to a halt.

It was a column of motorized lorries, moving from right to left along the sought-after highway. Dusk was beginning to darken the landscape, and the shadows thrown by the trees offered an added layer of gloom, but McColl was still astonished that none of the Germans noticed the stationary car in the side road, barely two hundred yards away. Astonished and very relieved.

THEY MADE GOOD PROGRESS AFTER that. The highway, though showing obvious signs of neglect, remained smooth and straight enough for driving without lights, and over the first hour McColl sustained a dizzying speed of fifteen miles an hour. Since any Germans driving toward them would be burning their lights, he thought he'd have time to get out of their way.

As they went through one small town, he noticed what looked like a school and wondered if Fedya had ever attended one. He asked him.

"Of course," Fedya answered. "When I was a child," he added. "But the teacher didn't teach us much. My mother said he was good in the beginning, but his wife died, and then he started drinking too much."

"So who taught you?"

"The priest taught us about God and Jesus and the devil. But my Uncle Rodion said it was all nonsense, that priests had always told that story to give themselves a living. He said they made things up because it was easier than working." He hesitated. "I thought the priest was a good man, but what my uncle said made more sense."

"Was your uncle a farmer then?"

"No, never. My father was a farmer, but my uncle hated it. When he was young, he went off to Siberia to work on building the railway there, and he never came back to the village to stay, just to visit his brother and us. Once he joined his Socialist Revolutionaries, he used to argue with everyone and hand out leaflets and try to persuade people to join his party." Fedya smiled reminiscently. "He told me lots of stories about his heroes. They all killed people who were cruel to the poor. Some were even women—have you heard of Maria Spiridonova?"

"I have." Caitlin had interviewed the woman on more than one occasion in the previous summer and had told McColl her story on the train to Aberdeen.

"She was his favorite. Anyway, he and my father were always shouting at each other, and my father got even angrier when the war started and Uncle Rodion told the men they shouldn't go and fight." Fedya was silent for a moment, as if reliving the family dispute. "My father went off to the war, and my uncle just disappeared. He was my mother's brother, but she wouldn't talk about him after that. Not until she got sick."

IT WAS AROUND FOUR IN the morning, and the recently risen moon was washing the land in pale light when they reached the outskirts of what seemed another village. But side roads appeared, and the buildings grew more substantial, darkening the road ahead. They were off McColl's map by this time, and instinct told him they couldn't be far from Ukraine's border with Lenin's Russia.

There was every chance this town would have some sort of German garrison, but he could see no lights or movement up ahead. He drove on at a slow, even pace, keeping the sound of the engine level. The dark street opened into a moonlit central square, then entered another virtual tunnel, twisting this way and that around a large church. McColl was admiring the onion-shaped silhouette against the Milky Way when Fedya let out a yelp and a very German voice screamed, "Halt!"

The shouted order came from behind them, and far as McColl could see, there was nobody up ahead. Several thoughts crossed his mind—that refusal might be fatal, that surrender might be too, that the border might be only minutes away. "Get your head down!" he told Fedya, lowering his own and ramming his foot down on the accelerator.

One second, two seconds. There were no shots.

Why the hell not? He glanced at the side mirror, expecting only darkness, but a light was moving on the road behind. Were they being chased?

He turned his eyes back to the road just as it vanished from sight. For a few split seconds, the airborne Pathfinder seemed confident of leaping the river but just as abruptly gave up the ghost, plunging nose-first into the glinting waters.

There was enough depth to cushion the car's encounter with the solid bed, but not enough to prevent their being thrown forward over the bonnet. After hitting bottom himself, McColl floundered around for several seconds and finally managed to get himself upright. The water came up to his chest, and there was no sign of Fedya.

A torch was waving to and fro on the broken end of what had been a bridge. "Put your hands up!" a voice cried in German.

The rear end of the car was still just above the surface. McColl waded back toward it, hoping against hope that the boy was still in his seat.

"Put your hands up or I shoot!" the man on the bridge shouted, just as Fedya broke surface with a cry of panic a few yards away.

"I must save my son!" McColl shouted back in German as he frantically waded toward the spot where the head had again disappeared. He was just thinking that the only way he'd ever find the boy was to walk into him when he did just that. Fedya seemed determined to fight him, but he finally managed to get the boy's head clear of the water.

Several torchlight beams were now focused on them. Fedya was breathing again, but there was no chance of escaping. As McColl carried the badly shaken boy to the riverbank, his thoughts turned to the possible consequences of their capture. He mentally ran through his options. Having spoken in German, could he claim to be one? No, because then his son would speak that language, and Fedya didn't. And since the Germans might retrieve Khristian Vissotsky's papers from the river, he needed to stick by that name. So . . . a photographer returning home to Moscow with his son after visiting an ailing sister in Kiev. It sounded feasible enough. But how had he come by the car, and why had he tried to run? What was he doing with the German gun, which they'd probably find in the driver's-side door?

His Service instructors had recommended keeping as close to the truth as possible. So his sister had a friend who had worked for the British consul, and the friend had told her about the car sitting in its garage, and what with the lack of trains . . . well, the consul had left it behind when he fled, and he'd seen no harm in borrowing it. Surely his German captors wouldn't get unduly upset on an Englishman's behalf?

As for trying to run away, who would stop for strangers in 1918 Ukraine? And he'd bought the gun for protection from some grand duke's nephew who'd run out of money, weeks ago in a Kiev bar. Yes, it was a German gun, but these days you could find a Mauser almost anywhere.

There were four soldiers waiting up above, all of whom looked on the wrong side of forty. "Keep your hands in the air," McColl told the boy. Their captors didn't seem trigger-happy types, but he didn't want to give them the slightest excuse.

Two of the men were gazing down at the almost-submerged automobile, already discussing how it might be salvaged. "Who are you?" one of the others asked, rifle raised.

McColl gave their names and confirmed that they were father and son.

"You are Russians?" the man asked, clearly surprised.

"Da."

"You speak German?"

"Da."

"But you are Russians?" he asked again, just to be sure.

"Da."

While one man covered them with his rifle, the other searched their soaking clothes for weapons. He found none but took the purse of coins that held all the money they had. Satisfied, he dried his hands on the front of his tunic. "Now you will come with us."

They were marched back to the church, then down a long side

street until they reached a pair of railway tracks. Beyond these McColl could see nothing but trees and open country, and for a minute or two he feared the worst. He was still wondering how to handle the situation—what should he say to Fedya?—when a light appeared ahead. It was a brazier full of blazing wood, at the gate to a newly built stockade.

One of the two men on guard was asleep, but other unlocked the padlock securing the latch, and McColl and Fedya were prodded inside. "We have done nothing wrong," McColl said in German, lest his silence be taken as an admission of guilt.

The Germans ignored him. The two who'd brought them walked off toward town, and the conscious guard started picking his nose.

Looking around, McColl could see tens of bodies spread across the beaten grass. All he could smell was shit, so he guessed they were sleeping rather than dead.

TWO FRESH SOLDIERS CAME TO collect McColl next morning. They didn't say what for, but since they'd emerged from what looked like the local command post, he assumed it was for questioning. "I won't be long," he told Fedya, hoping it was true.

Dawn had come an hour before, and McColl had been able to count his fellow detainees. There were almost a hundred inside the stockade. All were male as far as he'd been able to tell, but ten at least were boys of fourteen or less. Talking to some of the older inmates, he'd learned that most were peasants rounded up to do forced labor. The few whom the Germans had arrested for suspected involvement in resistance activities were also required to work but would probably be shot if and when their usefulness expired.

Most of the other prisoners were watching through the palisade as he was led toward the building. It was a combined cottage and barn, the latter containing a field kitchen and an open-sided dormitory for the men, the former an administrative office and living quarters for the man in charge. He was a young lieutenant, flaxen-haired and fine-boned, who looked like he wished he were somewhere else.

McColl was not offered a seat. "You speak German," the lieutenant said. It wasn't a question.

"Yes."

He answered the questions that followed with what he hoped was sufficient, but not excessive, humility. His name, his son's, his learning of their language while working for a German employer in Kiev. His and Fedya's reason for being on the road, and the parentage of the automobile now rusting in the river.

The lieutenant was interested in only one thing. "Your German will be useful," he said. "We have Russians we need to question," he added, "and if you help us in this regard for a week or so, then you and your son will be free to continue your journey."

McColl thought about asking whether his money would be returned but decided not to bother. He knew that the lieutenant had no intention of letting him go. "What about my son?" he asked. "Will he have to work?"

The lieutenant shrugged. "Some boot cleaning, laundry, cooking. Nothing too arduous. We are not savages."

Back at the stockade, McColl found that though one work party had already been taken out, the lean-faced Bolshevik named Ostrov was still there. He had come to introduce himself—and, McColl guessed, find out what he could—soon after their arrival the previous night. He seemed to exercise some authority over the other detainees, and McColl thought it prudent to explain what the Germans had asked him to do. "I agreed because I don't see what harm it can do and because they might take it out on the boy if I don't."

Ostrov gave him a long look, then nodded. "Some won't like it, but you knew that already."

"I won't let any Russian condemn himself," McColl promised. "Or betray anyone else."

MCCOLL SPENT THAT DAY AND the next with a work party, felling and chopping a line of trees a couple of versts to the north. On the third day, he was waiting to board the cart when one of the sergeants came to collect him, and McColl saw the looks of suspicion on his fellow prisoners' faces as the man led him away.

The lieutenant was sitting behind his desk. He gestured McColl toward a wooden chair, and a few moments later the sergeant returned with a well-dressed Russian couple. They looked around for seats and seemed surprised not to find any. The man was gray-haired and probably in his sixties, the woman about half that age with a mass of blonde curls that badly needed attention.

"Names," the lieutenant asked, with a nod toward McColl.

"Names," McColl repeated in Russian.

The man supplied them. Both, it turned out, were more than happy to share their life stories, particularly the most recent part, in which Bolsheviks had robbed them of everything they had. Except, that was, for the suitcases full of clothes and personal possessions that were still in the carriage on the other side of the river. Could the Germans bring the carriage across? If so, they would be on their way.

The lieutenant heard them out, his obvious boredom tempered only by fleeting sneers of contempt. "Tell them they can walk to Kiev," was his final ruling, one that McColl passed on with rather more joy than he should have.

The twosome looked stunned, and when the man opened his mouth to protest, McColl was fully expecting two new recruits for the work parties. But somehow the Russian managed to hold his tongue. A stiff bow, a curt word to the woman, and they were gone.

The newspaper on the lieutenant's desk reminded McColl that he had no idea how the war was going, and while they were waiting for another prisoner, he took the risk of asking. "It is almost over," the young German said shortly. "We will enter Paris in a few days."

"And then we can all get back to our families," McColl suggested, wishing he hadn't asked.

"Yes, of course."

A man was brought in, one whom McColl recognized from the stockade. Apprehended near a railway bridge by a German patrol, he claimed he'd been walking to the next town by the straightest route. As for the Bolshevik leaflet found in his bag—he couldn't remember where he'd picked it up, but he had to wipe his ass with something. The lieutenant was clearly suspicious, but if the Russian had followed the tracks with sabotage in mind, he obviously wasn't telling. McColl rather suspected he had been and did his best to edit out any telltale strains of defiance in the Russian's answers.

THE NEXT DAY MCCOLL WAS back with a work party, this one charged with laying carpets of logs where autumn would turn the roads to mud. Despite the lieutenant's optimism, it looked like the Germans planned on staying awhile.

The sun was hot and the work physically taxing, particularly for men who hadn't seen a decent meal in months. McColl was in better shape than most but still felt like collapsing the moment they got back to camp. Fedya, by contrast, seemed healthier and was eager to discuss his day. One reason for his fitness was the food he was scrounging and stealing, and after another boy was caught and flogged for bringing out bread for his older brother, McColl forbade Fedya to do the same.

One thing the boy *could* do in safety was keep his eyes open. Away from the camp all day and dead to the world all night, McColl had little chance of working out the German routines. And he needed to know them to plan their escape, to get the boy and himself out of danger. The camp regime could seem almost benign, but only because those in charge didn't yet feel threatened, and that might change at any moment. A local attack, news of major setbacks in France . . . who knew what might rouse the devil within? He'd seen it more than once in Belgium, seen it again at Chaplino Junction— he didn't want to see it here.

Any escape would have to be planned and executed under the noses of the other prisoners, and McColl wasn't sure how they would take it, or whom to approach for some sort of blessing. Having shared two work details and several conversations with Ostrov, he had gotten to know the Bolshevik better than anyone else. And it was Ostrov's influence, he suspected, that had saved him from suspicion, censure, and worse over his work for the Germans. If he was going to approach anyone, the Bolshevik seemed the best candidate.

✦ ✦ ✦

HE AND OSTROV WERE ON different details next day, and McColl was collected from his in midafternoon. One of the sergeants came for him on the unit's motorcycle, bouncing back along the dusty tracks with McColl's arms wrapped around his waist. McColl thought about throwing the man off but knew that his chances of keeping the bike upright would be minimal. And he couldn't leave Fedya behind.

This interrogation was conducted outdoors. The man to be questioned—a young Russian with floppy blond hair, a face set in stone, and a body that looked like it hadn't seen food in a week—was tied to a corner post of the barn, naked save for a pair of badly worn boots.

"At last," the lieutenant said, glancing up from his newspaper. "This man was caught with a bag full of dynamite. I want to know who he got it from and what he intended to do with it."

McColl put the questions into Russian.

The young man just looked at him, eyes brimming with contempt. He said nothing.

McColl repeated the question.

The Russian shook his head, and at a signal from the lieutenant the sergeant's bullwhip swished down across his back.

After the wince of pain, the slightest shake of the head.

"Again," the lieutenant said.

Rivulets of blood flowed on either side of the jutting shoulder blades. One of the watching German privates let out an audible snigger.

"Tell him this won't stop until he gives me some answers," the lieutenant said calmly.

McColl translated. He thought of adding that the German wasn't bluffing, but who was he to encourage betrayal?

The Russian seemed to know it anyway. The eyes first blinked, then closed; the skin across the cheekbones drew tighter with each cut.

Another ten strokes and the lieutenant signaled a halt. "One last chance," he said.

After translating that, McColl caught the hint of a smile.

The bullwhip sliced away at the bloody mess. McColl had just closed his eyes when the Russian made his first and last noise, a sort of "oh" that sounded more surprised than pained. The whole body shuddered, the legs sank and then gave way, until only the rope was holding the dead man up.

The lieutenant sighed with apparent frustration. "Cut him down," he told the sergeant, whose uniform was splattered with blood.

McColl took one last look at the lifeless body, wondering how the man had managed to stay silent. Even knowing that death was certain, McColl doubted that he himself could have done so.

THAT EVENING HE SPOKE TO Ostrov.

"Well, it's not that hard to get out," the Bolshevik agreed. "You could dig your way under the fence in less than an hour."

"So why aren't we trying?" McColl wanted to know.

Ostrov sniffed. "One of two reasons. When the Germans arrest people, they take the name of their villages and tell them that for every man who escapes, ten of their neighbors will be shot."

"They know I'm from Moscow," McColl pointed out.

"Well, they can't shoot ten of yours, then. But now we come to the second reason—there's nowhere to go. No village would take you in, and how would you live without food or money?"

"How far is the border?"

"More than fifty versts."

"That's not so far. What's there? Have the Germans built a fence?"

"I don't think so. They haven't had time. No, they man all the major crossing points—the trains in particular—but there's no great cordon of troops." He dropped the stub of his hand-rolled cigarette and ground it into the grass. "I'm sure there are places you can just walk across, but first you have to get there. Fifty versts is quite a way on the food they give us, and it's mostly open country. You'd have to walk it in the dark, at the end of a long day's work."

As they laid themselves out for sleep that night, McColl put the notion to Fedya. The boy was undaunted by the distance and the likely difficulties, but then eleven-year-olds were rarely the best judges of what they could do—McColl had vivid memories of being carried back down Ben Nevis after he and a school friend had embarked on an ill-considered winter climb. "We'll talk again tomorrow," he said.

WHEN MCCOLL RETURNED WITH HIS work party on the following evening, an excited Fedya was waiting. "I've got us some food," the boy said once McColl had collected his bowl of watery soup and no one could overhear them.

"I told you not—"

"I didn't bring it here," Fedya interrupted. "There's a place where the Germans pile up their rubbish, out behind the trees on the other side of their house. And when I was sent out with some stuff this morning, I realized there were places nearby where I could hide some food, and even if they found it, no one would know it was me. So the second time they sent me, I managed to wrap up two pieces of bread and hide them in among some roots. If I can do it again tomorrow and maybe the day after, then we'll have enough for a long walk, don't you think?"

"I do," McColl said. "You've done well." The boy's getting caught was an awful prospect, but so was staying where they were. Some risks would have to be taken, and, given their circumstances, it was Fedya who would have to take them. "But tomorrow," he added out loud, "promise me you'll be careful. If a day goes by without a chance, then don't worry about it. A few more days won't make any difference."

"I promise," Fedya said.

The boy was soon asleep, but anxiety kept McColl awake. After staring up at the stars for an hour, he reckoned his fellow inmates were making enough noise with their snoring to cloak the noise of a passing buffalo stampede, let alone some surreptitious digging. With only his hands for tools, he started a trial excavation by the adjacent fence and, once through the sunburned surface, found virtually no resistance. Ostrov had overestimated the difficulties, he thought. They could be under and out in less than ten minutes.

TWO NIGHTS LATER THEY WERE. It had been dark a couple of hours, and the light supplied by the crescent moon was just what the doctor ordered—bright enough to see by, dim enough to cloak their movements. Any inmates still awake showed no inclination to interfere, and the long silences that punctuated the gate guards' conversation suggested both were dozing off.

As already agreed, McColl and Fedya walked a decent distance away from the stockade before turning back toward the trees that stood behind the command post. A single kerosene lamp was burning outside the barn, but there were no lights showing in the cottage. Off to the left, the roofs of the town were silhouetted against a starstrewn sky.

McColl kept watch as Fedya retrieved the food from its hiding place. Once they'd stuffed the hunks of bread into their pockets, the two of them started walking, first across a succession of open fields, then down any track that kept the polestar on their left. An occasional bird flew over, cawing at the moon, but otherwise the silence was almost complete, and it took a while before they dared to talk. When it finally felt safe, McColl decided to share what he knew of the stars and constellations. It wasn't much, but Fedya seemed pleased to learn the names, which McColl had first heard on his ship out to South Africa, from a kindly old sergeant who loved astronomy. The man had died on Spion Kop, probably staring up at his favorite stars.

There was little to hinder their passage: the land was mostly flat, and those streams that had to be crossed were either bridged or easy to wade. They passed through several sleeping villages, but only one dog came out to confront them, and he beat a fast retreat when McColl reached down for an imaginary stone. Mile followed mile, and when dawn found them facing a fair-size river McColl thought they must have walked twenty.

There was no obvious way across—McColl felt too tired to risk the current with Fedya on his back—so he tossed a mental coin and headed north along the bank. After an hour a column of smoke appeared; another fifteen minutes and there were a dozen cottages, clustered on either end of a rickety wooden bridge.

It looked bucolic enough for safety.

As they approached the nearest cottage, a woman emerged in

the doorway, saw them, and ducked back inside. The man who took her place stood there watching for a moment, then, perhaps reassured by the sight of the boy, walked forward to his gate.

After exchanging good-mornings, McColl asked how far they were from the border.

"Ten versts. Maybe more."

"Which way is it?"

"Behind you," the man said, nodding in that direction.

"We're out of Ukraine?"

The man laughed. "I hope so."

"What's the nearest town?"

"Korop. Six versts up the river."

KOROP WAS SMALL, THE LOCAL soviet eager to help the Bolshevik photographer and his son who had escaped from German captivity. Despite an obvious shortage of food, a decent meal was provided. After eating this in front of an admiring audience, they were taken to makeshift beds in the local school and allowed to get some sleep. When morning arrived, a driver, horse, and cart were waiting to take them to Krolevets and the nearest available station.

The journey went slower thereafter, but the worst was clearly over. The committee in Krolevets was as happy to feed them as the one in Korop had been, which was just as well, given their subsequent three-day wait for a train and the much-interrupted ride to Konotop that followed, most of which they spent clinging to a carriage roof.

The next train was almost empty by current Russian standards, only eight to a compartment rather than the usual fourteen. Things got back to normal at Bryansk, and for the better part of two days and nights McColl had the boy on his lap. It was all extremely exhausting, but exhilarating, too. He remembered Caitlin saying how eager ordinary Russians were to discuss all the changes convulsing their country. In his visits home since 1914, the only real conversations about the war that McColl had overheard had all been started by bitter soldiers. But here on this train, inching its way toward Moscow, almost everyone had something to say. And perhaps even more surprisingly, most seemed ready to listen. And argue. Sometimes with a smile, sometimes not. Sometimes without much intelligence, sometimes with an almost heartbreaking natural wisdom. For the moment at least, the only thing lacking was cynicism.

Watching Fedya's eyes dart this way and that as the debates raged on, McColl had the feeling he was watching one child's education condensed into just a few days. He knew that the boy was clever—all Fedya needed was access to knowledge, and his uncle sounded like someone who would make sure he got it. The imminent prospect of their parting was more upsetting than McColl cared to admit, but it looked like he'd get the boy to Moscow, which had to be some consolation. In truth, it was the only thing he'd done in Russia that had left him feeling good about himself.

In that respect the next few weeks and months did not bode well. Only God knew exactly what Cumming had in store for him, but it was more than likely to be something that Caitlin would find reprehensible.

He wondered again if she was in Moscow. He wouldn't seek her out, but they might just run into each other. Half of him hoped they would, while the other half hoped she wasn't there, that she was safe in Brooklyn or London, waiting for the war to end, waiting for him to come home.

But that didn't sound like the woman he loved.

13
The Broken Pot

☭

The basement of the Cheka headquarters in Yekaterinburg was not where Caitlin had planned to spend the summer, but she had to admit that things could have been worse. The cell itself compared favorably with Colm's description of his in the Tower of London: it wasn't damp, there weren't any rats, and the bed was almost comfortable. The meals, though boring, were no worse than those she'd eaten in cafés the previous winter. It was surprising how quickly she got used to the smell of her own waste, and whatever it was that had bitten her all over during the first few days suddenly seemed to lose its appetite. The sky had never seemed more interesting than it did in her solitary ten-minute walks around the tiny inner courtyard.

She told herself she wasn't frightened, and most of the time she believed it. A misunderstanding, that was all. What had she actually done? They couldn't shoot her for being curious. Her friends would come through before long.

There was lots of time for thinking. She took mental walks around Brooklyn and Manhattan, conjured up memories of times with Jack, tried to get her thoughts about the revolution into some sort of order. On good days she understood why many of the revolutionaries she'd interviewed had looked back on their years of prison or exile with something approaching affection.

Caitlin knew she'd blundered on this occasion but overall saw no cause for regrets. She had tried—was still trying—to follow both her heart and her mind and try not to let either one trample all over the other.

She didn't blame the Cheka for her current predicament. With the czar in their care, of course they'd be jumpy. Who wouldn't? She had to be patient, had to wait. Sooner or later her friends would convince the men upstairs that their suspicions, though wholly understandable, were completely unfounded.

It took ten days. First she was brought to a bathroom, then given back her suitcase and allowed to change her clothes. Upstairs in the familiar office, her interrogator told her that references had arrived from both Kollontai and Volodarsky and that she was being released. He apologized for her incarceration, but only, she suspected, because a failure to do so might bring repercussions.

She thanked him anyway and accepted his offer of a ride to her hotel, where a new room had already been booked. On arrival she was informed by an overly obsequious manager that hot water was available should madam desire a bath. Madam did. Pushing her luck, she asked that copies of all the latest newspapers be brought to her room.

These did something to deflate her euphoria. When she read between the lines, trying to make sense of the often contradictory reports, one thing was certain—the Bolsheviks were losing ground. The Czechs had taken control of most of the Trans-Siberian east of the Urals and were now advancing up the Volga, having seized most of the larger towns downstream and formed an alliance with the local Mensheviks and Right Socialist Revolutionaries. In the south, General Denikin was building and training an army, and all around the Russian perimeter the country's erstwhile allies were stepping up the scale of their interventions.

It made for depressing reading.

After the last ten days, the temptation was to make the most of the local Cheka's anxiety and give herself a few days to recover. But the Czechs weren't that far from Yekaterinburg, and she needed to resume her journey while she still could. Kollontai had included a letter for the Cheka to pass on, telling Caitlin that she was currently on a propaganda tour, sailing down the Volga toward Nizhny Novgorod, addressing crowds at almost every town and village. Assuming that Caitlin was on her way to Moscow, would she like to break her journey and bear witness to the revolution in action?

After Vladivostok and the fraught journey across Siberia, after ten days in a cell and the woe-filled newspapers that lay across her bed, she rather thought she would.

THE NEWS GOT NO BETTER on the three-day journey to Nizhny Novgorod. During a twelve-hour delay at Perm, she heard that the Czechs, Whites, and Allies had together overthrown the Vladivostok Bolsheviks. Many of the latter had been summarily executed, and it seemed probable that many of those she had met would be among the dead. Caitlin found it hard to imagine that someone as vital as Zoya was gone, but how many young deaths had evoked that thought over the last few years? The graveyards were filling up with children.

Zoya might have escaped, but there were no grounds for hope where her friend Volodarsky was concerned. By the dim light of a lantern on the Vyatka station platform, Caitlin read the news of his assassination, the tears rolling down her cheeks as she stared blankly up at a star-filled summer sky. He had been gunned down in Petrograd by an RSR, presumably for political reasons. She could only hope that his "months of joy" had ended in only a moment of anguish.

She was still thinking about him when her train rumbled across the bridge over the Volga and into Nizhny Novgorod. Around the station and on the droshky ride into the center, she noticed a lot of military activity, but ordinary people were also going about their business, and there was none of that palpable tension that had afflicted most of the towns on her journey. In Nizhny Novgorod the enemy was still some distance away, which was certainly cause for relief. If he ever got this close to Moscow, the game would most likely be up.

Caitlin had telegraphed Kollontai from Perm, and a reply was waiting at the city soviet offices. The message, which was only a few hours old, informed Caitlin that her friend's boat would be arriving in Balakhna, some thirty versts upstream, the day after tomorrow. How she was supposed to get there wasn't mentioned, but she had all the next day to figure that out, and after finding a hotel room and eating a better-than-usual meal, she took herself off to bed.

It was a hot night, so she opened her windows wide, undressed, and let the incoming breeze cool her down. She could hear people talking in the street below, the occasional clatter of a droshky going by. The whistle in the distance was probably a train, the mournful horn a boat on the river. It might have been the Brooklyn of her childhood, and the commonplace nature of the sounds seemed to emphasize the distance.

She was a day away from Moscow, from the heart of a revolution that might well end in failure but could transform the world. Victorious or lost, it would change the lives of all who came within its compass. How it would change her own was still a mystery, but not one she felt in any hurry to solve.

THERE WAS NO TRAIN TO Balakhna and no boats heading upstream in the next few days, but a rough road ran close to the river and the local soviet found someone willing to take her. The driver was clearly annoyed at having been given the task, and after receiving monosyllabic replies to several cheerful queries, Caitlin stuck her tongue out at his back and settled down to watch the countryside go by.

The ride took six hours. Balakhna sat on the right bank of the wide river, backing onto flat, wooded countryside. The small town boasted a large paper mill and several beautiful churches, all of which had so far survived the change in political temperature. Since most of the buildings were painted in white or pastel shades, Kollontai's bright red agit-ship, moored at one end of the long jetty, offered a stark contrast. The paddle steamer was adorned with slogans and propagandist paintings, many on the theme of women learning to read and write.

Kollontai was in a meeting on board but hurried out to embrace her friend the moment it was over. Although there was a film screening in town that evening, she had time to show Caitlin around the ship, which had everything a modern propagandist could possibly need. Apart from the projectors and film reels, there were stacks of leaflets, a press for printing more, and a radio for keeping the ship in touch with party headquarters in Moscow. Plus, of course, around a dozen agitators, most of them female and young.

On their walk to the town hall, Kollontai gave Caitlin her take on the current state of the revolution. Despite Brest-Litovsk and her other differences with the party leadership, despite the strength of the opposition now rearing its hydra-like head across the country, Caitlin's friend was still full of optimism, and as the evening unfolded, Caitlin could clearly see why. The women who filled the hall, who sat enrapt as the film explaining the new approach to women's rights was shown—they were the reason. Watching the audience rather than the film, Caitlin saw few signs of dissent. The younger women's obvious enthusiasm was striking, the nervous optimism of their middle-aged mothers even more touching. And if most of the old seemed slightly more grudging, some were obviously won over. "If only the revolution had happened fifty years ago," one said, shaking her head with regret.

The questions afterward were mostly of a practical nature. What exactly were the rights of a wife under the new marriage law? In the case of divorce, who decided the fate of the children? Would the party make husbands do some of the cleaning?

It was more than an exchange of views. Committees were formed to deal with a number of issues, from setting up classes in literacy and women's health matters to the current lighting of streets and the future coming of electrification. This was revolution in action, Caitlin thought as they walked back through the darkened town. Making lives better. Making women's lives easier.

Kollontai had also been energized by the evening, but when their late-night conversation turned to personal matters, a different picture emerged. She missed Dybenko, whom she'd hardly seen since their wedding. Caitlin had heard one version of the story—how, ignoring the Treaty of Brest-Litovsk, he'd gone off to fight the Germans in his native Ukraine, refused party orders to desist, and eventually been arrested—and now she heard his wife's. Kollontai's was more subjective, a mixture of the anger, exasperation, and sadness that only a lover would feel. "I know he sometimes behaves like a willful child," she said, "but I miss his body next to mine."

As usual, talking about her friend's romantic partner caused Caitlin to reflect on her own. At least Kollontai knew where her man was, she thought, lying awake in her narrow bunk. Jack could be anywhere—in the few years she'd known him, he'd been to at least a dozen countries that she knew of, and probably some that she didn't. She missed him. She missed sex. And doubtless she would go on missing them both. As Kollontai had noted almost wistfully, "I know that everyone thinks I'm an advocate of free love, but in fact I'm remarkably faithful."

As am I, Caitlin thought. As am I.

SHE WAS IN BALAKHNA FOR almost two weeks, accompanying Kollontai and a few of the other agitators on their visits to a string of nearby villages. The farther they got from the river, the more dubious the response, but the sense of doing something truly worthwhile was always present. This was a story that Caitlin hoped would resonate back home, a message of hope for a world that seemed sorely in need of it, some positive press for the revolution when all seemed ranged against it. Who could argue against women learning to read and write? Who could deny that only the revolution had made such progress possible?

She took a boat downstream on the first day of July, sitting out on deck in the bright summer sunshine and watching the fields go by. She was hoping to reach Moscow for the final days of the Fifth Congress of Soviets, but there was no train from Nizhny Novgorod that evening or on the following day. While she was at the station, several trains rumbled through in the opposite direction, carrying units of the newly formed Red Army toward the battle fronts farther down the Volga.

A departure for Moscow was finally announced. Overcrowded and lacking a restaurant car, the train took more than three days to cover the two hundred miles, arriving at the capital's Kursk Station in the late afternoon of July 6. All the droshkies were gone by the time Caitlin reached their rank, but at least the trams were running—on her last trip to Moscow they'd been stuck in snowdrifts. As she rode into the center, the first thing that struck her was how normal the city looked. Seen from the Urals, the revolution had seemed close to collapse; seen from a tram on Pokrovka Street, it carried an air of rude health.

Or so she thought. As the tram waited to cross Pokrovsky Boulevard, she saw a couple dozen uniformed Chekists jogging northward, rifles in hand. They looked serious, some of them a little frightened, and she wondered where they might be going.

About ten minutes later, walking toward the front door of the Frantziya Hotel, she heard shots in the distance: a first, a second, a minor fusillade. What in God's name was happening?

Inside the lobby one man was loudly telling another that Count Mirbach, the German ambassador, had been assassinated. He didn't know by whom.

After getting a room—small, high up, with a view of the taller Kremlin cupolas—Caitlin rushed back downstairs and out onto the street. The Bolshoi Theater, where the congress was being held, was only a short walk away in Theater Square, and she hurried in that direction, eyes alert for signs of danger, ears pricked for the sound of gunfire.

The theater itself was ringed by Red Guards and Chekists, a machine-gun detachment facing the entrance. She walked toward the latter, press card in her hand, but the Chekist in charge simply waved her back. "The congress has been suspended," he said, merely repeating the phrase when she asked him why.

There was no one else to ask, so she walked back across the square, thinking she would watch and wait. As she passed a line of three parked cars, she noticed Yakov Peters sitting in the front one, smoking a cigarette and staring across at the theater. He saw her a moment later, and the smile that broke across his face was almost an invitation.

He climbed out to shake her hand.

"So what's happening?" she asked him in English, knowing how nostalgic he was for his years in London.

"The LSRs have gone mad," he said simply. "They've killed

Count Mirbach and taken my chief prisoner. Their people in the Vecheka—and don't ask me why we didn't get rid of them months ago—they're holding Dzerzhinsky at Pokrovsky Barracks. But their leaders are all in there," he said, pointing toward the theater. "So we've both got hostages," he added dryly.

"Spiridonova?"

"Oh, yes. She's spent the last few days calling for a new war against the Germans, and presumably killing Mirbach was how they hoped to start one."

Caitlin hardly knew what to think. "Are they actually trying to seize power?"

"Only they know that." He sighed. "They've always been more about gestures than anything else, and this feels like one more of those. If it is, they'll be sorry. We can't afford those sorts of games, not anymore."

They both stared across at the theater. "I posted the letter to your wife when I got to America," she told him.

"I know," he said. "I had a reply last month. Thank you."

Since he said nothing about her recent imprisonment, neither did she. "So what happens now?" she asked him.

He shrugged. "We wait. And now I must leave you," he added as a subordinate walked toward them.

Caitlin lingered in the square for a while, but nothing more happened. She decided to visit the Pokrovsky Barracks. These were about a mile to the east, on the innermost of the boulevards ringing the city center. Drawing closer, she expected to find a cordon, but it was a single soldier who stopped her, shooing her away with his rifle. When she didn't move, he lowered the weapon toward her and she had no choice but to retreat.

This time there was no Yakov Peters to explain the situation. She stood on the far side of the boulevard for several minutes, staring across at the mansionlike barracks and wondering in which of the rooms Dzerzhinsky was being held.

What were the LSRs doing? Peters's judgment—that they'd simply gone mad—seemed as good as any, but whatever their motives had been, the behavior seemed incredibly reckless.

She retraced her steps, first to the Theatre Square, where nothing new had happened, then back to her hotel for some food. It was almost ten by the time she'd eaten, and her legs rebelled at the thought of going back out. With any luck at all, nothing would happen overnight, and after the latest appalling journey she desperately needed some sleep. She requested a 5:00 A.M. call, then went up to her room and bed.

SHE LEFT THE HOTEL JUST before six. The Bolshoi Theatre was still surrounded, the LSR delegates still inside. Walking on, she found another ring of troops around the Pokrovsky Barracks, where the LSR Chekists were holding Felix Dzerzhinsky. Several pieces of artillery were lined up opposite the building, Yakov Peters and several subordinates standing nearby.

He saw her and walked over.

"Any news?" she asked.

"We have demanded their surrender," Peters told her.

"And if they refuse?"

He shrugged and gestured toward the waiting guns.

The besieged LSRs neither threw in the towel nor came out fighting. In midmorning the first shell was fired, chipping off a chunk of cornice. It didn't kill anyone, but to the watching Caitlin it felt as if something had died. The two parties who had made the revolution, who had ruled in tandem for several intoxicating months, were fighting and killing each other. And Kollontai and Spiridonova, the women who had most inspired her, were now on opposite sides.

AFTER SURRENDERING LATER THAT MORNING, most of the LSR Chekists were shot. The political leaders corralled in the theater were told they were under arrest, then led single file to the Kremlin, for incarceration in one of the citadel's barracks. Watching the procession of defiant Socialist Revolutionaries as it wound its way through the Nikolskaya Gate—the diminutive Spiridonova at its head—Caitlin felt nothing but sadness.

It took her three days to get an interview. Yakov Peters came through in the end, but only after making it clear what he *didn't* want her to write. "I trust you not to fall for all this "martyr to the revolution" nonsense. It's people like your friend Volodarsky who are the real martyrs."

On the morning in question, she was led through several inner courtyards to a small office opposite one of the churches. Two Red Guards stood sentry outside while she sat alone in the mostly empty room, waiting for Spiridonova. Her friend, when she eventually arrived, was wearing the familiar dark dress with white-trimmed collar. Her face was pale, the eyes a little feverish, but she looked healthier than Caitlin expected. Which was, on reflection, hardly surprising. The Bolsheviks would want the world to believe that Spiridonova was being treated decently, and who better to bear witness than a known friend and foreign journalist?

"It is good to see you," Spiridonova said after kissing Caitlin on both cheeks.

"And you."

"How long do we have?"

"They didn't say."

"Then I will waste no time. I am writing an open letter to the Bolshevik leadership. I am telling them, and the world, that we in the LSR leadership take full responsibility for the killing of Mirbach and that if they wish to punish anyone, it should be us. I know they have already killed several of our people in the Cheka—these men were simply following our orders and should not have been punished for doing so."

"What did the LSR leadership hope to gain from killing the German ambassador?" Caitlin asked.

"An end to their shameful peace. The people want to fight the Germans. In Ukraine they are doing so already. The Bolsheviks have betrayed us all with their wretched treaty—the Russian workers, the German workers. And that is only the half of it. They have betrayed the peasants, given them their freedom only to snatch it back."

There was more of this, much more. Listening to the other woman, Caitlin had the sense that months of doubt and frustration had come to a cathartic head, that Spiridonova and her party had simply had enough of compromise. And perhaps, she thought but didn't say, of responsibility. "But how are *you?*" she asked, hoping to separate the person from the politics.

"Me? I am ready for whatever comes. I could not have acted otherwise." A slight smile. "And I am glad you have come back to us. Are you glad that you did?"

"Yes, of course. But . . ." Caitlin sighed. "It hurts me to see you in prison, to see allies turn on each other. I am a stranger here, but it seems to me that a revolution with so many enemies can ill afford to lose its friends."

Spiridonova shook her head. "If a pot is broken, you cannot pretend it isn't. You have to make another."

That wasn't what Caitlin wanted to hear. "Do you need anything?" she asked. "I mean, I don't know if—"

"One thing," Spiridonova said. "If you could take a message . . . No, nothing political," she added, seeing Caitlin glance at the door behind her. "The people I live with—old friends—I would like them to know I'm all right."

"Of course."

Spiridonova provided the address of a house in the Arbat and then got to her feet. "I like to call time myself," she said, giving Caitlin another kiss. "It wouldn't do to let them think they're in control."

After a guard had escorted Caitlin back to the Nikolskaya Gate and her bag had been searched for contraband, she wandered around the huge Red Square, trying to shake off the sense of despondency. Would the Bolsheviks shoot Spiridonova? Surely they wouldn't be so stupid. If only someone would take her and Lenin and bang their heads together. Trouble was, they were both so sure they were right.

Caitlin walked out past the history museum and found the tram stop for the Arbat district. It was another perfect summer day, and the city and its people showed no sign of having been unduly inconvenienced by the LSR revolt. As Jack Reed had once told her, everyone might be affected by political developments, but usually it was only 5 percent of the population that actually noticed. It hadn't been true in 1917, but perhaps it was again. Perhaps there were only so many months of constant upheaval that any people could take.

The house in Arbat stood facing a little park, in which several children were playing under a watchful babushka's eyes. The house was small by Moscow standards and badly in need of repainting—a surprising home for one of Russia's most loved daughters. It took a while for someone to answer Caitlin's knock, and when a man did, the look on his face was one of suspicion. All changed when she explained the reason for her presence. He invited her in, and the woman who seemed to be his wife hurried to bring her tea.

"Maria says to tell you that she's fine," Caitlin said. "And not to be sad, whatever happens. She has chosen her path and has no regrets."

This was received with nods, as if such a message were to be expected. On a whim Caitlin asked if she could see Spiridonova's room.

They were happy to oblige. "The Chekists took two of her books," the man said as he opened the door.

"Is that all?" Caitlin asked, struck by the room's emptiness. A shelf held fewer than a dozen books, the wardrobe a handful of dresses. A framed photograph of Spiridonova and several other women—probably out in Siberia—stood on the bedside table beside an iron candleholder.

A monastic cell, Caitlin thought.

A few minutes later, emerging onto the street, she noticed a man standing opposite. As she walked back to the tram stop, she could hear his footsteps behind her, and once aboard the crowded vehicle she could see him at the other end. When she alighted, he did the same, but when she entered her hotel lobby, she looked around in vain. Whoever he was, he knew where she was staying.

Should she worry? She told herself not much, that doing a friend a favor was hardly a crime, even if that friend was currently held by the Cheka.

So why did she not feel reassured?

Up in her room, she began sketching out a piece on Spiridon-ova. It wasn't easy—she had no desire to malign her friend, but the more she thought about the LSR position, the more she believed it

was wrong. Did that mean that the Bolsheviks were right? Not necessarily. Maybe they were both wrong. Six months ago things had
seemed much clearer.

She had written only a couple hundred words when the peremptory knock sounded on her door.

She opened it with some trepidation.

"You will come with me," the Chekist said, stepping into the
room. Eyes lighting on the half-written article, he reached out a
hand for the sheets of paper.

THEIR DESTINATION WAS THE MAIN headquarters on Bolshaya
Lubyanka. Caitlin was kept waiting for almost an hour in a drab
reception room, under the watchful eyes of a young Cheka duty
officer. And if he wasn't mentally undressing her, then she was the
czar's mother.

Finally summoned to someone's presence, she was led down two
corridors and up two flights of stairs to an office overlooking the
large inner courtyard. The man in question was about thirty, with
hair already graying and dark circles around his eyes. Her unfinished article was lying on his desk.

"You speak Russian, yes?" he asked in that language.

She nodded.

"My name is Yuri Komarov, and I am the Second Deputy Chairman of the Moscow Cheka. You—correct me if I'm wrong—are
Caitlin Hanley, American journalist."

"I am." She felt nervous, but also more than a little annoyed, and
she did her best to hide both.

"You visited Maria Spiridonova in the Kremlin this morning, and
then you went to her lodgings."

"I did. Your colleague Yakov Peters arranged the interview—he's
an old acquaintance from Petrograd." Take that, she thought.

"I know," he said, clearly unimpressed. "So why did you visit her
home?"

"She asked me to. She wanted the people who live there to know
she's doing well. That's all."

He digested that, massaging the sides of his unshaven chin with thumb and forefinger, then picked up her scribbled pages and gave them a good long look. "You make her sound like a heroine," he said at last.

"Isn't she? Didn't Lenin say the other day that no one could impugn her integrity? If you can believe *Pravda*, that is," she added pointedly. She felt like scoring points, which was probably ill-advised.

He said nothing.

"She has been calling people to account for twenty years," Caitlin went on. "If she disagrees with the government, she won't remain silent."

He raised an eyebrow. "No one expects her to. What we cannot tolerate is her and her colleagues seeking to undermine the government by ordering the murder of a foreign diplomat."

Caitlin said nothing to that.

Komarov consulted another piece of paper. "You were here in the winter when restrictions were placed on the bourgeois press. Our opponents were using their money and their newspapers to spread lies about us, putting the whole revolution at risk. And you wrote that the restrictions, I quote, 'though regrettable, are both understandable and necessary.'"

"As a temporary measure, yes."

He sat back in his chair. "Well, I think we could agree that the revolution is in much greater danger now. We are surrounded by enemies, and they all want to kill us. The Germans are not our friends—of course they're not—but at this particular moment in time they're the only ones willing to let us be. And the LSRs want to provoke them into restarting the war. It cannot be allowed."

"I can see that," Caitlin said. And she did. If the Germans joined the Allied onslaught, then the revolution was doomed and the women of Balakhna could say good-bye to a better future. Why could Spiridonova not see it? For Caitlin's friend it was all or nothing, and there was a certain glory in that, particularly when the person concerned was so willing to put her own life at risk. But glory wasn't everyone's cup of tea, nor was staking one's life on absolute victory—most people would settle for something less if the only alternative was complete defeat.

And she was one of them, Caitlin decided. Sometimes a broken pot could be mended. "Is that all?" she asked Komarov, eager despite herself to give him nothing more.

He nodded and shouted for someone to lead her back out of the labyrinth.

SHE WROTE THE PIECE THAT evening, taking care to explain the motives and aims of both LSRs and Bolsheviks. And if she came down largely on the latter's side, it was not out of fear of the Cheka but because she felt they were mostly right. Power without principles was a thin gruel indeed, but there was always the hope of improving the diet; principles without power offered only a fleeting glow of self-righteousness before the beasts returned with their sharpened knives.

The Bolsheviks had not abandoned *all* their principles, and neither had Caitlin. She wouldn't lie for them. If the time ever came when they wouldn't allow her to write things she believed to be true, she would either quit the country or give up pretending to be a journalist. She had no objection to propaganda, but only if everyone understood that that was what it was.

Next morning at the Central Telegraph Office, she waited with some trepidation for the in-house Cheka verdict. Would they pass the article for export, or would there be another summons from Comrade Komarov? As it turned out, the acceptability of her views proved neither here nor there—the telegraph connections had been closed down, the one across Siberia by the Czechs, the one through Europe by the Bolsheviks, in retaliation for the latest British landings at Murmansk. There was no telling when either would reopen.

This was a blow to her sense of purpose and also to her pocket. As a correspondent she would still have received a salary; as a freelancer she was only paid by the piece. The money from Aunt Orla would last her a few more weeks, but she'd counted on staying longer than that.

Should she leave again? She already had sufficient material for a book—the trip across Siberia had provided enough on its own—but was that what she wanted to do? Sitting over newspapers in the hotel bar, she realized it would be like writing the first half of a novel, like recounting David's war with Goliath before they got around to exchanging their missiles.

Only that morning, news of a major rebellion in Yaroslavl had reached Moscow. The Czech Legion was still tramping all over Siberia and the Urals, the RSRs had seized another major Volga town with the help of some Bolshevik turncoats, and the British landing at Murmansk had proved more substantial than expected. One of the papers provided a list of those known to have died in the White takeover of Vladivostok, and Caitlin recognized several of the people she'd met and shared an evening with only two months before. Zoya was not among them, which was something.

No, she thought. This was it, the fateful summer, and she owed it to people like Zoya to stay. If she couldn't get her stories out, then she'd find some other way to help. Kollontai, she realized, had actually provided her with one of the latter. Inessa Armand was organizing a major women's conference for the autumn, and Kollontai had suggested that Caitlin write a piece about it. Kollontai had even given her a letter of introduction.

Next morning she walked across town to the old *Rabotnitsa* offices on Kamergersky Street. The socialist women's journal had ceased publication for lack of paper the previous spring, but the rooms in which it had been edited and printed were currently being used by Armand and her small staff of helpers. Over the last year, Caitlin's and Inessa's paths had crossed on several occasions, but they had never shared more than a few words until now. The Frenchwoman, who had lived in Russia for most of her life and who gossips claimed had once been Lenin's mistress, put on her glasses to read through Kollontai's letter. She was in her forties and, like all the Bolsheviks that Caitlin had met, looked weary to the bone.

"So what do you have in mind?" she asked.

Caitlin explained that the lack of a link to the outside world meant the story would have to wait. But was there any way in which she could help, any translation work that needed doing? Any typing?

Armand smiled. "We always need help, and yes, I'm sure we could find work for you. Where are you staying?"

"At the Frantziya. But it's too expensive. I have to move."

"Ah, I know we can help you there. There's a house on the other side of the river where several of our women live. Most are volunteers from the provinces, and the party gave us a home for them. I'm sure we can get you a room. There's no rent, but everyone shares in the chores."

At the end of the working day, two of the other women took Caitlin along. The room in the eaves was small but perfectly adequate. The house itself—a decaying mansion with over twenty rooms—was sparsely furnished but scrupulously clean; the other women, most of whom seemed younger than her, were full of welcoming smiles. Aunt Orla would have loved it, Caitlin thought.

When she returned from collecting her suitcase at the hotel, she sat around the kitchen table with several other women, discussing lives and work and boyfriends. She could have been anywhere, she thought, but quickly realized that wasn't true. It had needed a revolution to bring these women together and to give them a home like this one.

14
Selling the Past

It was Wednesday, July 10, according to the newspaper McColl picked up from the stand outside the station. If the cloud-free sky was any guide, a hot day was in prospect, but with the sun only recently risen, it still felt a trifle chilly.

Beside him Fedya was gazing openmouthed at the impressive station façade, reminding McColl of his own first trip to Glasgow. "They're only bricks," his father had said, sounding clever and missing the point.

"Is that a tram?" the boy asked, pointing a finger.

"It is. But first we need to know where we're going."

Several people at the stop were keen to help them out. One had heard of Grocholski Street and thought it was up near the Sukharev Tower. Others knew which trams to take down Bolshaya Tverskaya Yamskaya and which to change to on Sadovaya.

Their first streetcar was crowded with people riding to work. The smell of unwashed bodies waxed and waned, strong at stops, weaker as the vehicle gathered speed and sucked in the cool morning air. As they neared Sadovaya, McColl could see the Kremlin in the distance, its golden cupolas glinting in the morning sunshine. Pointing this out to Fedya, he realized again how much he would miss him. It might have been just a month, but in that time he'd grown to . . .

to what? To like the boy? To love him? A bit of both, he thought. McColl had no idea how it felt to have a son, but his mother had once assured him that he'd been more like a father to Jed than the real one ever had. Maybe being in loco parentis suited him.

From everything Fedya had said about his uncle, McColl was expecting to like Rodion Rozmirov. Assuming, that is, he was there. It was several months since the boy's dying mother had passed on her brother's Moscow address and God knew how many months before that since she had actually heard from him. The man might have moved several times by now, in or out of Moscow, in which case he'd take some finding. McColl imagined asking Cumming for a few weeks' leave to seek out a missing Bolshevik and smiled to himself.

Fedya was staring wide-eyed out the window. The crossroads at which they alighted was full of scurrying people, its imposing buildings plastered with posters and banners proclaiming the new promised land. As they waited for another tram, McColl took note of the numerous men, both in and out of uniform, who seemed to have nothing to do but watch.

Their tram arrived. Its driver thought Grocholski Street was one street up from Sadovaya, near the botanical gardens. "I'll tell you when to get off and which way to walk. Then you can ask someone."

They did as he suggested and eventually found the street. The three-story house at number 33 looked better kept than most, probably thanks to the middle-aged woman busily sweeping the steps.

Her eyes narrowed when she heard the name Rozmirov. "Are you relatives?" she asked after a lengthy pause.

"I'm his nephew," Fedya piped up.

The old woman cupped her face in her hands. "I'm afraid he's dead, my dear."

Fedya's face crumpled, and McColl could see him holding back the tears.

"He was killed in the fighting. He's buried in the Brotherhood Grave, in Red Square."

Inside, over tea, she told them a little more. While Petrograd's revolutionary struggle had lasted barely a day and been virtually bloodless, its counterpart in Moscow had lasted six and cost eight hundred lives. Fedya's uncle had been one of those killed, heading off one morning to join his Red Guard unit and never coming back. "The man who came to see us said he died during the street fighting, which was something. A lot of them were executed by the Whites before they got the chance to fight." She looked at Fedya. "He was a good neighbor," she said. "A good man."

"I haven't seen him since I was seven," Fedya replied. "But I wish I had." He glanced at McColl, eyes heavy with hopelessness. *What now?* was the unspoken question.

What indeed? There was no one else in Moscow with whom McColl could leave the boy. And if he could take him back to Bucha—which he couldn't—there was no one there to look after him. It would have to be a home of some sort—given how many Russians had died leaving children behind over the last few years, there had to be places like that. They were probably awful, but what other choice did he have? He would find the boy a good one.

Fedya must have guessed what was passing through McColl's mind. "I can look after myself," he said quietly as they started back toward Sadovaya. "Once I know where things are," he added, somewhat spoiling the impression.

"We'll see," McColl told him. "We're going to another house now, the one where I thought I might be staying. Maybe we both can. But when we get there, don't start asking questions, not in front of anyone else. Understand?"

"No, not really."

"Well, you don't need to. Just don't say anything, all right?"

"All right."

THE SAFE HOUSE WAS A longish walk away, north of the Sukharev Tower and market in the Meshchanskaya district. The houses here were smaller, grubbier, and closer together, the air full of smoke from nearby stations and yards. The address that Davidson had given him belonged to a wooden cottage someone had forgotten to pull down when the surrounding terrace was put up.

The tall, blue-eyed, chubby-cheeked young man who answered

McColl's knock looked like an Englishman in Russian clothes. Which he was.

McColl introduced himself with the appropriate pass sentence, and received the correct reply. "I've got someone with me," he said, gesturing toward Fedya, whom he'd asked to wait on the pavement.

The young man did a double take. "You mean that child?"

"Yes. A long story. He doesn't know I'm English, so we need to talk Russian. You do speak it?"

"Oh, like a native," the man said in that language. His grammar was correct, his accent appalling. "I'm Roger Bowers, by the way. Sergei Vasileyovich Bazarov to our Russian friends. And the Vecheka, of course."

McColl hoped the man's espionage skills were better than his Russian. He called Fedya over, and they all went inside. "I take it you need somewhere to sleep," Bowers said in Russian. "We have three empty rooms at the moment, but a couple of . . . of visitors are due over the next few days, so the two of you may have to share."

"We're used to it," McColl said dryly.

While Fedya was out back having a piss, McColl explained the situation. "We traveled here together from Ukraine. Fedya's parents are both dead, and he was hoping to live with his uncle in Moscow. But we've just found out that he's dead, too."

"So you're going to . . . ?"

"I've no idea. I'll have to find him somewhere to live. In the meantime . . . Look, he knows I'm part of a clandestine group fighting the Germans, so seeing men come and go won't seem strange. And I'll get it sorted out in a few days."

"Fine. I'm off to work now—I'm a projectionist at a cinema near the market, so I won't be back till around eleven. If anyone arrives and they ask for Boris Menzhinsky, invite them in and ask them to wait. If they don't ask for Boris, they'll probably be Chekists and they'll have the place surrounded." He laughed. "There's bread and tea in the kitchen, but not a lot else, I'm afraid. I'll see you later."

BY THE TIME BOWERS RETURNED, Fedya was asleep in their bed and McColl could pump his host for all the latest news. "I expected to find Moscow on a war footing," he told Bowers. "It looks as peaceful as London."

"Oh, that's because you missed all the fun," Bowers said, sitting down at the table. "God, I stink of cigarettes," he complained. "Some nights I can hardly see the screen through the smoke."

McColl poured him a glass of tea. "The fun?" he prompted.

Bowers smiled. "The LSRs had a brainstorm. They decided to go after the German ambassador *and* the Bolsheviks. They got Mirbach, but the Cheka got them. Spiridonova and all her chums are locked up in the Kremlin, waiting to see how much mercy Lenin has left. And while they were running riot here in Moscow, Savinkov's lot mounted a rising in Yaroslavl. Ended in tears, but our informers tell us the Bolsheviks all had their bags packed. Just in case."

"Were the two risings coordinated?" McColl wondered.

"Who knows? If they were, it wasn't by us. The French may have been in on the LSR business, but Savinkov's one of ours, and if he was coordinating with anyone, it was probably General Poole in Murmansk. If so, they got the wires crossed." Bowers grunted. "And not for the first time."

"What about the Czechs?" McColl asked him. "Are we backing them?"

"It was our gallant French allies who brought them on board, but they'll be fighting with us if Poole ever gets a decent force into Archangel. A joint front from there to the lower Volga, and then we all push west—that seems to be the general idea. Shove the Bolsheviks out of the way and get back to fighting the Germans."

"You sound less than convinced."

Bowers shrugged. "I've been here a while."

"And?"

The other man sighed. "Oh, I don't know. Don't get me wrong—I wouldn't lift a finger to save the Bolsheviks. But I like the Russians, and the last thing they need after what they've been through is a bloody civil war."

"But if that's the only way to reopen an Eastern Front . . ." McColl suggested, playing devil's advocate.

Bowers scratched his head and yawned. "Maybe it sounds like

an idiot's plan because I can't see the whole picture." He smiled to himself. "Why don't you ask the chief tomorrow? He wants to give you an official welcome. And no doubt put you back to work."

"Where and when?" McColl asked.

IT WAS EVEN HOTTER NEXT day, the sort of wet, clinging heat that McColl had always hated. Sitting on the wrought-iron bench, his Russian blouse stuck to his back, he found himself remembering Calcutta in 1915. He'd never known either of his grandmothers, but in the weeks before the monsoon he'd have sacrificed both for a working electric fan.

The empty bandstand was twenty yards away, the radial paths of Sokolniki Park fanning out behind him. And if he wasn't mistaken, the man striding in through the distant gates was Gerald Northcutt, the man in charge of Cumming's Moscow operation. The timing was right, and so was the newspaper under his arm. And Bowers had said he was tall.

McColl stayed in his seat while Northcutt did a circuit of the bandstand, just to be sure that no one had followed him into the park. In his seedy suit and badly scuffed shoes, the section chief looked like a low-level bureaucrat, which was doubtless the intention. Yet there wasn't much he could do about his face, which even behind a mustache and beard looked anything but Slavic.

Approaching him, McColl pointed at the paper and popped the prearranged question: Was there any fresh news from the Volga front?

"Some good, some bad," was the expected reply, the accent much better than Bowers's. "Let's walk," Northcutt suggested.

They headed up one of the paths, holding their tongues until certain that no one could hear them. To McColl's surprise, most of the trees and some of the wildlife had survived the winter shortages—he even saw a squirrel rocketing up the trunk of an ancient red oak.

When Northcutt finally opened the conversation, what he said was a shock. "I believe you know—knew—a woman named Caitlin Hanley."

"Yes," McColl said, and left it at that. Cumming had not mentioned Caitlin since her return to America in 1916, and as far as McColl knew, his boss thought their love affair over. Keeping an eye on his agent would have quickly revealed this mistake, but why would Cumming have had McColl followed when he was patently doing his job? So his occasional trysts with Caitlin should have escaped attention.

"She's here in Moscow," Northcutt was saying.

"Oh," was all McColl could manage as he tried to keep the involuntary leap of his heart from showing on his face. He knew he dared not see her, but still . . .

"She was on our weekly list of foreign arrivals," Northcutt said, answering the question that McColl was still trying to formulate. "And one of our people recognized the name and remembered her connection to you."

"I see. Well, she is a journalist, and this is a story."

Northcutt grunted. "She's helping to make them these days. As of this week, she has a job with one of their new women's organizations. But that's by the by. The chances of your running into her are pretty remote, but you never know. And what I need to ask you is this: Would she shop you to her Bolshevik friends? If the answer's yes, then for all our sakes we have to get you out of Moscow."

"No," McColl said shortly. "She wouldn't."

"You sound very certain."

"I am."

Northcutt gave him one more questioning look, then let the matter be. "Enough said, then. Let's get down to business." He paused as a walker went past in the other direction. "A couple of months ago, we acquired an antique shop in the Arbat district—at 27 Bolshaya Nikitskaya, to be precise—and one of our people has been running it. And making a profit, believe it or not. As he told me himself—when the rich are so desperate to sell, it's almost impossible not to. Anyway, he's needed in Ukraine, so you'll be taking his place, at least for a week or so. Maybe longer. It's a good cover, and you can always shut the shop when there's more important work to do."

"Okay," McColl said, imagining the scene if Caitlin walked in.

"Papers," Northcutt said. "Bowers says the ones you have—a pho-tographer, I believe—are good for a couple of days, so carry on using those while we find you some new ones. We try to use Cheka papers when we can—they get you in anywhere, and no one likes to challenge them."

A train was audible up ahead, and the end of the trees was in sight. "Time to turn back," Northcutt said, stopping and wiping his brow with an already damp handkerchief. "I used to think Russia was all about sleigh bells and snow," he added, in a tone that sug-gested he'd been badly deceived. "Bowers told me you have a young boy with you," he went on. "One you picked up in Ukraine?" he added, unable or unwilling to conceal a broad hint of disapproval.

McColl explained the circumstances of their meeting and Fedya's need to reach Moscow. "I thought he'd provide excellent cover, and I was right."

"Mmm. Where is he now?"

"Watching a film at Bowers's cinema."

"And what are you planning to do with him?"

"Find him a home."

"Good. As quickly as possible, please. If things go the way we want them to, you won't have the time to look after children. I'm not sure yet, but I should have a job for you early next week. Delivering money to one of our Russian allies. A group called the Trust—you know about them? They're people from the old regime, more reli-able than some of the others, but they need a little pushing."

"And they're prepared to fight the Germans," McColl assumed.

"Of course."

"How are things going in France? I've been out of touch."

Northcutt wiped his brow again. "It's hard to tell. The govern-ment's public position hasn't changed—victory's just around the corner. In private they're much more worried. The Germans have made a lot of gains over the last few months, and what with Russia dropping out . . . Last I heard, the General Staff still believe we can win, but not until 1920. If we manage to get the Russians fighting again, we could cut that short by at least a year."

"And can we?" McColl asked.

"We're doing our best."

"The Bolsheviks will have to go," McColl suggested.

"Of course. We need a government that wants to fight the Germans, and they've made it clear that they don't."

"Why not the LSRs? They're a lot more popular than the old parties."

Northcutt's grunt was dismissive. "Too late for that—they've overreached themselves this time."

"With French help?"

"Oh, I expect so. The French approach is a tad scattergun. Not a horse I'd have backed. That woman—Maria Spiridonova—what sort of young woman shoots a police chief?"

A brave one, McColl thought. One at the end of her tether.

"Hysterical," Northcutt was saying. "And the whole party takes after her. I think we'll stick with the old guard. Denikin seems sound enough, and there's an even better prospect in Siberia. Alexander Kolchak—used to be an admiral in the czar's navy. Factor in the Czechs and a few of our own and their shiny new Red Army will have a fight on its hands. The trick is in keeping the show on the road, and that's our second job. Providing links, keeping things coordinated, oiling the wheels with money."

"And the first job?" McColl asked, thinking he must have missed something.

"Oh, subversion. Above all subversion. If we can bring the leaders down, their precious Red Army will just melt away."

They were almost back to the bandstand, which a noisy group of ragged-looking children were using as the center of their racetrack. There were no adults in attendance.

"Moscow's full of them," Northcutt remarked, nodding at the children. "They play all day and do their thieving after dark."

McColl was wondering whether this was Fedya's future when the chief dropped his second bombshell. "Almost forgot to ask. Someone else that showed up on our foreign arrivals list—an American by the name of Aidan Brady. One of our people thought he might have been involved in the Sussex and Hampshire railway bombings right at the beginning of the war. Wasn't that one of your operations?"

"It was. And Aidan Brady was one of the eight men involved—the only one who escaped. He murdered two policemen that night." And tried to murder me in Dublin, McColl thought. He could still smell the moss on the quayside, the water like ice on his chest.

"Well, he's become one himself," Northcutt was saying. "The Cheka have taken him on."

"Have they indeed?" McColl muttered, his thoughts elsewhere. Two years before, at the height of the Easter Rising, Caitlin had saved him from a bunch of murderous republicans. He didn't know if Brady knew these particular men, but he was willing to bet they had friends in common. And if Brady had heard about the rescue, then Caitlin might well be in danger.

After Northcutt had commandeered a droshky and driven off, McColl walked slowly down toward Kalanchevskaya Square, still mulling the matter over. No decent human being would condemn somebody else for saving a loved one's life, but Brady wasn't a decent human being. He would see Caitlin as a traitor, to her brother and the wider cause. And he would see her treason as a God-sent opportunity, to prove his own credentials and to do what McColl thought he most enjoyed—killing his enemies.

In which case McColl had to warn her.

Or was he just looking for an excuse to see her? It seemed unlikely that Brady would know the details of what had happened that night in Dublin. Two of the republicans who'd been at the Mary Street house had died in subsequent days; the others were still in prison, at least as far as he knew. And even if Brady had somehow learned the details, he would surely think twice about meting out personal justice in Moscow, especially when the intended victim was a well-known supporter of the Bolshevik government.

There were also risks in warning her. If Brady knew nothing, then McColl himself was more of a threat to Caitlin. Meeting with a British agent would, if word got out, lay her open to espionage charges and possible execution. At best she would face deportation and an end to reporting the revolution that meant so much to her. She would never forgive him.

But could he take the risk of saying nothing? If Brady did kill her, McColl would never forgive himself.

The pros and cons kept outbidding each other as the hours went by. After visiting the safe house to check up on Fedya, he walked three miles across town to the antique shop on Bolshaya Nikitskaya. The proprietor was dealing with a customer—an angry-sounding middle-aged man who wanted more for his gold cigarette case than was currently on offer but who eventually gave up the struggle with better grace than McColl expected.

"Buying or selling?" the proprietor asked once the customer was gone. His Russian seemed as fluent as McColl's, and his angular face looked a lot less English than Bowers's.

"A little of both," McColl said, completing the password per Northcutt's instructions.

"In that case . . ." the proprietor said, flipping over the sign in the window, "you'd better come through to the back." He led the way, not speaking again until the door to the shop was closed behind them. "Sandy Luckett," he said, offering McColl a muscular handshake. "I think we once shared the lift at Whitehall Court."

"More than likely," McColl conceded. The other man's face was vaguely familiar.

Over the next half hour, Luckett explained the workings of the shop and went through the inventory. He had a long list of what he'd paid for the items and what he hoped to sell them for. The attention to detail was quite impressive but also seemed a tad extreme. Perhaps Napoleon had been right, McColl thought, and England really was a nation of shopkeepers. If so, he was glad he was Scottish.

There was less to say about their real job. After sharing contact protocols and emergency arrangements, Luckett gave McColl a rundown of the neighbors and local house-committee snoopers. And that was that. Luckett was bound for Kharkov and what he described as "rather different work." Sabotage, McColl assumed. Blowing up gasometers would certainly be a change from selling baubles.

After seeing him off and locking up the shop, McColl headed

back toward the safe house. He was passing the Sukharev Tower when it suddenly occurred to him that Caitlin could probably help when it came to the business of finding a home for Fedya. Over lunch in Fort William, she'd been full of the plans her friend Kollontai had for reforming the so-called angel factories and for helping mothers and children in general. If those plans had come to fruition and progressive new homes had been built, then Caitlin would know how to find one.

Was this just another excuse to see her? Perhaps. But if neither Brady nor Fedya alone could justify the risk, then maybe together they did.

He would have to find her first. He had thought of asking Northcutt where she was, but knew that such a query, no matter how casually expressed, would undermine his boss's belief that their love affair was defunct.

What exactly had Northcutt said about her current circumstances? "A job with one of their new women's organizations." That shouldn't be hard to track down.

SOON AFTER NINE THE NEXT morning, he and Fedya moved into the empty shop. He was beginning to think that telling the boy he was English might not be such a bad idea. It would stop him from wondering who people like Bowers were, stop him from asking questions like the ones he'd asked the previous evening, about where the supposed photographer had left all his equipment and how he had suddenly become the proprietor of an antique emporium.

What would Fedya say if he found out? He knew about other nations, and the idea of spying wasn't hard to grasp. He doubted that the boy would care one way or the other, but he might use the knowledge to get his own way—McColl remembered the night in Bucha when Fedya had threatened to wake up the village if he wasn't taken to Moscow.

But that was more than a month ago. They'd been through a lot together since then, and McColl didn't think the boy would deliberately endanger him. But unknowingly? That was a different matter. Perhaps it was better to wait and see.

Fedya was busy examining the stock. He already had a feather boa around his neck and was trying to unfurl an umbrella. As McColl was demonstrating the technique, their first customer came through the door, a youngish woman in worn but once-expensive clothes, with plaited blonde hair and a strikingly pale complexion. Looking and sounding nervous, she produced a small but exquisite icon from her bag and explained that her parents needed money to travel.

McColl examined the object with what he hoped would look like expertise. He had no idea what it was worth.

When Fedya asked to see it, he suppressed a smile and passed it over. "It's beautiful," the boy said simply after staring at the icon for several seconds. "You should keep it and tell your parents to stay in Moscow."

"We can't," the girl said sadly. "How much will you give me for it?" she asked McColl.

"How much do you want?"

"My father once said it was priceless, but I will take a hundred rubles." She said it almost defiantly, as if fully expecting refusal.

McColl thought about it, but not for long. "That sounds fair."

She almost clapped her hands in excitement.

McColl took the requisite notes from the desk, handed them over, and held the door open for the girl to leave. He thought it unlikely that Northcutt would appreciate his generosity, but then making people happy didn't seem to be his boss's stock-in-trade.

"Was it worth that much?" Fedya asked once she'd gone.

"I've no idea," McColl told him. "I felt sorry for her."

"So did I."

This one early customer was something of a false dawn—only three more came that morning. Two whizzed around the shop and were gone within a few minutes; the third spent half an hour squinting at every article on display, mumbling disparaging remarks as she did so. None of the three bought a thing.

When no one came between noon and three, McColl decided to close the shop early. He needed to register his and Fedya's residence in the district and thereby qualify them both for ration cards.

The government office they needed was farther west on Nikitskaya, close to its junction with Sadovaya. There were a lot of people milling around inside and quite a few in the relevant queue, but in the end the wait was less than an hour. A young woman with tied-back hair and an earnest face examined McColl's papers, added a new stamp, and filled out a ration card. The fact that Fedya had no papers was not a problem in itself, but she needed proof that McColl was his legal guardian to issue the boy a card of his own. It was apparently not unknown for people to hire a fictional child to gain them an extra ration.

McColl pleaded, but it was probably the stricken look on Fedya's face that won her over. "Oh, what the hell—you look honest to me," she said, reaching for another blank card.

On the steps outside, they examined their treasure. From that day forth, they could purchase a certain amount of bread, tea, sugar, and margarine or butter and eat in the local government canteens at a heavily subsidized rate.

"I have some things I need to do alone," McColl told Fedya, "but first I'll take you back to the shop."

"Just give me the key," the boy said. "I can't get lost on a straight road!"

"Once you—"

"I can look after the shop," Fedya insisted. "All the things are marked with a price."

McColl laughed. "Okay, you can sell stuff. But don't buy anything."

"I don't have any money."

"That's right. Well, if people have things to sell, tell them to come back later."

"All right. When will *you* be back?"

"I don't know. A couple of hours, maybe."

Fedya seemed happy with that. After watching him walk off, McColl went back into the government office and sought out the person in charge. He was finally ushered into a very full office, where a dark-haired man wearing spectacles was busy transferring papers from his desk to the floor. The "Yes?" was somewhat irritable.

McColl explained that his wife would be joining him in Moscow

put a note through the door, suggesting a suitable time and place. A park, perhaps. Or down by the nearby river.

CAITLIN ARRIVED HOME FROM WORK the next day to find a letter on the vestibule table and almost dropped her bag when she recognized the writing on the envelope. Ignoring cries of welcome from the kitchen, she hurried upstairs to examine the contents. Her "old friend Yakov" had just arrived in Moscow and urgently needed to see her. He proposed a meeting in the small park further down the street from her office, and said he would be there at noon, tomorrow, and each day thereafter until she came.

She stood looking out the window, working through the shock and the emotions the message had evoked. While her heart rejoiced at the thought of seeing him, her mind rejoindered that he wouldn't have come all this way to see her. And the same mind was acutely aware that women who worked for the revolution should not be keeping trysts with agents of the British Crown.

He knew that as well as she did. What the hell did he think he was doing?

She would go—of course she would—but only to tell him that they couldn't meet again. If only her heart would stop smiling at the thought of seeing him even once.

She was spared further inner turmoil by a shout from below—she had visitors. Aidan Brady had promised to look her up, and there he was at the foot of the stairs, along with Sergei Piatakov, the young man who'd shared her droshky and roller-coaster car on the night of Kollontai's wedding. The two men had met a few days earlier at the Cheka's military-enlistment center and had somehow discovered that they shared her acquaintance. Their unit was leaving for the Volga front in a week or ten days' time.

The two of them stayed only half an hour, and there was nothing in the conversation—which was mostly about the revolution and its current difficulties—to upset or annoy her, but Caitlin found the experience disquieting. She was used to men looking at her, but there was too much intensity in Brady's eyes. His stare was forensic, almost judgmental, for reasons she couldn't fathom. What had changed since their parting in Yekaterinburg? He had no way of knowing that she'd just had the letter from Jack.

Piatakov's stare was easier to bear—there was sometimes a look in his eyes that made her think of her junior prom. He was really quite sweet, she decided. His insistence on kissing her hand when they left seemed like something out of *War and Peace*—she doubted that such courtesies were given much space in the Cheka rulebook.

She felt relieved when they were gone and then guilty for feeling so. They would soon be risking their lives for the cause, and she might never see them again. Added to which, she could hardly blame Brady for being suspicious. When it came to Jack and herself, she'd lied to him over and over again.

Once back in her room, she reread Jack's message. The inner turmoil returned, the dance of contradictory feelings that never seemed to stop. How could she wish he hadn't come when she couldn't wait to see him?

THERE WAS NOTHING QUITE LIKE sunlight after rain, Caitlin thought as she waited in the park for McColl to arrive. The grass and leaves were glistening, the colors as vivid as one of the new expressionist paintings. It felt like a brand-new day, and she had to remember it wasn't.

When he came through the gate, the first thing she noticed was the Russian clothes. They looked strange on him, but doubtless only because she knew who he really was. A spy, she thought. My lover the spy.

He had seen her and quickened his step. He looked older, she thought as he approached. Or maybe just thinner of face. Like herself.

She had wondered how she should greet him, here, in Moscow, where so much else mattered. But in that moment nothing else did. They looked, they embraced, they kissed, as if the world were somewhere else.

"It's good to see you," he said.

She shook her head, if only to bring the world back. "Why?" she demanded, as all the mixed emotions his message had stirred came bubbling to the surface. "Why are you here?"

"Let's walk," he suggested mildly, offering his arm.

He must have known she'd be angry, Caitlin thought. She put her hand through his arm, feeling, for her, unusually unsure.

"Aidan Brady's in Moscow," he told her.

"I know," she said. "I met him in Vladivostok in April, and we traveled together for weeks."

"Oh," McColl said, somehow looking both relieved and deflated. "So he doesn't know about Dublin?"

"About me choosing you over them? No, he doesn't. We hardly talked about Ireland. He probably thought it would be painful for me."

"That doesn't sound like him."

"No, it doesn't, does it? Still . . ."

"I was afraid he might run into you here and mete out his own idea of justice."

She thought about that and had to admit that knowing what McColl knew, it was reason enough to seek her out. "How did you know he was here? Have you seen him?"

"I haven't. My people keep a list of all the foreigners here in Moscow. It's how I knew *you* were here."

"And how did you find me?"

"A long story. But I wouldn't have looked, let alone made contact, if I hadn't thought Brady might be out for revenge."

"He isn't."

"Good."

They ambled on. The park was filling up now that the weather had improved, and she couldn't help feeling a spring in her step. She stopped, turned toward him, and put a hand on each of his shoulders. "Now that Brady has brought us together, perhaps we should make the most of it. Do you have somewhere we could go?"

"Not where we'd be alone." He put his arms around her waist. "Which is the other reason I wanted to see you. I have an eleven-year-old boy I don't know what to do with. He's from Ukraine, and his parents are both dead. I brought him to Moscow because he thought his uncle was here, but the uncle's dead as well, so now he has nowhere to go. I can't look after him forever, and I was hoping that you might know of a home."

"You mean an orphanage?" Of all the things she'd expected from their meeting, finding a home for a Russian child wasn't one of them.

"I suppose so," he said, with obvious reluctance. "Wasn't your friend Kollontai going to shake up the old system and make it better?"

"She was. And to a point she has, although the way things are at the moment, it's not high on the government's list of priorities. But . . . well, I'll look into it."

"Thank you. As to us," he said, pushing her hair back from her eyes, "I don't suppose a hotel . . ."

"No," she said instantly. But why not take him back to her room? The others had all been out when she'd left, and having a man there was hardly unknown. Some nights the house sounded full of them. "We can go to my room," she said. "Just this once—you understand that? We can't keep meeting. I'm in enough trouble as it is."

"With whom?"

As they left the park and walked toward the river, she told him about her recent brushes with the Cheka, the one in Yekaterinburg that had been her own fault, the one here in Moscow for carrying Spiridonova's message. An ongoing affair with a British agent would certainly top them both, she said with some asperity. A swift deportation was the least she could expect.

"Then maybe we shouldn't," McColl said, slowing his pace.

The dismay on his face was almost comical. "I'm sure we shouldn't," she said, "but just this once . . ."

The house was no longer empty, but only one woman crossed their path on the way to Caitlin's room, and the stare she gave them seemed truly blank.

"She has terrible eyesight," Caitlin whispered, shutting the door behind them. "And she's always losing her glasses. I know," she added, seeing McColl's expression, "the bed is a trifle narrow."

"I'm sure we'll fit," he said with a smile, undoing the top button on her blouse.

"I'm sure we will," she agreed, feeling the familiar spike of desire. The remembered scents and touches, the sudden thrill of joining together—no matter how many times they did it, no matter how long they'd been apart, the ecstasy and sense of rightness never seemed to fade.

It was over far too quickly.

"Sorry," he murmured. "It's been a while."

"You don't have to hurry off, do you?"

"No."

"Well, then . . ." She laid her head against his shoulder. "I've been missing that."

"That?"

"You. That and you are synonymous."

"I'm glad to hear it."

She sighed and snuggled in. "What's the news from home? Your home, I mean. Jed and your mother."

McColl let out a deep breath. "It's been months since I heard anything. Jed was still alive in April, and that's all I know."

She pulled him even closer, and they lay there in silence for a while.

"Have you been in Russia all this time?" he asked eventually.

"No. I went home to the States in March and came back here in April. Across the Pacific. It wasn't so much fun on my own."

"How was the family?"

"Fine. Most of them—my dad was his usual disapproving self. It was good to see Aunt Orla, but the rest of the trip . . . I hardly recognized the place. They've shut down any debate about the war—all my old friends are either in prison or hiding their heads in the sand. And it's just about impossible for someone with views like mine to function as a journalist." She told him about the searching of the house in Brooklyn, gave him a précis of the trial in Chicago. "And I wrote several letters to you," she added. "I suppose they're still waiting in London."

"Yep."

She sighed. "So where have you been this whole time?"

"All over the place. After you left in November, they kept me dangling for a month, but I feel like I've been on the move ever since." He told her about Persia and Transcaspia, about the cotton and the oil and Audley Cheselden. He told her about the hostage shooting at Chaplino Junction, about Kerzhentsev and the gasworks bombing that never happened, knowing that she'd like the idea of him teaming up with a Bolshevik. He told her about finding Fedya asleep in the consul's Pathfinder and their time in the German camp.

"Where is he now?" she wanted to know.

"Minding the store."

"Store? What store?"

He described the antique shop and Fedya's natural way with customers.

She propped herself up on an elbow. "You're really fond of him, aren't you?"

"I am."

She had always believed he would make a good father, and suddenly, out of nowhere, the thought that they would never have children seemed to pierce her heart. Where had that come from?

She moved her hand down, with predictable results. "You seem to be ready again," she murmured.

This time it seemed to last forever, leaving them breathless and laughing, their hands and lips still reaching for each other, as if afraid to let go.

But eventually they had to, and Caitlin asked the question that both had seemed to be avoiding. What was he doing in Moscow?

His wry smile didn't bode well.

"The papers are full of British and French plots against the revolution," she said when he didn't respond right away. "There's been fighting around Murmansk between your soldiers and ours."

The "ours" was hard to miss. "I came to Russia to fight the Germans," he said. "And that's what I've been doing. In Transcaspia with the help of LSRs. In Ukraine with the Bolsheviks."

"And in Moscow?" she prompted him.

"I don't know yet," he said. "It's gotten complicated. There are things we are doing that are aimed at the Germans but might also hurt the Bolsheviks, and there are things we are doing that are actually aimed at the Bolsheviks. And the line between them isn't as clear as you'd think. I'm not trying to make excuses," he added. "All the things I've been involved with have been about beating the Germans, and if I'm asked to do anything else, I promise you I'll quit."

"But you said yourself that the line wasn't clear."

"It isn't."

"Then how . . . ?"

"All I can do is follow my conscience."

She stared up at the ceiling. She understood his dilemma, but where it did leave them?

On opposite sides.

"I'll do what I can to find a home for your boy," she said. "And I'll let you know what I've found out. But after that we won't see each other again, not here in Russia, not while you're doing what you're doing."

Sadness filled his eyes, but he took her hand and squeezed it. "Agreed."

15
Soldiers in Plain Clothes

The English Club on Tverskaya, which McColl had visited on several occasions in 1917, was boarded up and liberally plastered with revolutionary slogans. The latter were unreadable through the grimy tram window and the lightly falling rain, but the improvised name change was all too clear. It now read "Conspiracy" rather than "Club."

His fellow conspirator on this particular evening was sitting five yards farther down the car. He was dressed like McColl in blouse, trousers, and soft high boots, his cap more rakishly perched atop his thick blond hair. Northcutt had introduced him as Paul and stressed that they shouldn't acknowledge each other's presence until they reached their destination.

The point of the operation was wedged between McColl's knees— a battered leather suitcase packed with paper money. Bowers had delivered it to the antique shop that afternoon, and while Fedya was in the back, McColl had examined the contents, mostly out of curiosity. The ruble notes were old and grubby, and he couldn't help wondering where Northcutt had gotten them from.

Fedya had clearly been longing to know what the suitcase contained but had known enough not to ask.

Ah, Fedya.

Since Caitlin had offered to look for a home, McColl had been meaning to talk to the boy, but he hadn't managed it yet. There'd been no lack of opportunity—it was just cowardice on his part. He'd rehearsed his arguments, worked out what he'd say, but knew that the boy would be deaf to logic. Desertion was desertion, no matter how good the reasons might be.

He wished there were some other option, but if there were, he hadn't thought of it yet. The boy needed schooling. He needed someone to take care of him, someone who could and would stick around.

The tram crumbled across Sadovaya, narrowly missing a droshky that had strayed too close to the tracks. The rain had almost stopped, and the Triumphal Arch was visible up ahead. A long wall on his side of the street was lined with myriad copies of the same stirring poster, calling on the workers to defend their revolution. Could it be saved? Almost every day brought news of another Bolshevik reverse, and their papers had stopped printing maps of the fighting, presumably for fear of weakening morale.

He wondered again what the money was for. He'd asked Bowers, but the answer he'd gotten had been less than useful. "Take your pick," the other man had said. "Bribery, guns, and keeping their army fed if we're lucky. Buying back the nobles' jewelry if we're not."

None of which would win the war. The Germans wouldn't be bought off, and the Whites seemed far more interested in fighting their Russian enemies.

He'd promised Caitlin he would follow his conscience, but as she herself had told him once—people could decide what was right only when they had all the relevant facts. And he was far from sure he had them.

The tram was approaching the Triumphal Arch, the sunset behind it smudged with smoke from the station and yards beyond. A car was parked under the archway, two men leaning up against its bonnet. Chekists, most likely. Watching the world go by, wondering when to pounce.

The tram continued on up the Petersburg Chaussée, passing

the moribund racecourse on the left. When he caught sight of the Petrovsky Palace, its chimneys fired by the rays of the sinking sun, McColl reached for the suitcase and rang the bell.

This was one of Moscow's richer suburbs, which seemed strangely appropriate. Revolutionaries had traditionally held their trysts in the poorer parts of town, but in Russia's upside-down world they gathered in streets lined with trees and big houses.

Two turns to the left and one to the right were the instructions. He walked on, aware of Paul's presence some fifty yards behind. It was finally growing dark, and most of the windows he passed were lit, giving the streets an almost festive look. There was also a constant murmur of conversation, interposed with shouts and peals of laughter. Most of the houses had been split into flats and were now home to five or six families. Those owners who hadn't fled were probably grinding their teeth in the single room that the Housing Committee had allowed them to keep.

The Alexander Bar was on a corner of a four-way intersection, amid several rows of mostly vacant shops. Across the street two droshky drivers were sharing a smoke, their horses nuzzling each other with obvious affection. Behind them, in what had once been the Anastasia Hair Salon, a man was visible through the badly cracked window, working at a table in an otherwise empty room.

The bar itself was full of smoke, so much so that McColl needed several seconds to get his bearings. The furniture was bizarre, the seating a mixture of armchairs and iron benches, the counter a wardrobe laid on its side. From what he could see, the clientele was more club than pub—exclusively male, rather well heeled, and reeking of the past.

There were several different vodkas on offer, and McColl was announcing his choice when a Russian loomed out of the smoke. He was about thirty, with wavy dark hair and a military mustache. After slapping McColl on the back, he gazed expectantly into his eyes.

"I'm from Boris," McColl said, though an exchange of passwords already seemed somewhat redundant. "He told me I could get a game of *eralash* here."

"You can!" the Russian said happily, looking down at the suitcase. "No, seriously. What was it? Only on Tuesday and Friday evenings. That's right, isn't it?" He beamed. "I am Vasily. Come. We are in the back room."

He was drunk, McColl realized. Over the Russian's shoulder, he saw Paul enter through the street door. "My partner has arrived," he told the Russian. "We'll both come."

"The more the merrier!"

McColl rolled his eyes at Paul, who gave him a shrug in return. It didn't bode well, but sobriety hadn't been part of the deal.

The only occupant of the back room had wavy *fair* hair and a military mustache. "This is Viktor," the first Russian said. "And I am Vasily," he announced again, this time with a wink. "Not our real names, of course. He is Vasily and I am Viktor."

Both he and his partner laughed uproariously; the two Englishmen offered supportive smiles.

A Russian Tweedledum and Tweedledee, McColl thought.

"Have a drink," the original Viktor suggested. As with Vasily, an educated accent was recognizable through the slurring.

"We won't stay," McColl said, placing the suitcase on the table between them and opening the lid. The Russians were less impressed than he expected—not at all, in fact.

"That is good," Vasily said, as if receiving thousands of rubles were something he did every day. "But you must have a drink. And don't worry—the Chekists are tucked up in bed by this time of night."

Viktor had already poured four glasses. "To the czar!" he said once everyone had one in hand.

"To the czar," they chorused, and tipped them back.

Viktor giggled and poured four more.

McColl raised a hand. "To victory over the Germans!"

The Russians responded, but without much enthusiasm. "To getting our world back," Vasily muttered, suddenly serious, leaving McColl with the strong suspicion that it wasn't the Germans he wanted it back from.

He and Paul refused a third, saying they needed to keep their wits about them.

Vasily shook his head so hard that McColl was afraid it might fly off. "We have a droshky for you—it's waiting outside—so why do you need to keep your wits?"

"No—"

"A woman each, perhaps . . ."

"Some other time. We must go."

"If you must, you must," Vasily said sulkily. "And as for the Germans," he added, as if reading McColl's mind, "we will leave them to you and the Americans. We have our own battles to fight."

The droshkies were still outside, and McColl saw no sign of loitering Chekists. He doubted there were enough of them to keep a permanent watch on out-of-the-way places like this one. Or maybe there were too many Viktors and Vasilys. In either case he felt safe enough, particularly now that the money was out of his hands.

But he also felt far from happy. Drunk or not, Vasily could hardly have been clearer about *his* priorities. As the droshky made its way back toward the Chaussée, McColl just sat there in silence, angrily mulling the matter over.

"Why are we supporting these people?" he finally asked his companion in English.

"The enemy of my enemy and so on," Paul suggested.

"But who *is* our enemy now?"

"That's an easy one. Whoever the chief says it is."

"And that's good enough for you?" McColl asked, more aggressively than he intended.

Paul didn't seem offended. "We're just soldiers in plainclothes. We do what we're told."

McColl sat back in the rocking seat. He couldn't justify what they were doing. Not to the Caitlin who lived in his head, not to himself. Even as a child, he'd always hated the thought of doing as he was told.

THE DAYS THAT FOLLOWED THE one with Jack were difficult for Caitlin. It had been wonderful to see him, but also profoundly distracting. She found herself resenting him for turning up at all and castigating herself for letting his appearance cause such self-destructive turmoil in her heart. She loved him, she knew she did, but that didn't have to mean losing all sense of proportion whenever he danced back into her life.

She worked Monday, Tuesday, and Friday at the office on Cherkasski Street and had planned to spend Wednesday and Thursday getting her Siberian notes in some sort of order. She did get some of it done, but her mind kept slipping away from the task at hand and focusing back on him. According to Kollontai's "New Woman," which the party was republishing in a few weeks' time, passionate love was always a transient thing. So why, Caitlin wondered, was theirs proving so damned durable? And how ludicrous would that question sound to most women?

Maybe it was hardly ever seeing each other that gave their love no time to grow stale. Maybe, despite all their obvious differences, down deep they really were a perfect fit. She smiled at the thought.

She knew Kollontai's words by heart. The new woman "asserted her individuality," refused to simply "reflect" her beloved, put the expression of love "in a subordinate place in her life." And Caitlin had done all that. She was here, wasn't she, doing work that mattered to herself and others, not just sitting somewhere safe and sound, waiting for her man to come home? Then why was it so damn difficult?

McColl's debriefing was held in the Kazan Station's buffet late on the following day. There was only tea to drink and nothing at all to eat, but the place was crowded and noisy enough to cloak a conversation.

"I want you to meet up with Sidney Reilly," Northcutt said after McColl had completed his report. "We'll be putting a lot of troops ashore at Archangel over the next few weeks, and we expect the Bolsheviks to retaliate. They'll probably intern all British passport holders, so we're putting our best men underground while we still can. You're already in that situation, and you'll be joined by George Hill and Sidney Reilly. George is off in Ukraine at the moment, but Sidney's here, and I want the two of you to meet, set up contact routines, all the usual. He's using the name Constantine at the moment, and he's expecting to see you at the Tramble Café—at the intersection of Petrovka and Kuznetsky Most—at seven P.M. on Friday. He's a Jew, of course, but don't let that fool you. He knows what he's doing."

"All right," McColl agreed, wondering if Northcutt actually thought that most Jews didn't. He felt curious about Reilly. Over the years he'd heard about the man from several of his colleagues, and none had offered a neutral assessment.

"And you'd better smarten yourself up a bit," Northcutt added after taking at look at what McColl was wearing. "Reilly's a snappy dresser, and we don't want the two of you looking like an audition for *The Prince and the Pauper*."

THE FOLLOWING EVENING FOUND MCCOLL standing outside the entrance to St. Basil's Cathedral, idly staring across at the Kremlin, where Lenin was probably hard at work. It was a beautiful evening, much less humid than in recent days, and the setting sun was glinting on the domes of the churches within. In front of the wall, several families were laying flowers on the grave that held Fedya's uncle and hundreds of others. He should have brought Fedya, he thought.

The arrangement with Caitlin was simple—he would be here on alternate evenings, and if she had anything to report, she would run a hand through her hair and wait for him down on the towpath. If she didn't, she would just walk on by.

It seemed unlikely she'd have any news this soon, so McColl was surprised to see her glance across and lift a hand to her hair. He let her get fifty yards ahead, then followed her down the cobbled slope to the river. The iron supports were all that was left of the wooden benches, and she was sitting on one of the capstans that stood by the edge of the water.

She rose to greet him with a kiss, but her face seemed unusually somber. "Have you heard the news?" she asked, taking his arm and setting them both in motion.

"What news?"

"The czar's been executed," she told him.

"Oh," he said, for want of anything else. He wasn't surprised, and neither mourning nor celebration felt particularly appropriate.

"An official announcement was put out this afternoon. It happened three days ago. In Yekaterinburg." She looked out across the water. "I saw the place where they were being held, and I keep wondering where it was done. In the trees behind? In one of the basements?" She shrugged. "Not that it matters. She turned back to McColl. "My friends think it was to stop the Czechs from getting hold of him."

"That would have been awkward," McColl agreed. "What about the rest of the family?"

"Oh, they're all dead," Caitlin said.

"All of them? The children as well?"

"Yes."

McColl could see she was upset, but he wasn't sure why. "How do you feel about it?" he asked.

She gave him a weary look. "I don't know. Shocked. I understand why they did it, but still . . ."

"They couldn't afford to leave an heir for the Whites to rally around."

"Yes. That must have been one of the reasons."

"What others could there be?"

This time the look was slightly pitying. "Hatred. Revenge. Those millions of men he sent off to die. They all had families."

McColl nodded and wondered what the consequences might be. More bitterness was all he could think. People already knew which side they were on.

"I've been asking around about children's homes," Caitlin was saying. "There is a new Palace of Motherhood in Moscow, but it's for mothers and young children—your Fedya's much too old. There are lots of orphanages, but most are awful, and the government has hardly gotten started on making them better. But I have found one that's recommended. It's in Yauzskaya, not far from the Kursk Station. I've written down the address." She fished in her pocket for a scrap of paper and handed it over. "Most of the prewar staff was kicked out after the first revolution—there were terrible stories about the way the orphans were treated before. A local women's group took over, and they're still running the place. No one claims it's perfect, but everyone says it's the best available."

"How many children are there?"

"About two hundred."

"In how many rooms?"

"About thirty, I think. The children sleep in dormitories. But there's a canteen and a library, and there are women who give lessons. After the summer they hope to start sending some of the older children to one of the local schools."

"I don't suppose the children are allowed to go out on their own?"

"I don't know, but I wouldn't think so. How could you run a place like that if you let the children come and go as they pleased?"

"What's the age range?"

"No idea. Look, I told them about Fedya, and they say there's a place for him. All you have to do is take him there."

And hand him over, McColl thought. "I'm grateful," he said.

"You're welcome. Both of you." She turned to face him. "I don't know what else you're doing here—and I don't want to—though for the boy's sake I'm glad you came."

"But not for your sake?"

"I didn't mean—"

"I know. I'm sorry." He felt confused by her, by this woman he knew so well yet who sometimes seemed almost a stranger. "But it looks like the war might soon be over," he said, hoping she would say that then they could be together. She didn't.

"The fighting in France may end," she said, "and Germany may be defeated, but here the war will go on. The real war, the one that matters. You do understand that?"

"I do," he said with reluctance. Even though he'd known it was coming, it still felt like a blow to the heart.

"Take care of yourself," she said.

"And you. You know where to find me."

She smiled and put her arms around his neck. "I suppose for once that's true." They kissed and held each other close.

⤙ ⤙ ⤙

IT WAS BETTER LIKE THIS, she told herself as she walked away along the towpath. And most of her believed it. The new woman, she thought, crying the same old tears.

What other choices did she have? She knew what he'd wanted her to say, but she didn't want to raise his hopes with a promise she might not be able to keep. She was far from certain that she should have offered him any. Why could she not accept that being true to herself meant staying in Russia and that staying in Russia meant giving him up? She couldn't be a part-time revolutionary, any more than he could be a part-time spy. And even if he gave up spying, she couldn't give up the revolution, not without giving up on herself.

She wanted them both, yet more and more it seemed that it had to be one or the other. Passions came and went, but the work was forever—she could still hear Kollontai say it, three years ago in the house of exile high above Christiania. Her mind was convinced—could she bring her heart into line? One thing she knew—that emotional wrench would be easier once he was gone.

THE FACT THAT FEDYA HAD sold several items at a handsome profit during McColl's absence and was clearly feeling pleased with himself made it even harder to broach the matter of moving him into the home. McColl bided his time and waited to bring the subject up until after they'd eaten supper at the local canteen and enjoyed a leisurely walk in the warm evening air.

"Fedya," he began, once they were back inside, "I won't be here in Moscow for much longer."

The look of alarm was instant. "Why? Where are you going?"

"I'm going home."

Fedya looked confused. "But you told me you lived here in Moscow."

McColl hesitated. Telling Fedya his true identity was obviously fraught with risk, but he felt he owed the boy that much. "I come from England," he said, opting for simplicity. He doubted that

Fedya had heard of Scotland. "My government sent me here to fight the Germans. And now I have to go back."

"Why?"

"Because if I stay here, I'll probably be caught and killed."

Fedya looked stunned by that, though only for a moment. "So what's your real name?" he demanded to know.

"Jack McColl."

"Jack McColl," the boy repeated, trying it out. "I want to come with you," he said, a sliver of hope in his eyes.

"No, that's not possible," McColl said, watching it wither away. "I can't. I wish I could," he added, and part of him really meant it. "But I can't."

"Why not?"

"Lots of reasons. Because it's too dangerous. Because if you're caught with me, you'll share my punishment, like you did in the German camp—"

"But we escaped!" Fedya cried out, clenching his fists.

"I know, but next time we might not be so lucky. And, Fedya, you are Russian. This is your country. You speak the language, you know what it's like here."

"But . . ."

"I've found you a home—a friend of mine has. A home with lots of children, one where you'll go to school and learn lots of things."

"Why can't I just stay here? I can run the shop on my own."

McColl sighed. "I know you could. But someone else will be coming to run it, so you can't stay here. And the home will be better. It will."

"But I won't know anyone."

"Not at first, but you'll soon make friends," McColl said, wincing at the cliché. "The food's good. You'll learn things. And I'll visit you while I'm still here. And my friend will visit you after I'm gone. You'll like her." Caitlin had offered no such thing, but he knew she would if he asked.

Fedya was trying hard not cry. "When?" he asked.

"Tomorrow," McColl told him. It was better not to drag it out, he thought.

The boy let loose a single heartrending sob and turned his face to the wall.

McColl just sat there, wondering what, if anything, he could say or do to make things better. He told himself Fedya had fastened onto him and would do the same to others—boys of his own age, the women whom Caitlin had talked about. No matter how hard it seemed, things were better this way. McColl had no idea how long he'd be staying in Russia or how difficult it would be to get out when the time eventually came. And even if he could take Fedya to England, what would life be like for an eleven-year-old boy who spoke not a word of the language and whose whole world up to a few weeks before had been that of a peasant village? A fish out of water would feel more at home.

He knew he was doing the right thing, and maybe one day Fedya would, too.

THE NEXT MORNING THE BOY hardly said a word, either over breakfast or during the ride across town. McColl had wondered whether Fedya, in his desperation, might do something truly reckless, like vanish overnight or threaten to expose him as a foreign spy. But the boy seemed beaten down, which made McColl feel even worse.

The orphanage was a large pastel gray building on a narrow street off Sadovaya. It looked cared for, and McColl was pleased to see that those bars across the windows that were broken or missing had not been replaced. Once inside the front door, he found the lack of noise surprising, but the woman who welcomed them seemed kind enough. She ruffled Fedya's hair and took no offense when the boy pushed her hand away. "You'll like it here," she said. "Once you get used to it. I promise you will."

Fedya shook his head.

"It's better if you say good-bye here," the woman told McColl. "I have all the details your friend supplied, and Fedya can tell me about his family."

"They're dead," Fedya said, as if that closed the conversation.

McColl got down on one knee to face him. "I'll come and check up on you in a few days," he promised. "That is all right?" he asked the woman.

She nodded.

Without any warning, Fedya threw his arms around McColl's neck and clung on as if his life depended on it.

McColl hugged him back. "It'll be all right," he said. It was such a stupid thing to say, but somehow it struck a chord. Fedya allowed McColl to gently disengage them, then tried and almost succeeded in raising a smile.

"A few days," McColl repeated as the woman led the boy away.

Fedya didn't look back.

Out on the street, McColl wiped the tears from his cheeks and cursed the world and everyone in it. Another day, another fucking good-bye.

MCCOLL APPROACHED THE TRAMBLE CAFÉ cautiously, walking up Kuznetsky Most and spending several minutes watching the café from the other side of the intersection. It was doing good business, with hardly a moment passing before someone made use of the doors.

Most of the clientele were wearing suits, and McColl was glad he'd followed Northcutt's orders. It hadn't been easy, but an hour's rummaging through the shop's store of secondhand clothes had turned up a suit and a stiff-collared shirt that almost fit. The shoes were ones that Sandy Luckett had left behind, and after walking a mile in them McColl had a good idea why.

He was glad of something to do, something that took his mind off Caitlin and Fedya. It was five minutes past the allotted hour, and he'd seen no one who matched the description of Sidney Reilly. Which probably meant the man was already inside. There were no cars parked nearby, and McColl himself was the only loiterer. It looked safe.

He strolled across the road and in through the doors, then gave his eyes a moment to adjust. The café was busy and very smoky, but he doubted he'd have had any trouble recognizing Reilly even without Northcutt's description. He *did* look Jewish, and he *was* snappily dressed, but what made him stand out was the palpable air of self-possession. The large table in the corner—the best in the café—was his by right, and he'd spread himself accordingly, cloak on one chair, cane on another, newspaper laid across the table. While everyone else in the place seemed cheek by jowl, Reilly had room to swing any number of cats.

He rose to shake McColl's hand and suggested the seat by his own. "It's noisy enough that we can talk," he said once they both were seated. And it was—McColl had excellent hearing, and the men at the nearest table might have been miming for all he could make of their conversation.

Reilly offered his cigarette case and ordered brandies. "It's not a particularly good one," he admitted once the waiter had departed, "but it is the best in town. Outside the Kremlin, of course."

They discussed the current situation and the muted public response to events in Yekaterinburg. "A shame about the children, of course," Reilly said, "but their father was a weakling, and no loss to us. The Bolsheviks think they've wiped the slate clean, and they're right about that. But they haven't just wiped it clean for themselves. They're not the only ones who want a new Russia."

McColl took a drag on the Turkish cigarette. "They are in power," he said mildly.

Reilly sniffed. "They're hanging on by their fingertips. You know what happened on July sixth—the LSRs just froze like country rabbits in front of headlights. They sat back and waited, and Lenin's Latvians just rolled them up. But for twelve whole hours, the Bolsheviks were pissing in their pants—the Latvians are all they have, and they weren't sure of them. Neutralize them . . ." He opened his hands.

"How?" McColl asked.

Reilly smiled. "I'm working on that. Let's just say I have reason to believe we can turn them."

"Every man has his price?"

"In a way. When people say that, they usually mean money, and not every man can be bought with money. But with something else—a country of his own, for example—well, that's a different story. Everyone wants something."

"Do we have someone lined up to take over?"

Reilly took a gulp of brandy. "Savinkov's still the best bet, if we can get him back to Moscow. After Yaroslavl he had to make himself scarce for a while. But who it is doesn't matter that much—I could step in myself if it came to that. We just need someone to end this madness once and for all."

"And send the Bolsheviks back to Siberia."

"The lower ranks, perhaps. The leaders will have to be shot. After a trial, I suppose. But you can't take risks with people like that."

"No."

Reilly called for a refill. "Northcutt tells me you used to sell luxury automobiles."

"For six years. All over the world."

"Just the one?"

"Yes, the Maia. Beautiful car for its time. Do you know it?"

"I've seen it, but I can't say I've ever driven one. Be honest now—if money were no object, which car would you buy?"

McColl thought about it. "A Bugatti Type 13," he suggested eventually. "But he may have designed something better by now."

"Mmm." Reilly asked what McColl thought of the latest Daimlers, and for the next fifteen minutes the two of them traded opinions on the strengths and weaknesses of a dozen different automobiles. In an English pub, the conversation would have seemed quite normal and probably would have bored any female companions to death, but McColl found it strangely enjoyable. It was like a trip back in time and place, from desperate Russia to prewar England, from the life he led now to the one he'd led then. He wouldn't have swapped a life with Caitlin for one without her, nor the man he'd been then for the one he'd become, but these days simple pleasures seemed decidedly thin on the ground. And he really had loved the Maia.

Their talk was ended when Reilly noticed his watch and announced he had an "engagement." After they'd hurriedly gone through the various protocols and Reilly was getting up to leave, McColl realized that neither had mentioned the Germans. As they walked out onto the street, he asked the other man if he had any news of the war in France.

"Good as over, old boy," Reilly told him. "We've pushed the Germans back across the Marne, and London thinks they've finally shot their bolt. It might be all over by Christmas. Good news, eh?"

"Wonderful," McColl agreed as Reilly scanned the road for a droshky.

So what were they all still doing here in Russia? As if he didn't know.

THREE DAYS AFTER HER TOWPATH walk with Jack, Caitlin had another visit from the Cheka. This time they came to the women's office, and perhaps for that reason they were slightly less peremptory. Not that there was any doubt about the outcome—Comrade Komarov requested her presence, and a request from him was an order. As the three of them walked the short distance to the Cheka offices on Bolshaya Lubyanka—the Chekists slightly behind her, one at either shoulder—she wondered what she'd done this time.

She'd been meaning to ask for another interview with Spiridonova, if only to show that she hadn't been cowed, but hadn't actually done so. What else could it be? With a sinking feeling, she realized it had to be Jack. Had one of the other women reported his visit? And if so, why? Having sex was hardly a crime in itself, and who could have known that the man in her room wasn't a Russian acquaintance?

This time she wasn't kept waiting long. The same walk through the maze, and there was Komarov, the spider at its heart. A camp bed had been set up since her last visit, but he didn't look like he'd had much sleep. If you wanted to tire yourself out, she thought, then start a revolution.

"I understand you know an Englishman named Jack McColl," he said bluntly, his eyes alert to any reaction. His open shirt looked badly in need of a wash, but if he was dirty, he didn't smell.

How did they know Jack's name? was the first thought that crossed her mind. The only other person in Moscow who knew was Brady. "Yes," she said abruptly—she couldn't let Komarov think she was working on her answers.

"And you've seen him recently?"

A question or a statement? "Yes," she admitted, because if they knew already, then saying no would leave her no way back. "He came up to me on the street, and I took him back to my house."

"Why?"

"I didn't want us to be seen together."

"Because he's a British agent?"

"Because he *was* a British agent. I don't know if he still is. Not for certain."

Komarov smiled at that. "Did he give you any other reason for his being in Moscow?"

"He came to see me about a boy," Caitlin decided. When it involved her and Jack, she could neither risk the truth nor think of a workable lie.

At least her answer surprised Komarov. "What boy?"

She explained who Fedya was but denied any detailed knowledge of how he and Jack had met. "He told me he brought the boy here from Ukraine."

"Whereabouts in Ukraine?"

"He didn't say."

"How did they get here?"

"He didn't say."

Komarov gave her a skeptical look. "Why bring the boy to you?"

"He wanted help in finding the boy a home, and he knows that my friend Kollontai has been involved in reforming the old orphanages."

"And did you help?"

"I asked around, and someone recommended one."

She thought he would want to know who and which, but instead he asked where Jack was living. She told him she had no idea.

"He didn't tell you?"

"That's what I said."

"You used to be lovers, yes?"

"Yes."

"But not anymore?"

If Brady was the source, Komarov would know the story only up until 1914. "Not since the war began," she said. "The man deceived me."

"And arrested your brother, who was later executed."

She shook her head. "My brother told me before he died that Jack offered to let him escape. For my sake. So I forgave Jack for that. What I couldn't forgive was the fact that he'd deceived me about who he was."

Komarov steepled his fingers together. "If there was nothing left between you, then why would he expect you to help him with this boy?"

"He was desperate, I think. And he didn't want anything for himself."

Komarov shrugged that aside. "More to the point, why did you not report his presence to the Cheka?"

The big question. "Maybe I should have," she admitted. "I asked myself why I didn't, and there's only one obvious answer. No matter what happened later, we meant a lot to each other once, and I couldn't bring myself to give him up, not when I thought he might be shot."

Komarov gave her a long look, then seemed to reach a decision. "Did he have a beard when you saw him?"

"No."

"What was he wearing?"

"The usual things—breeches, a blouse, felt boots."

"A cap?"

"I don't think so. No."

Komarov leaned forward in his seat. "I could arrest you for consorting with the enemy. But I won't. I don't think you've been completely truthful, but I could be wrong about that. And in view of your services to the revolution—your writing and your current work for the women's section—I'm going to give you the benefit of the doubt. This time. There will be no second chance. If this man contacts you again, you will put the past where it belongs and report the matter to me. Understood?"

"Understood," she said. "I did tell him not to come near me anymore."

"Then you may have saved his life," Komarov said dryly. "Don't be tempted to do so again."

As she followed her Chekist guard back through the maze, Caitlin felt as angry as she could remember feeling. With Jack, for coming to Moscow in the first place; with herself, for knowing the threat it posed to her yet refusing to act on that knowledge. Well, Komarov had spelled things out in no uncertain terms. Her boyfriend's presence in Moscow, which had already risked compromising her work as a journalist, had almost put her in jail. And it wasn't over. She still had to warn him that the Chekists were on his trail, with all the risks that might involve. It was Dublin all over again, only this time she wouldn't be going home with him. That, she decided, was the one ray of brightness in the whole business—now that they were onto him, he'd have no choice but to leave.

ON THE AFTERNOON THAT CAITLIN was summoned by Komarov, McColl visited Fedya. He was asked to wait in the large room off the lobby, and the boy was then brought down to him, rather in the manner of a prison visit. But there were no bruises on Fedya's face, and he voiced no specific complaints. Yes, the food was good, the staff members were kind, the other children—well, some had been friendly, others not. "They say I'm Ukrainian because I come from there, but I'm as Russian as they are."

What was gone was the light in his eyes, and McColl had no idea how to bring that back. Maybe Caitlin would know. He would write and ask her to visit the boy as often as she could.

They talked about their journey to Moscow; they talked about the shop and some of the customers they'd had, but the only time Fedya showed any animation was in passing on what another child had told him, that England was full of Russian emigrants. He drew no conclusion from this but left McColl to draw the appropriate one himself. "When are you leaving?" Fedya asked hurriedly, when footsteps on the stairs suggested that someone was coming to fetch him.

"I don't know," McColl told him. "But I'll see you again before I do.

16
The Rotting Agent

☭

Three hours after visiting Fedya, McColl was passing Petrovsky Park at the wheel of a Cheka automobile, a red flag fluttering on the bonnet's left wing. Roger Bowers had picked him up in the Russo-Balt and was now sitting in the passenger seat, having cheerfully given way to the more experienced driver. He claimed he had almost run into a tram on Tverskaya, before narrowly missing two party officials crossing the road outside the Alexandrov Gardens.

The car was not all that Bowers had brought. There was now a cloth-wrapped pistol beneath McColl's seat and brand-new papers in his trouser pocket, attesting that Mikhail Krylov was a member of Felix Dzerzhinsky's organization. There were also Northcutt's orders for the evening. He and Bowers were to drive to an old inn some five miles outside the city, collect two crates of who-knew-what from a French intelligence officer, and deliver said crates to representatives of the Trust at a dacha in Arkhangelskoye some three miles farther west. They were already on the road to the inn—what began as the Tverskaya ran all the way to Riga under several different names—and Bowers was sure he could find the dacha without any trouble, so the mechanics of the operation seemed pretty straightforward. What worried McColl was the why.

He asked.

"As a favor to our allies," was Bowers's laconic response.

"But why would they want such a favor?" McColl wondered out loud. "Wouldn't it be easier—and less risky—to hand these crates over themselves? Why have two clandestine meetings when one would do? And using two cars doubles the chance that one will be spotted. Didn't Northcutt offer any explanation?"

Bowers seemed unconcerned. "Nope."

"Well, it looks to me as if the French are trying to put some distance between themselves and whatever it is these crates contain. Doesn't that worry you?"

"Not yet," Bowers said cheerfully.

They were approaching the city limits and that point on the highway where the Cheka inspected vehicles entering and leaving Moscow. But only at night, according to Northcutt's information, and in this at least he was proved correct—the makeshift cabin flew its flag but was otherwise deserted.

"And with any luck we'll be back before dark," Bowers pointed out as they motored by.

The sky was completely overcast, the evening hot and humid. The highway stretched ahead, lined by fields and patches of forest, delightfully clear of traffic. They passed through several villages, all of which would have seemed deserted if not for the smoking chimneys. Tucked inside their houses, the locals would be following the passage of the car, anxious as the noise of engine rose, relieved as it faded away. It was all about power, McColl thought. Power and the fear it always induced.

On nights like this in years gone by, the sense of excitement had always seemed strangely fulfilling, as if this were the life he was meant for. A simple adrenaline surge, perhaps, but it had always felt like more. No longer. Since Cheselden's death—and maybe even before—the thrill had disappeared. Maybe he'd grown too old for games, or maybe the ones he was playing here left too sour a taste on the tongue. If he wasn't fucking up the job, he feared he was fucking up lives, both others' and his own.

Time—or something less easy to measure—seemed to be running out.

Soon but not tonight, he told himself. The automobile was in good shape, which might have surprised its Cheka owners. One of Northcutt's Russian friends had secured the job of repairing Dzerzhinsky's cars, which gave the Service the chance to use them between repair and return. That and the papers—painstakingly prepared by the local forgery unit—had given Northcutt's men the freedom of the roads, at least in theory. McColl wondered where they got their petrol from.

The inn they were seeking finally came into view. It was a large, two-story building with high gable ends, and it had probably done a roaring trade in days gone by, catering to long-distance travelers in the pre-railway era and weekend trippers in recent times. Now it was deserted, the slope running down to the nearby river littered with twisted metal tables.

Where was the Frenchman? McColl did a three-point turn and parked the Russo-Balt along the side of the building. It would still be visible to anyone who passed, but that might even be a plus. The Cheka wouldn't be shy about advertising their presence, and neither should they be.

It was only a minute to seven, so the Frenchman wasn't late yet. McColl got out and circled the inn, stopping only to gaze at the Moscow River, half the width here that it was in the city. He had just gotten back to the car when he and Bowers heard the sound of another vehicle approaching.

It was a malachite green Delaunay-Belleville—one of the czar's, McColl guessed; he remembered that Nicholas had owned a small fleet before the war. It was an utterly gorgeous automobile, and he found it hard to take his eyes off it, realizing with a start that its current owner was offering a white-gloved hand.

"I am Riberot," the man said, as if others might claim the same. He was quite short, with shiny dark hair brushed straight back, a small mustache over thin lips, and darting black eyes. His companion, a fair-haired young Russian with vulpine features, was already dragging the first of the crates out of the Delaunay-Belleville.

"We must find a better place to rendezvous," Riberot was saying. "Somewhere closer to the city."

Leaving Bowers to soothe the Frenchman, McColl walked across to examine the delivery. The crates were nailed shut, but lines of glass jars were visible between the strips of wood.

"What's in the jars?" McColl asked Riberot in French.

"The ones labelled plum conserve have the rotting agent, the ones labelled cherry the poison. And you must make sure our friends know which is which."

McColl let that sink in. "And what do they mean to do with the stuff?" he asked, trying to sound like he didn't much care.

"You'll have to ask them that," was Riberot's reply. He looked at his watch. "I must be going. I have an engagement with an extremely beautiful woman." He looked at them both for a moment, as if expecting applause, then abruptly reached for the door of his car.

Who are these people? McColl asked himself. And what the hell was he doing running their errands?

As he and Bowers lifted the crates into the back of the Russo-Balt, lightning bloomed in the western sky. "Twenty-seven seconds," Bowers said after the ensuing low rumble of thunder. "Five and a half miles, give or take. We might beat it home."

McColl had other concerns but wasn't sure how much point there was in sharing them with his partner. "You heard what the Frenchman said?" he asked once they were back on the road.

"About the jams? Yes. Plum for rotting, cherry for poison. And this is where we turn off. Arkhangelskoye is about three miles down this road."

"I don't like it," McColl said as they turned onto the smaller road. The skies above were rapidly darkening, the flashes of lightning more frequent.

"It'll pass over."

"Not the storm. The job."

"Oh. Well, I suppose I can see your point. But if *we* didn't do it, someone else would."

Which was facile but probably true, McColl thought, steering the Russo-Balt through another somnambulant hamlet. He thought about going back to the inn and dumping the crates in the river but then realized that doing so might kill half the local population.

What were their Russian allies intending to do with the contents? As Riberot had said, he would have to ask them. Try as he could, he found it hard to imagine an acceptable answer.

He said as much to his companion, who was busy trying to read the sketched map that Northcutt had supplied.

"This is probably one of those times when it's better not to know," Bowers replied.

His matter-of-factness gave McColl a moment of doubt—was he overreacting? He didn't think so.

They were coming into Arkhangelskoye. High to their left, a mansion clung to the top of a hill, its white façade standing out against the dark gray sky. Ahead of them the lane wound slowly downhill, passing widely spaced cottages with lightless windows and smokeless chimneys. These dachas were the weekend retreats of Moscow's middle and upper classes, most of whom had more pressing concerns in this particular summer.

The dacha they sought was right at the end of the lane, a neat white cottage almost engulfed by a long-neglected garden. The overgrown lawn sloped down to the river, which was here about thirty yards wide. Two weeping willows stood sentry on the bank, on either side of an exquisite summerhouse.

There were no waiting Russians.

"What time are they supposed to be here?" McColl asked Bowers as he drew the car to a halt.

"In twenty minutes," Bowers said, looking at his watch. "We gave it an extra half hour in case the French were late."

Lightning flickered through the trees to their right, and this time the thunder was more crack than rumble.

"I'll take the red flag off the car," Bowers said, opening his door. "No point alarming our friends."

McColl sat there for a moment, then reached beneath the seat for the pistol. Sliding it under his belt and the hip-length Russian blouse, he got out of the car. "I'll check the area," he told Bowers, who was still unraveling the string with which the flag was fastened.

After walking around the cottage, McColl made his way to the edge of the river and watched a cluster of broken branches slowly drift downstream.

Was he overreacting? He didn't think so. This was a step change, what the Americans called a whole new ball game. For almost five years, he'd done the jobs that Cumming and others had asked him to do, and though he'd often had his doubts about the politics, he'd never stopped believing that the war was worth winning.

But this was something else entirely. Delivering poisons to a warring group of Russians—and it hardly mattered which one—did nothing for King and Country, except perhaps tarnish them both. How could it help the British war effort? If these people succeeded in bringing down the Bolsheviks, it would take them months to reestablish an Eastern Front, assuming that they actually wanted to. And if Reilly was right, the war in the west would be over by then.

This was Russian business, and as far as McColl could see, neither Reds nor Whites posed any threat to Britain or its people. If forced to choose sides, he would probably have opted for the Reds, if only because Caitlin believed in their revolution. He didn't share all her political opinions—far from it—but he had learned to trust her heart.

But what could he do? What if he went back to Bowers and told him he'd decided not to hand over the crates? If Bowers tried to stop him, was he prepared to hold off a colleague at gunpoint and if necessary put a bullet in one of his legs?

The storm was moving closer, raindrops stippling the surface of the river. One step at a time, he told himself. Maybe Bowers would listen.

He never got the opportunity. McColl was halfway back to the car when a moving light appeared in the distance, and it was only a matter of moments before he heard the trotting hooves. Now he had the Russians to deal with as well.

There were two of them in the horse-drawn carriage, one of around middle age, the other a good deal younger. Both were wearing blouses and army breeches, with guns in leather holsters hanging from their belts. As Bowers and the older Russian exchanged passwords and introduced themselves, McColl tried working his way through the possible consequences of pulling his gun on them all. Too many imponderables, he decided. Anything could happen.

The rain was falling faster, the older Russian producing a key from his pocket. "We should drink a toast," he said, pulling a bottle from the back of the carriage and tucking it under his arm.

The door unlocked, they followed him in, McColl feeling strangely calm. The air was stale, the furniture covered in dust, but everything seemed to be there—this particular dacha was still awaiting its looters.

The older Russian found four porcelain teacups and poured out generous measures.

Toasting the czar was now a matter of toasting his memory, but the emotions kindled in some Russian breasts seemed stronger since his death.

There was no second glass, though—these two seemed more professional than Viktor and Vasily. Together they might be more than a match for McColl, in which case these might be his last few minutes. He rather hoped not.

The rain was making a racket on the roof. "Not the weather for an open carriage," the elder Russian said. "We won't be leaving until it stops. But there's no point in you waiting. Give us the stuff and you can drive back to Moscow. Safe and dry in your Cheka car."

"What's the stuff for?" McColl asked abruptly. He could see that Bowers was wishing he hadn't, but he wanted an answer.

And rather to his surprise, the Russian proved willing to give him one. "It will give us victory," he said simply.

"How?" McColl persisted, trying to sound more curious than judgmental.

"If they cannot feed the people, the people will overthrow them—it's as simple as that."

"And the poisons?"

"Ah. We didn't want to use them, but they left us no choice." He leaned back against the windowsill and reached inside his pocket for a half-smoked cigarette and a match. "In the north all the food for Petrograd crosses one of two bridges to reach the city, and once we blow them up, the city will starve. Simple, eh?" He lit the cigarette stub. "But Moscow is different—there are too many ways in and out, too many bridges to destroy. We cannot stop the movement of food, so we have to stop the production. If you have brought the amount our expert asked for, we can do that. There will be nothing to harvest this autumn and no beasts to slaughter for two hundred miles. Moscow will starve."

McColl took a deep breath. He'd had his answer, and it wasn't one he could live with. This man, this oh-so-reasonable enemy of the Bolsheviks, was intent on depriving an entire city of its food. The city where Caitlin and Fedya lived.

This really was the end of the line. The war was virtually over, he'd done his duty by Jed, and a Service willing to condone such a thing was not one he wanted to work for.

He felt, for a few short moments, an overwhelming sense of relief.

"No," he said, as much to himself as the others.

"No?" the Russian asked. He was about six feet away and partly shielding his partner.

"McColl . . ." Bowers said warningly.

The gun snagged in McColl's belt and wouldn't come loose. As he struggled to free it, the Russian's expression shifted from bemusement to anger, his hand to the holster at his belt.

They fired at almost the same instant, but McColl took a step to the side as he did so. The Russian's bullet embedded itself in the wall, his own in the Russian's chest.

By this time the younger man's gun was clearing its holster, and McColl shot him as well.

They fell across each other, like a cross marking the spot.

"Jesus Christ," Bowers was saying, disbelief in his voice.

McColl ignored him. The elder Russian had taken a bullet to the heart and was definitely dead. The younger one's wound was a little higher, and he would probably live. McColl knew he should finish him off and also knew that he wouldn't. Even if he could bring himself to do it, what would be the point? Sooner or later the Trust would be out for his blood.

Bowers was just staring at him. "Why?"

"You heard them. They were going to starve a city to death."

"It's a war! People die."

"It's not my war. It never was."

"I think you've made that clear enough. Northcutt will have your guts for garters." Bowers sighed. "If I were you, I'd disappear for a while."

"I wasn't thinking of staying around," McColl said mechanically as he tried to work out what he needed to do. "Help me carry the body to the car," he said after a few moments.

"Why?"

"Just do it. We don't have all night."

For a moment he thought Bowers would refuse, but after one shake of the head his colleague took hold of the legs and the two of them carried the corpse to the car, where they wedged it on top of the crates. While Bowers was wiping the blood off his hands, McColl reached in and took his colleague's gun from under the passenger seat.

"What are you—" Bowers began to object.

"You can have it back when we get to Moscow," McColl told him. He handed Bowers the small red flag. "See if you can fix it back on."

Bowers gave him an angry look but did as he was told.

The rain was slackening off, the rumbles of thunder fewer and further between. The Russians' horse was shuffling this way and that in its traces, as if keen to get going.

"Time to leave," McColl told Bowers once the flag was reattached.

"What about the other Russian?"

"We'll have to leave him where he is. Someone will see the horse and carriage." And if nobody did, it was hard to feel sorry for someone prepared to kill thousands of women and children.

The car started the first time—Northcutt's mechanic was good at his job. As McColl steered it up the lane and out of the village, Bowers sat there shaking his head, seemingly more surprised than angry.

The other man's silence suited McColl, who was trying to think ahead. He knew what to do when they got back to Moscow, but after that was a blank. The Trust people would be on his trail once they knew what he'd done, but they probably wouldn't find out for a while. How would Northcutt react? He would see McColl's action as a betrayal, but would he see it as treason? McColl had heard of one colleague in Russia who'd refused a direct order to kill the Bolshevik nationalities' leader, Stalin, and who'd only been sent home as a punishment. Was his own crime worse? It probably was. Killing allies and wrecking their operations was a very active form of dissent.

Even if Northcutt was sympathetic—which McColl very much doubted—the Whites and the French would be demanding some sort of reparation. He couldn't see Northcutt killing one of his own, but he could see him looking the other way after pointing his allies in the right direction.

All of which would take some time. McColl had to leave Moscow—had to leave Russia—but not like a panicky thief in the night, and not without saying good-bye to Fedya. The thought of seeing Caitlin one last time was tempting, but she had made it crystal clear that she didn't want another meeting.

So that was it. He would go to the orphanage early next morning and then get out of the city. In which direction? Not north—Northcutt had several agents with the British troops in Murmansk and Archangel. Not east, where the Czechs and their French paymasters blocked the way, nor west, where the Central Powers were still in control. So south it had to be. Another journey across occupied Ukraine, or perhaps farther east, through the Caucasus and down into Persia. One last adventure, at no one's behest but his own.

They were back on the highway by this time, and as they drove past the abandoned inn, Bowers stirred in his seat. "So what's your plan?" he asked.

"I plan to drop you off when we get to the city."

"And after that?"

"I'm going home. If there's music to face, I'll face it there."

Bowers thought about that for a moment. "I've heard worse ideas," he admitted.

Twenty minutes later they were approaching the Cheka checkpoint. This time it was manned.

"I hope you know what you're doing," Bowers muttered as McColl brought the car to a halt and carefully placed the gun where his hand could easily reach it. A shoot-out with the Cheka might end badly, but surrender certainly would.

There were two Chekists, both armed with pistols. They looked surprised not to recognize McColl or Bowers. "Comrades, where are you from?" the first one asked.

"Yauzskaya," McColl answered, handing over his identification. That was the Cheka unit that their papers said they belonged to, but the area in question was on the other side of the city.

The Chekist noticed the discrepancy. "Then what are you doing so far from home?"

"Look in the back," McColl told him. "There's a dead White who we chased all the way to Tushino. And some poisons he and his bourgeois friends were planning to put in the city's water supply. We need to report this, comrades. To the director."

The Chekist took a quick glance at the corpse, then waved them on.

"Very clever," Bowers conceded. "You've lived up to your reputation."

"My reputation?" McColl echoed.

"As one of Cumming's favorites. That's what Northcutt told me when he knew you were coming."

But not after this, McColl thought, feeling a twinge of regret for the first time that evening. It had been fun while it lasted. Most of the time.

After they'd passed the Brest Station and crossed Sadovaya, McColl looked around for somewhere to stop. Rather to his surprise, people were still out in numbers. It was, he realized, earlier than he'd thought—this particular day seemed virtually endless.

He found an empty stretch of pavement and pulled over. "You can get a tram from here," he told Bowers. "Once you're on the pavement, I'll drop your gun out of my window—you can pick it up after I'm gone."

Bowers reached the door handle. "Any last message for Northcutt?" he asked.

"Tell him we should be better than that," McColl said shortly.

Bowers climbed out and put his head back in the window. "Don't tell anyone I said so, but good luck."

Not a bad man, McColl thought as he drove on toward the center. But not a very good one either.

Where to leave the car? Although the idea of parking it outside the Cheka headquarters on Bolshaya Lubyanka had a certain appeal, that was probably pushing his luck. He had wanted to leave an explanatory message, but he had neither paper nor pencil and saw no obvious place to acquire them. He assumed that the stuff in the jars wouldn't actually look like food, and if anything shouted "handle with care," it was a corpse wedged in on top. The Cheka would work it out.

Approaching the inner ring, he noticed the Pushkin Monument off to his right and decided that was the spot. He parked the car close up against the plinth, where no one could look inside it without actually crossing the road, and strode off down Tverskoy Boulevard. The shop was about a mile away and should be safe for a few hours at least—more than enough time to pack what he needed and find somewhere safe to spend the night.

The streets were still full of puddles, but the sky was rapidly clearing, and by the time he turned onto Bolshaya Nikitskaya, the moon was dimly glowing behind the thinning clouds. As he neared the antique shop, he noticed a figure standing in the shadows on the opposite side of the street and abruptly slowed his pace. How could Northcutt have gotten someone here so quickly?

Whoever it was took a step toward him, and he realized it was a woman. One step more and he knew it was her.

"WHAT ARE YOU DOING HERE?" he asked, meeting Caitlin in the middle of the empty street.

"Can we talk inside?" she said, with no attempt to hide the anger in her voice.

"Of course." McColl unlocked the door and ushered her in. "The back room's better," he said, opening the connecting door. Once he'd closed it behind them, he struck a match and lit the kerosene lamp.

"I won't stay long," she said coldly. "I came to warn you, that's all. The Cheka are looking for you."

"How do you know?"

"I was called in and questioned by a man named Komarov. Brady must have seen you on the street and told the Cheka. It must have been him, because Komarov thinks we parted in 1914 and hadn't seen each other again until last week."

"How do they know we met the other day?"

"I admitted we had. He asked me, and I couldn't take the risk that he already knew. I told him you'd only come to see me on account of the boy, that you wanted my help in finding an orphanage."

"Did you tell him Fedya's name?"

"I can't remember. I don't think so."

"And the name of the orphanage?"

"No. He didn't ask. I'm sure of that. But what does it matter? It's you who's in danger, not the boy. You have to leave."

"I was planning to leave tomorrow, but not on account of the Cheka. I killed a man this evening, a member of the Trust—you know who they are? Well, they'll be looking for me when they find out, and so will my own people." He smiled. "Some servant of the Crown. As unreliable as you could wish for."

She couldn't help returning the smile. "For what it's worth, I'm glad."

"It's worth everything," he said shortly. "But you must go now. If the Cheka finds you here, you'll never talk your way out of it."

"I'll go in a minute. Tell me why you killed this man."

McColl went through the story as quickly as he could.

"You did the right thing," she said when he was done, and she resisted the temptation to ask the obvious question: Had he really not known what kind of men he was working with? She asked if the shop would be safe for that night.

"No, but I'll find somewhere else."

"Where?"

"I don't know yet."

"You can't stay with me. The Cheka might be watching the house."

"I know."

"Why not leave now? There's always hundreds of people sleeping at the stations—you could hide among them."

"I have to see the boy before I go. I promised him I would."

She raised her hands in exasperation. "Jack—that's crazy. I'll go see him and explain why you couldn't. He'll understand."

"I would like you to visit him after I'm gone, show him that somebody cares. But I have to see him before I go."

She accepted defeat. "All right. But where will you spend the night?"

"I don't know. But you really should go. Please."

"I will." She had to admit it: over the last few days, and especially over the last few hours, having him gone from Moscow had been high on her list of wants. But now that the moment had come, the prospect of a lasting separation was hard to bear. She wouldn't go back on the choice she'd made, but there was no denying the cost. "I might be here for years," she said, determined to be honest.

"However long it takes," he said, but he looked like he'd been hit.

"I can't ask you to wait for me," she said, more coldly than she intended.

"You don't have to," he told her almost reproachfully. "I'll be faithful," he added lightly.

"Don't say that!" she said. "I don't want you to be, not in the way that you mean. I don't want you to put your life on ice."

"But . . ."

She saw the question in his eyes. "Look, we love each other. After all we've been through, how could either of us deny it?" And it was true, she thought, but not the only truth. Their love for each other wasn't the whole of their lives, wasn't all that they were. "I do love you," she said, sounding almost surprised by how much she meant it. "And if we never see each other again, remember that," she added, sounding more desperate than she intended.

"We will," he said.

He clearly wanted this conversation over, and she could understand why. It suddenly felt as if door after door were closing.

"Write to me when you can," he told her.

"I will."

She put her arms around his neck and looked him in the eyes. "Be safe," she said. "Say hello to Scotland for me."

The embrace and kiss were all too short, the parting only sorrow.

AFTER CHECKING THAT NO ONE was observing the shop, he watched her walk briskly away up Nikitskaya, wondering if he would ever see her again.

A passing droshky brought him back to the present. Could he risk staying in the shop? He didn't think so. Back inside, he crammed his meager possessions—a spare set of clothes, a copy of *Dead Souls* he'd found in the shop, the letters Cheselden had written to Soph— into a battered suitcase that Luckett had left behind. The Cheka papers went into his pocket; the other two sets—which might still prove useful—he stuffed inside the book. The Webley went back in his belt, where the folds of his loose cotton jacket concealed it.

After locking up the shop and pushing the key under the door, he stood on the pavement assessing his options. Caitlin was right about the stations being crowded, but they all had Cheka offices. It was warm enough to sleep in one of the parks, but they had Cheka patrols, whose members might wonder why a fellow Chekist was living like a peasant. A hotel would make more sense. With his brand-new Cheka papers, he could demand a room with a view.

He didn't get the latter, but the staff at the old Berlin Hotel did seem keen to please. The room was clean, the bed surprisingly firm; there was even a fire escape outside his window. It would do, he thought. He felt safe for the night, and—considering the outcome—strangely satisfied with the way he had handled matters since Bowers had first picked him up. All except for the meeting with Caitlin. The last for God knew how long. As he lay there unable to sleep, her words kept coming back, words with too many possible meanings, some of them hopeful, most of them not.

HE WAS AWAKE AT DAWN. Rather than eat breakfast in the hotel, he walked back to the canteen where he and Fedya had eaten most of their meals and where his presence would not seem unusual. As he devoured his bread and jam, he thought about the talks they'd had and how many times the boy had mentioned sharing the future. Whatever problems he'd had growing up, McColl had at least been blessed with a brother. He'd never felt truly alone, as he imagined Fedya now did.

His thoughts turned to Jed, who he prayed was still alive. There was more than a chance he might not be—in surviving as long as he had, his brother had already beaten the odds. And of course he might be maimed—a leg or an arm gone, his sight stripped away, his lungs burned out. It was hard to imagine. The picture McColl carried around in his head was over four years old, of a Jed who was young and full of himself, a Scottish Peter Pan eager to battle the Kaiser's Captain Hook.

A posse of Red Guards crowded into the canteen, interrupting his reverie. These men were Russians and looked it, but physiognomy apart, they could have come from anywhere on earth—many populations were pushed to the limits of endurance by a heartless system and stupid, reckless rulers. The difference was that the Russians had fought back, and now here they were, wearing red armbands and hoping to build a brand-new world. Would they make their revolution work? Would the rest of the world even let them try? McColl suspected it would end in blood and tears, but that was who he was. He hoped he was wrong. All peoples came in shades of good and bad, but he'd come to admire the Russians and their instinctive generosity. They deserved better, and he hoped they got it.

It was almost eight o'clock. Outside, the sun was up above the horizon, the sky as clear as it had been for most of the summer. As he walked up Tverskoy Boulevard, he noticed that the Cheka car was gone. Two Chekists were guarding the spot where he'd parked it, for reasons best known to themselves.

People were hurrying to work, ordinary people in ordinary clothes, some of them smiling, some of them not. It was hard to believe that the Bolshevik realm was now a shrunken remnant, surrounded on all sides by vengeful enemies. They might not last the summer, he thought. Vasily and Viktor and all their friends would be back; Lenin and his would be swinging from lampposts.

Approaching the end of the narrow street on which the orphanage stood, he slowed his stride and cast a cautious look around the corner. At first he'd been surprised by the Cheka not asking for Fedya's current whereabouts, but later it had made more sense. If McColl had only used the boy for camouflage, then why would he want to see him again?

The street was empty. As he slowly walked down it, McColl scanned the windows and doorways for watchers. None were apparent.

The same woman was sitting sentry in the lobby. She was uncooperative until McColl flashed his Cheka identity, then almost too willing for words. The Cheka were striking too much fear into ordinary people's hearts, McColl thought. And the chances of their rediscovering any human kindness in the midst of a civil war didn't seem that good.

He was shown into the familiar room, and a few minutes later Fedya walked in through the door. He looked healthy enough to McColl and even a little happier, or was that wishful thinking?

He sat the boy down and explained that he was leaving Moscow and couldn't say when he'd be back. "I said I'd come and tell you, and here I am. Is there anything I can do for you, anything you want me to tell the people who run this place?"

"Are you going back to England?" Fedya asked.

"Probably, but I don't know when. Eventually, yes."

"Take me with you."

"I can't. We've been through this—"

"Please."

"I can't. Fedya, men are hunting me, and I won't take you into that sort of danger."

"You did before."

McColl couldn't help laughing. "You gave me no choice, remember?"

"It will be easier for you to get away if I'm with you—a foreigner would not be traveling with his son."

It was probably true. "No," McColl said. "This is your home now. This is your country."

He expected more of an argument, but Fedya just hung his head for a moment, then abruptly got to his feet. "Good-bye, then," he said, before almost running across to the door and hurriedly pushing through it.

McColl sat there for a moment, exhaled loudly, and followed him through the door. Fedya and the woman had both vanished, so he let himself out onto the still-empty street. What had he expected—hugs and smiles?

He started walking. His first idea had been to cadge a lift on one of the farmers' carts that came in and out of the city, then catch a train from somewhere farther down the line. But on reflection it seemed better, and easier, to catch the first available train from the Kursk Station and get out of Moscow as soon as he could. Brady would have given the Cheka a description, but what could that contain other than average height, average weight, brown hair and eyes? As one of the Service instructors had told him, his distinguishing feature was the lack of one. And his Cheka papers should see him through any routine check.

It wasn't a long walk to the Kursk Station, and most of it was down Sadovaya. He tried not to hurry—only a fugitive would rush in such heat—and he tried not to think about Fedya or Caitlin. Trouble was, each kept passing him back to the other.

The station appeared on his left, a long white building with two large domes in the middle, smaller ones at either end, and a wide open space in front. The latter was full of people—families, it looked like, as if several trainloads of Volga refugees had all arrived together—and McColl was some twenty yards from the edge of the crowd when he heard the shrill voice shouting, "Yakov!"

It was Fedya's.

The boy must have followed him all the way from the orphanage.

Heartsore and exasperated in equal measure, he turned to see the side of Fedya's head erupt in blood and bone.

"No!" he heard himself shout as the boy collapsed in a lifeless heap only five yards away.

There were two men walking toward him, both with guns in

hand. One seemed familiar, and a split second later he knew. Aidan Brady without a mustache.

It was lucky the suitcase was in his left hand, leaving the right to ease out the Webley and get off a shot, after both men had missed him with theirs. Ignoring the shrieks in the crowd behind him, McColl took aim at Brady's heart and hit him in the knee. As the American went down, McColl adjusted his bearing and put a bullet in the other man's chest.

Ahead of him people were scattering, away from the wounded and dead, away from the broken boy, away from guns and what they could do.

Behind him the crowd was drawing back into itself, hoping he'd leave it alone.

He turned and strode toward the wall of people, wondering how his legs were still working, how his body was bearing its millstone of grief.

It parted before him, and myriad faces—fearful, excited, even admiring—invited him through their improvised guard of dishonor.

17
Roller Coasters

There was no mention of the boy's death in the newspapers, and it was several days later when one of Caitlin's colleagues mentioned the tragic shootings outside the station. After other acquaintances had supplied enough details to convince her that Fedya had died that day, she took a deep breath, walked down to the building on Bolshaya Lubyanka, and requested an interview with Comrade Komarov.

Much to her surprise, she was shown up to his office. More astonishing still, he looked pleased to see her.

"I've been expecting you," he said.

"Why?" she asked, though on reflection it wasn't hard to guess.

"It was you who told me about the boy."

She sighed. "How did he get shot?"

He told her that it had been an accident, that two of his men had followed McColl from the orphanage, hoping that he would lead them to other foreign agents.

"But how did you know which orphanage?" she asked without thinking.

He let that go. "We checked them all for new arrivals. It wasn't difficult."

"I suppose not," she said, a sickening feeling in the pit of her stomach.

He continued the story. "The area around the station was crowded, and my men were afraid they might lose the Englishman, so they drew their guns and moved in to arrest him. And then the boy rushed past them, shouting out a warning. Shots were exchanged, and he was caught in the crossfire. Two women died as well."

"Who was it that shot the boy?" Caitlin asked.

Komarov shrugged and looked slightly uncomfortable. "We're not sure—different witnesses tell different stories. Does it really matter?"

Yes, she thought, it did. But she knew there was no point in pressing the matter. "How did McColl escape?" she asked.

"He just disappeared into the crowd. We had the station cordoned off in a matter of minutes, but somehow he got away." Komarov's sudden and unexpected smile seemed almost playful. "I don't suppose you've heard from him."

"No," she said, smiling back. She got to her feet and thanked him for his time. He was human for a Chekist, she thought, as she made her way back to the street. They would need people like him.

IN THE WEEKS AND MONTHS that followed, things turned nasty. The Allied invaders, who now included Caitlin's countrymen, opened up several new fronts, and the fledgling Red Army suffered several alarming defeats before Trotsky and his young generals managed to stabilize the front. Closer to Moscow, Allied agents launched a series of successful attacks on oil installations and food trains, stoking fears in the city of a cold and hungry winter. The Cheka's unmasking of the Lockhart Plot, a British plan to subvert the Bolsheviks' Latvian guard, was followed by another attempt on Lenin's life, one that was almost successful.

Any one of these events might have proved the final straw—together they broke every bone in the camel's body. The Bolsheviks, once lenient to a fault, went to the other extreme, letting the Chekas off the leash to maul and crush all opposition. Hundreds were shot—thousands, according to some—and that was just in Moscow. There were positive signs—Spiridonova was still alive, despite her ties to the woman who'd almost murdered Lenin—but they were few and far between. The revolution was choking on blood.

The reaction was mixed among Caitlin's Bolshevik friends. Some thought it was about time, that bending over backward to be fair had gotten them into this mess, encouraging their enemies and putting the whole revolution at risk. Some said a killing spree could never be justified—hadn't abolishing the death penalty been one of their greatest achievements? Others worried about the long-term consequences. Remember what followed the guillotine in France, they said. Did they want a Red Napoleon, a Red Genghis Khan?

Caitlin agreed with them all, and like everyone else she hoped that the terror would soon be over, that once the civil war was won, destruction would again give way to creation and the openhearted spirit of the early months would be restored. She immersed herself in work. Her journalistic career was in abeyance, every bit of her energy going into the all-Russia women's conference that was scheduled for November. Just spreading the word was a major endeavor in a country so splintered by war, and getting the delegates to Moscow was a real logistical nightmare.

Kollontai finally returned. Her political reputation had been damaged by her errant husband's chronic indiscipline, but she still had more determination than any ten of her comrades. Caitlin had missed her political energy and had missed her more as a friend. As someone who knew about Jack.

"What else could you have said?" Kollontai asked one night in the otherwise empty office. The conversation in the back room of the antique store was etched in Caitlin's memory, and she'd just repeated it almost verbatim. "What else?" the Russian repeated. "That you loved him more than life itself and would follow him to the ends of the earth? You don't, and you haven't. You love him—of course you do. And from everything you've told me, I'm sure he loves you, too. But the love between you is something you both create. You're its authors, and you mustn't become its victims. Especially you, because nine times out ten that's what happens to women."

Caitlin relived that conversation for several days, the same thoughts and feelings drawing circles around her brain until she felt like screaming. There was nothing else for it, she decided one evening. She had to really end it, cut him out of her head.

The letter was written that night, stamped and sent off early next morning.

She went back to work.

SAUCHIEHALL STREET WAS PACKED WITH people as far as the eye could see. Most of the soldiers were still overseas, and those present were vastly outnumbered by women, children, and the elderly. Most of the bairns were happily waving their Union flags, and many of the women seemed almost hysterical with relief, but the eyes that tugged at McColl were the ones that mirrored the cost. So many men had fallen, and still the band played on.

He hadn't wanted to come, but his mother had insisted. "We have to celebrate the peace," she'd told him. "Think how happy Jed would have been."

Jed was dead. After four years in the trenches with hardly a break, he'd finally picked up a wound that was serious enough to merit a fortnight back home. And there, like so many others that fateful September, he'd caught the Spanish flu and died.

His mother had borne the shock better than McColl had expected. For five days she'd hardly stopped weeping, but once the funeral was over, she had consciously pulled herself together. "I know a lot of women who've lost all their sons," she'd told him, "and one of mine's still here. So I'll count my blessings and get on with my life. That's what Jed would have wanted."

McColl had stayed on in Glasgow meaning to look after her, but it soon became clear to both of them that they were looking after each other. Now it sometimes felt as if she were all that stopped him from floating away.

In October he'd finally heard from Cumming—a summons to the Whitehall Court aerie that at first he'd thought to ignore but then decided to honor. For one thing he was curious, and for another he knew he owed the old man something, if only an explanation. So he'd taken the train south on a bright autumn day, assuming he wasn't en route to prison, but not completely certain.

Cumming had been brusque as ever. He had listened to McColl's version of what had happened in Moscow, interspersing a few nods and grunts, then asked for a detailed account of his escape. Getting in and out of Lenin's Russia was "becoming a trifle tricky," and the Service was keen to learn from McColl's experience.

And that had almost been that. There was no way that McColl could ever be reinstated—initiative was all very well, but Cumming couldn't have his agents deciding who they were and weren't prepared to work with, especially in the middle of an operation. And of course a pension was out of the question.

But there would be a medal. For his work in India, Cumming had added superfluously—McColl had not been expecting one for his service in Russia. It would be in the post in a couple of weeks, which was probably for the best. His mother would not appreciate his dropping it into the Thames.

As a parting shot, Cumming couldn't resist asking after Caitlin. "That Irish-American girl. Is she still in Moscow?"

"I believe so," McColl had answered shortly.

"You're not in contact?"

"No."

Cumming had shaken his head, perhaps in admiration. "She does get around."

She did, and McColl had lied about the lack of contact. A letter had arrived in late September, but his joy had been short-lived— she'd sent it from Japan almost six months before. After bathing in its love and affection, McColl had admonished himself for being so foolish. The letter was like one of those stars in the sky that appeared to be shining so brightly but had actually burned out aeons before.

Several weeks later a second missive had proved his point. She had given up journalism completely and taken a full-time job with the government women's organization. And since there was no prospect of her leaving Russia in the foreseeable future, she didn't think it fair to keep him dangling. So she was setting him free— not, of course, that he wasn't free already. He would know what she meant. She did love him, but love and life sometimes led in different directions. She hoped he'd understand.

He did. It was over, at least as far as she was concerned. All he could do was accept it. And maybe, given time, he would.

But not yet. As he stood there in Sauchiehall Street, surrounded by revelers, acceptance was not on the cards. Of her defection or of anything else. Others might see cause for celebration, but the dead were no less dead for being invisible. If all the corpses were stacked in rows, they would fill this street to the rooftops, this street and thousands of others, more valleys of death than Tennyson ever dreamed of. The noble six hundred? How about the noble six million?

Ours not to reason why?

Like fuck.

At least the dead *were* dead. How could the survivors ever recover?

Not that McColl felt guiltless. Far from it. Not a day went by he didn't see Fedya's head exploding, or Kerzhentsev wheezing his last, or Cheselden smiling that stupidly innocent smile. The flu had taken Soph as well, and the letters to her were still in McColl's suitcase.

He had left his own trail of dead, and for what? A better world? The one he'd imagined only five years before seemed more like a joke than a prospect.

THE CONFERENCE WAS A TRIUMPH. Three hundred women had been expected, and four times as many turned up. They came from all over Russia, the young and not-so-young, the poor and the formerly rich, wearing everything from overalls to veils. The sessions were sometimes stirring, frequently enraging, and almost always inspiring. There was even an unscheduled visit from Lenin, who gave a short speech pledging his support for full women's rights, something no other leader on earth had done. When the conference broke up, few of the delegates traveled home with any intention of letting things stay as they were.

It didn't make up for the terror—of course it didn't—but as far as Caitlin was concerned, the conference offered the proof she needed that her revolution was still alive.

Two days later she boarded a train for Petrograd, where she had the task of persuading Lenin's disciple Zinoviev that the women of the world deserved their own section in the new International.

The journey passed by faster than expected, partly because the train showed a marked reluctance to submit to the Russian stereotype, but mostly on account of the company. She hadn't seen Sergei Piatakov since he and Brady had come to see her in July. He was joining a newly formed Red Army regiment in Petrograd and had recently returned from the fighting on the Volga. He had some news of Brady. The American had suffered a serious knee wound back in the summer but was more or less fit again now and running a Cheka unit in the recently recaptured Samara.

Their train reached Petrograd soon after midday, and with her first meeting fixed for the following morning Caitlin went out for a nostalgic stroll. It was almost a year to the day since her arrival from England, and as on that occasion the city was wearing its first cloak of snow. After visiting a favorite café—the variety of fare available was much reduced, the welcoming smiles the same—she hailed a droshky and asked its surly-looking driver to take her out to Luna Park.

"It's shut," he told her, but she insisted on going regardless.

Once there he waited while she walked around the roller coaster, its structure coated in ice, the cars frozen hard to the rails.

It was ten months since the wedding, ten months in which the happy couple had hardly seen each other and mostly argued when they did.

It was four years and more since she and Jack had ridden the one on Coney Island.

She slowly walked back to the waiting droshky, thinking about the letter she'd received from her aunt a few days before. It had made her so happy; it had made her cry.

Sometimes she was sure she was doing what was right, and sometimes she feared that she hadn't a clue.

Historical Note

With historical fiction the question often arises as to where the history ends and the fiction begins, and I feel it is incumbent on authors to at least take a stab at explaining their own approach. The most important thing, to my mind, is that the historical context—by which I mean everything from political events to food and clothing—should be as accurate as possible. Some will disagree with my judgments—history, after all, is often a matter of opinion. Others will gleefully point out the odd mistake, and as someone prone to schadenfreude myself, I can hardly complain when they do.

My account of the year that followed Lenin's revolution is, of course, partial—it reflects my fictional characters' interests and beliefs as much as it does the totality of actual events. I have included real people in the story, some in passing, others in more important ways. Alexandra Kollontai, Pavel Dybenko, Yakov Peters, Maria Spiridonova, and V. Volodarsky were all prominent figures in the revolution and its aftermath, and Mansfield Cumming was the head of the British Secret Service at this time. I hope I have portrayed them accurately and not had them do anything too uncharacteristic. The journalists who appear—Jack Reed, Louise Bryant, Bessie Beatty, Albert Rhys Williams, Arthur Ransome, and Morgan Philips Price—were all real people, and I have made frequent use of the vivid accounts they left of their time in Russia. Louise Bryant's *Six Red Months in Russia* best captures the hopes that the revolution inspired in its first year.

The main characters—Jack McColl, Caitlin Hanley, and their families; Audley Cheselden, Semyon Kerzhentsev, Fedya, and Aidan Brady—are all fictional, as are Yuri Komarov and Sergei Piatakov, who have only minor roles here but who will figure more prominently in the fourth and final book of the series.

The activities of the British and French intelligence services in Russia, Ukraine, and Turkestan at this time were many and varied, and they were carried through by a bewildering variety of organizations and groups. I have simplified this somewhat and fictionalized those working on the ground, but all the schemes alluded to—including those intended to cause mass starvation—are part of the historical record. Michael Occleshaw's *Dances in Deep Shadows* is the best and most thorough account.

The events chronicled in the United States—the state persecution of those who opposed the war, the hobbling of the press, and the political crucifixion of the IWW union—are not inventions.

With the end of the grisly Soviet experiment now more than a quarter of a century in the past, the inspiration provided by the original revolution—one that captivated millions of men and women in the interwar years and beyond—is not easy to understand. Those wishing to do so should read Victor Serge's *Memoirs of a Revolutionary*, a beautifully written account of the political and emotional roller coaster that Lenin set in motion in 1917.